A Quantum Hijra

by Dawoud Kringle

"A Quantum Hijra" ISBN 9780615765693 Dawoud Kringle

Leilah Publications

First Printing : 2013   Second Revised Edition: 2017

Leilah Publications Phoenix AZ, USA 85008

leilah@leilahpublications.com

leilahpublications.com

Introduction

I bear witness that there is no deity worthy of worship except Allah, and I bear witness that the Prophet Muhammad (Peace be upon him) is the servant and messenger of Allah.

It is with great pleasure that I present this second edition of A Quantum Hijra: a Sufi Science Fiction Story.

While writing the first edition, I was under the impression that there is a noticeable vacuum of work written from an Islamic perspective. I believed I was alone in interjecting Islam into the literary genre of science fiction, and conducted myself under this assumption. I have since learned, to my delight, that this is not true. Many Muslims have written brilliant science fiction.

Suddenly, I found I was part of a community.

The response to the first edition has been gratifying. Many people have shared with me their experiences and feelings of reading QH. I was humbled to learn how deeply my work had affected people's lives. For this I am truly grateful.

This second edition attempts to smooth out some of the rough edges of the first, and clarify the storytelling. A few large revisions had been made, but the essential story remains.

The story presents, among many other things, the extrapolation of what extraterrestrial Islamic civilizations of human origin would be like, and how they would evolve over thousands of years. I had nothing to use as a model except my own imagination and powers of extrapolation.

2

In writing this, I found I could not entirely avoid the presence of my own personality. In fact, I took considerable license in applying bits of pieces of quasi-autobiographical elements to several of the characters herein. I could not resist. That said, there is no single character that is "me."

Despite our best efforts, we are victimized by our propensity to perceive Allah's creation not as it is, but as we are. One becomes great only insofar as one is able to free oneself of such constraints, and understand reality on its own terms as Allah, highly glorified is He, has designed it. I'm still struggling with this; and pray I be forgiven my shortcomings.

This book is an aggregate of interconnecting situations that the main character experiences, spanning centuries, that interconnects to form a coherent whole. The story is treated with considerable poetic and literary license, and often functions as parable. I experimented with liberal use of subtexts that would appear, disappear, and reemerge transformed later in the story. There were a few other devices I used that took considerable liberty with orthodox literary forms. I expect some people will dislike the book for that reason. In fact, some of the ideas presented herein may be conceptually and ontologically alien and incomprehensible to some people.

Throughout, I make indirect references to copyrighted material. Care has been taken not to violate these copyrights. The characters in this story do not exist, although a few are inspired by real people. The most obvious is Sheikh Yusef

Lateef, who was inspired by Dr. Yusef Abdul Lateef (the master musician, author, educator, and artist, whom I was acquainted with and who was responsible for greatly inspiring me).

I make absolutely no claims that what the characters say are true. Some of the opinions expressed by the characters in these stories are not my own. Some are.

Be forewarned. There is absolutely nothing within this book that I have intended to be in any way prophetic. The details surrounding the future, the Unseen, the Day of Judgment, and the like, I have absolutely no exclusive or accurately detailed information and refuse to speculate. The reader will also find what appears to be arcane knowledge about religion, politics, history, spiritually, and the interpretation of the Qur'an. While I have taken considerable artistic license to share some of my opinions with the public, I do not claim that these things are absolutely true.

Let me be clear: this book is fiction, nothing more. I refuse to be held responsible for the reactions of whoever may be unwilling or incapable of understanding and/or accepting this.

The following people deserve thanks for their contributions and assistance, or inspiration in completing this book. The Prophet Muhammad (may peace be upon him) and all his companions and family, Dara Shardya (whose generous permission to shamelessly plagiarize his own work has been of incalculable value to me), everybody on the Sufis Without Borders yahoo group, Frank Herbert, Irving Karchmar,

4

everybody at the Mosque of Islamic Brotherhood, Masjid Farrah, the old Sufi Book Store in New York City, Wahid Azal, Jeff Slatnick and everyone at Music Inn, NYC, Sharif Abdul Aziz (who always believed in me, and taught me many things: although perhaps not what he intended), Imam al-Hajj Talib Abdur Rashid, Imam Salihou Djabbi, every musician and writer whose work ever moved and inspired me, and every friend and stranger who showed me kindness and support in my hours of need.

Special thanks are due to my wife Akosua "Kosi" Gyebi , without whose herculean editing and objectivity, this second edition would have been impossible; and to Joshua Seraphim and everybody at Leilah Publications for their help, support, and for believing in my humble efforts.

Finally, thanks to you, dear reader. You're having purchased this book and taken the time to read it means more to me than I can express.

I salute you all, and thank Allah for your lives.

Dawoud Kringle

Prologue

Destiny writes its inexorable poetry on the essence of our lives. We read this poetry every moment. It's the same story we've heard again and again, echoing through the ages. There is no other story to tell.

As Talib walked to the class, he found himself drawn into an unveiling of memory, a remnant of the experiences of his distant former life, and former self. Mastery of memory was a technique taught by the Order, and one could learn to summon memories at will. On occasion, a memory came up unbidden. This was one of them.

"In the beginning, I was not aware. All humans begin this way; in total ignorance and darkness; a Ruh (Breath / Spirit of Allah) attempting to make sense of a new human experience. Slowly, I struggled toward the light. I began to understand. Yet understanding becomes painful. One must, from time to time, discard what one had held on to. We hold what we love. But we don't always love what we need. Or need what we love. Many of us would rather die than face this.

"I was Russell; a young American. I was born into it the same way we were all born into whatever we were born into. I had no choice. It seemed like such a long time ago,,,

6

"Russell fell in love with a dream. Russell sold himself an ideal around which he built his life. His ideal was very firmly entrenched in the time and place of his life. It held him prisoner; he fell in love with the intoxication of his imprisonment.

"One day, Russell began to learn about pain.

"And Light,

"And freedom,"

Chapter 1. Growing Pains. April, 1994.

It was raining outside. Russell Peterson hated the rain.

It had been the kind of day in which everything seemed to go wrong. He'd had a fight with his girlfriend, Denise. It seemed to him that she just wanted to do whatever came into her head to make him angry. She left his apartment hours ago, after much yelling, cursing, and things said in the heat of anger that neither would forget (nor forgive). The tension from the fight hung in the apartment like a fog. He'd also received a phone call from his agent: several shows his rock band was booked to do were canceled. This did nothing to improve his mood; he needed the money. Then he discovered a crack in the headstock of his favorite guitar. This meant an expensive repair job that may or may not do any good. To top it off, it was his birthday today; he was 27. He didn't want to celebrate and didn't want anyone to know it was his birthday.

Something else was bothering him. Something he didn't know how to articulate, even to himself, let alone face.

The phone rang. Russell waited until his answering machine let him know who was calling. "Yo, Russ, it's me. Eddie. You there? Pick up." Eddie Gilbert was the drummer of the rock band.

Russell picked up the receiver. "Yeah. I'm here."

"Russ, man, what's up?"

"I'm having a bad day. I should've stayed in bed. What're you up to?"

"Nothing, dude. You ready for tomorrow?"

Russell snorted "Didn't Pete call you?"

"No. What's up?"

"That fool didn't call you? The gigs are canceled."

Eddie let loose a string of semi-coherent obscenities. After his profane verbal ejaculation, he asked why.

Russell scowled. "Some drama with those people in Boston. They screwed up the money, or don't want to pay us or something. I don't know. I don't care. Why should I give a damn?" He was almost yelling.

Silence. "Yo, Russ." Eddie said, "You don't sound too good. Something bothering you? You OK?"

Russell took a breath. "Yeah. I'll be alright."

"You feel like having a drink?" Eddie asked.

"Yeah. Meet me at Rocco's."

Eddie chortled; "Man, you must be in a funk if you want to go to Rocco's. I'll see you there in a couple hours."

"Cool." He hung up the phone.

Russell looked around his apartment. It was a mess. It was always a mess when Denise wasn't around. The window of the small living room looked out at a dismal abandoned section of Queens, New York. He stood and looked out for a moment. The sky was a steel gray. The rain obscured much of the landscape, but not enough for Russell's taste. This desolation, so characteristic of much of America, reflected the condition of his spirit with an eloquence that left him cold and defeated.

Turning his back on the window, he walked into his tiny kitchen and opened the refrigerator.

Cold pizza and beer. Good enough.

Eating the pizza, he walked back into the living room. His eyes fell on a spiral notebook on the bookshelf across the room. It was music manuscript interspersed with writing paper, photocopies of documents, and magazine articles. He didn't want to see it. He wished he'd never seen it. He wished he never met the man whose handwriting filled these books. He wished he'd never read those crazy books that he was told to read. *Why did I let him into my life? Why do I keep that shit in my house?*

After eating the pizza, he put on his shoes and a jacket, grabbed his keys and left. The rain was falling harder now. He ran to his car, a beat up '78 Ford Mustang, and jumped in. It was cold and damp. *Damn! I play for big audiences and my record is selling. I can't afford a better car than this? Where's all the money at?* he thought, shaking his head.

On the way to the bar, he grabbed a random tape from the pile on his dashboard and put it into the stereo without looking at it. As the music started he realized his mistake, and reached to stop the tape. His hand fumbled, and he poked and jabbed at the buttons violently. He had forgotten about that tape. The music on it was the last thing he wanted to hear. Not now. Finally, he got the tape out of the tape player, threw it on the floorboard and turned on the radio, set to a local rock station. The intro to Van Halen's "Atomic Punk" filled the car. *Good,* he thought to himself, *something I like. Not the bullshit he used to make me listen to.* But the pounding drums, flashy guitar gymnastics, and the vocalist's howling and caterwauling held none of their old power to pacify him. The exhilaration was gone. He didn't want to admit it to himself, but it was a grating noise to him now, and he was resentful of the man who had done this to him, who had taken so much away from him.

Russell turned the corner a bit too fast and almost scraped a parked car. Still, he managed to find a parking space. Running out in the rain he made his way to the entrance of Rocco's bar. The neon beer signs beamed a lonely welcome to him, beckoning him to enter the special oblivion of the drunkard. As he opened the door, he was greeted by the smell of stale beer. The pungent aroma always held a special place in Russell's memory. It never failed to remind him of good times long past. Alcohol had always been a part of his life ever since his childhood when relatives would visit and the adults would be drinking. It seemed like the alcohol would make them more open to him; friendlier. Now alcohol and drugs became his spiritual nourishment, his elixir of life. It dominated his existence and he welcomed it, because all else was failing him.

Yet this too, despite his refusal to admit it, was entering an advanced state of decay. At times, he simply could not drink the anger and pain off his mind. Tonight, it seemed, was going to be one of those nights. This was not good. He was known to sometimes either become violent and abusive or emotionally depressed at such times. It was, however, too early to tell whether he would pick a fight or sit in the corner weeping. He would have to simply get falling-down drunk before he could determine this. One thing was certain: tomorrow he would need to drink a beer so that he could function through his terrible hangover.

Once inside, he looked around. Not many people inside. Good. He didn't want to be around a lot of people. He sat at the bar and waited for Eddie. After ordering a beer, he walked to the jukebox. The lumbering 7/8 bass line of "Money" by Pink Floyd poured from the speakers. Same old songs he'd been listening to for years. He was tired of them. Cursing to himself, he wondered how it had come to this. He had never felt this way about the songs he'd always loved. When he was a teenager it seemed like he and his friends worked hard to build something. It was the voice of their culture, the soundtrack of their lives. When Russell learned to play the electric guitar, he felt like he was doing something important. Now everything carried with it a feeling of futility, emptiness. Everything he loved and valued suddenly became ugly, idiotic, and devoid of meaning. It made no sense to him; why was this happening? What had gone wrong?

Eddie walked in just as Russell finished his beer. "Dude!" he greeted.

"What's up, Eddie" They shook hands. Eddie sat down.

"Chilling." They ordered a round of beers. Russell ordered a double shot of Jack Daniels. "You must feel like getting hammered, Russ."

"Man gotta do what a man gotta do" retorted Russell.

Just then "Solitude" by Duke Ellington came on the jukebox. Eddie looked up and said "Who the hell put this crap on?"

"I did!" Russell snarled. "You got a problem with that?" They sat in an uncomfortable silence until the drinks arrived.

"Bottoms up," said Eddie.

"Asalaam Alaikum," Russell said with a sarcastic lilt in his voice.

Eddie looked at him. "Salami an' bacon? What the,,,?"

"It don't mean nothing. It's something my guitar teacher used to say."

"You wanna know something? You been actin' weirder and weirder since you started taking lessons from that crazy son of a bitch." Russell looked at him, wanting to get mad. He couldn't.

"I'll tell you something else," Eddie continued. "At first you started to play better. Don't get me wrong, you still play great. But after you been with that old fart for a while, I don't know, man. What you been playing ain't rock 'n roll. All the crap he laid on you messed you up." Russell stared at Eddie. He didn't know whether to agree with him, curse him, or punch him out. He remained silent, drinking his beer faster. He swallowed the Jack Daniels silently.

Eddie continued. "Whatever went down between you and him must have been something heavy. You ain't been the same since. Everybody knows something is wrong. After we got our record deal and did that first tour, things were looking up. Then you started taking lessons from that guy. Everything went downhill from then on."

Eddie ordered another round of drinks, and looked at Russell. Now his voice was less angry, less confrontational. He said "I don't get it, Russ, what happened? Tell me, man. I'm your best friend. I can't stand to see you like this."

Russell looked off into the distance. After a silence, finally Russell said "You remember when I first met him?'

Eddie said "Yeah. Kinda."

"I'll never forget that as long as I live.

Chapter 2. So it begins.

Russell was on the Lower East Side in Manhattan. It was raining. Russell hated the rain. He had to meet someone at a restaurant and pick up a contract. The meeting had gone well and now Russell realized he had the whole night free. It was 9:15 P.M.

He walked around. He hadn't been to this neighborhood for years and had never been very familiar with it. As he walked, a peculiar looking coffee shop caught his attention. He walked in and ordered an espresso. He wasn't much of a coffee connoisseur, but he wanted to try one. He sat down in a chair and sipped his espresso. The strong nutty bitter taste asserted itself to Russell's taste buds in a way he'd never experienced.

This coffee shop was one of those places where the furniture was mismatched, where East Village "Artists" hung out (a handful of them actually had talent), and where the occasional poetry jam or musical performance took place. Such places would open, enjoy a few years of popularity, and then close. Occasionally, one would stay open for many years.

Russell was no poetry fan. He liked rock 'n roll, and didn't spend his time on much else. He used to laugh at the poets. Their poetry sounded like nonsense to him. A good rock tune made more sense to him; it was more direct. Simple. No allegorical non-sequitur. There was something in the artistic endeavors of such people that seemed to him slightly emasculated. He saw such people as being weaklings and cowards.

Fortunately, there were no poets reading on the small stage. There were three chairs, a small amplifier, a microphone on a stand, a guitar case, two keyboards on a stand, and assorted percussion instruments. This aroused Russell's curiosity. Who could this be? He built a cynical picture in his mind of a hippie folk singer strumming some simple chords and singing "sensitive" songs. He decided to stay; he felt that this would be good for a laugh, something he could tell his buddies about. He'd seen the sign in the window. Someone named Hassan something or other was scheduled to play. *This should be hilarious*, Russell thought to himself.

Several people came in and sat down. By now the place was three quarters full, but a quiet, serene sense of anticipation hung in the air. Somehow, the door attendant forgot to ask Russell for the admission price, an oversight which he found amusing. They had been playing some jazz on the stereo: "Crescent" by John Coltrane. Russell knew nothing about jazz. beyond a vague idea that you had to be "good" to play it, but all the jazz he ever heard sounded like a bunch of notes to him.

Suddenly the music faded out. The audience became quiet. A man walked to the stage. He was a swarthy Italian about 45 years old with a beard and a profile that looked vaguely reminiscent of a Native American. He had short dark hair which was graying, and wore a gray jacket and loose fitting black denim pants. He looked to be in good shape. His movements were fluid, slow, and deliberate, but very easy. His movements seemed to say that he moved slowly by choice; there was no need to hurry. A man followed him; a dark skinned African American wearing colorful, loose fitting clothes, and a strange brimless hat with ornate embroidery. To Russell, it looked like one of those hockey-puck looking things the Jews wear, only bigger. A tall man, of similar age, whose racial origins Russell couldn't identify, sat at the keyboards. Reaching into his guitar case, the Italian man picked up his guitar. Russell looked at it: it was a semi-hollow body. It had a scalloped fingerboard, beautiful mother of pearl inlay of a mesmerizing geometric design which resembled something organic, and a simple pickup configuration. He had never seen a guitar like this before. It was obviously hand made. He resolved to ask him about it later. The African American sat down in front of one of the congas. There were a variety of other percussion instruments which Russell couldn't identify within easy reach, including tablas, cymbals, bongos, shakers, bells, a small gong, a tom, Tibetan singing bowls, and electronic percussion equipment. The man reached over to the tablas and let his fingers dance briefly on them, creating a flurry of notes that reminded Russell of a hummingbird's wings.

The Italian sat down and greeted the audience. "Asalaamu Alaikum" he said.

Huh? What the hell did that mean, Russell wondered. *Is this guy going to speak Russian all night?* Some of the people in the audience, mostly African Americans, responded "Wa Alaikum Asalaam."

The man said "For those of you who don't speak Arabic that means Peace be upon you."

Great, thought Russell: *he's a towel-head hippie. What the hell am I doing here? This guy better be good.*

The man continued "My name is Hassan Rusticcelli. This is Malik Scott on percussion. On keyboards is Sharif Cunningham. Let's begin, shall we?" There was scattered applause.

Suddenly, a chord seemed to slash its way into the air like a bolt of lightning. It settled into a hypnotic groove that Russell found himself drawn into. He felt the air charged with an energy he'd never experienced. The melody asserted itself. Along with the slow, relentless rhythm, it demanded one's attention. Then the guitarist began to take a solo. His guitar sang haunting melodies; his fingers executed lightning fast runs which tied into the sounds of the other instruments, weaving in and out of the rhythm and harmony of the song. It was more than the "hot guitar" Russell was used to. There was something else here; there was a reality about it. The man was speaking with his instrument. He was telling a story. His story. All stories. Russell was forced to look at the essence of this man as it was presented in his music and there was an agonizing beauty in its sincerity. The other musicians were also deeply engrossed in this musical adventure. They were actually communicating with each other. Russell had never thought this as an abstract goal, let alone an achievable possibility. Yet they were doing it, and it seemed not only impressive, but necessary. As if the world needed the music these men were making. As the song continued the keyboardist took a solo, then the man with the percussions. He fascinated Russell. He seemed to play several instruments simultaneously. He weaved in and out of the rhythm, playing several time signatures at once, without losing the groove. At times he swore he could hear melody lines coming from his drums. Russell wondered how this man was doing it. The song built to a climax; the three musicians playing what seemed a statement of the most absolute of truths; the most absolute of realities. It was as if the secrets of heaven and earth were revealed to him, and he couldn't comprehend it, couldn't bear the burden of the beauty and majesty the music was telling him about. The air in the coffee shop was charged with an energy and a power that terrified him. What was happening? This was only music, only entertainment. It wasn't supposed to have this kind of power.

The audience applauded loudly and sincerely when the song ended. Russell sat drained, exhausted. He remembered a story he heard as a child in Sunday school about Paul going to Damascus and seeing a vision of Jesus, and being knocked off his donkey by what Jesus told him. This must have been what it was like. He felt like he'd been emptied of everything and filled with - what? He didn't understand what he was experiencing.

Suddenly, they began the next song. Russell realized that they'd only played one song! He didn't know how much of this he could take. A whole set of this might kill him. He wanted to leave, but he couldn't. He sat and listened. The song they were playing was a ballad. A blues unlike the blues Russell was familiar with. A slow, pulsating rhythm carried lush, ornate chords which sculpted sonic arabesques.

The lyrical and indomitable melody seemed to reach into him. It pulled out memories he'd forgotten, didn't want to face, and had worked hard at forgetting. He began to sob. Burrowing himself in his chair and hoping nobody would see or hear him, he tried to stop. He couldn't. This music was telling him the truth about himself, and it was painful. Ironically, these were not at all bad or shameful things, but he had a facade, an ego, and an image that was being systematically destroyed. He began to hate what was happening. The feelings of regret, longing, gratitude, a sweet sadness, and an assurance (from where?) that all would be well, all was forgiven, was not in keeping with the persona of a young rock star.

The set continued song after song. The mind numbing display of virtuosity was hard enough on him; the effect the music had on his spirit was devastating. When the set ended, Russell sat staring ahead, drained. The second set took him to even further heights of agony and ecstasy.

After the performance, when the musicians were packing their instruments away, Russell walked up to the guitarist. Waiting for the other people to leave him he walked up to him.

20

"Excuse me, mister?"

The man looked at Russell. His face radiated serenity. His eyes were clear and well defined with a steady gaze. "Yes?"

"Ah, I really, ah, liked your show." What did he want to say? He couldn't remember.

"Thank you." The man said. "You're a guitar player, aren't you?"

Russell said "Yeah, that's right! How did you know?"

"I can tell. My name is Hassan. Yours is?"

"Russell."

"I'm pleased to meet you Russell." He held out his hand. Russell shook his hand. It was very strong, and it felt like there was electrical power going through the man's whole arm.

Russell said "Man, your guitar is nice. Where did you get it?"

"A friend built it."

"No kidding." Russell wanted to continue the conversation, but it seemed like there wasn't much he could say. "Your music," Russell stammered "I never heard anything like it. It was like, ah, I don't know, man. Something happened. I never felt like that before." He felt a little foolish.

Hassan smiled. "Thank you. I'm glad you liked it." He continued to pack his equipment. Russell stood and tried to think of how to continue the conversation.

Hassan had strapped his belongings to a hand cart and put on his jacket. Picking up an umbrella, he said "It was nice meeting you. Peace."

Russell blurted out; "Listen, ah, Can I ask you something?'

"Yes. What do you want to ask me?"

"Ah. Umm. Can I, uh I mean, do you give, like, guitar lessons?"

Hassan looked closely at him for a few seconds. He seemed to see directly into Russell's soul: as if he knew more about Russell than Russell knew about himself. Finally he reached into his pocket and took out a business card. Handing it to him, he said "Call me. We'll discuss it later." He walked away.

Later, he left the coffee shop. It was still raining. He looked at his watch; it was 1:30 A.M. He walked aimlessly around the East Village. It was at that hour when the East Village's vibe gives way to something dark and hungry. On the corner of East 7th street and Avenue A, he heard a jazz group playing somewhere in the upper floor of a building. There was a saxophone calling into the night. It was crying, pleading for love, for redemption. It was a prayer. Finally, he headed to the subway train. The ride seemed much more of an ordeal than usual.

When he got home, he picked up his guitar and tried to play it. It was useless. The instrument which had once expelled a flood of sound at its master's command was rendered impotent and powerless. It mocked him. It insinuated creative sterility, something which would have enraged him, had his heart not stated that there was undeniable truth in this accusation. He put it back in its case and tossed it in the corner, then sat on his bed, fighting the urge to weep. Something had happened that night. He was dimly aware of having left something behind, having passed a point of no return. He smoked some marijuana, opened a can of beer, and turned on his TV, trying to forget what had happened.

*****

Eddie sat, listening to his friend's story. "Damn. That's not what you told us. You said--"

"Yeah, I know," Russell broke in. "I said I heard this cool guitar player. I didn't know how to explain what happened. You would've thought I was kidding." He took a swallow of beer. "Or crazy."

"Yeah. I see what you mean." Eddie sat for a while, meditatively sipping his beer. "So you called him."

"Yeah. About a week later."

Chapter 3. Not what we thought it would be.

Russell picked up the phone. The dial tone droned insistently in his ear. He hung up the phone and paced around his apartment. He had no idea what he would even say to this man. Finally he picked up the phone and dialed the number.

"Yes?"

"Hello, Hassan?"

"Speaking."

"It's me. Russell. The guy you met at your gig last week."

"Yes, I remember. How are you?"

"I'm cool. I wanted to talk to you about the guitar lessons"

"Yes, of course," Hassan said. "Lets meet tomorrow."

"Where?"

"The same place where we met. At 5:00. Is that good for you?"

"Yeah. I'll be there."

"Good. See you tomorrow. Asalaam Alaikum." He hung up.

Russell walked into the coffee shop and looked around. He saw Hassan sitting at a table talking to a tall African man with a beard and colorful clothing. They were speaking in Arabic, which Russell didn't understand.

"Hi." Russell said.

Hassan looked at him, smiling, rising and extending his hand. Again, the powerful handshake.

"Glad you could make it. Russell, this is my friend Muhammad." Muhammad stood. He was tall, with broad shoulders, jet black skin, and a warm smile which lit up his dark face. Something about him insinuated itself into Russell's consciousness; it was a feeling of being in the presence of an indefinable energy. It was quiet and serene, yet indomitably powerful. He wore a light blue jalabiya and a white kufi with gold embroidery. He held out a massive hand.

"I am very happy to meet you Mr. Russell," Muhammad said in a deep, resonant voice with a musical Senegalese accent. They shook hands. *Damn*, he thought. *This guy's got a strong grip too*. He then held Russell's hand in both of his, bowed slightly, then released it and touched his right hand to his heart and forehead.

Russell didn't know what to make of this.

"The hour is getting late for me," said Muhammad. "I must be on my way. Insha Allah we will see each other again soon."

Hassan said "Insha Allah. It was good to see you again, my brother. Asalaam alaikum."

"Wa alaikum asalaam, wa rahmatuallah" Muhammad replied. They hugged and Muhammad left. Hassan sat down, gesturing for Russell to do the same.

"So," Hassan began, as Russell sat. "You want guitar lessons."

"Yeah. I like the way you play. I want to learn how to do that."

Hassan sat back, looking at him with his hands clasped at his chest. "Do what, exactly?"

Russell said "You know, what you were doing. What happened when you played. The energy in the room. I want to know how to do what you can do."

"Why?" Hassan asked, with a penetrating stare that was unnerving in its cool, relaxed manner.

Russell hesitated. *Why? How do you answer something like that?* "You know," he stammered. Hassan said nothing. This irritated Russell. "I want to be able to do what you can do," he blurted. "That's all. Ain't nothing else to it. I want to use it in my band."

Hassan leaned forward slightly. "You play rock music, don't you?"

"Yeah." Russell said.

Hassan sighed. "There is a reason why I am asking all these questions. The thing you are asking me to teach you is not something that you can just learn in a couple of lessons. It isn't often that I take students. I don't need the money. When I do take on a student, it's because I see something in him or her that tells me that this person is worth my time. I teach a complete system of music which ties into a complete system of thought, a complete system of life. If all you want is someone to show you 'licks' or 'riffs,' go buy a magazine. Don't waste my time. If you're serious, we can get started. Be forewarned: I guarantee you will make progress, but you will find that the progress you make, the things you learn, and the skills and knowledge you acquire come with a price. And I'm not talking about money. You may have to part with something you *think* you love."

Russell sat staring at the floor unable to meet his gaze. He didn't understand. Pay what? What was he talking about? *Well,* he concluded silently, *I think I'll just take some lessons with him. I don't have to "pay" nothing other than the fee for the lessons. He may be a great guitar player, but this dude must be two bottles short of a full six pack. I hope he don't belong to no cult.*

"I want to take lessons with you." Russell said. "How much do you charge?" Hassan told him. It was less than Russell expected.

He said "Good. When can we start?"

"How about next week? Friday, 7:00?"

"Cool," Russell said.

They shook hands. "Glad to have you aboard, Russell" Hassan said. "Can I treat you to an espresso?"

"Sure. I'd love one."

*****

Eddie looked at him. "Man, if some dude laid some crap like that on me, I'd have told him to go to hell. Why did you go along with it?"

Russell finished his beer. "I don't know. I thought I was gonna get over on him. I thought I'd just learn some stuff on guitar, some tricks or something. I didn't expect it to turn out like it did."

"You know," Eddie said, "you never did really tell me what those lessons were like."

*****

Russell looked at the address he'd written on the piece of paper again. It was a loft in Soho; an old building. He wasn't familiar with this neighborhood, but he managed to find the place. He was buzzed in, and soon found himself walking up five flights of stairs. Cursing and out of breath, he knocked on the door. It was ajar.

"Come in; it's open," Hassan called from inside.

The loft space was a large, sparsely furnished, yet comfortable place. It smelled of patchouli incense. There was a sofa, a few tables and chairs, a kitchenette and dining table, several musical instruments, a stereo, a computer, and recording equipment in one corner, cushions and several Persian rugs on the floor, and two chairs facing each other by the window. Pictures with Arabic calligraphy hung on the wall, along with some photographs. A large partition blocked off the bedroom area, and a massive bookshelf dominated one wall. There were also small rugs near a corner which were all pointed in one direction.

Hassan was in the kitchenette boiling water. Standing next to him was a beautiful, slim African woman wearing a multi-colored head wrap, and a long, colorful, loose fitting dress. She held her head in an erect posture.

"Welcome to my home, Russell!" Hassan said, shaking his hand. "This is my wife, Amina."

"Hi," said Russell timidly. Normally he would have shaken her hand or even kissed her on the cheek, but he felt instinctively as if he had no right to make physical contact with her. Her black eyes (or violet? Russell couldn't tell. It was almost as if they were changing color in front of him) shined with a luminescence that contrasted her smooth dark skin. Her lips, which looked like they were carved from dark mahogany, moved with a mesmerizing fluidity when she spoke, accenting her high cheekbones, and displaying her perfect teeth. Her garment hung loosely from her shoulders, the line of her neck and a fraction of her right shoulder open to the world were almost intolerably beautiful. She possessed an elegance that was beyond the considerable physical beauty focused through her face by the garment that protected her. She was like a queen.

She smiled; her smile was warm and modestly, almost motherly. "Asalamu Alaikum" she said in an indefinable African accent. "Would you like some tea?"

He didn't usually drink tea, but he nodded his head. She brought him a small wooden vessel with silver trimming from the kitchen. It held what looked like a thick stew of green leaves in hot water, and a silver straw sticking out of it.

"What is this?"

"Yerba mate, from South America. It's very good for you." Amina left the room, as Russell wrestled for a few seconds with the final image of this extraordinary woman.

Hassan motioned for Russell to sit down at the window. There was a music stand in front of him. *Great*, he thought, *now I have to learn to read music*. He picked up his guitar and plugged into a small practice amplifier. His fingers began picking out notes as he waited to be tortured. Hassan sat opposite him quietly observing, his guitar propped against the window. There was a look of disapproval on his face. Disapproval and something else.

It was pain.

"No," Hassan said. Russell paused, and then with bravado attempted a more complicated lick. Hassan recoiled. "No! Please! Stop it!" Hassan exclaimed.

Russell froze, speechless.

"Do you know what you were playing?"

"Yeah. Riffs. Leads."

"No," Hassan huffed. "You were playing nothing. It had no structure, no beauty, and no meaning. You were not making music; you were throwing noise around indiscriminately. Furthermore, your hand positions are sloppy, and your fingers are clumsy, weak, and uncoordinated. Never play that again."

Nobody had ever insulted his playing before. Russell wanted to be mad, but instead he was crushed.

"I didn't think there was anything wrong with what I was doing," Russell said. "People like what I do."

"I'll bet," Hassaan said, shaking his head. "Let's start with your hands. They're all over the place. Your fingers are weak, but stiff like overcooked sausages. The faster you play, the more disorganized you become. When you play fast, you do so because there must be played a series of notes in quick succession. They serve a purpose to the music, not to your ego. *Weedlee weedlee weedlee weeeeee!* That's not music! You must eliminate the 'rock guitar' syndrome of nervously flapping your fingers around like a goldfish that jumped out of the aquarium. Did you ever see a Bruce Lee movie?"

"Huh?"

"Bruce Lee. The martial arts master."

"Yeah, but what does that have to do with guitar?"

"Watch him. When he throws a punch or a kick, he doesn't wave his arms around like some drunk in a brawl. He goes for a minimum of movement. He economizes all motion. No movement happens without a purpose. And he's relaxed, not stiff. This is what you must work towards achieving. Let's correct your hand position. By the way, do you read music?"

Russell winced. *I knew it!* "No," he admitted, shrinking.

"Do you know much about music theory?"

"No."

"Well," said Hassan, "We'll have to do something about that," as he put on his eye glasses.

Oh boy, Russell thought.

It was a long lesson. Hassan put him through exercises which were as tiring and tedious as they were meaningless to him. At one moment, when Hassan was standing and looking out the window, Russell played a wrong note. "That should be a B flat, not a B," Hassan called out without taking his gaze from the window.

"You weren't even looking at my hands!" Russell marveled.

Hassan was silent for a moment. "You gonna try it again, or no?"

But this is not even rock 'n roll, Russell thought to himself. *How am I even gonna use this?*

Hassan turned and looked at him. "Any time you're ready." Russell obliged, pretending not to have been momentarily intimidated.

After an hour and a half Russell's head was spinning and his hands were tired. He was relieved when Hassan finally said "Let's call it a day."

Thank God, he thought.

Hassan smiled at him, reading his mind. "Russell, I know this was hard to deal with," he said amiably, "but we must get you familiar with this so that it becomes second nature."

"Why?"

"Because then we can begin the Real Stuff. By the way," he added quietly, "where do you get your information about music?"

Russell said "From the radio, you know. And from magazines. And clubs."

"Like that one that's in your guitar case?" It was the latest issue of "Guitar World." A picture of the members of a famous rock group sneered at him. "Get rid of it. If you have any old issues at home, throw them out. They're not worth the paper they're printed on. And stop listening to the rock / metal stations. It's mostly noise. It'll only damage you."

Hassan's matter-of-fact nonchalance left Russell speechless. How dare this crazy old man attack his music!

"What's wrong with my music?" he blurted out, finally finding his words. "I've been listening to it for years! It hasn't damaged me or anyone else! What makes you think my music is no good?"

Hassan looked at him; again with the penetrating stare. There was, however, a hint of tenderness in his look, and in his voice. "It gives me no pleasure to attack you. All I tell you is what I have learned from bitter experience. I used to play rock music years ago. I could explain why I think it's damaging, but you would only interpret it as an attack. After we have worked together for a while, you'll understand what I'm really telling you. Then you can make up your mind as to how to interpret my statements. I will say this: you and a lot of people think that music is nothing more than an intangible art form which exists for no reason other than entertainment. This kind of thinking will ruin you, and everyone you come in contact with. Music is inherently powerful. Make that the starting point of all your thoughts."

"I gotta go," Russell said after a tense silence. He handed his teacher the fee for the lesson.

"Thank you," Hassan said. "Practice what I showed you. Next week we'll move on to something else."

"Yeah, sure, dude." Russell said, and walked out the door and down the stairs. He stopped at the outside door. It was raining. He cursed. Bracing himself to walk out into the downpour, he heard the door behind him open. It was Hassan. He handed Russell an old, but functional umbrella, and without a word disappeared, moving up the stairs with astonishing speed.

Chapter 4. Unexpected Perks and Pains.

The lessons continued.

Russell was learning a lot. Sometimes they would analyze one of the songs Russell wrote, and he would gain an insight into songwriting that was miles ahead of what he'd ever thought he was capable of. His technique improved greatly. Learning how to read music wasn't the boring task he thought it would be. His soloing was becoming more fluent and musical. Everyone who heard him noticed and commented on it. The knowledge he was acquiring seemed to flow into him, as if to fill a vacuum.

At other times, he was completely confused by his lessons. They analyzed jazz songs by Monk, Coltrane, Mingus, Wayne Shorter, or Miles Davis; or excerpts from symphonies by Bartok, Scriabin, Stravinsky, and Rimsky-Korsakov (which Russell didn't care much for). Hassan attempted to demonstrate how to use their concepts in an improvisational setting. Sometimes he would teach him something about the music theory of Arabian, African, or Indian music. He gave Russell things to read; magazine articles, photocopies out of books.

Upon arriving for one lesson, Hassan told him not to unpack his guitar. While Russell stood confused, Hassan went to the other side of the room, opened a large strange shaped case and pulled out a sitar. Hassan handed it to him and said "Play it." He tried, but couldn't get much out of it. Hassan showed him some techniques on the strange instrument, and after a while, Russell managed to play some melodies on it. The rest of the lesson consisted of him attempting to play a variety of exotic instruments that Hassan had lying around his home, such as string instruments that operated on very un-guitarlike principles, wind instruments that made bizarre and comical noises, and percussion instruments that sounded nothing like what he thought a drum should sound like.

"I don't expect you to be able to play these instruments" Hassan said. "I'm just introducing you to different methods of making music. The electric guitar is not the beginning and end of all music," he added with a chuckle. Later, Hassan put on a tape of a singer named Pandit Pran Nath, and after listening for a while, Hassan told him to "play like that." He couldn't come close, but Hassan didn't seem to mind. Russell actually had fun trying out all those weird instruments, and said so. At the end of the lesson Hassan refused any payment.

Another time, Hassan handed him a pencil, some manuscript paper, and a book of Rumi's poetry. Telling him to open the book to page 63 he said "Put this to music. I'll be back in two hours." Then he left. Russell sat dumbstruck. During Hassan's absence he thought about looking around the apartment a bit, but resisted the temptation to invade his teacher's privacy. Upon his return, Hassan said "Play what you came up with." Russell hadn't done much. Hassan told him to keep working on it, and then sent him home. This time, he accepted payment.

Sometimes he was told to listen to tapes of music that Hassan had compiled on a cassette. None of it, except a few obscure songs by Jimi Hendrix (songs Russell had never heard before, but liked) was the least bit familiar to him. This included jazz, Indian raga, Arabian, Mongolian singers, Pygmy music, Chinese music, symphonies, Qur'anic recitation, and environmental recordings. One was a recording of sounds from outer space that the Voyager space probes had recorded. Hassan told him to "find the music in it." Russell was very confused by all of this.

One night Russell called to cancel the lesson. He had a bad cold. Hassan told him that he would come to his home, and that the lesson would be free (sometimes Hassan would knock a few dollars off his fee. Occasionally, when the lesson was unusually "exotic", or if Russell's playing particularly pleased him, he waived the fee completely). Unable to resist the offer he agreed; giving him directions to his home. When Hassan arrived, they skimmed through the contents of the previous lesson. Russell was grateful; he hadn't the strength to withstand his teacher's usual rigors. Hassan suggested taking a break, during which he offered to make tea.

"Damn! You like your tea, don't you," quipped Russell.

Hassan chuckled. Handing him a cup, Russell stared at the tea: it smelled strong, and tasted stronger. "Yech! You trying to poison me?" Hassan laughed again and said "Not this time. It's an herbal expectorant; it'll help your cold. You have any honey?"

When they resumed the lesson Hassan took the acoustic guitar he'd brought and tuned it to an open tuning.

"Are you going to play in an open tuning?" Russell asked.

"No. You are." Hassan replied, handing him the instrument.

He showed Russell a few strange sounding chords, and then taught him to play them in a time signature which was unfamiliar to him. After Russell mastered the rhythm to his teacher's satisfaction, Hassan took a strange looking wind instrument from his bag.

"Where did you get that thing?" asked Russell.

"Overseas." Hassan said unhelpfully, and gestured to Russell to play. After the song picked up some momentum, he began to play the strange sounding instrument; using a scale which he never heard before. *Sounds like snake-charmer music*, thought Russell; *I hope the neighbors don't bug out*. As the improvisation progressed, Russell began to feel light headed. His vision became sharp and his color perception became more pronounced. He lost all concept of time. The bodily discomforts which tormented him disappeared. His mind became clearer than it had ever been. His thoughts were free from confusion. He sensed an understanding of new truths, like a great spiritual awakening. His perception of his body, the instrument in his hands, the man blowing into the exotic pipe in front of him, all disappeared. He was one and at peace.

After the song ended, and Russell came to his senses, he looked at the clock. To his amazement he realized that over three hours had passed, and that he was soaked with perspiration.

"Man! That was something!" Russell gasped. "Did you put acid or something in that tea?"

Hassan laughed. "No such luck, young man."

Suddenly, Hassan looked very tired. "Get some rest. Call me when you feel better." He left.

For about a half hour Russell tried to get himself together. He took a shower. His nose ran profusely, coughed up a lot of phlegm, and spent a lot of time in the lavatory. Finally he fell asleep, exhausted. He had a long, very vivid dream. He was standing in a great clearing with a small group of people. He was tearing bits of rags and dirt from his clothes and throwing them into a fire. Overhead, the stars were moving in an ever changing series of patterns. The planets were close enough to reach out and touch; he could have held the stars in his hand. He and the people he was with were waiting, anticipating a wonderful event.

When Russell woke up, he realized that his cold was gone. This amazed him; his colds usually hung on for over a week. Russell automatically associated his recovery with his teacher's visit, but wasn't precisely sure why. He called Hassan.

"Yes?"

"Hassan. It's Russ."

"Russell! Asalaam Alaikum. How are you my brother?"

"My cold is gone. How did you do that?"

"Yes, I know," Hassan said.

"Man, you gotta teach me how to do that!" Russell said.

Hassan replied "No."

Here we go again. "What? Why not?"

Sighing, he said "Russell, what I did last night requires years to learn. I can't teach it in a few easy lessons. You're not ready. You may never be ready. I have to slam this door in your face, and I know how much it annoys and hurts you. I'm truly sorry. Do yourself a favor; never ask me to teach it to you. When and if you are ready, I'll teach it to you. Or you'll figure it out without my help. But only when the time is right, not a minute sooner."

There came a time when Hassan began to take him places. These were always places which were unfamiliar to him, and whose purpose for the most part eluded Russell's understanding.

One evening Hassan took him to a mosque. Russell sat on the floor and tried to take it all in. The Arabic speech made him uncomfortable as he didn't understand a word of it, although some of it was translated for him. He wasn't used to sitting on the floor. His legs kept falling asleep. The prayer ritual was completely incomprehensible. The whole thing left him uncomfortable, but he had to admit, the people were polite, hospitable, and friendly, not at all like the Arab terrorists and Black Nationalists he'd seen (or imagined he'd seen) on TV. Later they brought out some food. Most ate with their fingers, but there were plastic forks for whoever wanted them. The food was spicier than he was used to but he liked it. As they left, an Egyptian man named Mustapha gave Russell a copy of a translation of the Holy Qur'an. He was struck by the gesture; the man seemed to be humbly bestowing a gift of fantastic value upon him. It would be a long time before he would look at this book.

Once, after Russell came back from a brief and successful, yet uneventful tour with his band, Hassan gave him an address in Harlem and told him to meet him there, and bring his guitar. He took the train to 145th street, and walked to the location. Nothing was familiar about this neighborhood; the buildings, the music blasting out of windows and cars, the faces of people walking or standing around, the authoritative stance and body language of the men, the unfamiliar movements and shape of the women, the clothes, the aromas of strange food coming from West Indian and African restaurants, everything frightened and intrigued him. People were talking. They were speaking English, yet he understood little of it. People would walk into dark doorways and he would wonder what secrets were concealed within those labyrinthine corridors. Sometimes people made eye contact with him. A man would nod to him, with a half smile. Russell would nod back, and continue on his way confused. *Aren't they supposed to hate me?* Unlike many of his friends, he was not given to racial prejudice, but he'd also never ventured far outside of his own subculture, and didn't understand its cause, nor how it manifested in America. His main exposure to African Americans (with the exception of the very few who ventured into his hangouts) was from the television or the movies.

This was different. Life was following an unmistakable rhythm here. Russell could almost count the beats of this rhythm. He saw desolation in the run down, burned out buildings grouped incongruously with new, well maintained buildings and stores; and felt a tension in the air that was threatening; dangerous. He also saw a joy and a pride which he didn't understand. He perceived an alternative tradition arising from a history he was never taught. The worst part of it was that he was the stranger. He didn't like being a stranger.

Upon arriving at the place he walked inside and saw Hassan. He and his teacher were the only European-Americans in a sea of black bodies, although there were a couple of Japanese people there as well. Hassan seemed completely at ease here as he introduced him to some of the other people in the room. The unexpected friendliness of the people who greeted Russell left him even more alienated.   This evening there was a jam session scheduled. This was "jazz." Russell watched and listened sheepishly. These musicians, like his teacher, were in command of a frightening amount of musical expertise, which they wore very casually but with a proud and protective undercurrent.

After about an hour, Hassan wrote some chord symbols on a piece of paper. Handing it to Russell he said, "This is the song that they're playing." It was "Impressions" by John Coltrane, a song with a very simple modal jazz structure of two chords: D minor 7 and Eb minor 7. Hassan asked if he could follow what was going on. He couldn't, but said yes. Hassan told Russell to go to the bandstand, plug in and play after the next soloist was done. He did as he was told. The soloist he was meant to follow, a young trumpet player, ran through the changes like a master. Hassan looked at Russell when the soloist was done. *Here goes nothing*, Russell thought.

He fumbled through the song, hardly able to make sense of what the rest of the band was doing. The bass player didn't ride the tonic like a rock bassist would. He played all the notes of the chord. The drummer didn't keep a steady beat, but rather added fills in strange places. The pianist played unnatural chords at odd times. He didn't know how to play against any of this. He tried playing the things which had always worked in his band. They didn't sound right here. His guitar was designed solely for heavy rock music, and couldn't generate a tone suitable to this music. Soon he got lost and couldn't find his place in the song. This was a two chord song and he couldn't handle it. His face turned red. The faces of the others in the room were dripping with emotion, some with pity, others with barely concealed disgust. He couldn't look at them. He was unprepared for the demonstrative mannerisms of Harlemites. He tried to keep playing, but the bass player got up and walked off the bandstand. The song had officially fallen apart. He unplugged his guitar and left the bandstand.

As he walked off, Nur Abdullah, a man who had been playing saxophone gently said to him "You ought to work on your technique. It's weak."

Russell said nothing and continued to his seat. Hassan was standing at the bar talking to the piano player. Gesturing to Russell to join them, he introduced the man: "Russell, this is Nurideen."

Nurideen said to him "Yo, I'm sorry we lost our cool up there, little brother. Hassan was telling me you're his student."

Russell said "Yeah,,, sorry, I sucked. I never played this kind of music before."

Nurideen said "Don't feel bad; everyone goes through what you just went through."

The two men continued to speak in this vein. Phrases such as "Trial by fire", "It's how you learn", "Take your lumps" and the like, filtered through Russell's roiling emotions. Russell wanted to say something, but didn't know what to say. He was grateful for the kind words, but they made him uncomfortable. He wanted to leave immediately.

Hassan said "I'm going to go for some dinner. Would you like to join me? Let me make up for the hard time I've been giving you."

"Sure."

Hassan took him to an Ethiopian restaurant. He had never eaten this kind of food before, and he wasn't sure he liked it.

As they ate Russell said "Why did you do that to me?"

"Why do you think?" asked Hassan.

"You enjoyed it, didn't you? You put me up there to humiliate me! Those people were laughing at me!" Russell poked at his food with the injira bread. "Why can't these people eat with a knife and fork like everyone else? What is this slop you're making me eat? What's in it? If we're going to have breakfast, let's have bacon and eggs."

Hassan said "Lower your voice. You're in a public place."

Russell sat, fuming.

"What you are experiencing is called cultural shock," Hassan continued. "It's also called growth. You're at a dangerous place in your life. You could lose everything. There are a lot of other crisis situations you may expect. You will find your perceptions and concepts of the world and yourself to have changed. I advise you to change along with it."

"I never wanted to change a damn thing! All I wanted was to learn some stuff on guitar. All this 'mystical' and 'cultural' crap you're laying on me ain't doing me no good! Why are you wasting my time with this bullshit? What good will it do me?"

"Wasting time?" Hassan further lowered his voice. "I warned you that what I was going to teach you would cost you. What you were in love with would have destroyed your life."

Hassan took a bite of his food, and then continued. "By the way, I know that you thought you were deceiving me. You only deceived yourself. Whether you realize it or not, you have passed a point of no return. It was destined to happen. You can't stop now. To go back would be fatal. You've been living in an insulated world. You know your subculture, your music, your small circle of friends and associates. Nothing else. If you remain where you are you'll end up in a spiritual and artistic cul de sac which you can't break out of. Then the 'fashion trend' changes and you can't change with it. Then, after the managers, agents, and record companies are finished robbing you blind, you'll spend the rest of your life sitting in a neighborhood bar, drinking yourself into a stupor every night waiting to die, telling your 'Guess who I used to be' stories to anyone who will listen. If you're lucky, you may have a brief moment back in the limelight in some 'where are they now?' presentation. This is where you you're headed. You may still end up there. It's up to you.

"I'm trying to show you the way out of that and into something better. You remember the reaction you had when you first heard me? Remember how you wanted to be able to do the same thing? This is the price you pay. This is how it's done. Nothing else works. The process of maturing is not so much the acquisition of more and more tidbits of knowledge as it is a stripping away of the non- essentials."

After a pause he added "By the way, for your information, you should be nauseated at the idea of eating bacon and eggs. Especially bacon. Pork is not fit for human consumption. Don't eat it; it'll kill you."

He punctuated his last point with a bite of his food, which he seemed to very much enjoy. He used Russell's silence as an excuse to eat heartily. Russell hardly touched his. More than halfway through his doro watt, Hassan broke the silence. "You're going on another tour soon, aren't you?"

"Yeah. Listen, I have something to ask you. The night before there's going to be a jam session at one of my hangouts. You wanna stop by?"

"I'd be delighted" Hassan said, with an amused smile.

*****

This session was at a rock club in Queens. When Hassan walked in Russell was standing near the bar drinking a beer. *I wish he'd stop drinking,* thought Hassan. Russell was having a good time though; now he was in his element. He was an important person here, and although Russell was not given to excesses of egomania, he enjoyed the attention.

The jam session started. Hassan wore earplugs the whole time. Though he smiled and was friendly and polite to everyone he spoke to, he also looked bored and irritated.

After a while he was called to the stage. He took an old Stratocaster out of the case and plugged it into an amp. The band called a blues in C#. Hassan started the song, but insisted that another guitarist take the first solo. *He's good*, thought Russell, listening to the shredding of the first solo. He stopped himself from thinking *but Hassan is better*. He knew Hassan could hold his own here but almost hoped he'd mess up, unlikely as that was.

His hope was dashed when Hassan's turn to solo came. Russell was astonished; he was fantastic! Everyone stopped what they were doing to listen, even the bartenders. The other guitarist stood with his mouth hanging open. That same feeling came into the room that Russell knew so well; Hassan was doing it again. He interspersed strange, altered chord melodies reminiscent of Sun Ra with intense blues licks. As part of his solo he played a series of melodies using nothing but feedback, of which he displayed an absolute mastery. At another moment he played the guitar with his teeth, and then laughed as though it were a joke. At the climax of his solo, he played a note that had a devastating effect upon everyone; the entire room vibrated with the power of that single note.

That one note would reverberate in Russell's head for the rest of his life.

After the song Hassan went to the bar and ordered an orange juice. Several people came up to him and congratulated him, asked questions, and asked for his phone number.

During the conversation, Hassan mentioned that he didn't play this kind of music anymore.

When asked why, he said "Because there's no challenge and nothing left for me to explore. The music they call 'alternative'; the so called 'new' music is the same thing people were playing 20 years ago. The only thing that's different is the technology and some of the drugs. I want nothing to do with the rock 'n roll lifestyle. I left that behind years ago and I don't want to go back. There's nothing there that either contributes to my spiritual and artistic growth or conforms to my spiritual beliefs. Besides" he smiled "I'm getting too old for this nonsense."

The people listening to all this didn't know how to take it. A young woman began to make a whining, nagging defense of the music she loved. Hassan stared at her: she seemed to wither away from him.

Not long after this Hassan said goodbye and thanked Russell for the invitation. "I must admit; I enjoyed myself, although this loud music and confusion is very uncomfortable. The loud noise upsets my digestion; I must leave. See you tomorrow?"

"Yeah! I'll be over at 7:00. Yo, you played great, man!"

"All praise is due to Allah." Smiling shyly, Hassan departed.

*****

The house was dark and very quiet when Hassan arrived home. A small nightlight from the kitchen and a few candles cast faint illumination. Amina approached him from the bedroom. They kissed.

She looked at him intently. "Are you alright?"

Hassan smiled. "I'm OK. I guess the loud music didn't agree with me."

Amina said "Please don't go back to such places. You are always telling me to be careful with music. Look at you now! You are a wreck!" she exclaimed in the rich contralto and thick Senegalese accent her voice assumed when she was upset.

"I can't fool you," Hassan said somewhat sheepishly.

"No, *husband*, you can't. Besides, you stink of beer and the cigarettes and the dope they smoke." She sighed. "Are you coming to bed or do you want to read a bit first?"

"I'll come to bed after I wash up and have some tea. Do you want some?"

"I'll make it. You wash up."

After changing his clothes and washing his beard and hair, he went to the kitchen. He watched the water as it boiled.

"You smell better," Amina said. After a pause, she said "You are concerned about your new young student, yes?"

"I am," Hassan admitted, as she poured the water for the tea. "I knew the minute I met him that he was out of sync with himself. I soon realized that Allah must be preparing him for something. I worry about him, a little."

Amina said "Allah guides and protects whom He will. And He loves His creation. He loves you, my love. Have faith that Allah is the best to know and the best to plan. I have faith that Allah will guide both of you. And remember: I have faith in you too."

She paused a moment and said "I want to tell you something I never told you. Before we were married, I saw in a dream that you would rise to great heights, and help others to do so. What you build will benefit all the worlds, and last until the Day of Judgment. I knew then that you are a good man, and that you are my man. So, do not worry. Everything will be fine in the end."

50

The vast color spectrum of her eyes shined with a luminescence that rivaled the candle in the middle of the table. For a moment, Hassan saw past the lovely face of his wife, the magnificent body he enjoyed so much, and the closeness they shared. He saw her Ruh which was reflected in what his bodily senses perceived. It was a timelessness that held a promise that was beyond words, beyond action. Even now, as the light faded, and his beloved wife remained in its wake, he mourned for what he saw as the world pulled him back. But he would never forget.

Hassan smiled at her. "You're right, as usual." He paused. "Its times like this that I am reminded why I married you." She smiled. They embraced, their essences drawing toward union, and walked towards the bedroom.

The two cups of tea were forgotten until morning.

A few days later Russell ran into Hassan while downtown on business. Hassan walked Russell to the train. "Tomorrow you're going on your tour. How have the rehearsals been progressing?"

Russell said "Good. I've been trying to use some of what you taught me. Sometimes it doesn't work; sometimes it does. I used some of it on the record too."

"Good" said Hassan, "There's something else I have to tell you."

"What?"

"You're going to be in the thick of your 'rock 'n roll' world. One of two things will happen. You will either forget about everything I taught you, or you will find that you will need to utilize the things I've been teaching you. If the former occurs, it may do a great deal of damage to you musically and spiritually which you will not be able to perceive even if I point it out to you. If the latter occurs, you may find your new found knowledge to be incompatible with your surroundings. You will see the lifestyle as being something other than what you once knew it to be. It will be frustrating and traumatizing: be ready for that."

Russell felt an inexplicable twinge of pain, identical to the feeling of guilt and dread he'd felt as a child when he did something wrong.

"I'll be alright," he said, half to himself.

"Have a good time, Russell. May Allah guide you safely. Remember your promise to call me, and to read that Qur'an my friend gave you." They shook hands. Hassan said "Asalam Alaikum."

"Take care dude."

*****

Eddie was beginning to show the effects of the beer he drank. He discreetly sniffed some cocaine, and offered some to Russell, which he took.

"Yo, that tour was weird," Eddie said. "We all tried to figure out what was wrong with you."

Russell said "Yeah. It was weird alright. I never thought we'd get through it."

Chapter 5. An Aborted Attempt at Escape from Destiny.

The night before the tour, Russell didn't get much sleep. What little he got was sabotaged by a disturbing nightmare. He was in an abandoned building. Rats ran around his feet. A large snake was coiled around his arm. He tried to get the repulsive reptile off him, but it kept coiling around his arm. Russell had a grip on its head so that it couldn't bite him. He dared not let his grip loose.

The alarm clock rang from the table across the room. He woke with a start and tried to catch his breath. His heart was racing and he was drenched in sweat. He staggered into the shower. When he got out, he called a car service to take him to the band's rendezvous point. He got dressed and ate while he waited for the car to arrive.

The band had rented a bus for their tour, which was parked at the rendezvous point. Upon arriving, Russell threw his suitcases in the back of the bus. The instruments and amplifiers had been packed in a separate truck, which was driven by the band's roadie named Mark Kovacelic, and another roadie, Joe Palionelli.

Eddie walked over to him, put his arm around him and said "You ready?"

"You bet," said Russell, unconvincingly.

Eddie offered Russell a can of beer, which he accepted. Curt Janovic, the band's bass player was sharing some marijuana with Keith Keller, the lead singer. Both looked visibly intoxicated. It was 7:30 A.M. The sun was shining.

They piled into the bus and claimed their individual territories. The stereo was playing an old Black Sabbath tape. An aging member of the Hell's Angels motorcycle club who worked as the group's driver and road manager, known only by the name Jimbo, lit a cigar and roared "And away we go!" as the bus, followed by the truck pulled out.

Soon the small caravan was driving on the interstate. No one had any idea where they were except Jimbo, whose knowledge of the American highways was profound; he seemed to know every inch of the continental United States. As usual, Keith passed out. Curt locked himself in the lavatory, and later came out even more stoned, and sat down in an almost comatose state. Eddie and Jimbo began the first of a long line of debates wherein Eddie would offer an opinion on subjects about which he knew nothing, and Jimbo constantly bringing the conversation around to either sex or his experiences in prison or Cambodia during the Vietnam War.

Many hours later, Jimbo had put on a mixtape of Hank Williams and David Allen Coe. ("Hank and Dave understand what life's all about!" Few had the nerve to argue with him.) Keith was still unconscious, and Curt had followed suit. Eddie was reading a pornographic magazine and drinking his sixth beer for the morning. Russell's mind was foggy from the beer and marijuana. The boredom and the close quarters with these, his idiosyncratic friends, was irritating him. He wanted something to do. Suddenly he remembered the Qur'an that Hassan told him to bring with him. Pulling it out of his bag and opening it at random, he began to read.

" *Oh you who believe! Intoxicants and gambling, (dedication of) stones, and (divination by) arrows, are an abomination, of Satan's handiwork: eschew such (abomination) that you may prosper. Satan's plan is but to excite enmity and hatred between you with intoxicants and gambling, and hinder you from the remembrance of Allah, and from prayer: will you not then abstain?"*

He turned the pages.

"It may be that Allah will grant love (and friendship) between you and those whom you now hold as enemies. For Allah has power over all things; and Allah is oft-Forgiving, Most Merciful."

"Yo Russ! What'cha readin'?" Eddie blurted out.

"Mind your business," he said with a dismissive snarl.

Eddie lurched forward, grabbing the book.

"Lemmie see it." Opening it and glancing at its contents, he began to read it out loud in a drunken parody of a Southern televangelist.

"As to those who are rebellious and wicked, their abode will be the fire: every time they wish to get away therefrom, they will be forced thereinto, and it will be said to them: "You taste

the penalty of the Fire, the which you were wont to reject as

false."

Eddie and Jimbo began laughing out loud.

Jimbo said "I didn't know we was gonna have a born-again Bible banger on this tour! If Ida known that, Ida chased all that Jack Daniels with holy water!"

Eddie sputtered with laughter yelling "Halleluliah! The boy done got religion! He's saved! Praise the Lord and pass the Budweiser!"

Russell said "Shut the hell up, Eddie." Eddie ignored him; continuing his puerile monologue. Russell repeated himself; "I said, shut up!"

Eddie said "When did you start readin' th' Bible?"

"Hassan reads it. He says it's from God. And it's not the Bible; it's the Qur'an."

Eddie said "So what? It's all the same. Someone wrote that crap so they can keep people ignorant and suck money out of them. I'd rather listen to some rock an' roll. That's what's happenin', Dude."

"Yeah," Russell said, "Like that Penthouse you're reading is gonna educate you."

Eddie picked up the magazine and said "Ain't nothin' wrong with a little sex, Russ. You keep readin' that crap and you won't even know what to do with a shkafooza when she drops her bloomers for you."

At that moment Jimbo roared "We're here!"

They pulled into a driveway. Everyone piled out of the bus. Jimbo went inside to announce their arrival to the staff of the large rock club where they were playing. Everyone was in a festive mood, except Russell.

Later, after everyone had eaten, and the sound equipment was set up and checked, the band was lounging in the dressing room. A woman from a local radio station was interviewing Keith. Curt looked half asleep and was nodding his head. Everyone was exhausted.

Russell said 'Yo, we're all wiped out and we gotta play this gig! We can't go on like this."

"Not to worry" said Curt.

He took a packet of cocaine out of his pocket and poured some on the table. He used a credit card to divide the pile of powder into four equal piles which he arranged into lines. "This'll wake us up," Curt slurred.

Rolling a dollar bill into a tube, he sniffed the powder up his nose. The drug's effects hit him immediately; he stood up wide eyed, and sniffed and wiped at his nose. He handed the bill to Eddie who indulged himself gleefully and noisily. Russell followed suit, hoping he wouldn't be too nervous to play. Keith walked over to the table and took his share while the woman from the radio station tried to continue the interview. Soon the group was a bundle of nervous energy.

Russell took his guitar out of its case and began to play. His fingers seemed to be charged with electricity. He fought to gain control of his instrument; but the drug seemed to have other ideas.

Eddie came up to him and said, "Man, your hands are shaking like a Catholic virgin on her weddin' night."

Russell said "It's the coke; I must've did too much." He was grinding his teeth and fidgeting; his mind racing from one crazed thought to another.

Eddie said "Maybe Curt has something to take the edge off. Yo! Curt! You got anything for Russ?"

Curt felt around in his pockets and pulled out some pills. "Take these" Curt said.

Russell refused "I'll be OK." *Damn*, he thought, *this guy's a regular pharmacy*.

When it was time to go on stage they were greeted by an enthusiastic audience, but Russell was not enjoying himself. The band didn't sound right. Eddie's timing was off, Curt's playing was sloppy, Keith was so off-key that Russell could count on one hand the number of notes he sang in tune. *Funny, I didn't notice this before.* Russell's own playing was a nervous jumble of notes and noise. It seemed that the worse the band played and the more obnoxious they acted on stage the louder the audience screamed for them. He wondered what Hassan would've said.

After the show the band went back to the dressing room and fell to the case of beer that had been placed there. The road crew was packing and loading the equipment. Russell sat in silence.

Eddie bounded up to him. "Great show! This is how a tour should start! We did it again, Russ!"

Russell said "We sounded like absolute shit, and you know it."

Eddie said "What? I thought we sounded great. The audience liked us. What's the problem?"

"Don't tell me you believe that. We played like amateurs. We were out of tune, the rhythm was off, the amps and sound system sounded like a transistor radio. We weren't playing good music. We just made noise."

"So what if we hit a few bum notes? You think we gotta sound like Beethoven or somethin'? This is rock, man! We don't need to be perfect. We just gotta do what we do."

Russell shook his head, silently searching for an escape from whatever it was he was feeling.

As if on cue Eddie handed him a bottle of vodka. "Here, Dude. Drown your sorrows."

The next day Russell woke up on the floor of the bus. He was wearing the same clothes he was in the day before. His head was pounding. His stomach was churning violently. His vision was blurred, his hands numb and shaking and his mouth tasted like the inside of one of Jimbo's boots. He stood up and the bus began to spin. The pounding in his head got worse.

Keith looked at him and said "The dead hath risen."

"Where are we?" Russell croaked.

"Just outside of Springfield, Illinois" Jimbo announced. "Chicago is coming up soon. You better git yerseff together, cowboy."

Russell stumbled to the lavatory. Crashing inside, he fell to his knees and vomited violently in the toilet.

Curt said, "Don't worry Russ. I'll have you in shape for the show. Get some rest."

"Hey Russ! You hungry?" Keith said, holding out a half eaten McDonald's bacon cheeseburger and fries. Russell looked at the offensive piece of fast food and ran back to the toilet. Everyone laughed.

"Here" Eddie said, holding out a can of beer. "Drink this. It'll reestablish your biorhythms." Russell drank. Moments later he seemed to feel better, but was still in no shape to do anything but sleep.

Later, in the dressing room of the venue they were playing, Curt took Russell aside, looked at him and said "You need help." Leading him into a dark staircase, he pulled "The Pouch" out of his bag and poked through it. This was the first time he had seen the inside of "The Pouch." He almost wished he hadn't. There was an eighth of an ounce of cocaine, small packets of some unidentifiable powder, a bag of marijuana, a bottle of pills mixed indiscriminately, and an eyeglass case.

Curt said "You still got that headache?"

"Yeah."

"Take these" Curt said, handing him some capsules. This time he took them, washing them down with a beer. Curt then offered him some cocaine, which he also accepted. Thanking him, Russell headed to the dressing room and prepared for the show.

Again the show was terrible.

Again the audience loved it.

Again the band thought they were master musicians.

Again Russell couldn't stand himself.

Later they went to a hotel. A group of people came with them. Soon a full fledged party was in effect. Everyone was drunk, high, or both. A young woman took off her top and bra. The result was a noisy and messy orgy. Russell walked out of the room. Standing outside, he looked at the stars and moon. *What's going on here? Why do I hate this?* Normally he would have been in there indulging himself. Now he couldn't wait for the tour to end. And this was only the second day! How would he get through this?

He looked at the far wall of the building. There was a pay phone. Obeying an impulse he walked to the phone and picked up the receiver. Dialing the number he knew by heart, he waited for the operator.

A moment later, Hassan was on the phone.

"Asalaam Alaikum! How are you? How's the tour so far?"

Russell said "It's OK. We're in Chicago. The shows have been well received."

"How have you been?"

"I'm OK."

Hassan paused "Are you really? You don't sound so good."

Russell said "I'm fine. Really. It's just that,,," He trailed off. Hassan waited. "I don't feel like it's going the way it should. We played like shit. They liked us anyway. The guys don't even know how bad we sounded. They, I mean, Damn! This ain't working! It doesn't feel right."

Hassan said "Is there any way you can get out of this obligation?"

"No. I gotta finish the tour" Russell said. "Hassan, this isn't right. Something's wrong. I don't feel like a part of this, but I'm stuck in the middle of it."

"Russell," Hassan began "what you're going through is exactly what I thought would happen. There isn't anything you can do right now except fulfill your obligations and stay out of trouble. After the tour you can chill for a while and decide what you're going to do. Or, you could leave now and let the chips fall where they may. Its up to you."

"I can't leave."

"Well, it's your call. I know it may be hard to believe, but I know exactly how you feel. If you need to talk, I'm here."

"Thanks. I'll stay in touch. Look, I gotta go. Take care."

"Ma Salaam." He hung up.

Russell stood silent. *The only way I'm gonna survive is to play this game*, he thought.

Eddie came out. "Yo! What're you doin' out here? The ladies are asking for you." A young woman wearing too much makeup and not enough clothes came out.

She said "Come in and join the party Russ. I wanna play." She giggled idiotically, took him by the hand and led him back to the room.

The tour progressed like that for the next three weeks.

Sometime in the middle of the fourth week, Keith rummaged through Curt's "Pouch" and got inebriated by show time that the band was convinced he wouldn't live through the show. Afterwards Curt beat him up. It took Russell and Jimbo's combined efforts to pull him off. They took Keith to the hospital, where he stayed overnight. Nobody pressed charges. The next day, both Jimbo and Mark got several speeding tickets trying to make up for lost time. The next week Keith had had his way with a woman who later told him in front of everyone that she had AIDS. Keith gave her a beating which sent her to the hospital. The incident was highly publicized. Jeff Michael, the band's manager, flew out to meet the band and gave Keith a lambasting that resulted in a fight and almost caused the demise of the band.

Another night Russell's equipment refused to work. He had to borrow an amplifier, which did not meet his requirements. Eddie disappeared one night. He was found the next day in another city with no recollection of how he got there. The next night one of Russell's guitars and several pieces of the band's equipment were stolen. Curt disappeared more than once, and often asked for a "loan" which was never repaid. Somehow, though, he always had plenty of drugs.

Once, Curt mentioned that he had some acid. Russell had never taken acid before. An hour after taking what was considered three times the normal dose, he had to go on stage and play, while hallucinations and weird delusions filled his mind. The guitar in his hands was a rubbery and botanical machine. It made noises that mocked him and sent waves of uncontrolled vibrations pounding out of his amplifiers. People became ugly, slimy, slithering reptilian monstrosities that laughed and leered conspiratorially at him. At the hotel after the show, the TV was showing the movie "The Exorcist." This didn't help at all. He ran to the bathroom and locked himself inside, but couldn't find the light switch and sat in the dark for hours. Outside the door, his band mates banged on the door and shouted incomprehensible things at him. He spent the night trapped in a labyrinth of demented nightmarish mental images, with no reference point to anything he'd previously understood to be reality.

The next day he was physically and psychologically drained. He had nothing left with which to function. But he plodded on. He had no choice.

Ironically, the band had never enjoyed more public acclaim. The rock press, for the most part, treated them well, and seemed amused by their antics. Their record was selling well, and, according to Jeff, the band was making money, though no one but Jeff seemed to have access to any of it.

Finally, Russell decided to give Hassan another call.

"Yes?"

"Yo, Hassan! It's Russ. What's up?"

"Asalam Alaikum, Russell. I'm fine. How are you?"

Russell said "Good. We're making it through the tour. It's been hard, though."

"I've been reading the paper. Has it been as bad as they say?"

"It's been worse. But we're hanging in there."

Pausing, Hassan finally said "Russell, you should think about quitting the band. You may want to think about starting your life with a clean slate."

"What?! What're you saying?"

"I'm serious Russell. I see what this is doing to you. I'm not stupid. I've seen it destroy stronger people than you."

Russell was livid. "What do you know about what I'm going through? I broke my back to build what I have here,"

Hassan broke in "So someone else can make all the money and leave you with a substance abuse problem and a lot of debts you'll never escape? Russell, you're not stupid, you can see what this is doing to you. You can see,"

"Shut up!!" Russell yelled "I know exactly what I'm doing! This is my life! This is what I do! This is what I am! It's all I know! And you want me to give it all up so I can sit around playing the same bullshit you play?! I'll tell you what: go to hell and take all that bullshit you believe in with you!! How does that sound?"

He slammed the receiver down and stormed off to the hotel. Upon arriving in his room, he took his Qur'an and all his other reading material and threw them in the garbage.

The tour continued as it had been. A blur of half remembered sensations, eruptions of violent arguments over meaningless controversies, empty and almost repulsive sexual exploits, and a desperate pursuit of sensation. Russell made sure he was at least marginally intoxicated during every waking hour. He accepted the flood of compliments aimed at him for work he knew was substandard. He drank, smoked, swallowed, and sniffed whatever was offered him. He accepted every invitation from any woman wasn't who offered. Anything to keep him from thinking about what he was doing long enough to exercise a modicum of self introspection.

He did everything he could to avoid sleep. When he did sleep, he was plagued by terrifying nightmares. He almost always woke up screaming, to the annoyance of whoever was nearby.

Interviews he gave to magazines and radio betrayed a self loathing and a subconscious desire for self destruction. His band mates were only vaguely aware of this. The band's manager saw it and didn't care. Russell once overheard him talking on the phone: "Who? Peterson? Yeah, I know! So what if he does? He can sodomize a dead goat in Macy's window for all I care! As long as I get my 15%, and whatever else I can grab, I'm happy. Believe me, there's plenty more where he came from."

One night when they were playing one of their last shows in Los Angeles, Russell went looking for Curt. Walking from door to door in the venue he called out "Curt! Where are you?" He opened a door marked "maintenance", not knowing why. Once inside, he saw Curt and an anorexic looking woman sitting on the floor propped up against the wall. Neither was moving.

"Yo, dumbass. We're leaving. Let's go." Curt didn't move. Russell walked up to him and noticed a needle sticking out of his arm. A chill ran through Russell. He tried to speak; it took half a minute for words to come out of his mouth.

"Curt. Please be alive, man." He reached out and felt his jugular-- no pulse.

"Curt! Curt! You can't be dead, man! You can't!" Russell noticed the faint smell of death coming from his friend already. He ran out of the room looking for someone. He kept saying "Oh shit! Oh shit!" over and over as if it were a mantra. Turning a corner, he slammed into Eddie and Jimbo, spilling their beers.

Jimbo bellowed "Hey! Watch it!"

Russell said "Curt's dead."

Eddie and Jimbo stared at him.

Jimbo said "Where is he?"

Pointing to the open door, he said "In there."

Jimbo walked into the room and inspected the bodies and then calmly called 911 on a nearby phone. He searched for Curt's pouch and flushed the remaining drugs down a toilet, then gave the pouch to a roadie with instructions to dispose of it somewhere outside the building.

The police arrived and were followed by a hoard of press people. Paramedics came and, minutes later, notified the coroner's office. Russell was questioned endlessly by everyone from the police to the press. He and Eddie were both in shock, but did what they could to remain in control of themselves. Jimbo, by contrast, was calm and incredibly helpful; his military experience came in handy at such a time as this. Keith was near hysterics and was of no use to anyone. Jeff called from New York, and told the band to come home when the police were through with them, but didn't fly out to help.

After five of the most hellish days the surviving band members ever experienced, they loaded the bus and truck, and headed home. "Make your asses comfy, boys," Jimbo said, armed with a bottle of black market amphetamine, "No sleep 'till New York." He put his beloved country music on the stereo. Nobody else was in the mood for country music, but nobody dared argue with him.

The three musicians sat in silence.

Finally Eddie said "So. Where do we go from here?"

Russell said "We gotta keep going. We gotta get another bass player, and keep the band alive."

Keith said "I don't know, man. I think we aughta, y'know,,," he whined.

Russell got mad "What're you saying? You think we should break up?!"

Keith said "Russ, we can't go on without Curt! How would it look? It sounds so cold blooded."

Russell stood up and screamed "We are not fucking breaking up! I'm not gonna take any of this! We didn't come this fucking far just to give up!"

Keith said "I'm just saying, Russ, think about --"

Russell interrupted his sentence with a fist to his face. Eddie tried to pull him off the frail singer and got a hard right backhand to the temple for his trouble. The scuffle continued until Jimbo pulled the bus to the side of the road, grabbed Russell, and threw him out the door.

Russell landed on the grass and gravel with a thud. Jimbo picked him up off the ground with one enormous arm, and with the other he slapped Russell in the face, hard, before bellowing "Cool out!" and tossing him back down again.

With his lips slowly curling away from what remained of his teeth he said "This is what we're gonna do. We're gonna drive home. When we get there, we gonna rest for a few days. Then, we'll all of us meet up and decide what to do. You got that?"

Russell said nothing. He stared at the enormous barrel chested man in front of him wearing the leather vest that said "Hell's Angels M.C. New York" and the tattoo on his arm of a heart with a dagger thrust through it above a scroll that said

"Trust Me." He looked at the scar across his face, the calluses on his knuckles, and the scuffed motorcycle boots. He glanced at the bulge in his shirt that suggested a concealed weapon. He stared at the eyes that stared back at him with no trace of the capacity for fear of man or beast. He wondered how he would beat him in a real fight.

Discretion being the better part of valor, he decided not to try.

Jimbo poked him in the chest with a finger and said, "Don't make me ask you a second time, kid."

Russell said "Yeah. You're right."

Jimbo brushed some of the dirt off him, kissed him on the forehead, put his arm around his shoulder, and said "Let's go home."

*****

Curt's funeral was a circus. The rock music community treated the attendance of the funeral as a status symbol to be coveted. Half the people there were there to be "seen." Russell was constantly accosted by people, asking questions, requesting or demanding interviews, offering drugs, asking if a replacement had been selected and offering to be that replacement. A fat, impotent, and thoroughly despicable looking Catholic priest with beady eyes and oily pasty skin gave a long rambling sermon amounting to absolutely nothing of any relevance to Curt's life. Curt's gentle, sincere, hardworking Midwestern parents were there. They seemed on the verge of a breakdown. Russell felt bad that they had to be exposed to this. Jeff was there, doing more business than mourning. "We must put this behind us and go on. Curt would have wanted it that way." Eddie was drunk, but not completely out of control. Keith had regained his composure and played the part of superficial moody rock singer to a tee.

After the burial, the band members were given a date and time for a meeting which would be held at Jeff's office. Everyone agreed to attend.

The meeting went more smoothly than was expected. They all agreed to find a bass player as soon as possible and continue. Several possible replacements were auditioned. They agreed unanimously upon a man named Jack Nicholson (no relation to the actor, and the recipient of an almost infinite variety of jokes). Two days later, a press conference was called to announce the replacement, and the band's intention to continue the tour the following month. The first show would be in Boston.

During this time, Russell mostly kept to himself. Although his intake of intoxicants was not as abundant as it had been on the tour, he was never completely sober. He refused to answer the telephone, and almost never returned the calls he got on his answering machine. He played his guitar only during rehearsals which, mercifully, were keeping him very busy.

One day he had to drive to the East Village to pick up some marijuana and cocaine from an acquaintance. He passed by

Hassan's apartment building. The sight of the building reminded him of what Hassan had said to him about quitting the band. The thought infuriated him. He ran over the memory of the phone call, the lessons, and all the things his teacher had said to him, again and again. His memories seemed to arouse his anger; Russell somehow placed the blame for all his recent misfortune upon Hassan. How else could he know this would happen?

"How dare that crazy old man tell me to quit? Forget it! I don't need his shit anymore."

That afternoon his girlfriend Denise visited him. They fought. Eddie called him. They met later at a bar. They drank and talked.

*****

The night at Rocco's Bar wore on. Eddie was drunk. So was Russell.

"Russ, I been thinking," Eddie said.

"I thought I smelled something burnin'," Russell interjected. After a brief pause they both laughed.

"Yo, serious, Russ, man. We been through a lot. I mean a lot. We seen some shit that woulda make anyone crazy. When Curt died, I thought that was the end. Especially after the fight we had. I'm glad we got through it. You helped hold the band together, Dude."

Russell said "Eddie, ain't nothin' gonna take this thing from me. I been fightin' for it so much; so much, man, I can't tell you. I been going through some changes like you wouldn't believe. I gotta hold on. This is all I got. Without this thing I ain't nothin'. Life ain't nothin'. Nothin' ain't nothin."

Eddie said "We all been going through some changes."

"No, man, I mean even during the tour. I had some weird shit going through my head. I thought that what we were doing was wrong. And you wanna know what? I called Hassan and talked to him, and he said that I should quit the band! That half-a-hump said I should quit the band! Like all I gotta do is throw my life away just cause he said so."

Eddie sputtered with laughter. "Russ, you gotta get rid of him."

"I did," said Russell. "I told him to go screw himself. Eddie, I don't know anything else. I don't have a damn thing in my life but this. If I lose this, I have no life."

Eddie said "Don't worry. We gonna live forever. We ain't never gonna die. Bartender! Another round! My friend's buying!"

After a while Eddie said "You know what? We aughta go get Jack and initiate him in the band by way of brewski libations. I'm gonna call him."

Eddie called him. Russell sat in silence. "He's at home, in Jersey. Let's go get him."

They walked out. Russell asked Eddie "You know how to get there?"

Eddie let out a noisy belch. "Yeah. I'll bring my car around. Follow me."

Russell climbed into his car, started the engine and waited. Seconds later, Eddie came around the corner. Russell put his car in gear and followed him.

As they drove through Manhattan, Russell put a favorite tape in the stereo by the German heavy metal group Accept. Singing along with Udo Dirkschnider's screeching lyrics about violent political uprising and sadomasochistic sex, he followed Eddie through some strange detour that he seemed to be making up as he went along. Russell thought to himself, *Everything is finally cool. Everything is finally going the way I want it. All I gotta do is keep going the way I'm going now. Things are working out great.*

Suddenly, as they came to the intersection of Bowery and Delancey, the light turned yellow then red. Eddie drove through the red light at about 45 mph. Whether he didn't see it, ignored it, or passed out at the wheel, nobody ever found out. An 18 wheel truck was entering the intersection at the same time, and Eddie's car slammed into it. Russell stopped his car and stared in disbelief for a few seconds before running out of the car. "Eddie! Eddie!" he screamed. Eddie was lying with his chest against the steering wheel. The windshield was smashed and splattered with blood and pieces of flesh and hair. Eddie's head was bent at an unnatural angle. His eyes stared straight ahead at nothing.

Russell backed away from the car. He held his hands against the sides of his head. His mouth was open, but no sound came out.

Chapter 6. Grabbing at a Rope.

There were several eyewitnesses, two of whom called 911. Soon the distant sound of sirens faded up from the distance and dominated the air. Flashing red and blue lights splashed an eerie illumination on the hideous scene. Russell barely moved. He stood and stared as the police examined the wreckage. He stood and stared as the EMS pulled Eddie's body from the car and placed it in the ambulance. He answered the police mechanically as they questioned him. After a while, Russell was told he was free to go.

As Russell walked slowly to his car, a policeman asked him "Are you gonna be alright?"

"Yeah. I'm fine," Russell said weakly. He got into his car and drove around Manhattan aimlessly. He had no idea where he was, where he was going, or what to do. His mind was blank. He parked his car near the George Washington Bridge. Staring over the Hudson river at New Jersey, the full impact of what had happened hit him. His best friend was dead. His career had just come to a grinding, screeching halt. Everything he valued was gone. Nothing was left except a feeling that he had done something wrong, that he had been lying to himself and that he had believed every word of his lie. He stumbled out of the car and fell to his knees. A cry of pure anguish tore from his body. Confusion and pain radiated through every part of his mind. Memories ran past him with blinding speed, and yet he missed nothing; he saw his life for what it was. His head buried in his hands, he wept uncontrollably.

He staggered to his feet with a single recurring thought: *I can't live like this another minute*. How could he continue? How could he rebuild a shattered life? How could he live with the knowledge of the spiritual wasteland he'd made of himself? Wiping the tears from his eyes, he walked up to the bridge, and looked down at the cold, polluted water.

"Russell!" It was Hassan. "Russell, what are you doing here?" asked Hassan.

"Leave me alone," Russell slurred, not looking up.

"Answer me, Russell, what are you doing here?"

"What difference does it make? I ain't got nothin' left."

"What are you talking about?" asked Hassan.

"Just… just go away and leave me alone. I have to..."

"You have to what?" There was a silence. "Wait,,,, you weren't going to jump, were you? You weren't going to kill yourself?" There was more silence. One or two lonely cars sped by. Russell held his breath for a moment, unable to form words or meet his teacher's gaze.

Hassan shook his head. "No. No, you weren't," he concluded.

Russell finally spoke. "I… I gotta do *something*, man! I mean, I gotta change *something*! I can't live like this!" A sob escaped him and soon he was weeping again. "Eddie's dead! He got killed in a car accident about an hour ago! I ain't got nothing! My best friends dead! My band's dead! My life's dead! I gotta do something, man! I gotta,,,"

"I'm sorry about your friend, Russell," Hassan said.

A gust of early-winter wind tore at their clothes. Russell felt nothing. Hassan shivered.

"It's cold out here. Let's get some coffee in you," Hassan said, and guided Russell towards a diner a few blocks away. It took two shots of espresso to calm the shaking of Russell's hands.

"You've been drinking."

Russell scoffed "What are you even doing here?"

"To tell you the truth, Russell, I'm not sure. I just suddenly got this urge to take a walk through Washington Heights."

"Whatever, bro," Russell sighed. He was empty. His vision was still blurry from the residue of the tears he hadn't the strength to wipe dry.

After a moment of silence, Hassan leaned forward in his seat. "I don't know if I ever asked you this," he said in a quiet but authoritative voice "but do you believe in Allah?"

"Huh?"

"Do you believe in God, Russell?"

"Yeah, I guess. So what?"

"Did it ever occur to you that your life was being guided? All the tribulations you have suffered and all the anguish you've felt have happened for a reason. Your life is valuable, Russell. Too valuable to throw away on meaningless nonsense. Too valuable to destroy for nothing."

"Destroy? What's left to destroy? My life is over."

Almost smiling, Hassan said "Do you think that you have some kind of pedigree on suffering? You don't want to see the real reason for all the things you have gone through. I saw them before they happened to you. Allah had something great in mind for you, a destiny greater than anything you ever imagined. You fought against it, but you can't fight it. You saw it, but you told yourself to ignore it. Allah cannot be ignored. Least of all by someone He loves as much as He loves you."

Hassan's words permeated his brain and body slowly, like water soaking through a sponge. "He loves you." "Allah cannot be ignored." Next followed the words of the Qur'an. No, not the words, but the experience of reading them while surrounded by booze, drugs, and toxic music. He could feel in his body again the sensation of self-deception. The thud of the Qur'an hitting the bottom of the garbage can when Hassan suggested that he quit rang in his ears. The noise of the tour rang in his ears. Jimbo's phone call to the police rang in his ears. He covered his ears with his hands, but the noise only got louder.

Suddenly, in a cataclysmic flash of understanding, Russell saw what he was running from. It all finally made sense to him. He experienced a moment of clarity like the ones he'd experienced before he strayed from his path. All the information he'd taken in finally came together as one. All time was one. And even as he desperately clung to this moment it began to slip away. This gift, even in its transcendence (no, it wasn't transient: he was) seemed a part of the lesson.

Hassan sensed what was happening. He dared not interrupt.

Finally, Russell spoke. "Hassan? Is this how it works? Is this what we go through? It's too much,,, too much,,,"

"I know, Russell. I know." Hassan stood and Russell followed. The men hugged. Russell wept. For several minutes he could do nothing else.

"I'm tired of fighting," he declared, taking his seat again with tired determination. "I want to be a Muslim."

Hassan sat as well. "You realize that this is no small thing? You're making a contract with Allah. Are you ready for that?"

"Yes. I'm ready. I'm not running away anymore."

Hassan smiled; he understood what Russell meant. He said "Repeat after me. As Shadu an laa--"

"As... Shadu an laa--" Russell stammered slowly.

"--illaha il Allah--"

"--illaha il Allah--"

"--wa Ash shadu anna--"

"--wa Ash shadu anna--"

"Muhammadan rasulullah."

"Muhammadan rasulullah. Haha, what did I just say?"

"You said 'I bear witness there is no god but Allah, and I bear witness that Muhammad is the messenger of Allah.'" He motioned for Russell to repeat this as well.

"I bear witness there is no god but Allah, and I bear witness that Muhammad is the messenger of Allah."

Hassan hugged him again. "Welcome to Islam my brother!"

*****

That night, Hassan had a dream that he was playing in a nightclub, one of the places Hassan wouldn't play anymore. One of the patrons was a man engaged in a poker game. He was a large Sicilian, vaguely resembling an old friend of one of Hassan's uncles. His hair was jet black, and oily, his lips looked like strips of raw veal, and his eyes were the very quintessence of "dead eyes." He was smoking a cigar.

Suddenly, the room shattered. Hassan found himself in a foreboding swamp. The sky was an unnatural shade of yellow. The distant hills looked volcanic. At a short distance, the man was sitting at a table, still smoking his cigar. In front of him was a chess set. Standing on either side of him were two women dressed like stereotypical Arabian harem-prostitutes.

The man stared at Hassan with an unnerving smile. "Vinnie! My old friend. Long time no see."

Hassan knew he shouldn't speak to this man, but answered him anyway. "My name is Hassan."

"Whatever you say, old friend," the man said.

"You're not my friend."

"Now, now. Is that any way to behave? Remember who you're speaking to: I'm Fire! You're dirt," the man said with a chuckle. "You know why I've paid you this visit?"

"You haven't taken much effort in hiding. I'm a bit surprised at your lack of subtlety."

The man said "I don't always need to hide. By the way, that 'music' of yours was impressive!"

"Is there a point to all of this?"

"You bet there is, mudpuddle," the man countered, gesturing at the chessboard in front of him. "I'm not happy with that little friend of yours. The insect you call Russell-- I had big plans for him. You really did a number on that little prick. You should feel proud."

"I did nothing," Hassan said. "All praise is due to Allah."

The man's greasy and abrasive laugh slithered through the swamp. "This false modesty does not become you. Your pride is so obvious I can damn near smell it on you! You enjoyed playing 'Guru'! Be honest with yourself for once, Sheikh Hassan Salami Gonnasavetheworld. I know what I am. What are you?"

The man leaned forward and said "You know I'm right. You aren't doing anything for Allah. It's all for yourself. And it should be. You think He don't know this? You think He doesn't understand this?"

Hassan exclaimed "A'oudo Bilahi minash Shaitan ir-Rajeem! La Hawla wa lakuwata illabillahil ayhul azeem! I have nothing to say to you! I'm not a part of any game you play, and whatever I do, whatever I am, I owe you no explanations." He swept the chess set off the table with a backhand motion.

The man stood up, furious.

Raging, he said "I hate all of your kind! Everything was fine before you came here! We had the earth and all that was in it! We built and did things you couldn't imagine! Nobody worshipped Allah more perfectly than me! Then along comes Adaam! The "Vicegerents of Allah"? Prostrate before you? Was that some kind of joke?! You are all nothing but glorified fertilizer! If you could see yourselves for what you really are, you'd take the bombs I taught you how to make and drop them on each other just to enjoy a quick death! Make no mistake: this isn't over yet! I've got plans for you and that pet earthworm of yours!" The man's face became distorted with rage, and no longer resembled that of a human being. The table collapsed. The women became dogs. "I'm standing between you and the Kingdom of Heaven! You'll never get past me, you scum sucking pig!"

Finding a sword made of light in his hand, Hassan jumped on the man and slashed him. He woke with a start. His wife was still asleep. He got out of bed, stood up, spit three times over his left shoulder and said again "A'oudo billahi minash Shaitan-ir rajim." He went to the bathroom, made ablutions, and prayed. He prayed for a long time.

That night Russell had a dream. It was vague, indistinct. Some activities have been happening around him that he couldn't remember; people, and places. But toward the end of the dream, a person or being of some kind, very powerful, yet compassionate and not threatening, spoke to him, saying "Wake up and meet yourself."

He got out of bed and looked out the window. In the glass he saw his reflection. He saw himself. He saw Talib Ali. Outside a light rain was falling, like cool tears of joy.

Chapter 7. A Closer Look Inside and Outside.

Talib was speaking to a group of teenagers.

It was part of the duty and training of all Warriors that they should teach. Talib was especially effective at this. His students listened to his history lesson with rapt attention

"It is sometimes difficult to describe what those days were like. I read the history books, like you did. And yes, I was there. But my perspective is not that of a historian. It is that of an individual participant. There is a big difference between the two."

Chapter 8. Wake up and Meet Yourself.

It was Friday, December 19th, 2003.

Talib dug through a drawer where he kept his old phone numbers, business cards, and the like. He would know the item he was looking for when he saw it. Could it have been so long since he'd spoken to his old mentor that he couldn't remember the man's phone number? While continuing his search, he thought about how he'd let so much time pass since he spoke to Hassan. They'd drifted off in different directions.

Here it is, thought Talib, as he found the old worn business card. Holding it in his hand brought back a flood of memories. It seemed like another world. Even the person he had been was now a stranger.

He picked up the phone to call Hassan. He dialed immediately, so as not to give himself time to have second thoughts. He was still unsure about what he would say, or even if he wanted to speak to him. Hassan had a way, he knew from experience, of looking directly into his head. There was no deceiving the man. No thought, it seemed, could be hidden from him. How would he look now, under Hassan's scrutiny? Especially now, since so much more was expected of him?

The phone rang. Once. Twice. Thrice. Maybe he's not home. *Should I leave a message? Does he have an answering machine?* He was almost hoping that he wasn't home. Just before the fourth ring, the phone picked up, and that old familiar voice answered.

"Yes?"

"Hassan?"

"Speaking."

"Its Talib. Talib Ali Peterson."

There was a brief pause, and then Hassan exclaimed "Alhamdulillah! Asalaam alaikum wa rahmatuallah! How are you? Where have you been for so long?"

"Wa alaikum asalaam wa rahmatuallah. I've been surviving. And you?

"Alhamdulillah. I've had my ups and downs. Just like everyone else."

"How's Amina?"

He paused. "She died three years ago of leukemia."

"I'm very sorry to hear that."

There was a brief awkward silence.

Finally, Hassan said "Let's meet. We should talk. Get caught up."

"I'd like that! Where and when?"

"How about my place? Next Saturday night?"

"Great. I'll need your address."

After giving him the address, Hassan said "It'll be good to see you. I'm looking forward to Saturday."

"Me too. I'll see you then. Asalaam alaikum."

"Wa alaikum asalaam wa rahmatuallah."

Saturday night came. Talib found the building with no difficulty. It seemed so strange to be there again after all this time. The neighborhood was different. Art galleries, expensive looking restaurants, and other businesses had invaded the formerly foreboding area. Yet, here and there, a few vestiges of the old neighborhood still held their ground; and one would be a poor New Yorker not to notice it.

Upon arriving, Talib remembered the five flights of stairs in the building with no elevator. He rang the buzzer and was immediately buzzed in. He stopped at the door of Hassan's apartment. It was ajar, a silent gesture of welcome. He reached for the doorknob and took a breath. He walked in.

"Hassan! Asalaam alaikum"

"Wa alaikum asalaam wa rahmatuallah" said Hassan's voice from the other room. "Come in. Make yourself comfortable. I'll be right with you."

Talib walked over to a chair near the big window. He turned and looked over the apartment. It had changed. The musical instruments and equipment were still there. But there seemed to be something strangely utilitarian about the place. One knew instinctively that there were no women in residence here, and somehow there seemed to have a harder edge to everything. With the exception of a large cactus, the plants that were there before were gone. The massive bookshelf seemed somehow less tidy than it had been. The pictures on the wall were a bit dusty. Everything was reasonably clean and orderly, but now a shabbiness and almost hoary atmosphere had taken over. Even the aroma was different; incense still permeated the air, but it seemed musty and worn. For a moment Talib was overcome by the spectacle of the ravages of time; and reluctantly wondered how his own life would fare under similar scrutiny.

Finally, Hassan walked into the big living room. He was speaking on his cordless phone. He waved to Talib, and walked to the phone unit.

Hassan hung up the phone.

The two men looked at each other, and then hugged.

Hassan held Talib at arm's length. "Look at you! You're so different. No longer the crazy kid I knew back in the old days."

"Well" Talib said "I may still be a little crazy,,," He smiled.

"No, seriously. You don't know how much you've changed. Your vibe is so much more harmonious."

Talib smiled shyly. He didn't see it at all. "Well, Alhamdulillah. You're looking good."

Actually, he did. He was still in good shape, or appeared so. He still had the physical strength Talib remembered. But somehow he seemed slower and slightly stiffer. His hair and beard were dominated by gray. It seemed like he'd put on a little weight as well. His eyes were still sharp and clear, but changed somehow; probably by sadness.

"Please, sit down. Would you like some tea or something to drink?"

"Tea will be fine, thanks."

Hassan went to the kitchen to make tea. Talib sat and looked around again at the apartment. The place spoke of a masculinity that was rough around the edges and somehow incomplete. A stoic and resigned acceptance of inevitable loneliness.

Returning with a cup of hot tea in each hand, Hassan set them down on a coffee table near the sofa. "Please, sit down," Hassan said, gesturing towards the sofa.

Talib sat down.

"So" Talib began "Where do we start?"

"You first," Hassan said with finality. He was still as sharp as ever; deflecting what was obviously a great deal of curiosity from Talib.

"Well,,," Talib began, with a preparatory deep breath.

"Not long ago, I was sitting in the basement of the mosque. A brother from the East was talking to me. But I was just not interested in hearing his babbling. I mean, I knew what he was going to say before he said it. His ideas about Islam were so superficial. I realized he had nothing to offer me. I was wasting my time.

"I learned a long time ago to be careful what information I give these people. I have no need to be told a dozen times that I need to pray five times a day. This man didn't realize that he was talking down to me. He was one of these guys who couldn't grasp the idea that an American, especially a white American, could possibly know anything about Islam.

"And I learned never to tell anyone that I was once a rock musician. I'm tired of the lectures on the evils of music, and fed up with talk about Cat Stevens becoming Yusef Islam.

"I'm not saying I'm ready to quit Islam, as you probably guessed, but I know that there is something greater than what I found so far. I'm looking for the Next Level of Understanding. That's why I came to you."

Hassan thought about it. "Why didn't you come to me sooner?" Talib was silent.

"Seems to me," Hassan said, "that you have found yourself in a spiritual cul de sac. It may be time for you to let go of something and move on."

"Yeah," Talib said, "But I don't know how. I don't know what to do."

"You'll do what needs to be done," Hassan said. "Would you like something to eat?"

For the rest of the evening, they did not speak of Talib's spiritual crisis.

Later, as Talib put on his coat to go home, Hassan said "There's a Sufi dhikr ceremony that is held every Thursday at a mosque downtown. You ought to check it out."

"I will," Talib said, without thinking. Then he realized that he'd have to go through with it. The stern warnings of Salafi Muslims who were fearful of the potential religious deviations of the Sufis echoed through his mind. Now, he was committed to going.

When Talib walked into the Sufi mosque for the dhikr the following Thursday night, he immediately felt at home – and uncomfortable. In an indefinable way, he was thrown off balance by the very noticeable difference between this gathering and the Sunni mosques he was accustomed to. It brought up a resistance within his ego, and a challenge to the image of Islam that he'd accepted.

Almost without preamble, the dhikr got underway. The Sheikh was sitting upon a black sheep skin rug. Several white sheep skin rugs formed a circle in the center of the mosque. There were more people than rugs; but the rest sat close by. The Sheikh spoke. His words opened up things that Talib hadn't realized were right in front of him his whole life. It was as if he was being reminded of something he'd forgotten long ago.

Then the dhikr began. He joined the congregation chanting the names and praises of Allah. It seemed to create within him an awareness of a higher reality, a place wherein everything was more real than real. It was an experience of a beauty and state of being that was both attractive and frightening. It exposed every atom of his "self." And he found his mind and his ego rebelling.

But he knew that he'd found something he was looking for.

*****

The A train thundered and bounced through the tunnel. Talib sat, reading a book on Islamic heresy. The book was a gift from Hassan; one of his "metaphysical jokes" no doubt. But the essays were interesting.

He put the book in his shoulder bag and suddenly got off the train after it had stopped at a station. He wasn't sure why he got off there, but the door of the train closed and there he was. As he looked around, and cursing his carelessness, he realized that this was the west 4th street station.

Walking out of the train station, Talib headed west. He wasn't precisely sure where he was going, but he needed to take a walk, and this seemed as good a neighborhood as any.

The street was much like any in this neighborhood. Restaurants, apartments, bars, stores, etc. Young men were playing basketball in the court he'd passed at the train station. All types of people walked about, engrossed in their own world; seemingly oblivious to the myriad subcultures vying for domination around them, and unaware that none of them would ever achieve anything more than a superficial power base that would be swept away forever.

Suddenly, Talib's attention was drawn to a store. It was situated in the middle of the block, and stood out incongruously. Obeying an impulse, he walked in.

It was a run down, hoary looking place, cluttered and organized in a system that only the store's manager would ever understand. There were musical instruments from every part of the world. No culture was overlooked, and all were at least marginally represented in this eclectic collection.

A gentleman looked up from repairing a harmonium to address Talib.

"Hi. May I help you?"

"Hi," answered Talib. "I was just looking around. You have quite a collection here."

"Thanks," the man said. "Let me know if there's anything I can do for you."

Talib crept around the cramped little store. He marveled at the variety of instruments; to his embarrassment, he couldn't identify many of them.

One particularly strange looking instrument had a quality that attracted Talib. He asked the man what the instrument was.

"That's a sarod. It comes from India. What instrument do you play?"

"I used to play guitar. I had stopped for a while, but I've been messing around with it again recently. I may get back into it again."

"Wait a minute," the man said. "Aren't you Russell Peterson? My son has one of your band's CDs."

Talib smiled, a little embarrassed. "Yeah, that's me."

"I heard you stopped playing. Something to do with converting to Islam."

"Yes, I had. I guess I had to leave it alone for a while."

The man nodded his head and said "I know what you mean. Sometimes we have to do these things. By the way, my name is

Jeff." They shook hands. "Anyway, you were looking at the sarod. Would you like to check it out?"

"OK" Talib said, unsure of what he would do with it.

Jeff took the instrument down from the hook on which it was hanging. Reaching into his pocket, he pulled out a large plectrum. With a dexterity and grace one would not expect from hands that were calloused and scarred from working with hand tools all day, he tuned the instrument (by ear, no less) and began to play.

Unknown to Talib at the moment, Jeff was playing Rag Desh Malar; a "standard" raga. The music seemed to awaken something in Talib that had been dormant for a long time.

"Here, you try it." Jeff said, handing Talib the instrument. Talib took the instrument and sat on a stool. He showed him the basics on how to hold and play the instrument. Amazingly, the strange instrument felt comfortable, almost familiar. Talib began to play it, not knowing what he was doing. He managed to find a few melodies, and even found a few chords (something not normally played on the instrument).

"Wow. That's beautiful!" Talib said. He sat and played it for a while longer while Jeff tended to other business.

After a while Jeff returned. "So, what do you think?"

"How much is it?"

The price was reasonable. Talib seriously considered buying the instrument, but had his reservations.

"Where would I go to learn how to play this?" Talib asked, remembering with illuminating irony the last time he'd asked for music lessons.

"I could teach you," Jeff answered.

Talib paused thoughtfully. "I'll take it," he decided finally. "Can we begin lessons tomorrow?"

Chapter 9. A Beautiful Invitation.

Talib walked through a rainy Thursday night. He didn't mind; it had been a long time since it had rained, and it was needed. He stood under his umbrella waiting for Hassan.

Things had been going well with his music in recent years. After a year of intense study and a series of well received performances, his name was becoming known again. He'd begun performing at larger venues, such as colleges, libraries, museums, and theaters. He'd recorded CDs that were well received in the New Age and World Music markets, and had distribution in the US and Europe. He'd even done some short tours of Europe, Russia, and Japan. He'd begun work on his next CD, and speculation amid the aforementioned markets abounded as to what he would do next.

How strange it all seemed to him! His earlier dreams had been painfully crushed, yet now they were replaced with a success that was as comfortable as it was unforeseeable. Years ago, he would have laughed at the idea of doing what he was now doing. Now he couldn't imagine himself doing anything else. *Allah is truly in charge*, thought Talib.

As Talib was lost in thought about this, Hassan approached him. "Asalaam alaikum" he said.

"Wa alaikum asalaam" Talib replied. "You look like you got something on your mind."

"You're very perceptive," Hassan said with a smile. "Do you have a gig tonight?"

"No. Why?"

"I'm going to a meeting with some brothers and sisters with whom I have an ongoing project. I'd like you to attend."

Talib knew Hassan long enough to recognize the symptoms, He was about to lay something heavy on him.

They took the train to the Williamsburg section of Brooklyn. Talib tried to get some information out of Hassan about their destination and what he might expect when they arrived. Hassan was not helpful.

After arriving in Brooklyn, and passing through an affluent and populated area, they walked through a deceptively desolate looking block of warehouses. Hassan walked up to a green door with "786 Productions Inc." ornately painted in white letters. He took out a key and opened the door and walked in. Talib followed him in and closed the door.

Up a flight of stairs there was another green door. Hassan unlocked this door as well and the two men walked in.

Inside was what looked like a recording studio, except that its design was very different from that of most studios. There were a variety of instruments neatly arranged, and an assortment of new and vintage microphones covered with silk cloth. Against the south wall was the window to the control room. There were also cushions and small tables arranged, with rugs, and tapestries and abstract paintings on the wall. Incense burned in one corner.

"Have a seat. I'll be right back" Hassan said.

Talib sat on one of the cushions. Hassan returned with seven men and four women. They sat down in a semicircle around him and faced him. *He* was the purpose of the gathering. After everyone exchanged the customary salaams, Hassan introduced the group to Talib.

The first man was named Sadibou Ndao. He was a tall West African man with a steady gaze that correctly suggested a perceptive and calculating intelligence, coupled with serenity and kindness. He was a master singer and percussionist, with a doctorate in molecular biology. Next to him was a Japanese woman named Tchakiko Muhammad. She was a mathematician and botanist who played keyboards. She was also Sheikh Suliman's wife. The next man was Bilal Abdul Kareem, an African American; who played several instruments, taught several styles of martial arts, and co-owned a small real estate and contracting business. Next to him was a Russian named Jamal Postatnik. He was a master of the oud, saz, and bass, and held degrees in audio engineering and filmmaking. The Indian woman next to him was a singer, accountant, and marketing expert named Aisha Yasmin Khan. To her right sat her husband Uthman Khan; a percussionist, ney and shenai player, and astrophysicist. Next to her was Maryam Jalil, a woman who played piano, and ran her own book publishing business. Next to her was a young Irish woman named Zeinab McKormick, a lawyer who did consulting for an entertainment law firm and played cello. Malik Scott and Sharif Cunningham, the percussionist and keyboardist who played with Hassan that first night he heard him were there. Finally there was Sheikh Suliman; a Master Musician - singer, multi instrumentalist, composer, artist, poet, and author who owned the studio and the building they were in. He also owned a share of a small incense manufacturing business, and a share in a precious metal recycling and refining business.

All were accomplished composers and improvisers, master poets, trained in yoga, and the Sufi arts. They exuded a vibe suggesting that he was in the company of very formidable individuals. Yet all seemed to welcome Talib as one of their own. Aisha, Jamal, and Maryam all complemented Talib on his CD, stating that they listened to it regularly.

After tea had been made and everyone was comfortable, Hassan said "I imagine you are curious to know what this is all about. There's something I never told you about me. Perhaps Sheikh Suliman would like to explain?"

Sheikh Suliman took a breath and began.

"This group of people constitutes a part of a Sufi order unlike any that you may be aware of. The Order has a total of 776 members from all over the world. We are called JAZ, and the Order has been in existence for almost 25 years. We are led by a democratically elected council of Sheikhs. I have the burden of being one of the leaders.

"We are involved in a long term project that will outlive us. We are attempting to find an absolute music. This is a music that exists outside the confines of style, culture, or historical period. It would be a truly "autophysiopsychic" music, a music of "all the worlds." Do you remember when you first heard Hassan? You once mentioned about feeling a power. That is the tip of the iceberg compared to what we're attempting to achieve.

"We have had some success, but are nowhere near attaining our goal. We have produced recordings, and written essays about our endeavors. In fact, we have quite an archive. But we knew from the start that we would be passing our work down to succeeding generations.

"The Order follows some protocols, and has some rules. For instance, any member can play whatever he or she wishes outside the Order, and these may involve collaborations with Order members, but our collective efforts must be for the Order's stated purpose. We are non-profit, and in the US, incorporated under a 501-c3, and depend upon contributions and volunteer work to exist. A few sympathetic people have made sizable donations to us. We occasionally raise money by putting on concerts; but these concerts are by invitation only. They are not open to the public.

"We believe that the general public is not ready for what we are attempting to do, even with what little we have achieved in the past. While our Order and its work are not secret, we discourage members from speaking about us to the uninitiated. Most would not understand us. Some among us believe that no existing culture can withstand exposure to our music.

"We also practice other arts and sciences. Things most people would not understand, and may, out of ignorance, interpret as evil. They are very dangerous, but our use of them is not. You must know this; because mastery of these arts and sciences is essential to our goals; both individually and collectively."

Talib broke in "Are you asking me to join?"

Sheikh Suliman and Hassan smiled. The others chortled a little in sympathy. "Yes," Hassan said. "I made your reputation and credentials known to our members. All have approved your entry. Are you interested?"

Talib smiled. "You know, it seems that every time I agree to go along with you on something, I get put through the ringer one way or another. Are you gonna turn my life inside out again?"

"Of course!" Hassan said with a smile. Everyone laughed.

Talib looked at him, and looked at the people that surrounded him. Instinct told him that this would be another of those milestones. Once passed, there was no turning back.

"I'll do it," Talib said, amid a chorus of "Alhamdulillah."

The group rearranged their seat cushions into a circle around Talib and Sheikh Suliman. "We're going to initiate you into our group. This involves an ordeal and experience. You must pass through this. Your consciousness will be altered. You must not be frightened by anything that happens."

The group began to chant a rhythmic dhikr, with sparse instrumental accompaniment. Jamal had set up a microphone and began recording the event on a laptop. "First, close your eyes," Suliman said. Talib did so.

"Concentrate on your breathing. With every breath, take in light and let the light penetrate your whole body. When you exhale, spread the light that's in you to the whole universe, and at the same time expel impurities in you. Do this and concentrate on it until you can't perceive anything else."

"Now," Suliman continued "I want you to picture yourself walking through a labyrinth. Tell us at every step of the way what you see and hear. Take your time."

Talib sat for a moment and silently "looked" into his imagination for a cave of some kind. It took some effort. He wasn't sure how to "see" anything like this, so he imagined in his mind's eye what such a thing would look like. When effort failed him, he simply let go. Then he saw it, almost as clearly as if by his own eyes.

Finally he spoke. "I see a cave, a tunnel. It's dark, and the walls are lit up from somewhere behind me. The walls and floor and ceiling are wet, like there was a stream or rain nearby."

Suliman said "Walk through the tunnel."

Talib began to walk. He could no longer hear the dhikr of the group. He could no longer feel the floor under him. He felt the ground of the tunnel under his feet and felt the cool humidity on his skin. All that remained of the "outside world" was the sound of Suliman' voice.

"I see an opening ahead. I'm walking toward it." He paused. "I just came to the opening and I'm standing at the edge of a cliff. Off in the distance is a valley and mountains beyond it. The sky is a strange color: it's a kind of pinkish purple. I don't see the sun. The plants and trees are moving like animals. There are no shadows. There's some kind of building on the side of one of the mountains. It's built into the side of the mountain.

"I want to go to the building, but it's so far off and I have no way off this cliff."

"Just go," Suliman said, from what seemed like a long way off. "Don't think about distances or heights."

Talib braced himself, and then "willed" himself to go down to the valley. To his astonishment, he began to fly toward the ground.

"I'm at the bottom and I'm walking toward the mountain. All around me there's the plants I told you about. I can't tell what's close up or far away, my sense of distance and dimension is all changed. There are rocks and little monuments all around here, and I see shapes moving around, like people or elves or some kind of thing like that. But they go away when I try to focus on them. It's all very pretty, like a fairy tale or something.

"And the plants and rocks are all alive! They talk to me. It's like they can talk, but not like a person talks. They talk, I don't know, by putting feelings into you, feelings and thoughts that you know are not from inside you, but they are felt inside. And like everything that happens to them is written or recorded in them. It's weird. I don't know if I understand them.

"The ground is alive too. Everything is alive! And it's all talking to me. I wonder if the trees and rocks that are in our world can talk, but we can't hear them."

Back in the "real" world, Suliman and Hassan smiled at each other.

"I just arrived at the mountain. The building is like a big temple with pillars and long corridors. There's a big staircase leading up to the main entrance."

Suliman said "Go into the building."

Talib obeyed.

"There's a long hallway with columns on each side. The ceiling might be a mile high. There are doors, big massive doors all around. They're talking like the plants and rocks did. One door is saying "Stay away" and another door asks me to open it. Others are talking too, but they don't have anything to say to me."

Suliman said "Find the door that feels right to you, and open it and walk in."

"I just walked in and the door disappeared. There's no sign of it anywhere. I'm standing at the edge of a large arena. The walls are so far away I almost can't see them. All around me are big slabs of stone that are arranged in ranks. The sun seems to be kissing blue mountains in the distance. The sky is gold and rose now, with thousands of stars and eleven moons. I can't tell how big this arena is; it seems like it's a big place, yet I feel like I can hold the whole place in the palm of my hand.

"Wait-- one of the slabs is rising in the air. It's coming toward me."

"What are you feeling?" Suliman asked.

"Fear. I'm scared of that thing! It looks like it wants me for something! I don't want to go near it."

"Let it come to you. Don't be afraid," Suliman said.

Talib waited for the object to come to him. As it got closer, he realized what it was.

"It's a book," Talib said. "It's *my* book. My whole life is in that book. I'm the book and the book is me. It stopped in front of me and it's just standing there."

Suliman said "Is it on your right or your left?"

"Neither. It's right in front of me. Like it's waiting for something. It's judging me, accusing me of something! I gotta get out of here! I can't take this!"

"Don't run from it," Suliman said. "Stay where you are."

Talib fought his desperate urge to run. "The book is opening. There are things on the pages, shapes, images, like what's in my memory. It's all connected to everything, like a spider web all across the sky. And it's all inside me, like lines running through me. Little waves of energy are passing through all the lines, and it's causing ripples in the whole world. Everything I do, everything I think, is all running in and out of the whole universe! I didn't know I had that kind of power!"

Talib stopped for a second.

"There something else here. On either side of me, there are two, I don't know what. They're not men. They're some kind of beings. Spirits or angels or something. They're my angels! They know who I am. They know what's in my book. Wait. Now they're moving toward each other. They're merging together into one person and they have my book in their hand. And now, it's trying to reach for me. It's pointing at me. Everything is changing. The lights! The colors are moving. It's touching my forehead, between my eyes, inside my head,,,"

Talib fell silent. His body shuddered and tears streamed down his cheeks.

Suliman said "Talib. Can you hear me?"

"Yeah" Talib said breathlessly.

"Return to your body. Open your eyes, Do it now."

Talib opened his eyes. He looked around and met the patient gazes of the people surrounding him. It was as if he'd never seen with these eyes before; like the whole world was brand new and he had been washed clean of all preconceived ideas about what his senses were telling him.

"Hold out your hands," Suliman commanded.

He obeyed. To his astonishment, they were bathed in a wall of blue light. The light moved with him, as though he were generating it himself. All around him little whorls of light emanated from him. He saw this with his physical eyes. So did everyone else.

Suliman sat up and said "Welcome."

Everybody smiled warmly, and welcomed him amid a chorus of praises to Allah.

*****

It was Friday afternoon, two weeks after the Eid.

Sheik Suliman, with whom he'd had coffee after jumma, had given him a small book and several copies of the Order's newsletter. "You will need to read these," he'd said. "This is the book that outlines what the Order is about, and there are several back issues of the newsletter. This should get you up to speed. My business card is in the book. If you have any questions, you can call or email me."

Now he was home. After his dinner, Talib flopped onto his couch and began to read with hungry anticipation:

The Order of Jaz has an ongoing project in the works. We are searching for an absolute music.

No doubt you have noticed in your interaction with your brothers and sisters in the Order that we make extensive use of musical forms and theories from all cultures and historical periods. Unlike many people in these times, we have a real reason for doing this. When one attempts to incorporate musical influences from other cultures, one must have a reasonably clear understanding of exactly what one is using, and why: i.e., a particular scale or instrument, it's proper use, function, and significance. This is important not only if one is going to use it in the same manner in one's own music, but especially if one is going to change its use and function in its new context: something for which one must be aware of the attendant responsibilities. Proper knowledge of outside cultural influences is not only essential to comprehension, but as a sign of respect to the original culture. This is something which we all too often overlook. The mutual sharing of cultural influences is an act of love, not rape.

When utilizing outside cultural influences, one must make the intention to give something back. While this is not always possible, or practical, it must hold a place of supreme importance in the intentions behind our endeavors. Cultural and scientific accomplishments are a great treasure because they represent the essence of a people's knowledge. Knowledge resembles love in that the more you give away, the more it increases.

The next logical step would be to find a focal point where all forms and styles of music share a common bond. The first place to look is in the physical properties of sound. The "Natural" scale found in the harmonic overtone series has been elemental in the foundation of many systems of music.

There are techniques that will prove valuable in the building, modification, or extension of a musical tradition. When examined against the traditions of previous systems, one will find parallels and similarities between the traditional and new. The works of cultures, languages, and individual composers are dialects, and that their basic elements have remarkable similarities. Musical elements from different cultures have interchangeable characteristics.

There is a parallel in physics, and the work of John W. Keely; his observations of natural phenomena he calls the Neutral Center. The Neutral Center is the center of introductory action necessary in all operations of nature. This is to be found in all rotational systems: e.g. atom, molecule, planets, stars, DNA molecule, etc. It is an indestructible unit around which all that is recognizable as matter is built. It is immovable and indestructible, and bears the burden of the mass of the universe. Its attraction condensed matter and its negative attraction forms nodes in its energy flow. These continue to meet in a center of sympathetic coincidence, which is recognizable as the permanence of form and matter. This concept, when applied to music, gives us both the tonic upon which modal music is built, but also allows the formation of an axis giving cohesion and form to extended chromatic harmony, rhythmic variations, and melody that exploits harmonic consonances and dissonances as the result of liberal use of microtones, and the effects they produce.

It must be understood that the entire universe exists, like music, in a state of constant tension and resolution. All tensions will resolve, and all resolutions will eventually grow to "beget" tensions. This is the yin yang principle, the cycle of death and rebirth, the ebb and flow of all things. The musician whose music does not resolve must know that it will resolve within the extra musical environment. One has caused a change to occur, and this change, like all others, will have universal repercussions for which he/she will be held responsible.

You are at liberty, in fact are encouraged, to use musical elements of any cultural tradition, provided you have a justifiable reason for doing so. Non-Musical concepts or elements as inspiration for your music, such as geometry, astronomy, chaos theory, fractal geometry, subatomic physics, quantum mechanics, and other sciences may also be employed. Techniques of other art forms such as poetry, painting, cinema, architecture, or abstract sculpture may avail themselves to translation into your musical concepts and practices. The principles of the martial arts are easily applicable to music.

One must be very much concerned with communicating a strong emotional / intellectual / psychic effect upon the listener for a specific purpose. While we may use any means at our command to accomplish this, we are always mindful of the attendant responsibilities of these effects. Many among us have refused to use a specific musical technique, device, or sound simply because it has no place in, or contradicts the message we attempting to communicate, or we feel it would violate our moral or spiritual responsibility to our listeners.

Talib flipped forward to a random page:

Each of you must develop your own procedure for the exploration of the reality of music. While there exist absolutes within the art and science of music, there is to be found therein an infinity of diversity-- an inherent dynamic that allows for almost infinite interpretation. We are not averse to innovation in the arts. Far from it! We have dedicated a great portion of our lives to it. Yet I advise the reader and musical seeker to examine with brutal honesty one's motives when treading on this path. The "Self" must always be in subservience to a greater purpose. The artistic ego is a demon with which we must always do battle - but it is also a wild beast which we may train to do our bidding. Jesus is quoted in the Gospel as saying "Seek ye first the Kingdom of God and all His righteousness, and all else shall be added thereunto." You will be well advised to apply this advice to your musical endeavors.

Ignore this at your own peril.

The practitioner of our music is, in our times, in a somewhat hostile environment. He or she must behave like a warrior. He or she must be able to adapt to an ever changing set of circumstances. Every performance and recording is a temporary autonomous zone: an oasis in the desert he or she is crossing.

He flipped to the end and read the last paragraph:

We are a reflection of the Divine. We are a mirror of the Supreme. Our music is an action that echoes throughout the entire Throne. There is no difference between music and the universe; they are one. May Allah guide us in our work, and may our music be useful to Him, accomplish His purpose, and be a service to His human creation.

He could tell he'd have his work cut out for him. *Hassan, you've done it again*, he thought. He poured himself another cup of tea and started the book again from the beginning.

*****

As time went on, Talib's music career began anew, and was making good progress.

When Talib recorded and released his fifth CD, its release was accompanied by a world tour. This tour involved not only the US, Europe, and Japan, but also Indonesia, Malaysia, Egypt, Morocco, Senegal, and the UAE.

At the last minute the government of Iran permitted him to do a solo performance in Tehran. This was accomplished as a result of great pressure from the Iranian people, who saw Talib as a hope for the future of Islam, and a healing of the rift between them and the US. While the Iranian government didn't see this, nor were they at all concerned with his music (which they couldn't understand), they saw this invitation as politically advantageous. Talib didn't care; he had his own agenda. The performance was received with tumultuous accolades; but when he returned to the US, he was "debriefed" quite severely by US authorities. The experience, including a blatant and sloppy "good cop / bad cop" performance, would have been amusing had Talib not been convinced of the very real possibility that he would never see the light of day again if the officers interrogating him (without charges) decided he was guilty of treason or conspiracy to commit terrorist acts - in the form of a single musical performance. He had few legal rights because he couldn't afford the necessary legal council. The experience left him with a shaken idea about the "freedom" that his government's spokespeople were always talking about. Shortly afterward, a friend of his informed him of the possibility of performing in Kabul, Afghanistan and Baghdad, Iraq. Talib jumped at the chance.

Unlike many artists, Talib not only allowed, but encouraged bootleg recordings of his concerts. Occasionally, he would even supervise the recordings himself, and let the people have them for free. Eventually, he started "bootlegging" himself. He would record his own performances, and upload the mp3 to his website as a free download. The arrangement actually had the unexpected side effect of stimulating sales of concert tickets and "official" CD releases. Some people in the music business disliked this; and some celebrities made public statements (all of whom had heavy major label support) denouncing this practice. Others supported him, and his mode was imitated by many artists.

The music on his newest CD was, in some ways, a departure from what he'd been doing. Yet most of these changes were too subtle for most people to notice. He was simply utilizing what he'd learned from his fellow seekers in the Order. For example, one piece he did had him soloing in a pentatonic mode over what was essentially a hybrid of hip hop and dub drum rhythm, with some sparse percussion and a minimal bass ostinato and synth pads. But the subtle shades of the tuning, which he worked out using something he learned from a CD by Mark Deutsch, created a subliminal effect that was as powerful as it was subtle. He'd also analyzed some recordings of the Master Musicians of Jajouka, and the Gwana Masters and employed what he learned from them in a song that sounded deceptively like "smooth" jazz.

He achieved a "cult" status with his audience. He could not fill a venue of more than 500 people (not counting festivals where there was already a built in audience). But his audiences were not only loyal, they were spread out all over the world. He had staunch admirers on every continent on earth except Antarctica. Some of his followers were a bit overzealous; including a few who treated him like a spiritual leader. This was the last thing Talib wanted, but there was little he could do about such people. Many times he found himself in the position of actually advising people on personal or spiritual matters. To his astonishment, he found the words that poured from his mouth in such encounters to be exactly what these people needed to hear. Many times people said, or he heard later, that he helped them or that he understood exactly what was happening. Talib was astonished because he rarely had any idea where any of this came from.

Along with the recordings, concerts, and collaborations Talib made with members of the Order, he began to study music theory in earnest. He made rapid progress, and in a short time he was developing his own theories about music. His writings and musical compositions that demonstrated his theories were submitted to the Order. They were received as valuable contributions. The catalytic nature of his ideas, i.e. the evident fact that they would lead the way to greater understandings, which Talib hinted at, were to prove indispensable.

He found that, quite unknown in his earlier life, he had a natural talent for writing, linguistics, and mathematics. This was valuable to him, and to his contributions to the Order.

One of the greatest of these contributions was the tuning system he developed that would entrain itself to the harmonics of the human nervous system. These could be systematically calibrated to cause the human nervous system, and its subsequent organs and systems, to respond in any way the musician chose. His knowledge of Indian Raga was the cornerstone of this; but he also made use of the works of Mark Deutsch and W. A. Matthieu. He even experimented with Deutsch's technique of training the mind and ear by systematically working out the mathematical formulas of these subtle tunings, and playing recordings of performances of ragas and other music using these and similar tunings while he slept. This was detailed in a brilliant thesis he submitted to the Order that explained how musical forms could produce moods and emotional associative reactions in human beings no matter what cultural imprint and musical associative patterns they already had. After this, Sheikh Suliman used his influence to help Talib earn a degree in music from Juilliard.

*****

During this time, Talib and Zeinab McKorrmick married.

Zeinab was the kind of woman who naturally possessed but strictly restrained an intense inner passion. Many people thought her to be staid and reserved; she was never seen without her hijab. Few bore witness to the depth of her emotional nature. Yet there was a calculating intelligence balanced by a deep sense of loving kindness behind it. Her restraint was in reality the residual effect of the mastery of her passions, not the repression of them.

One day Talib called Zeinab and asked her if she'd look at a contract he was offered, as embers of the Order often did. They sat on her couch and discussed the contract for an hour, after which she offered him coffee, apologizing for not doing so sooner. Hastily, she went to her kitchen to make the coffee. When she returned, her hijab was partially undone and her hair was uncovered.

She was more beautiful than he'd imagined. Her long red hair cascaded around her soft, shapely shoulders, and her skin, a solid, yet silky ivory, seemed to absorb the light around her and reflect it inward. Her flawless figure spoke sublime poetry to every level of his being. Not a word was exchanged between them. Speech was neither necessary nor possible.

The attraction between them was stronger than either would have admitted before this. But now, they understood and accepted the reality, and decided, right then and there, to stop deluding themselves. Within minutes, they went to Brooklyn, walked into the headquarters of the order, and insisted that Sheikh Suliman perform a marriage ceremony immediately. Two witnesses were drafted. Afterward, Talib took everyone out for dinner. That evening, he and Zeinab jumped into his car, and apart from a vague email informing Hassan that they were OK, were not heard from for three weeks.

The details of this impromptu honeymoon remained a mystery forever. Neither he nor Zeinab ever discussed it; if it was ever brought up, they smiled conspiratorially to each other.

Their marriage had a number of mutual advantages. Her experience with law and business was useful, and she eventually became Talib's manager. (He had been managing himself before; his experience with Jeffrey Michael made him wary of artist managers.) She restructured his business operation for more efficiency, (later, she would joke that he ran his business the way a bachelor cleans his apartment), found ways for him to cut costs and introduced him to a brilliant accountant named Yusef Bailey who had the uncanny ability to find tax deductions in the most unlikely places. She even played cello on one of his recordings, even though she had no interest in performing publicly. This was, in later years, seen as a loss; she was quite good. People who cast derision upon Talib for being a Muslim created rumors that he forbade her from performing in public. Nothing could have been further from the truth. He tried encouraging her to share the stage. She refused, and had her own reasons for doing so. Though disappointed, Talib respected her decision.

As time went on, their marriage had its ups and downs. There were a few tragedies. A fire in their apartment destroyed some of their valuables, including a hybrid instrument Talib built by hand. Less than a year later, Zeinab got pregnant; and three months into her pregnancy, she miscarried. They were devastated. Talib took good care of Zeinab during the crisis; he felt he had no right to do or feel anything that interfered with discharging his responsibility as her husband in her hour of need. He would be strong for her no matter what. But a few weeks afterward, when they were alone and the situation settled, he broke down and wept bitterly and inconsolably for a long time. He'd really wanted that child.

There were also Talib's occasional performances in potentially volatile places, such as during his world tours. Zeinab was not at all happy about this. She felt that Talib was sometimes unnecessarily reckless, an adventurer who often leaped before he looked.

But all in all, it was a wonderful marriage. They were happy together - in fact, they were madly in love with each other. Although Talib loved to travel, when they were separated they only wished to be together again.

The only thing that really puzzled Zeinab was Talib's cat -- a big black male he'd named Brunabulax. Talib never explained the cat's name to anyone. He and Zeinab called him Boo, and Boo commanded great attention from Talib. When he was home, the two were inseparable. Boo liked Zeinab and vice verse. But there was a strong bond between Talib and Boo that Zeinab sometimes found a little bizarre. Talib and Boo talked to each other, after a fashion. When Talib was away, Boo clearly missed him and was never completely happy until he returned.

Chapter 10. A Subtle Dance.

Talib was out tending to some errands. His cell phone buzzed (how he hated that thing – and often contemplated throwing it away, if not for some measure of usefulness it occasionally offered). It was a text message from Zeinab. She was going to be late for dinner. The message ended with a private joke of an intimate nature.

Just then, Talib saw Sheikh Suliman on the street, and called out to him. After exchanging salaams, Sheikh Suliman invited Talib for tea at his apartment. They walked a while, engaging in small talk.

They arrived, and sat down to their tea.

For a long time, they were silent. An indefinable and inexplicable mood of sadness overtook them.

Finally, Sheikh Suliman spoke. "Any true master knows that the student is the property of Allah. To have them around our short lives is a great blessing. Like the Prophet (sas), the true teacher is a mercy from Allah. Real mercy is not easy to learn. It appears from time to time in its purest form, but we rarely recognize it as such, because we see it through our own distorted perceptions. And the knowledge it encompasses has to be carried by the illuminated beings in this world and the other ones by their blessed presence. There's no other way. True Faith is a dimensional shift in consciousness, and experience of certainty so direct that it arises straight from the heart, bypassing the mind and the emotions. It is a revelation of the soul, not a subscription to a premise or a concept."

Sheikh Suliman took a sip of his tea. "How can this be taught by books or lectures? It can't.

"Knowledge that flows through presence is a 'Bright Moments.' We are amazed when we are in the presence of the people who witness Allah. Some even have a chance to be their disciples. They are like a child filled with innocent hopes and aspirations - and raw darkness - running towards their father for attention and approval. The soul / nafs / self, is like a child. There is a special ontological symbiosis from the master and disciple which holds the Great Secret. This is a delicate tether, but it's powerful enough to connect us to the Prophet (sas). A relationship of a master and disciple is being nurtured and inspired to grow, and when the master leaves, the child experiences great separation anxiety. Some separate from the master and some do not.

"Most teachers are false: I know, I've been around enough of them. Tragically, they don't know they are false. They think they are doing God's work; but in the end, they generally devolve, without exception – Sunni Muslim, Shi'ite Muslim, Sufi, Hermetic, Zen Buddhist, Thelemite, Jewish mystic, new age fundamentalist, it doesn't matter. It is all the same with them. I learned only one thing from spiritual teachers - if they don't teach you to leave them, they are false.

"Egoism, emotionalism, the urge to transform yourself into a 13th Century Persian gentleman, etc.; in the end, they're all illusions and mean nothing. Turbans, beards, fancy rituals, and devotion to a lodge or teacher don't make a Sufi. It is the heart of the Master who teaches you to leave - once the student is well on his way to be a Master. The momentum that Allah placed in the universe and in the heart will do the rest."

Thus ended the conversation. All that remained of their visit were pleasantries and courtesies, after which they parted ways.

They would never see each other again.

Chapter 11. The Journey of No Return.

It had been a trying day. Talib and Zeinab had been attempting to book a tour in South America. Such work is difficult enough, but he was having problems with his contacts in Brazil. Some obstacles involving visas had to be dealt with. Afterwards, he got into a long and spirited debate with an acquaintance of his, a Muslim named Kalil Warrenson who followed Imam Warith Deen Muhammad, regarding the pros and cons of NAFTA and President Obama's involvement with it. Talib was worried; he didn't like the idea of the North American Union one bit.

That night, while Zeinab slept, Talib was playing his instrument alone in his home. He'd learned an arcane raga from a man from India who had connections with his Order. He had told him all kinds of strange stories about it, and appended all kinds of vague warnings. He called it "the sacred forbidden music." Talib had been a little hesitant to play it (Zeinab wanted nothing to do with it, and asked Talib to never play it. She called it "Woman's Intuition"). But he'd decided to experiment with it.

He'd played it for thirty nine consecutive nights; tonight would be the fortieth.

He was always doing things like that. After he accepted Islam, he found he had a natural talent for conducting rituals. He tended to make everything into a quasi-ritualistic act.

Zeinab thought it was beautiful, although she sometimes teased him about it.

He was deep into the music. It allowed him to enter another state of consciousness. This happened to him often, but this time the music produced an especially intense depth of meditation.

The melodies insinuated themselves into the time and space he was in.

Rhythmic patterns, melodic movement, and harmonic structure intersected with subtle primordial forces of the universe known and unknown to human consciousness.

Suddenly, he felt weightless.

An energy / state he had no concept to define and no words to explain enveloped him.

The room folded and twisted into itself.

His body became a shimmering liquid that poured itself up a tunnel.

Time and space melted together, then became meaningless.

The "self" of Talib Ali Peterson disintegrated.

*****

Zeinab woke up with a start. She'd imagined she'd seen a flash of light. The atmosphere in the place was,,, unbalanced. Nothing seemed natural. She went into the living room where Talib had been. The room was in disarray, and objects seemed to have moved toward a central point in the room.

Talib was not there.

*****

Hassan woke suddenly from a dream. Fighting to regain control of his physical senses, he looks at the clock. 3:27 am. After taking a few deep breaths, he walked into the other room, and phoned Sheikh Suliman.

After one ring, Suliman answered "Yes?"

"Asalaam alaikum. This is Hassan. I'm sorry to have waken you, but I had a dream that you should be told about"

A yawn. "I know. I had a dream too. It was about Talib Ali."

"We should meet"

"Is noon at my home good for you?"

"Yes. Call the others; including Zeinab. I'll see you then. Asalaam alikum."

"Wa alaikum asalaam."

Later, the leaders of the Order met at Suliman's home.

"Ikhwan," Suliman began "it has been revealed to us through our dreams and firasah that our young brother Talib has met with an unusual experience. Has anyone else had any unusual dreams?"

All of the members there took turns sharing their recent dreams and visions. All verified that this indicates a uniform revelation regarding Talib.

Hassan sighed. "He's gone."

"Will he ever return?" one of the men asked.

"It's possible. We should perhaps make plans for his return. But I fear we may have the rest of our lives to wait."

Sheikh Suliman said "Preparation for his return is a good idea. We will preserve the records of what happened. I will also prepare a message for him that will be preserved in our archives.

"Allah has revealed in the Qur'an, 70:3 ' ,,, *from Allah (who owns) Ma'arej The angels and the Spirit ascend to Him in a day, the measure of which is fifty thousand years.*'

"Ma'arej. Ascending into space in a geodesic line. Wormholes" said Imam Bilal, who had been visiting from San Diego. He was in awe.

"Yes" Hassan said "The Prophet used a wormhole once in the Isra wa Me'raj, Allahu alim."

"He's been taken outside space-time; he's gone, and he's not coming back for a long time." There was awe in Sheikh Suliman's voice.

Zeinab's wept inconsolably. The men wept too.

Not long afterward, Boo died. Presumably from a broken heart. Zeinab never had another cat.

*****

The police investigated Talib's disappearance. They could find nothing, and they could not make sense of Zeinab's testimony. Fortunately, no criminal charges were made and called it an open verdict.

His detractors and enemies were glad to be rid of him.

Zeinab was financially set up. Since she and Talib had joint control of their finances, she had no worries. She made sure that Talib's musical legacy survived. His notoriety continued to grow, and his music sales increased as rumors and legends about his disappearance flowed among admirers and detractors alike.

Unknown to either of them at the time, Zeinab was pregnant. The boy she gave birth to, Talib Jr., would grow up to be a great man, following in his father's footsteps. The men of the Order became his "Official Uncles," and saw that he would have good male role models and support.

Zeinab never remarried. As is the case with the widows of many great men, her heart belonged only to Talib and no other man could ever assume that mantle.

Chapter 12. Much Later.

The revolution was showing unmistakable signs that the Believer's victory would be inevitable. Mars was almost in their hands. The Earth's corporate world order governments were weakening. Centers of military and economic power were targeted first, followed by industry, media, and education.

The Believers, as they were informally called (they had no real formal structure as is defined by any previous model: their enemies had many other names for them, none of which accurately described them) were held together by a belief in the application of spiritual principles to social order.

This was the result of the human race having found itself in a peculiar state of bondage unlike any that had existed in history. A capitalist technocracy, a corporate world order that functioned at the direction of an oligarchy nobody could identify held dominion over the earth. Its totalitarianism was so effective that it convinced most of the population that it was, in fact, living in a state of absolute freedom. The reality was, the only freedom they had was the freedom to act irresponsibly. The implementation of this horror paralleled a descent into a spiritual malaise that humanity struggled for centuries to emerge from.

The decision to stand against the corporate world order was a difficult one. There were enough examples in history of the disasters military action creates when done for the wrong reasons. And many of those who were amenable to joining the resistance suffered from hearts full of fears and viscous intentions that made them no better than those they named as enemies. Organizing the resistance and implementing the revolution was more difficult than executing it.

The artistic works of the Believers (somehow, they found time to sustain this) became popular among many young people who found the manufactured art of the corporate world order to be boring and insubstantial. Rebellion among the youth increased, despite several ingenious attempts to either suppress or assimilate it.

The Believers avoided the use of weapons of mass destruction. Their avoidance of innocent civilian casualties was executed with unprecedented genius. The attacks on the CIA headquarters at Langley, VA, the destruction of the Verichip Corporation, Monsanto, the attack on the World Bank headquarters, Mossad headquarters in Israel, and several others of the like succeeded without collateral damage.

However, there were other attacks that were felt by the general population. For example, Fox News was targeted; their equipment, computer databases, and financial resources were either confiscated or destroyed. After Fox could no longer function, the people no longer had their disinformation to poison their world view. Other news services, and many entertainment outlets that produced mind-numbing TV programs or video games that served no purpose beyond diluting human intelligence and perception were similarly attacked. Most people suffered from what can only be described as withdrawal symptoms. Some people reacted violently from having been deprived of their sitcoms, professional sports, Play Stations, and Facebook. There were some riots; but none of them knew who to direct their frustration against. The resources of government and law enforcement were thus diverted to put down these riots, and couldn't concentrate on the Believers. Quite often, the police used deadly force against protesters, which increased the hatred the general population had against their leaders.

The Believers had the advantage of not being identifiable by any paradigm the corporate world order was capable of labeling and classifying. This had, however, an unfortunate side effect that many innocent people were unjustly targeted as "potential assailants" and incarcerated or killed. Eventually, people fought back.

Some factions among the police and military in the US (which, by this time, were almost indistinguishable) deserted their posts when it became clear that the people they were protecting had stolen their pensions, social security and IRAs and condemning their families to economic slavery. They realized they were fighting against the wrong group of people.

A faction of the Believers had recently enjoyed a great victory under Sheikh Suliman's leadership. Rome and Vatican City were recently conquered, and now under Muslim rule. The secret archives of the Vatican were being examined under Sheikh Suliman's supervision. Several of the caretakers had, upon realizing the archives would fall into Muslim hands, attempted to destroy some cache's of documents. Fortunately, this was prevented, and most of the documents were recovered. The histories, artifacts, and bodies of work the Church succeeded in keeping secret from the world for a while were astonishing. They would be busy examining this new treasure for decades.

Similar caches of secret information were confiscated in England, Egypt, China, and the North American Union. A pattern was emerging that, while of little surprise to those knowledgeable of this, a lot of dark places were now illuminated; and many questions were being answered. The Believers immediately published everything. This had the effect of weakening their enemy's position. After some of this information became public, many former supporters of the corporate world order defected and allied themselves with the Believers.

China was showing signs of internal dissension at all strata of its society. This was not apparent at first, but after a while, a three sided civil war erupted. When this happened, Russia, who had its own internal troubles, closed its borders. India, Bangladesh, Pakistan, Tibet, Nepal, Cambodia, Vietnam, and Indonesia united to repel the Chinese. Mongolia found itself in the crossfire, and its government fell. Mayanmar fell to civil war, and the Chinese took advantage of this, driving a wedge between the allied forces of Southeast Asia. Chinese and Mongolian refugees streamed into Kazakstan, Uzbekistan, and Afghanistan, and migrated into Europe.

In Africa, a Pan African congress was assembled from the remnants of the African National Congress that consisted of a Muslim majority that rejected any alliance with Saudi Arabia. Ties with China were almost completely severed. Military forces consisting of animists joined forces, and a trans-national war between the two almost completely covered the continent. Christian populations joined one or the other. Eventually, the Muslim alliances emerged victorious. In the end, Africa became economically and politically autonomous.

In South America, a civil war in Brazil upset the political stability of the whole continent. The Believers formed alliances with indigenous tribes and nations throughout South and Central America.

While this was happening, several natural disasters plagued the world. Earthquakes, tsunamis, floods, famine and disease hit many populated areas.

The Believers had prevented an attempt on the part of Israeli radicals to smuggle a nuclear weapon into Mecca. Instead of the device reaching its target, it was detonated just outside Petah Tikva. Details were unclear as to how the device was detonated, as the Believer's orders were to prevent detonation, and confiscate the device so it could be disarmed, but it was generally believed that the Mossad was behind it. Civilian casualties among innocent civilians were enormous. When the Arabs heard about this, they invaded Israel, joined by the Palestinians, Jordanians, and Syrians. Owing to weakened strategic positions, sabotaged communications, and a clear warning not to interfere, the NAU was not able to help them. Within two weeks of concentrated fighting, Israel lost 92% of its territory, and its military was decimated. Strangely enough, civilian casualties were minimal, and refugees began to travel to Europe. The Believers did not interfere with this, provided the Israeli refugees made no aggressive action toward anyone, and even offered military protection if dhimmi status was unconditionally accepted. With no remaining military power to speak of, the surviving government of Israel tried to negotiate a truce. This was refused, and they were told they must unconditionally surrender.

In the NAU the Believers officially recognized the nations of the Sioux, Lakota, and other Native American nations that had survived genocide, and offered alliances with them. These alliances worked out well for all concerned.

Eventually, a group of Believers decide to make a daring move. They set up a network of similar minded Muslims to leave the earth and colonize the moon and Mars. This began what later historians would call the Second Hijra. Some of these were former members or sympathizers of Al-Qaeda, ISIL, and others who'd become discontented with the direction these organizations had gone, and saw this as an act of repentance.

When they arrived, they learned that the Elite had already set up several bases of operation on the moon and Mars. This necessitated that the Believers develop new skills. Before long, they could travel to the moon and Mars almost as easily as anyone. They had their own vessels. Occasionally, they either bribed non-believers to bring them off world, became skillful in faking "documentation" and hacking into computer systems to travel wherever they wished. They were equally skillful as stowaways.

Most Sufis and other communities based in pursuit of spirituality had no aptitude for war. The question of consequences of such actions was argued among them. What, for example, of the inevitable casualties among noncombatants? What of environmental concerns?

After the Believers began traveling in space, some groups arose in later years that opposed the Martian terraforming project on the grounds that the planet should be preserved in its pristine condition. Others were opposed to the whole idea of space exploration; believing that humans belong on earth and nowhere else. Some of these people formed radical groups, and their exploits are well known.

However, the Believers engaged the corporate world order forces on Earth, the moon, and Mars and won. The war on Mars lasted two terrestrial years. A great percentage of the enemy's wealth and resources were confiscated and attempts were made to divert them into different directions that attempted to ennoble and enrich all of humanity.

After building the means to survive, and protect their world, they announced to Earth what they have done, and declared independence. The superpowers and corporations of the world were weakened, but still in place, and they were angry. The threat of another war hung above the newly independent Martian nation. Their propaganda networks made the Believers look like mad terrorists - while the corporate world order planned and financed terrorist attacks against innocent civilians.

Eventually, there were more wars among the population of Earth, pestilence, famine, etc. Several of the sub-governments of the Earth collapsed, and the Sufi government of Mars assumes control. The earth was rebuilt through a massive "re-terraformation" program in an attempt to repair the damage that mismanaged corporate culture had done to the earth. Within a few years, they announced that the Earth may regain its autonomy; provided that no aggression is taken against the Martians. Then humanity underwent a Great Awakening. Humanity renounced much of its evil – for a while. They headed towards the stars, and built new civilizations.

One of the things the Believers did that nobody expected was to seek out men and women of specific bloodlines that had ruled the world for centuries. Each person would be dealt with as the individual merited; there would be no genocide. Many were spared, and among these, some allied themselves with the Believers, and accepted Islam, and in a few cases even intermarrying.

But some purges among them were necessary to remake the world.

*****

Zev Shorin was in a holding area, awaiting execution. He'd been arrested, tried and found guilty of crimes against humanity. Shorin had been a very powerful member of the Elite, and abused his position in unspeakable ways (including suspicion of planning and directing the failed attempt to use a nuclear weapon on Mecca). Now, he was in rags. Dirty. Hungry. Without power, resources, influence, wealth, or authority.

Taking time from his part in planning the invasion of Area 51 in Roswell, NM, Sheikh Suliman had assisted in the last part of capturing Shorin, and oversaw his interrogation and trial.

Sheikh Suliman and Shorin sat opposite each other, staring each other down. Shorin had proven himself a formidable adversary. His leadership was brilliant. The two men had been fighting for a very long time.

Shorin respected his enemy. And hated him.

Sheikh Suliman finally realized, ruefully, that he was too old to fight anymore.

Finally Shorin spoke. "We've been through alot, you and I"

Suliman said "Indeed we have."

"Before we bring this to a close," Shorin said "I owe you something. I'm going to let you in on a little secret.

"We sought power for the sake of power. Sure, we enjoyed "perks", so to speak. But we wanted power. And we must be the ones to have it! You were too weak minded to see that there is no god but man. And only the strong among us can be gods on earth. Who else but the truly strong could do what we did? We controlled everything; the economy, industry, the political arena, media, education, and public opinion. Every war served a twofold purpose; to adjust business and distribution of resources, and to cultivate psychic energy for us to harvest.

"Don't deceive yourself, and don't play dumb. You know *exactly* what I'm talking about."

A mutual hate thick enough to cut with a knife filled the room as the two men stared at each other.

"You could have had it too," Shorin continued "but you were too scared of this idea about some kind of deity that would punish you for what you wanted to do deep in your heart. Even our perks, what you would see as perversions, were such that people like you were too contaminated with your pathetic and timid morality to enjoy. It will stifle you. Your inability to accept the idea of state as substitute for God will leave you impotent, and with your hands tied forever.

"And now you're winning the war. Congratulations. But I shall tell you what's going to happen. Your people will soon find you will have to employ the exact same methods of running whatever government you create that we did. And for the exact same reasons. You won't be able to avoid it. There's no escape from the patterns and hard realities ingrained in this universe, and you know it. It has always been like this and it always will. The dynamics of power are not answerable to any pathetic ideology, like that bullshit you say you believe in. They are no more changeable than mathematics.

"You will find this out sooner than you think. And when that happens, you will realize that you and I are exactly alike except in one respect. *You are a coward and a hypocrite!* If you finally assume power, and you establish whatever government you envision, remember this conversation. *I've been here before, and I will return!* Remember always that I am daring you to look in a mirror. You will find me staring back at you.

"If you want my advice, stop deluding yourself."

Sheikh Suliman listened calmly, silent for many moments, his face betraying no reaction, no emotion. Finally he spoke.

"It is true that such dangers exist. And we will have to be aware of it every moment. We are not safe. Such is our Jihad."

Shorin rolled his eyes and snorted in disgust.

Ignoring him, he continued "And among our descendants will be some who will succumb. And the Jihad will begin again. But you failed in one respect. You mistook appearances for reality. You sought the keys to heaven, the power of the spirit. But what you achieved trapped you in a cul de sac you couldn't escape from, or even identify. We were the necessary agents of Allah's creation re-balancing itself, and casting you and your kind off as excrement."

"So!" Shorin broke in "You think you cleansed the universe by defeating us,,,"

"Please!" Sheikh Suliman said, half shouting, half laughing. "That 'excrement' is part and parcel of the universe you thought yourself master of. Don't you see? You missed every important key point when formulating your doctrines. So did all your ancestors. You were deceived by your own dividing and divisive egos. You really had no other god than this; even though you sought guidance by the whispering envious one. And it all came to nothing. You are the greatest failure in human history!"

Shorin glared at his enemy. Spitting on the floor in front of the Sheikh, he said "You bore me. Please be so kind as to finish what you started."

Sheikh Suliman took a slow breath. He was not angry. In fact, he was almost sad. So much great potential wasted. Such intelligence! Allah knows what he would have done had he been rightly guided. That which awaited Shorin and his kind on the other side was too horrible to contemplate. And it was all his own doing. But the inevitability of how these events must unfold was at the forefront of his mind. All the things that happen, good and bad, are part of a great series of interrelated events, none of which is fundamental in itself. Only in perceiving their self consistency are these events seen for what they are. The Believer is also compassionate and merciful; as these are Allah's attributes and must be cultivated and emulated.

But he had to do what he had to do.

Signaling to the young men waiting outside, they took Shorin outside.

A heavy, cold rain was falling. The wind gusted in painful bursts. Thunder cracked in the distance.

Five other men waited outside.

After their grim duty was finished, and Shorin's remains disposed of, they returned to their families. Sheikh Suliman returned to his modest dwelling. He lived alone while on earth. A pot of soup waited for him in his fireplace, a small fire offering a comforting and consoling heat and light to the room. He felt the weight of decades on his heart. He'd seen so many painful things. So much misery and destruction. He felt worn out, stretched thin.

After a bowl of soup, he felt better. But the mood was on him still. He thought of his long gone friend Talib. At such times, he often went deep inside himself, and far outside himself, and spoke to him.

"Little brother." he began "You have been spared some horrors that I have had to live through. Allah was merciful to you. But whatever you must now face, I pray you stay strong. Remember what you truly are. You will have all the help you need. May Allah protect you!

"Oh Allah! We are so fragile! These bodies and minds haven't the stamina for eternity – but our Ruh constantly impels us toward eternity! Where does our certain knowledge go when we die? Where do our memories go when our brains crumble to dust?"

Late that night, he rose to make prayer. He was taken by the sudden inspiration to do so. He made his ritual ablutions, and stood on his 60 year old, almost threadbare prayer rug. Reciting Surat-ul Fatiha, and Ayatul Kursi from the Qur'an, he then made his bow, then the prostration on his forehead.

A constriction gripped his chest, his breath seemed to fall into a deep chasm. His vision blurred, then sharpened to a clarity he'd never experienced. His body suddenly felt distant, disconnected, irrelevant. Silently, gently, the Angel of Death greeted Sheikh Suliman as a friend and took him home.

His body was found in that position the following morning.

Chapter 13. Impermanence and Continued Transformation.

Talib continued his lessons to the young students.

"You cannot imagine what it was like to live under such conditions. Living for an ideal became almost impossible not only to enact, but to even communicate. Language itself was manipulated and degraded. One couldn't survive unless one allows oneself to become contaminated by these processes wherein all value was measured in terms of marketing and commerce.

"The problem was that many people just couldn't understand that they were slaves, and couldn't understand who was enslaving them. This caused a great deal of consternation. The politics of the "hard line" Muslims of the time were in many way little better than the other power structures of the time. The most terrible aspect of the totalitarian state is that it forces those who fear it to imitate it. The main difference was that while the others were based on capitalist acquisition, theirs was based on theocratic oligarchy. There were, as may be expected, some intriguing exceptions; and those who answered to the former description were scarcely aware of their shortcomings. Thus is the danger of religious extremism.

"It was decided to initiate an active resistance against the Elite that did not include the hard line Muslim groups. Alliances with different Muslim groups, including some hard

liners who were beginning to question their leaders; as well as non-Muslims who were dissatisfied with the status quo were secured. Yes, Rhaulq?"

A young man straightened up, but remained seated. "How did interplanetary government evolve after the revolution?"

"Good question" Talib said. "The question of how humanity would govern itself was debated after the possibility of planetary settlement became a practical option. An Ashura convened with representatives from all of the worlds. Various ideas and governmental theories were proposed and analyzed.

"The idea of a single government spanning all of the inhabited planets was rejected. Given the immense distances between planets and the almost infinite diversity of cultures and races, and the fact that this diversity would intensify the impracticality of the idea was obvious. It was decided that each planet would have its own government or governments. Each would have its own autonomy. There would be, however, a general set of laws that all planetary governments would agree unconditionally to abide by.

" The Khaliphite Government in this age gave birth to offshoots that seemed, more or less, consistent throughout most of the civilized worlds. Smaller communities, orders, guilds, tekkes, and the like rose and operated in a semi-autonomous fashion. It bore a slight resemblance to the feudal systems of old earth. Yet conflict with the central khaliphite was rare; they mostly operate in a synchronized, and almost symbiotic fashion.

"One of the unexpected results of interstellar space travel was that the human body would undergo dramatic changes. This was due to the removal of human beings from their indigenous environment. These changes were eventually perceived on not only the obvious physical level caused by changes in gravity, subtle differences in atmospheric conditions, biological changes in food manufacture, meteorological conditions, and the like, but in the subtle energies of the human body. This unexpected metamorphosis was caused within the Latif al Sitta. Other traditions called it chakras, chi or ki energies of the human body. There were also drastic changes in the influences of environment which included what previously could only be described in astrological terms These caused cataclysmic upheavals in health, longevity, diet, and even psychology. It would be some time before many cultures would develop the necessary sciences to live with the criteria of the new planetary and interstellar ecosystems. To complicate matters, each planetary settlement had its own specific array of variables in this area. This made all but the most general of scientific principles in this area exclusive to each planet. Even some science was not interchangeable.

"Emigration from one environment to another presented interesting problems. While it was possible for people to travel from one planet to another, specific environmental conditions would occasionally cause difficulties on the traveler. Acclimation to different gravities was a big problem. The

possibility of disease was watched very carefully. Some diseases were imported or created by the transfer of individuals or groups from one planetary system to another. Some of these were very serious. Other variables completely prevented one group or race of people from traveling to some places; and some found that they couldn't survive anywhere other than their own world. Some people actually developed allergies to some planets.

"The psychological changes this brought about were as varied as the number of worlds that would be settled. In the case of the diseases, for instance, there arose among some communities legends of foreign races and attitudes of racial exclusivity. In some cases, certain races and nationalities were refused admittance to specific worlds for no reason other than fear of diseases or cultural influence that had no basis in reality. This was, however, always disguised with political and cultural facades"

One of the students raised his hand. "You had mentioned changes in the chi of the emigrants. Is this connected in any way to astrological science?"

"Another good question" Talib said. "Back on earth, Albert Einstein published a scientific document outlining what he called the 'gravitational constant'. This meant that all bodies exerted a change in the gravitational field of the entire universe. Some bodies were of such distance that the change on the physical level was negligible. yet the physicists of old failed to take into account the changes wrought upon the subtle body,

the qi, Latif al Sitta, or whatever other name you wish to append to it. When science started to understand the forces and manifestations of Allah's artistry that only religion and mysticism are capable of labeling and classifying, they understood that there was a truth hiding under the shirk and quasi-mystical nonsense that polluted most archaic forms of astrology. It is now a science, no different from physics or chemistry.

"I should like to point out that it was Islam that succeeded in removing all traces of shirk from astrology. This was based in the writings of Muhayyideen ibn Arabi and others of distant antiquity. In the past, all attempts to label and classify the energies that constituted these sciences eventually fell into the trap of psychological archetype. Thus the element of shirk and idolatry found fertile ground, and the science degenerated into 'fortune telling'. Islam removed this danger, and a new science was born. Now, science, religion, art, mysticism, psychology, philosophy, and politics, are not looked upon as being separate and incompatible things. They form a symbiotic system wherein all components support the whole structure.

"Time and space are a much stranger thing that we may realize. In fact, it was these subtle energies that caused me to be here."

A pause. "But I didn't understand until much later" Talib chuckled, and his students did likewise.

Chapter 14. A Stranger in a Very Strange Land.

When Talib Ali Peterson awoke, it took him several minutes to regain awareness of himself.

For a long time, he fought with the overwhelming sense of disorientation. He hadn't felt like this since his days of using drugs. After regaining some coherence, he fought to focus his awareness on his surroundings. It wasn't easy. Nothing looked familiar. He couldn't remember where he had been before falling asleep - or rather, losing consciousness.

Finally, he sat up and looked around. His eyes fought to focus upon objects in the room.

"Now what?" he finally managed to ask himself, when language returned to him.

Looking around, he was seized by a sudden wave of fear. He was lying on a bed in a strange room. It was illuminated by lights that were embedded in the ceiling, but whose precise location he couldn't identity. There were two doors; one led to what he took to be a shower. Getting up on his feet and walking to the door, he noticed that his body didn't seem to weigh the same as it had. Putting this down to whatever caused him to lose consciousness, he tried the other door. It was locked. At the opposite wall, there was a large window made of some semi-opaque material; a faint blue light coming from it. It too was locked.

The whole room seemed oblong and asymmetrical. The whole shape and feel of the room was like nothing he'd ever seen before. Even the door and window was shaped in a way that almost required effort to identify it as a door and window.

Near the window, there was a table with a notepad on it. He picked it up, thinking it would tell him something. To his shock, it was filled with some writing in a variation on Arabic or some Semitic language with what looked like a cross between mathematical symbols and hieroglyphics along the right hand side of the pages. Even the paper was of a kind he'd never seen before. Thin as an onion skin, but incredibly strong.

He sat down. Shock began to ebb away, to be replaced by naked fear. Where am I? How did I get here? Am I a prisoner?

Suddenly, the door opened. Two men walked in. Both were wearing colorful robes and small headpieces. One of them looked Scandinavian, with black Asian shaped eyes. The other was an African man with green eyes and shiny black hair, streaked with strands of gray. Both men were tall and thin, yet powerfully built. Their ages eluded Talib's estimation, although the African man was clearly the elder. The man spoke first. He seemed to be asking questions in a language that was liquid and musical, punctuated by occasional gutturals and hard consonants. Not wanting to show fear, Talib said "My name is Talib Ali Peterson. Where am I? Why I was brought here?" The two men looked at each other and exchanged brief speech. Talib thought he recognized the word "English."

The Scandinavian said "Wait, please" (with his heavy accent, it came out sounding like "*Wahyt Pl'hyyss*"). Then they left the room.

Well, thought Talib, now at least I'll have some answers. He thought of the fact that none of their actions or the tone of the man's voice were threatening or intimidating in the least. Just then the door opened again, and a nondescript man brought in a tray of food and set it down; leaving without a word. There was a dark kind of bread with a hard crust, several kinds of fruits (none of which he'd ever seen before) a piece what of looked like cheese, and a bottle of some clear liquid. Suddenly realizing he was ravenously hungry, he tried a bit of each experimentally. They were all delicious. The cheese and one of the unfamiliar fruits, a violet colored thing about the size and shape of a small pickle, were especially to his liking. The beverage was water, with what tasted like essence of cranberry and mint; and something else he couldn't identify.

An hour or so later the door opened again, and one of the men who'd been there before, the big African, entered. He was holding a small vaguely rectangular silver object in his hand. As he towered over Talib, he spoke again in that liquid language, and the object spoke to him in English.

"With the name of Allah, the Merciful Benefactor, the Merciful Redeemer, I extend to you the greetings of peace. Welcome to our city. I wish to apologize for the inconvenience and discomfort you have experienced."

Talib thought *Well, at least he's a Muslim*. "Wa alaikum asalaam. Where am I? How did you bring me here?" As he'd half expected, the translating device in the man's hand "spoke" in the strange liquid language.

The man continued "A man fluent in your language has been summoned to explain to you where you are and how you arrived. In the meantime, we ask for your patience. All your questions will be answered. Please make yourself comfortable. If there is anything you wish, it will be provided. Peace be upon you." He left.

Suddenly, Talib felt extremely tired. A wave of fatigue washed over his body and mind. For a moment he considered the possibility that he'd been drugged. But no; this was simple exhaustion. He lay on the bed, resolving to sleep lightly, in case he had to wake suddenly. However, in two minutes he was in a deep sleep.

*****

Rashidevqov Malik; a Second Master of Communications and Ancient and Classical Languages; as well as a respected poet of some fame and great talent, hurried into the Healing Center. He had been told that there was an emergency situation, and that his assistance was needed. The nature of the emergency was not revealed. Since it was the Master of Medicine himself who had summoned him, he had no doubt that it was serious. Stopping to catch his breath, he asked the receptionist where the Master's office may be found. Following her directions, he came to a large unmarked door, knocked, and walked in.

The office of the Master of Medicine was an impressive sight despite its deliberate avoidance of ostentatious show. The large oak-koa hybrid wood desk with its onyx and Martian silver inlay was, nonetheless, somewhat scarred from abundant use, and covered with symmetrical piles of papers, books, and micro-computers (or what a 21st century man would understand as such). To the left of the desk was a massive bookshelf; filled to near bursting with books, scrolls, and recordings of every description ranging from the inexpensive to classics and antiques. Against one wall was a semi-circle of cushions surrounding a small table. In the table's center was an ornate, but rarely used hookah: a handmade gift from his great-great-grandchildren. A large window behind the desk showed a beautiful view of the ocean. Breathtaking paintings adorned every wall. All of them were the work of the Master of Medicine himself.

The room seemed to become smaller as Sheikh Muhammadu Mbenga-Reid stood to greet his guest. The colors of his djalabia providing a perfect balance of unity and contrast with the colors in the room. Another man with a thin beard and red skin, and wearing a hooded djalabia currently popular among scientific researchers, stood with him.

"Asalam Alaikum Wa Rahmatuallah" Mbenga-Reid and his guest said. "Allow me to introduce Professor Apukanasawaka Radh'hammad."

Rashidevqov broke in "Wa Alaikum Asalam Wa Rahmatuallah. I am familiar with your work, Professor

Akiradh'hammad. My brother was a student of yours when you taught advanced theoretical phenomenology at the university. He spoke highly of you."

"Your words do me great honor, Sheikh Rashidevqov. I have heard of your work as well. I especially enjoy your poetry. Allah be praised for allowing us to meet; and in the company of my brother Mustapha." This last was more than the customary honorific; the two were related by marriage.

The men settled on the cushions on the floor, enjoying the coffee with cinnamon and ghuyrah that was brought to them.

After a few minutes of pleasantries, Sheikh Mbenga said "I must apologize for the secrecy in bringing you here. A most startling and amazing event has occurred"; he paused, and glanced at Prof. Radh'hammad.

For the next three minutes Prof. Radh'hammad explained what had happened, describing how a space / time wormhole opened and deposited what he called "travelers" among a group of scientists attempting to measure an unusual energy signature they'd detected several days before.

Rashidevqov was almost too astonished to react.

Sheikh Mbenga added "There were three people, all men, who had come to this place and time through the phenomenon. Only one survived." He and the others paused, silently offering a prayer.

"After decontaminating him, we put him in rooms normally assigned to patients with illnesses of the mind. He had been in a mild coma, but woke up earlier today."

"This is an incredible thing!" exclaimed Rashidevqov. "Now I must ask you: why did you send for me?"

"Your expertise in the ancient languages was an important factor guiding our decision" Radh'hammad said. "We feel that the use of a translator alone will contribute to their sense of isolation. Personal contact is very important. There was also your record and reputation in the academic circles. You come highly recommended."

Mbenga-Reid said "We would like you to guide him into becoming a part of our society."

Rashidevqov thought about this for a moment. This was a very serious responsibility they were offering. Doubtless the compensation would be generous. But to guide a man like this into their society! How does one begin such a task? The risks to the man's psyche were enormous. There was also the added danger that the man's ideas may contaminate social order. Rashidevqov didn't think this likely, but it must be considered.

But to turn away from a fellow human being in such a time of need was unthinkable for a Believer. "I accept the assignment" he said.

"Alhamdulillah!" both elders exclaimed. Sheikh Mbenga said "May Allah guide you to success! The resources in my care are at your disposal."

"As are mine" added Prof. Radh'hammad.

The next quarter hour was devoted to the working out of several details. Living quarters would be provided for Rashidevqov, if they were needed. Later he called his wives,

Firouzeh and Anjjeliqh. He did not enjoy being separated from them; and they and their children were equally unhappy on such occasions. But they understood. They wished him peace and success. He thanked them; promising to keep in touch, and to be home as soon as possible.

Now it was time to meet the man in his care.

*****

Talib awoke with a start. He heaved himself into an upright position; fighting his way back to full consciousness. Looking around, he noticed the door to what looked like a water closet was open. On a small table near the door, there were clothes and towels. He hadn't noticed them before. After availing himself of the toiletries, he tried on the clothes laid out for him. It consisted of a light green robe, undergarments, and shoes (seemingly a kind of loafer). Normally he wouldn't presume to wear another man's garments; but his own clothes were beginning to get a little ripe. To his surprise, he found the clothing to be very comfortable, to fit him perfectly. On the table there was also a small crystal vial of what turned out to be some kind of scented oil. It smelled wonderful, at once musky, with a floral aftertone.

Just then there was a knock on the door. After Talib called out to enter, a man walked in. Like his earlier visitors, the man was very tall. He was, Talib estimated, half East European, half Arab. His brown hair and beard had a very thick texture. His eyes were the darkest blue Talib had ever seen: almost violet. He was dressed similarly to his earlier visitors. Talib noticed that he did not carry one of those strange devices that the man had.

"Asalamu Alaikmum" the man said. He continued in English (with an indefinable accent that, to Talib's ears, sounded like Moroccan Arabic, Russian, and Scottish fighting with each other) "May peace and the mercy of Allah be upon you. My name is Malik Rashidevqov."

"Wa alaikum asalaam. Talib Ali Peterson. I'm pleased to meet you" he said with cautious formality. They shook hands.

Rashidevqov continued "I am honored to welcome you to our community. I have also been charged with the responsibility of seeing to your comfort. I believe we should begin by my explaining where you are, and how you got here. Before I do, I suggest we have some breakfast. I imagine you are hungry."

"I'm famished!" exclaimed Talib; relieved that he wasn't, he'd began to suspect, a prisoner.

Rashidevqov had never heard the word "famished" before, but had little doubt as to its probable meaning; and his guest's assertion carried with it a sense of comradely humor. This was a good sign.

Food was brought in. It included a different kind of bread than the one he'd had before. It resembled sourdough, but was lighter. There was a soft cheese in a porcelain bowl. It had a sharp odor and taste, not unlike cheddar, but with a basil-like aftertaste. There was also honeycomb sprinkled with what Talib guessed was dried lavender, fruits that he couldn't identify, and some kind of meat marinated in a thick, spicy sauce that lay upon a bed of rose petals. There was also more of the scented water, and coffee which was very strong and dark and had essence of some unfamiliar spice.

After they had eaten, Talib said "That was excellent! Thank you. I especially liked that small purple fruit. And I've never had meat like that before. It was very good."

Rising, Rashidevqov said "Now, it is time I explain where you are and how you got here. I ask that you follow me very carefully: this will be difficult to understand, and to accept.

"Tell me today's date"

Talib answered "December 21st."

"And the year?"

Talib looked at him in confusion. "2012. How could you not know? What's this got to do with why I'm here?"

"I'll explain momentarily." Rashidevqov continued "Long ago, my people learned how to travel great distances. This mode of travel was unlike any that had been attempted before. We learned how to travel from one place to the next almost without occupying the space between the two points. I'll explain the principles of how this works later, but for the moment I'll leave it at that."

"What?!" asked Talib. "Are you talking about Star Trek or something?"

Rashidevqov had no idea what "Star Trek" was; and couldn't imagine how to answer this. "I promise" he said "that I am not lying or insulting you. In time, I will prove everything I say. For now, please allow me to continue.

"As time went on "Rashidevqov continued "we began to exploit this new technology. We began to explore, and later colonize places which were previously inaccessible. We traveled to the planets. Later, we traveled to the stars."

Rashidevqov paused, allowing his words to sink in. He tried to proceed carefully, as he wasn't quite sure how much his guest would know of space travel.

He continued "In our travels we have encountered various natural phenomenon which the greatest scientists of your,,,," he paused, searching for the right word. "Nation had no knowledge of. One of the rarer phenomenon is when a "tunnel" opens up; causing a bridge between two points in time and space. We understand the basics of how and why this happens, but the phenomena cannot be conjured at will. The factor of time is too unstable and unpredictable; and the danger that history may be artificially altered makes this unacceptable. Anyway, matter can be caught in this. On rare occasion, organic life is so transported. Once in awhile, that life survives."

Rashidevqov paused again, looking at Talib, his right eyebrow raised slightly, hoping he'd take the hint.

Suddenly, Talib said "Are you saying that I,,,"

"Yes" Rashidevqov said. "According to your calendar, it's May 6th, 4461. You are on a planet orbiting a star in the constellation you know as Orion."

Before Talib could speak, Rashidevqov stood and walked to the window. He opened it (without any visible act of unlocking it) and said "Look. See for yourself."

Talib walked unsteadily towards the window, almost frightened of looking outside. Finally he arrived at the window and leaned out.

The first thing Talib noticed was the smells. An odor came past him. The odor was like a humid forest in the morning; with a lime-like overtone. This, however, was not the least bit unpleasant and actually attracted him. This was followed by another which he couldn't describe; it being so incredibly alien to anything in his experience.

As he looked out, he noticed they were on the third story of a building. To the left of his view the sun was just coming up. It was not high enough on the horizon that he couldn't look at it. But it almost seemed to be too big. On the horizon were mountains; sharply defined by the sunrise. Dark clouds drifted by. Ahead, and stretching out to the sunrise, was a forest of strange trees. Their thick trunks and palm-like tops waved in a gentle breeze. Here and there buildings of strange, almost aerodynamic architectural design rose out of the foliage; their shape blending with the natural essence of the forest. Some were pyramids. To the right was a dark green ocean, and its waves and motion gave the impression of a liquid of thick consistency. A flock of bird-like creatures flew across the sky. They were not yet clearly visible; but their movements were unlike any he'd ever seen: not quite like a bird and not quite like a bat. Their call was not unlike a violin; but with unusual overtones. The stars were still visible. To his astonishment, he could not find a single familiar constellation. Some of the stars shined with an intensity that exceeded anything in the sky he was familiar with.

Talib noticed a light reflecting off the ocean and leaned a bit out the window to see what it was. It was the moon. But it was too large, had an unmistakable orange tint to it, and it was dotted with tiny lights arranged in patterns too symmetrical to be natural. Then he turned around and looked up and saw another moon! It was bright silver, smaller than Earth's moon, and shaped like a potato.

Talib turned his back on the window. He sat down, too shocked to speak. Rashidevqov sat at a polite distance from him.

"It's true" Talib said to himself quietly.

Rashidevqov gently spoke "I can't begin to understand how you feel. But don't worry" he said, somewhat clumsily. "You are among friends."

For a moment, Rashidevqov sat silent. Here before him was a man suffering in a manner which (probably) no sentient being ever suffered. It was a mystery why Allah had willed this to happen. He stood up and began to pace back and forth.

Rashidevqov sat patiently. He knew that Talib would have to work this out.

"My world,,," Talib said. "What about Earth? What has happened since I was gone? When can I return?"

Rashidevqov said "Unfortunately, there will be no transportation to Earth for some time. This planet is independent. You should know that a lot has happened in the last 2449 years. You would not recognize your world if you return. None of the governments or nations that you knew still exist. Even the geography has changed."

"Does the United States of America still exist?" Talib asked; almost desperate for some point of reference he could understand.

"No. It's been gone for many centuries." Rashidevqov continued "The history of the earth is full of cataclysmic events which we have, by Allah's mercy, survived. I will tell you more in time. For now, the most important thing is that you adjust to what has happened. The entire community is willing to welcome you. Try to understand that Allah has allowed you to survive the experience for a reason. Allow me to welcome you to the world of Uq'Dyill. You will need to have a medical examination. Afterwards, would you like to see our city?"

"Yeah." Talib said, blankly.

The medical examination was uneventful.

As they left the building, Talib wondered out loud "How did I survive this?"

Rashidevqov said "We don't know, beyond the obvious: it was the Will of Allah. How else could it have happened?"

The two men walked out of the building. Before they'd left, Rashidevqov procured one of the translating devices for Talib. He said that it would be on semi-permanent loan to him, until he no longer needed it.

Talib attempted to look calm and slightly disinterested. He failed miserably. The sun was well over the horizon by now, and the sky was a light bluish purple. Both moons were still visible. A light breeze was blowing. The weather was warm and comfortable.

They walked on a paved walkway through a garden of sorts: beautifully manicured and filled with stone sculptures. Talib asked about the design of the sculptures. Rashidevqov replied in his own language, and the translator rendered it "They are based on a combination of anionic, non-anthropomorphic metaphysical symbolism combined with a system of mathematical models based on ancient chaos theory equations and fractal geometry which, like quantum mechanics, transcend the limitations of Newtonian linear physics."

"Cool" Talib said. Rashidevqov wasn't sure if he was referring to the whether or using a colloquialism. He would ask him later.

Up ahead at a distance was what looked like a town square (yet there were no squares here). Various other walkways weaved through the large garden, occupied by robed people of all sizes, ages, and races. Some of the races he couldn't identify; including several that didn't exist during the 21st century.

Then Talib noticed the women. They dressed vaguely like classic Arab or Persian women; but with some elements Talib traced to fractal patterns and post-psychedelic / entheogenic art, and others he couldn't identify. Their clothes ranged from simple, to colorful and ornate; and either could be found on young or old, and any race. One thing they all had in common was an unmistakable air of dignity about them. They were like queens, every one of them. All of them had some kind of beauty; some more indefinably so than others; but all were beautiful.

People worked, walked, socialized, and sold their food and wares (some of which were everyday items that would have not been too out of place in his time. Others were incomprehensible to him. What, for example, were those teardrop shaped glass objects with the strange shaped pieces of metal embedded in them used for? They were being handled with too much care to be mere ornaments). Twice, they passed pavilions where old men were seated, surrounded by children, or young adults. Once he saw a group of men discussing the contents of a large book (was it the Qur'an?). Once they came across a physical fitness or martial arts class of sorts. A group of people were involved in a complicated and physically demanding exercise that left Talib amazed. What was even more amazing was that this class was taught be a small man whom Talib estimated to be in his seventies; and whose strength, speed, and agility were far superior to his students. Yet others were praying, meditating, or engaged in some ritualistic activity the purpose of which Talib could not even guess. For example, there was a group of people who sat in a circle humming and intoning in some strange kind of harmony while making hand gestures like sign language with their eyes shut. What were they expecting to accomplish?

As they continued to walk, Talib attempted to observe how these people lived with each other. There was no sign of class division. Some people were obviously wealthier than others, or possessed specialized skills, or were in some sort of position of authority. Yet the sharp division between them seemed non existent. Nobody appeared opulently rich or desperately poverty-stricken. The groups of people who had their own subcultures did not provide friction in social interaction: indeed they seemed to be components of a greater whole. The people were interacting with a harmonious efficiency that was too natural to be called mechanical, and too deliberate to be called organic. Yet it seemed like they were intensely individualistic. Eyes shined with intensity of observation and superlative intellect; yet with kindness, respect, and brotherly love. Voices spoke, in many languages, with clarity of purpose; a poetic beauty combined with intellectual efficiency. Even the children showed this quality while they played and expended their excessive energy on intricate games. Each person seemed a nation, a law unto himself. This did not, as one would normally expect, interfere with social order. On the contrary: social order seemed to depend upon it. Each person enjoyed what appeared like absolute freedom. Yet nowhere was there any evidence that this freedom was ever abused.

After a time, Talib noticed that the people even moved differently. There were some who moved with slow, serene, and deliberate movements. A few people walked as if they were accustomed to taking great leaps and bounds across rocky terrain. Some walked with a swinging, almost avian, movement. Others glided swiftly and effortlessly across the walkways. Occasionally, when two or more people were speaking they would use hand gestures that gave no clue to the content of the conversation. The overall body language, while not totally alien to Talib, was certainly different. It had obviously undergone some great changes. Talib reflected on the possibility that this was the result of adapting to extraterrestrial environments. It would be some time before he could read the gestures (and perhaps even facial expressions?) of these people. The thing that Talib found truly disturbing was that not one of them moved like a 21st century American.

It began to occur to Talib that these people were not just "different" from his own people. They seemed to have an entirely different mode of logic by which they based their thought processes. He accepted that things would have to be different some 24 centuries into the future. But for it to be so alien; to owe, it seemed, almost nothing to his own world from which they'd come from, was almost more than Talib could grasp.

After a while, Talib began to take serious note of the technology.

His first exposure was, of course, the translator. Talib asked how it worked, and Rashidevqov explained that it was a device with circuits that operated on a semi-organic principle. It archived information on all known languages. When it "heard" intelligent speech, it would cross reference the words to whatever language it was calibrated to, and translate it into an audible facsimile of human speech. It had an internal electrical power supply which could infinitely regenerate itself, or convert light or temperature changes into electricity (with 100% efficiency). Rashidevqov added that the semi-organic aspect of the device was actually restricted technology. There were strict guidelines about building a machine in the image of the human mind.

Rashidevqov told him, as a formality, that he was, by law, forbidden to reproduce the device or others like it. Talib assured him that he wasn't likely to attempt to do so.

As they walked toward the center of the city, Talib saw other examples of mind bogglingly advanced technology. There were a number of vehicles that silently rolled past on larger, wider roads, floated like balloons, or flew in the air at astonishing speeds. He saw platforms with people standing on them, which seemed to float inches above the ground. Upon one platform, a man walked under an arch of some kind. When Talib looked again, the man was gone. There was no sign of him anywhere. He decided that his eye had been deceived. At intervals there were places at the side of the roads and walkways that had booths. Upon closer examination, Talib saw that people would touch buttons and lights on a panel, and then talk to an image of the person. This was obviously some kind of videophone. Rashidevqov told him that it was possible for anyone to talk to whomever they pleased at any distance; provided they had a compatible device on the far end.

Yet there were some whose telepathic abilities made the use of these devices unnecessary. Often times, people simply "knew" when someone wanted to meet him or her. They would "know" the message being sent to them. Rashidevqov hinted that this was a skill that could be cultivated.

"Could I talk to someone on Earth on one of those videophones?" Talib asked.

"Possibly" Rashidevqov sighed. "But there are factors involved which make it complicated to arrange. You'd also have to interface a translator within the communication system if the other person doesn't speak archaic English. It's a very expensive operation. And you would need a very good reason for doing so; otherwise, you risk not having anyone who will wish to talk to you."

"You mentioned something about 'my" calendar,,," Talib said

Rashidevqov said "Yes. By mutual agreement of the inhabited worlds, a standard year is equal to 1.613 terrestrial years. Each world also devised their own calendars according to the astronomical characteristics of their star systems and planets. A system of adjustments and allowances were also devised to compensate for the effects of relativity upon time and space due to the great distances between worlds."

The architecture of the buildings was, like those he saw when he first looked out the window at the hospital, in perfect harmony with the natural surroundings. Some buildings were small and simply designed and decorated. Others were larger and more complex than a cathedral. The purpose of most of them was pretty obvious: there were homes, shops, small academies, and even what Talib took to be a theater. There were some whose purpose eluded him. Few buildings were taller than three stories although there were a few towers, pyramids, and spires here and there. And all had that asymmetry to their design that left Talib slightly disoriented.

During the walk he also saw what he took to be machines and inventions whose purpose and the principles by which they operate were beyond his understanding, or even his ability to describe without sounding like a madman. Rashidevqov's explanations were not helpful; as he had no reference points to work with that Talib would recognize. Sometimes the translator would render a word into English, but he couldn't make the connection. Other words the translator flatly refused to translate.

Rashadevkov would occasionally have need of using his translator to explain himself.

"What about the vehicle that you navigate among the stars? The space ship?" Talib asked

"Well" Rashidevqov began " in your time it was believed that matter cannot travel faster than the speed of light. If we were to travel at this speed from earth, it would take over four years to reach the nearest star. To complicate matters, time itself is altered. It slows down when matter travels at such speeds. This is unacceptable where interstellar travel is concerned. So after years of theoretical work, and experiments, it was learned that the best method would be to alter the dimensions of space itself. We would manipulate gravity, and several other natural forces and energies found near and between stars; all of which is merely converting these energies into the spacecraft's velocity and other power needs. Anyway, the resulting man made phenomena would essentially "fold" the space between two points, and simultaneously step "outside" the confines of three dimensions. This allows us to travel great interstellar distances at will. Even then, these voyages sometimes take a long time. The act of folding space cannot occur too close to a star.

"And time itself is a much stranger thing than you think.

"As you may have guessed, the pilots who navigate these vessels are not only highly trained, but must undergo special preparations of the body and mind. Then they may safely operate these vessels. An untrained and unprepared person couldn't hope to survive an attempt at navigating the stars. In fact, almost all of them belong to a coalition of spacefarers. Often this vocation is passed from parent to child. Others are allowed to join after passing the training I mentioned. They are from all the civilized worlds, and no government or financial institution is allowed to gain exclusive control over them. Our charter of the worlds dictates that if any government or group of people attempt to do so, all other ruling bodies would automatically unite and declare war on them. The spacefarers themselves are not allied with anyone."

"What about other stars?" Talib asked. "You said there are settlements on other star systems."

"Yes" Rashidevqov replied. "We have cities and nations on nineteen planets orbiting stars other than Earth's sun. We have scientific outposts on several other planets which are too hostile for human life, and are presently not possible to terraform. We have also explored other stars and planets. Our scientists and explorers have detailed records of almost 9% of the galaxy."

"We had to take into account the moral responsibilities of such action. If, for example, we find a planet that suits our needs, but clearly belongs to someone else, we must leave it alone."

Talib dared not guess what "someone else" might imply.

Rashidevqov continued "And what about the living things that would already be there? We may have dominion over the "lesser" creatures, but this doesn't give us license to do whatever we wish with no thought of the consequences."

After a pause, he continued. "You must understand something. In your time, the more scientifically advanced you became, the more you thought yourselves to be beyond submission to Allah. In this society, the more advanced we become, the more we are convinced of Allah's omnipotence, greatness, and mercy. For us, it's a matter of scientific fact as well as religious belief. It almost turned out differently. We could have been destroyed by our own arrogance. It has happened to the greatest civilizations the Earth has ever known. We are constantly concerned that it could still happen to us."

Navigating among the stars. Re-forming planets. Communicating at astronomical distances. He felt very small.

Yet other things he saw were not much different than that of his own time. People rode bicycles (of unusual design, but they were bicycles nonetheless). There were lampposts at regular intervals. A gardener tended an area of the foliage using not some fantastic machine, but a regular pair of pruning shears. There were even people riding horses, camels, and occasionally some other kind of animal that clearly was either the result of some strange kind of breeding, or had no terrestrial origins at all.

"The simplest method is always the best" Rashidevqov said, when he was questioned. "Certainly, more advanced devices could be made, but some people prefer to do their work this way. The results are the same, if not better. You will find artisans whose tools are almost exactly the same as in your time. You will also find some whose tools are the most advanced that humanity has. It's largely a matter of personal choice, or what the situation calls for. The gardener over there with the pruning shears; look at his work. What machine could improve that? There is a man on the far side of this city named Slatniq who makes musical instruments. He is acknowledged as being among the greatest in history. Yet most of his tools are somewhat primitive. On the other hand the people who oversee the maintenance of our community's space vehicles utilize our most advanced technology. The people responsible for the planet's environmental maintenance also use extremely complex technology; though they mostly approach their duties from a strategy of non-interference. They too are artists. It all depends on the individual. A tool is only as good as the hand that wields it.

"When you review history, one of the things you will find is that humanity almost allowed itself to become enslaved by the machines they made. Rather than being masters of the technological process, many became components of it: and lost their humanity. We have, Masha Allah learned from our past mistakes." After a pause, he added "and I pray we never again forget."

Just then they came to a large building. It blended so well with the natural landscape, that Talib didn't notice it until they were almost upon it. It was three stories high, and very wide. It was carved out of a single, enormous shiny marble-like rock indigenous to the planet. The architectural design and technological methods employed in its construction had no parallel in anything in Earth's antiquity. They entered the cool, beautifully designed and decorated foyer area of the building. Looking around, Talib guessed that this was some kind of institution of learning. He asked Rashidevqov about this.

"Yes. There's a lounge over there. Would you like to rest first? You look tired."

In truth, he was. The long walk, after his recent ordeal had taken its toll on him. He was even further fatigued by the strain on his mind from the sights he'd seen, and the intellectual concepts he had envisioned. Rashidevqov, on the other hand, looked in robust health. Talib asked him about this.

"We exercise regularly, most of us practice martial arts, are careful of the food we eat, and we fast regularly. Our medical sciences are in harmony with our bodies. We do not pollute ourselves with harmful or unnecessary substances. The environment of this planet, combined with the way we live keeps us in good health. How old are you, my friend?"

Talib replied "I'm 51. And you?"

"I am, in terrestrial years,,," He paused and thought for a moment. "92."

Talib stared at him.

"The first man you met, the Master of Medicine, is 143. This is the blessing we receive from understanding how our bodies work, and not going against the way Allah had designed them. We also get this effect from this environment. I imagine it may have a similar effect on you after a time."

Just then the air was filled with the sound of a man calling the Adhan in a melodic voice. This was not like any adhan he'd ever heard before. The words were correct, but the melody was totally unfamiliar to him. It wasn't at all like the Egyptian influenced muezzins of his time. The scale it was based on had no parallel in any terrestrial music that Talib could identify and had harmonic overtones, like the throat singers of Tuva he'd heard.

The method of prayer held no surprises for Talib. After prayer, they continued to walk.

One of the things Talib noticed was the strange architecture. It possessed a quality that could only be described as simultaneously biological and aerodynamic. With the exception of the occasional pyramids of varying sizes, there were no squares, rectangles, triangles, or any such shape; although occasionally a structure might come to a crease or a point. He would later learn that the people here considered such shapes in their architecture to be, at best, aesthetically displeasing and at worst aggressive and threatening. Walls curved inwards or outwards at seemingly irregular intervals. Doorways vaguely resembled vaginal openings. Windows had no defined shape, yet somehow allowed light into the dwelling in a way that didn't lose consistency with the movement of the sun. Steeples, minarets, and towers swept upwards like birds in flight. Courtyard flowed seamlessly into building, which flowed seamlessly into neighboring building. Divisions of property lines were indistinct. People rarely argued over such things, as it was considered bad manners. And every single structure was in perfect harmonious balance with its natural surroundings. All the buildings were asymmetrical; yet not a single one failed to trace its logic to the Golden Ratio.

There was also a few examples of buildings that were organic. Several centuries earlier, someone revived an idea by an obscure artist in the 20th century that it was possible to manipulate plant life in such a way as to produce dwelling places. Trees and other forms of vegetation were either cultivated or genetically bred to grow into structures that not only provided shelter, but even food. Rashidevqov explained that there were hundreds of such "buildings" on the planet.

What impressed Talib on a near subconscious level was that the very shape and feel of the buildings implied a simultaneous backwards and forwards flow in time; as if past, present, and future were one and the same. He remembered something Hassan once mentioned about k-mesons and positrons.

Talib inquired about the architecture and Rashidevqov explained; "The architecture of a pyramid is conducive to energy transformation. This energy exists within and without the body and the corporeal world. It is a step beyond the old Chinese concept of feng shui. When we find it necessary to build something, we take into account the calculated changes that will occur within the next several thousand standard years; but only Allah truly knows. We also design them so that maintenance and redesign of the building suits anticipated and unexpected change."

"But why build something that will last so long? You're not going to be around to see it" Talib asked.

Rasheveskov took a breath. Despite his education and his experience with Talib, he had difficulty thinking like a 21st century Western man. He said "Why build something that will last only a century? Was not your society unstable? Was not your economy parasitic? A long lasting structure will contribute to cultural stability. The ancient Egyptians knew this; and they lasted longer than your society did. And the structures remember. The atoms and subatomic particles remember. All things are Written. Allah remembers."

Talib thought about it. The idea of stabilizing society through a complete, holistic economic plan that manifested itself in all areas of life had simply never occurred to him. He also realized how selfish he and his society had been. They cared nothing for succeeding generations.

How long would it take for him to unlearn that selfishness?

*****

After lunch, the two men walked a while. They'd passed through a wooded area. Talib noticed some plants that had qualities unequalled in any terrestrial plant. He was suddenly amazed that he was seeing actual extraterrestrial life. One plant that caught his eye was a slender blue stalk with orange thorns. At intervals, it bloomed into a rose like flower, but the stalk continued. These plants grew only in the joints and crevices of larger plants and trees. They never grew out of the soil. Rashidevqov noticed Talib's interest in the plants and warned him not to touch them; they secrete a sap that irritates the skin. But they are useful in that they are carnivorous and eat insects that would otherwise overpopulate and damage the ecosystem, and make things difficult on humans.

Presently, they came to a clearing, and the edge of a cliff overlooking a large valley. In the distance, the sun was setting. Along the edge of the cliff at a distance and at intervals in the valley below, people were standing or sitting, and facing the sunset. Talib put on a pair of dark eyeglasses someone had given him.

They sat down, facing the sunset. It occurred to Talib that this was not the sun that had shone on his world all his life. He was looking at something that was, to him, completely alien. It insinuated a great pressure upon his mind, and spoke of the vastness and enormity of the universe. He had, of course, given this some thought before. The idea wasn't new to him. But it had been an abstract idea. Now, it was something that was in his immediate environment – or rather, he was in its environment. He was the alien here.

How many other sunsets were there in this universe that he could imagine but couldn't see? What other wonders existed that no human eye could ever behold? The idea weighed upon him, pressed upon his mind. He was intoxicated, overwhelmed by the idea.

Rashidevqov said "You are about to see a planetary eclipse. This is a large gas giant we have named Thuul. It is larger than Jupiter in the mother system, and it orbits the sun closer than earth's orbit. Its gases feed directly into the sun. Our planet is further from the sun than earth is from its sun, and we travel in the opposite direction from Thuul. This eclipse happens about every seventeen year. Masha Allah, it happened upon your arrival!

"After the eclipse, we will have to return to take shelter; the gravity of Thuul will cause a violent storm. Afterward, the world will be refreshed."

By now, a great multitude of people were assembled and waiting patiently for what was to come. The sun was lower now, and the atmosphere around it reflected a spectrum of unearthly colors. Iridescent shades of blue, gold, and a violent shade of scarlet shimmered at the edge of the world. At its outermost edge, touches of vermilion and violet hovered indistinctly.

Just before the sun had touched the horizon and set for the night, he saw a sight he'd never thought he would see in his wildest dreams. A large dark disk has moved into the side of the sun, just over the left side. As it grew it seemed like a stream of multicolored vapor spiraled out of it and receded into the now diminishing sun.

It had come out of nowhere. Such a large body that gave no evidence of its arrival; suddenly challenging that majestic star and the unutterable beauty it painted upon the horizon for domination of the sky of this world. Yet it all coalesced into a perfect dance upon the stage of this enormous, yet incredibly tiny corner of the cosmos.

The sky darkened. As the sun receded, the illumination from the stars increased. The moons were behind him. They seemed quite close together (this was an illusion; their orbits were quite distant, and while eclipses occurred, they rarely got close to each other). Their reflected light was bathing the landscape in a strange glow. The land around them was aglow in soft colors; all colors perfectly visible, yet blended and none immediately recognizable.

A subdued silence fell upon the whole world. The wind stilled. No creature made a sound. No human spoke. Even small children and babies were silent. Time itself paused, as if gathering its thoughts, or acknowledging the significance of this moment, a significance that surpassed all understanding.

Talib then noticed someone sitting next to him at a distance of about a meter and a half. He was a kind looking man, with features indistinct in this light. He wore a green robe. He looked at Talib, smiled and, in a low voice, said in English, "There are Signs in this for those who have wisdom." After a pause, he added "We will meet again soon." Then he winked at Talib and grinned. Talib was, at the moment, too engrossed by the astonishing display of Allah's creation to notice that the man had spoken in his native language.

Finally, the disk relinquished its selfish hoarding of the sun's light. As Thuul moved out of the way, the sun had almost set below the horizon.

The sunset had been beautiful. Light reflected off Thuul and cast shimmers of color onto the indistinct horizon. The sky was awash in hues of gold and rose that evoked a peculiar feeling in Talib. It was an emotional response he had never experienced, and one he had no words for. To the opposite direction, the stars in their secret constellations, and the two moons shone fiercely through the stark and almost aggressive indigo. Talib thought briefly that it was as if Allah were deliberately displaying a virtuoso performance of His power for Talib's entertainment. But then he checked himself; the idea seemed too close to blasphemy. Yet, a feeling of humorous understanding came through him in a subtle wave, as if some immense power were smiling at him.

After sitting meditatively, Rashidevqov silently motioned to make a prayer. Talib joined him; still overwhelmed by what he saw.

The man in the green robe was gone.

Rashidevqov led Talib into a shelter. It was in a place deep under the building where he'd woken. He took a moment to use a communications device to make sure his family was safe elsewhere in the same shelter. Satisfied that they were (and arrangements were made to meet later). There were many other people there; and all were calm and comfortable. Talib noticed that they faced what must be an incredibly violent storm with serenity. Many were sitting comfortably and making dhikr; or tending to duties and making dhikr at the same time. He felt a bit ashamed of his own nervousness; which must surely be obvious to those around him.

The storm began.

A frightening roar came from outside the shelter, and was heard throughout the whole structure. This was followed by a moment of silence, and then rumbling and howling of wind. Loud cracks of thunder would cut through the noise. Everyone sat in silence and waited. Rashidevqov sat silently as well. Their attitude toward the storm was either they would survive or Allah was calling them home. Either prospect was equally probable and equally accepted.

Talib sat and collected himself. So much had changed in so little time! He had returned to his music, joined an obscure Sufi order, been transformed by all manner of initiatory experiences, revived his career, entered a marriage where he and his wife were madly in love with each other, was suddenly transported through time and space to a very strange yet wonderful civilization, witnessed a natural phenomena on an alien planet, and was now hiding from a storm of devastating magnitude with a group of people who regarded it as lightly as a spring shower! What could be next?

As if on cue, Rashidevqov asked "I am curious; what did you do for a living on earth?"

Talib answered "I was a musician."

"Alhamdulillah!" Rashidevqov exclaimed. "Our culture very much appreciates music. You should have no problem earning a living. We must find you a suitable instrument. I beg you the honor of purchasing your new instrument myself"

Talib offered a gentlemanly protest, but Rashidevqov refused to take no for an answer. "We also have a number of musician's groups. One of which is the respected Order of the JAZ. Their origins are from old earth."

Talib looked at him. "I was a member of the Order of the JAZ."

The two men looked at each other in silence for a moment.

Finally, Rashidevqov said "I must arrange some introductions."

After about four hours, the sound of the storm began to diminish. A very human sigh of relief passed through the shelter. Shortly, Rashidevqov's family arrived; a female voice spoke from a distance.

"Malik! Asalam Alaikum!"

Both men turned. There were two women standing at a small distance. One was a woman in her late thirties, by Talib's estimation. She was of indeterminable race, and had large dark green eyes that complemented her bright ivory complexion. Ringlets of curly dark red hair were barely visible under her head covering. The other looked African. Her skin was as dark as it is possible for a human being to possess, but her eyes were unlike any Talib had ever seen. They were an almost fluorescent blue, with a not unpleasant shade of reddish orange where the whites would have been. Their shape was almost Asian, but curved sharply upwards at the corners. Her nose was wide and flat. Like her companion, some of her hair was visible; but hers was twisted into thick dreadlocks, a few of which fell from the multi colored head wrap she wore. Both women's lips were large, and perfectly proportioned, offsetting their high, sharp cheekbones. Their dresses were loose fitting, and very colorful; seemingly made of some kind of silk-like material that reflected light in a pale glow. Both women exude an elegance which suggested royalty; and were distractingly beautiful. They smiled radiantly at Rashidevqov.

They were accompanied by four young children and a male teenager. The teenager was tall, and had facial features which resembled Rashidevqov's, except that his skin was very dark, and his eyes resembled the African woman's. He seemed competent and self assured beyond his years, and left one with the impression that he was completely trustworthy. The children, two boys and two girls, resembled the women and the teenager; and were dressed in the same kind of colorful clothing everyone else wore. They were utterly charming, and very intelligent.

They came up to the two men, and Rashidevqov advanced upon them. He held out his arms and embraced both women briefly; and, in what was doubtless a custom peculiar to this culture, passed the palms of their hands over each other's forearms as they exchanged tender words, which Talib's translator didn't pick up. The teenager and Rashidevqov embraced, and the children clamored for his attention; which he gave them; smiling and laughing.

Rashidevqov said "Brother, I want to introduce you to my wives. This is Anjjelliqh." The African woman smiled and nodded. "And this is Farouzah" The other woman smiled and nodded. "These are my children: Khalad" The teenager shook his hand. "These are Rasheema, Djunal, Mda'ud, and Amandla."

All four children said "Asalam Alaiukm" in unison, smiling at Talib.

Talib smiled at them and said, holding out his translator, and hoping it was properly set "Asalaam alaikum. I'm very pleased to meet you all."

Some brief conversation followed. As they talked, everyone careful not to speak at once so the translator wouldn't be confused (except the children; who had to be reminded of this from time to time), Talib got to know the family. Anjjelliqh was, as Talib understood it, a master of theoretical mathematics. Farouzeh owned a small business that designed machinery used by astronomers. Rashidevqov stated, with obvious pride, that an astronomical body that she had discovered was named after her. Khalad was a student of music. From his description, this music was used in an almost purely medicinal capacity. One of the musicians who were scheduled to perform tonight was Khalad's teacher. Khalad mentioned that his teacher, in addition to being a master of both medicinal and art music was also a practitioner of "Djjil'arghinab'vhaqq": which was translated by Talib's device, as the "forbidden-tone/spirit-music/truth": a subject of which he spoke with sight awe.

Khalad asked Talib if it was true that he was a member of the Order of JAZ. The translator almost imitated the tone of the young man's voice. Yes, he replied. It is true. "Sheikh Suliman himself conducted my initiation ritual. Hassan Rusticcelli was my friend and music teacher for a long time. I knew them well. I'm going to miss Hassan. He was truly the best friend I ever had" Talib said this casually; and the family's reaction was as if he'd casually mentioned that he had dinner with Hazrat Ali ibn Talib, or Sheikh Muhayyideen ibn Arabi the night before last.

" You knew Sheikh Suliman and Hassan Rusticelli! That must mean that you're THE Talib Ali Peterson! This is incredible!" Khalad exclaimed. "We must inform Sheikh Lateef immediately!" Rashidevqov advised him to wait until after the storm settled and people returned to their homes - after all, Sheikh Lateef was an old man.

While this was happening, Talib was suddenly overcome by a wave of homesickness. He had been so overwhelmed by sensations and had little sleep; the reality of the situation had only now hit him emotionally. Before he could stop himself, he began to weep. He missed his beloved wife, his friends, his family, his cat. He missed his world, the only world he ever knew. In an instant, the intoxicating novelty of his surroundings fell away, and it struck him that everything he knew and was acclimated with was gone. He would never see his own world again. Never.

Rashidevqov understood, as best as he was able, what was happening. His wives reacted with their womanly instincts; they held his hands, and Anjjeliqh allowed him to cry on her shoulder. The small children stopped what they were doing and asked what was wrong. Rashidevqov motioned for them to be silent. They obeyed, but were just as concerned. Khalad had returned, and for a moment couldn't understand what was happening. He was still overwhelmed with the news he'd received and it took him a moment to realize that this man had been through a series of traumatic experiences.

Rashidevqov, Firouzeh, Anjjeliqh, and Khalad looked at each other and a silent decision had been made between them. They would invite Talib to stay with them until he found a place of his own.

Finally, Talib regained control of himself. He began to apologize, but they all told him it was alright. "I pray that you understand that you are among friends" Rashidevqov said. As Anjjeliqh attempted to dry the material of her dress, she added "We know you have been through a lot. We can't imagine the trails you have faced! You are not alone, brother Talib."

Firouzeh added "We would like you to stay with us at our home. It will be good for all of us. Please don't refuse."

Talib nodded in agreement, and smiled through his tears.

At that moment, little Rasheema, ran up to Talib, hopped into his lap, and hugged him. The innocent sincerity she showed was more powerful a medicine for his soul than anything he could have imagined. "It's OK" she said, as the translator rendered her small voice into English. "I cry when I'm scared too."

After about four hours, the sound of the storm began to diminish. A very human sigh of relief passed through the shelter.

After the storm, the people walked outside. Everywhere people were making vocal exclamations of thanks to Allah for having allowed them to survive. There wasn't as much damage to the buildings as had been anticipated. News services reported that worldwide, injuries were minimal. The plant life had been hit hard, but their natural resiliency necessitated only repairs to farmlands, parks, and clearing of what was called "cultivated public areas." The wild life areas that were never 'developed" were largely left to their own powers of regeneration. Rashidevqov's family went home, and he and Talib returned to the hospital, where a tree was being removed from the top of the building. No damage had been done to the building; but people were concerned that they may not be able to save the tree.

Rashidevqov informed the hospital that Talib would be staying with him indefinitely. The administration had no argument; and thought it an excellent idea (Sheikh Uthman Ulyutah, a well intentioned, but cranky, old man with an abrasive exterior scolded Rashidevqov as an idiot for not thinking of the idea sooner.)

All of Talib's worldly belongings were the clothes on his back and the items in the pouch around his shoulder. He went with his new (and only) friends to their house.

It was a good sized house; one that would provide a comfortable home for a sizeable family. The outside, despite its size and aerodynamic shape that most architecture here had, was remarkable in that it appeared unremarkable. When he went inside, however, it was quite beautiful. The colors, shapes, furnishings, and even the light and space was all designed to inspire a feeling of comfort and peace. There were works of art that were stylistically unlike anything Talib had seen (most of these were the works of the members of the family or friends).

In that moment, when he was looking up at a skylight, he stepped on and almost tripped over a toy one of the children left laying about. Some things never change.

The house and surrounding land produced most of its own food, water, and energy. This was the standard design for homes on this world. Talib described how things were on earth in his day. They found the idea of having to pay a utility company for water and electricity, etc. downright bizarre.

Talib got settled in, Rashidevqov took him aside.

"Brother," he began "there's something I want to ask you. I'm not sure how to ask, or what the question means. Nor am I sure what I will do with your answer. But you told me something that I truly did not understand. Now I must ask, if I may."

"Sure" Talib said. "Ask me anything you want."

Rashidevqov paused, and then said with great solemnity "What is 'Star Trek?'"

Talib laughed so hard he couldn't catch his breath for a long time.

*****

The next day Rashidevqov brought Talib to an office of some kind.

"I have brought you here "Rashidevqov began, "to introduce you to some people. They will assist me in helping you become familiar with our society. There are some things regarding us that you will need to know. We will help you get started."

"I can't thank you enough for everything you've done for me" Talib said with

true sincerity which was not lost on Rashidevqov. Occasionally the terror of being in such unfamiliar surroundings was almost more than he could bear; although he did his best not to show it.

"Alhamdullilah. Masha Allah" Rashidevqov said. Then he stopped, looked up and around; as if he heard something. Then he closed his eyes and took a deep breath.

This left Talib confused, but he followed Rashidevqov.

They were lead to a room that contained the usual assortment of cushions and close-to-the-floor tables; and several pieces of what Talib took to be electronic equipment. What these had to do with education, he couldn't yet understand, although he assumed they were some kind of information storage or media playback devices. In one corner was a tea service. In another corner was a brass urn with the same kind of incense he'd smelled here yesterday. Talib wondered why they would take such pains to make these places smell so decorously. Then he realized that these incenses had specific meaning or function.

"Tell me something" Talib said. What kind of government do you have here?"

Rashidevqov said "It's something akin to a theocracy. There is a khaliphite that is specific to this planet. The lower levels of government are an aggregate of religious, mystical, scientific, or philosophical orders. These orders have an economy, military, governmental hierarchy, ruling and ruled classes, and the like.

"But our government could probably be thought of as almost a feudal system, except that the 'houses' are not governed by families but by ideals. Principles that are believed to be greater than our ideas of self."

"What about wars?" Talib asked.

"There are still wars. But there are very few large scale wars like in your day; and none have happened on this planet, Masha Allah. They are usually much smaller, and observe special protocols. A territory is marked out for the sole purpose of war, and two groups of elite warriors meet in this territory and fight. They almost always confine themselves to the use of handheld weapons. Sometimes they fight among themselves for their own reasons. The fighting rarely goes beyond these boundaries. No innocent people are involved. But there are people who are, by nature, warriors. This is the best way to let them be what they are. They have their wars and their honor; and disputes between nations are settled."

Talib thought a moment, and said "It's like the gladiators of Rome, I guess. More than just some kind of football game."

Rashidevqov thought for a moment. He vaguely knew what football was, but has difficulty drawing the same parallel between that and war. Finally he said "There are no more professional or commercial athletics. There are only warriors who fight real wars in honorable contests based on high ideals and competition for the gain of their people, and" he paused, searching for the right word, "amateurs who amuse themselves."

A man and a woman walked in and sat down.

The man, a young Aryan with light reddish-gold hair spoke. "In the Name of Allah, the Beneficent, the Merciful, I offer you the greetings of peace; May peace and blessings be upon you.

Welcome to our abode of work. My name is Jihad al-Mukhtalak. We have been contacted about your situation and your needs."

The woman looked Hispanic or Mediterranean with violet eyes. She was old, and her skin seemed almost greenish-gold; and Talib couldn't tell if this was an effect of the lighting, or her actual skin pigmentation. She gave a similar salutation and introduced herself as Aisha Bhzillasha'ah. She said "I would like to emphasis that there is no precedent to your situation. There is so much for you to learn. We hardly knew where to begin."

"However" interjected al-Mukhtalak "we had some literature in your language prepared for you. This will cover the basics. Let's have a brief look at it."

The "brief look" lasted over eight hours. They had taken a break to make their prayer, then the session resumed. Talib was convinced that they'd covered every aspect of society.

"I have an idea" Rashidevqov said, when they returned to the house. "If you are not too tired, we can have dinner at the nearby park. There will be a musical performance."

"I'd love to attend" Talib replied. "I will need to rest first." He sat down, heaving a sigh.

Rashidevqov chuckled. "I would imagine that it has been a difficult day."

"No! You think?" exclaimed Talib, then laughed. Rashidevkov chortled; knowing it was some kind of a joke, but didn't quite understand it. Talib said. "I'd really like to go. I think it would do me good to hear some nice music."

"Very well" Rashidevqov said. "I will go to my room and refresh myself. I'll be back in a few hours. Ma'a Salaam."

After Rashidevqov left, Talib walked to the balcony of the house. The sun was well below the horizon, yet a hazy bluish-gold remained on the horizon. The stars were out, and Talib wondered which of them was home. Or will this be my home? Talib asked himself. If I stay here, or if I go back to an Earth centuries older than when I left it, I will not be home. I have no home.

Just then Rashidevqov knocked on the door, and announced himself.

Rashidevqov said "Shall we go?"

"Yes" said Talib. "I should warn you" he added "that I have no money,,,"

"My brother, "Rashidevqov said, smiling "You are our guest. I assure you that you need not concern yourself with such things."

The family convened and they all walked out.

Once outside, they took a different walkway than the one they had in the morning. Talib had an excellent sense of direction, and subconsciously made mental notes of the local geography.

Soon they arrived at the place where the concert would be presented. It was in the middle of a large garden. A fountain stood at the center of the square. Rock sculptures were scattered about and some were part of the fountain. Flowers of species unknown to Talib were arranged in almost fractal patterns. Their colors bathed the eye in shades of impossibly beautiful hues. All about, at intervals were torches and incense burners. The aroma of the incense blended in perfect harmony with the smells of the flowers and the nearby ocean. People sat on cushions on the ground, with small tables around them. To the left of the entrance was a buffet table with the exotic foods that these people seemed to thrive on. A small group of men and women were tending to the food, and offering assistance to whomever needed it. A few people were smoking from hookahs; but from the smell of it, it was not tobacco, hashish or opium. At the far end, sloping downward, there was a stage with a covering supported by slender pillars. There were also curved panels erected at the parameters of the stage; which enhanced the acoustics of the performance area. Silk sheets covered what Talib guessed were the instruments that would be played.

"Come" Rashidevqov said "Let's have some food."

At length, they all got themselves a plate of food, and found a place to sit together.

Suddenly, the musicians took to the stage. Assistants preceded them; removing the silk sheets from the instruments. Four men and a separate group of two men and three women took to the stage. All were wearing white robes and headpieces, with embroidery of various colors and designs; which was actually indicative of their station and accomplishments. One man, of indeterminable race, whose hair looked like reddish brown dreadlocks, sat with a strange stringed instrument; which had two necks, and dozens of strings arranged at several angles. It seemed like a sitar, acoustic bass guitar, and harp combined in the same instrument. A man of unidentifiable lineage sat before several percussion instruments. A very tall, powerfully built light skinned African sat before a small table arrayed with several wind instruments. A man who looked Chinese or Mongolian sat in front of some kind of keyboard instrument. The others were vocalists, and sat at one side of the stage.

After about a minute, during which time the audience became quiet, and the musicians had made some last minute adjustments on their instruments, the African raised his hand. Bringing it down, the percussion began a medium tempo beat in rhythmic groups of seven beats. The keyboardist faded in; and several sounds simultaneously emerged from his keyboard: one deep and penetrating, the other shimmering and crystalline. The strings came in and provided a complementary counterpoint to the keyboard. They were bouncing unusual harmonies off each other. Notes that seemed out of tune actually created "beat" frequencies in absolutely perfect synchronization with the rhythm of the percussion. It created harmonic consonances that were more pure than anything Talib ever heard.

Then the African picked up a small, slender pipe with a flaring bell that curved slightly upwards, and began to play. It

196

cut through the dense tapestry of sound and rhythm that filled the air of the space. The melodies it played spoke of ancient, timeless truths. How loud it was! Such a tiny thing making such an indomitable sound!

Then the men began to sing. Their voices would have put to shame any opera singer of Talib's time. The women joined them; their voices possessing timbres unlike any Talib had ever heard. Suddenly one of the men began to sing two, then three notes simultaneously; like the Tuvan throat singers. The women followed suit, and soon their strange harmonies were interwoven with the harmonic and melodic structure of the instrumentalists.

As the composition progressed, the music became more intense. Not unbearably so, but it required an effort on the part of the listener. One did not, it seemed, passively listen to this music; one did so actively, and became a part of the performance. Sounds seemed to come from all directions at once. Melodies swirled about him; above and below him. Harmonies reverberated from behind him and blended with the other sounds. It was far from anything Talib was accustomed to – and he had, by this time, quite exacting standards. This music, it seemed, had always existed and would always exist. It would have been the music of a master's master in any time or place. Bach would have wept upon hearing this music.

Suddenly the music seemed to ebb away. It faded like the incense smoke that held its olfactory dominion. The audience applauded; a quiet thunder of appreciation.

The second piece they played largely consisted of long notes and phrases. It seemed concerned with impressing the effects of harmonies and intervals upon the listener. The time signature was of a cycles of 23 beats at 80 bpm. Yet, the startling effects of the extended harmonies and the anticipation of the melodic movement made the piece anything but boring. The dynamics employed throughout were both startling and seductive; it was quite different from minimalism, yet used minimalist building blocks in a way Talib never dreamed.

The group played three more compositions; one was based upon an old folk song from a long extinct nation on another world; the next, a slow, moving lament which brought tears to many eyes; the last an up tempo piece which afforded each musician and singer the opportunity to display by turns his or her improvisational virtuosity. At one point the string player played something strange and complex which summoned laughter from everyone. The bandleader chuckled and smiled with obvious amusement. Talib didn't understand the joke.

The concert ended with a man introducing the master musicians. "

Then everyone sat down, and turned their attention to their own parties. Talib was still caught up in the throes of the amazing musical performance. Later, Talib saw members of the audience placing coins in a large bowl as they left. He assumed this was how the musicians were paid.

Khalad nudged his father, and gestured to his right. One of the musicians, the tall African, was headed their way.

Everyone at the table rose. Khalad seemed intent upon exhibiting great politeness and reverence towards the great musician. "Brother Talib" he said "This is Sheikh Yusef Lateef; my teacher, and First Master of All Music."

"Asalam Alaikum Wa Rahmatuallah" Sheikh Lateef said, extending his hand. "News of the unusual circumstances which brought you to us has reached me. Allow me to bid you welcome to our community, and to extend my hopes for a happy and prosperous life here."

Talib was touched. "Thank you very much. Your performance was magnificent! I've never heard music like it"

"All praise and gratitude is due to Allah" Sheikh Lateef said. His manner and bearing were that of a king. Dignity, kindness, and indomitable intellect all radiated from the man.

Farouzah invited Sheikh Lateef to join them.

As he sat down, he said "I fear that I will not be able to stay but for a moment. There is to be a session tomorrow night, and I must prepare. Khalad, I assume you understand what I mean."

Khalad said "The Djjil'arghnab'vhaqq?"

"Precisely" said Sheikh Lateef. Turning to Rashidevqov (the elder) he said "With your permission, I would like Khalad to assist me in tomorrow's session. I believe he's ready."

Rashidevqov paused, and asked "Are you quite certain? It is very dangerous."

Sheikh Lateef said "The risks are real, but I would never expose him to it unless I was convinced that he was ready. And as you know, it is a necessary part of his training. Tomorrow's session will be less risky than usual. I recommend it. The experience will strengthen his immunity."

The two women looked frightened, and looked to Rashidevqov as if to plead with him to forbid it. Finally Rashidevqov turned to his son and said "What are your thoughts on this?"

With youthful determination, Khalad said "I'm ready for it."

"Then, may Allah guide you to success."

"Thank you, father" Khalad exclaimed. Khalad's mother and step mother struggled to conceal their disapproval.

Sheikh Lateef said "I have much preparation to do early in the morning, and should be on my way. Ladies; I advise you to prepare his recuperation for the day after tomorrow; it will be a trying experience for him. My friends, I am happy we've seen each other again. Brother Talib, I hope to see you again, and pray for your success" Rising, he said "Asalam Alaikum Wa Rahmatuallah."

"Wa Alaikum Salaam Wa Rahmatuallah" everyone said in ragged unison.

After they left, Talib asked "I don't understand. What is so dangerous about this music?"

Rashidevqov said "I'm no expert in music, Perhaps Khalad should explain." He looked to Khalad.

Khalad began "About 500 years ago a congress of musicians from all the planets developed The Djjil'arghnab'vhaqq. They used a synergy of elements of all known music. The Order of

200

JAZ pioneered research into this music as early as the 21st century, old Christian era.

"What they succeeded in developing was music so powerful that the human body reacts by purging impurities and diseases. This music would also affect the mind in such a way that the normal mechanism which permits us to perceive thoughts, memories, and sense impressions one at a time would be disabled. The barrier between the conscious and subconscious mind is also removed. One would experience these things all at once. There are medicinal uses of this music in controlled environments, and under strict supervision. Many illnesses have been cured this way. Occasionally it can be used to open the mind to higher levels of awareness. This music can also have effects upon physical objects. But if you casually listen to this music without preparation or supervision, you could die or go insane."

Khalad could have gone into greater detail, and part of him wanted to very much. But he didn't want to bore or annoy his father's guest.

Talib said "This is really interesting. I'd like to learn more"

Khalad said "You will. It was your work that made it possible."

*****

The next morning Talib woke up refreshed and full of energy and enthusiasm. He hadn't felt this good in a long time.

After bathing and dressing, he went into the hall and began headed for the room where Rashidevqov and family were already beginning their breakfast. A cushion at the low table waited for him, and Firouzeh gestured for him to sit.

Talib said "Asalaam alaikum. How are you today?"

"Wa alaikum asalaam. I feel fine; all praise is due to Allah. How did you sleep?"

"Like a baby. After a night of sawing wood, I feel wonderful this morning."

Rashidevqov looked at him, with a slight smile.

"Is something wrong?" Talib asked.

"Oh no" Rashidevqov said. "It's the expressions you sometimes use. I've never heard them before. I think I understand most of them, but it is truly educational for me, especially in my field of expertise"

"I wondered about that" Talib said. "The study of ancient languages must be difficult if there is no way to hear or speak them with a person who uses them in everyday speech."

"Exactly" Rashidevqov agreed. "I have often wondered how accurate my understanding is. There are also colloquialisms, and cultural variables which the scholars might have omitted from their books. Fortunately, recordings still exist: a surprising number, considering the events of the centuries following the time when you were brought here."

Talib became pensive. This was something which he was concerned about: historical events. These would be of great importance: since they would be so heavily influenced by the work his people had done. Something inside him was filled with dread at the thought of learning what accomplishments his people have wrought; although he was not sure why he felt this way.

As if reading his mind, Rashidevqov said "As I told you yesterday, we will be reviewing the events of the history of humanity. Arrangements have been made for this at the academy we visited yesterday."

Just then a woman entered the room.

As the two men made themselves comfortable, a woman walked in. She was a small dark skinned Jewish or Bedouin looking woman, about five feet tall; wearing a black hijab with gold floral embroidery. It covered everything except her face and hands. She was old: in her eighties, by Talib's estimation (which in this world was probably terribly inaccurate). But her eyes were sharp; with a steady, intense, and penetrating gaze who would have been completely unnerving, had she not carried with her a sense of kindness. Yet she was clearly no one to be trifled with (and nobody ever did).

"Asalam Alaikum Wa Rahmatuallah" she began. "My name is Sheikha Rasheema Tomaktah Y'ishmael. I am a First Master of Historical Preservation. I am pleased to welcome you to our academy."

Sheikha Y'Ishmael summoned a servant, who brought coffee. She said "We will instruct you on the history of humanity since your time on earth. We would also eventually like to interview you to learn more about your time. You could help us a great deal in this"

Talib nodded his head in affirmation.

"There is something else" Sheikha Y'ismael continued. "It is something that is important for you to know"

Great, thought Talib ruefully. Another major shock.

"I don't know if you have been told by your hosts and benefactors, but records of your former life survive. Among these records is the account of what they believed happened, the fate of your friends, family, and your wife. And a personal message to you."

"What?" Talib said. "They left me a message?"

"Yes. I don't know how many in the past centuries read this message. Few thought that you would ever return; although Sheikh Suliman was convinced you would. But it is addressed to you; and you've waited centuries to read it.

Sheikha Y'ishmael turned to a cabinet, and removed a book and a small black leather folder. They were covered in dust, and the folder looked very old. She placed the two items on the table in front of him. "Take all the time you need" she said, and left the room.

For a long time, Talib stared at the book and the folder. he was actually frightened to pick it up and look at it. For a moment, he thought that it would be comical if it was written in a language and script he couldn't read.

He reached for the book, and opened it. *Well*, he thought. *At least it's written in English.*

He began to read. It was, indeed, English, but in a dialect that was about 180 years after his own time. There were several passages whose meaning he had to extrapolate. Several times he came across a word he simply could make no sense of. One of which was "termashahidi"; which described the political assassination of a spiritual leader by order of kuffar leadership. Another was "refrefyd"; the refusal to accept an RFID implant. Another was "dalantilii" which was the use of logic and reason to counteract the effects of shirk dialectic.

The Order survived a series of crisis from the political upheavals that happened during the twenty first century. They not only preserved their work, but contributed to it and developed it. Often as an underground movement, because the government became so paranoid and despotic that they'd consider the Order dangerous. Some of the members were arrested and tortured for no reason other than that they were Sufi musicians.

Eventually, the Order's records and works were smuggled off planet. On the Martian colonies (this was news to Talib), they could practice their work with greater freedom, despite the harsh conditions of life and the presence of the war there. New members were accepted, and their work spread throughout the newly settled worlds.

He read on. Sheikh Suliman had to resort to militaristic acts to support the Believers, as they were known, and to preserve the Order during the revolution and its work. He became a brilliant military strategist. He died at the age of 82. The cause of death was not mentioned, beyond it being "beautiful." His successor, Sheikh Abdulqadr Koneig, whom Talib never met, was assigned the task of leading the Order. He was a composer, who wrote all kinds of works, including ten symphonies that used techniques and instrumentation that could only be described as revolutionary. His office continued until he died at the age of 79.

Hassan Rusticelli continued his work with the Order, and put a great deal of effort into continuing the work that Talib had begun. He died at the age of 75 from congestive heart failure.

His friend Jamal Postatnik was murdered by Blackwater International. The culprits were never brought to justice (in this world). Maryam Jalil and her husband were attacked by a neo-fascist cult called Youth for Trump when she was overheard expressing an opinion they thought contradicted their ideas of political orthodoxy. She survived; but as she was pregnant at the time, she miscarried. Her husband died of his injuries.

Talib made a silent prayer for his friends. As he did so, he found himself momentarily overcome by what may be called "survivor's guilt." He saw no reason why he should have been spared and those closest to him suffer in these terrible ways.

He found his own name. He smiled. An accurate (but, Talib thought, excessively flattering) account of his work was listed. His "unexplained disappearance" was shrouded in mystery. Sheikh Suliman insisted that, according to visions he had, Talib Ali would return one day. At times, his name was invoked as a rallying cry when the Order faced what looked like an insurmountable obstacle. When they would face hardships, they would remind each other to "be ready for Talib's return."

He was a "legend." *Unbelievable*, thought Talib.

Then his eyes fell on the name Zeinab McKormick Ali. Talib closed his eyes a moment. He was frightened to look for a moment. His beloved, the great love of his life, would be reduced by the ravages of time to a footnote in history. Only Allah, and he would know the true depth of this woman's beauty of spirit. Only Allah and he would know the passion, pain, and poetry of love that they shared. That was, he knew, enough. But his love for Zeinab demanded more. And he was visited momentarily by a slight feeling of guilt. What if she suffered? What if she needed him, and he was powerless to help her?

He read. The history listed the work he knew she'd done, and continued after he was gone. It was quite impressive. It seemed that after an intense period of mourning, she threw herself into her work; and also made herself the biographer and preserver of Talib's music. His music sales had increased, and Zeinab was well off.

At the time of Talib's disappearance, unknown to both of them, she was pregnant with what was to be Talib and Zeinab's only son. She named him Talib, after his father. Eventually, she was offered the job of treasurer of the entire Order; a job she performed in an exemplary manner. The Order made her a Sheikha. A few words about her personal life were included. She was spared most of the horrors of the wars. She moved to a

Sufi community in South Dakota, located just inside Lakota territory that had officially seceded from the US, and lived a quiet life. She died of natural causes at the age of 74, never having remarried.

He wondered what happened to Boo. A cat would not merit a place in historical record.

His son Talib jr. grew up to be a pianist. He synthesized Asian and western classical music, and became a virtuoso improviser on pianos tuned to alternate systems of intonation. He married a Chinese woman named Ling; a Hui who came to the US in her teens. They had four children. Talib Jr. was killed by Zionist militants who were connected to a cult led by an insane Rabbi.

The entire genealogy of his descendants was here.

He read on, skimming through what he knew he'd have to read in detail later. There were histories, names that he didn't and couldn't know; but who accomplished great things. To his astonishment, he learned that Malik Rashadevqov was one of his decedents! He wondered if he was aware of this.

There were also great problems, controversies, power struggles within the Order; fitna and more fitna, But the order survived.

He closed the book and set it aside. Then he reached for the folder, and opened it.

It contained a laminated handwritten letter addressed to him.

Asalaam alaikum, wa Rahmatuallah. When you read this, and I don't know when that will be, I will be gone from this world.

Allah informed me in a dream that you were taken from us in a way that was unlike others before you. You would travel vast oceans of time and distance. I meditated on the dream and made dhikr to try to understand what I was told. Understanding eludes me.

Little brother, when Hassan brought you to us, I was so happy. You don't know it, but you carried a Light within you. It was obvious that Allah had plans for you. We could all see it.

There were so many things I wanted to share with you. So much we still needed to teach you. Are they lost to you? I pray Allah makes these gifts available to you, and more!

Know that there are some among the Sufis who are struggling against the misuse of powers that lay dormant within human beings. For centuries, we have been guarding them, marking time. Protecting these secrets from their misuse by the profane. Soon these secrets will be known to you. I'm sorry I couldn't be the one to share them with you. It would have been a great pleasure and honor to do so!

We have held our peace about many thing, and marked time. When you return, the world will be much different than when you left. But by then, Insha Allah, the world may be ready for this.

As you read this, doubtless Allah is placing you further on your Path. I have no doubt that you will find what teachings and gifts I was unable to give you. You will find them, and more; and take them to places we couldn't. It is too late for us; you will walk the Path we couldn't.

Keep the Dhikr of Allah foremost in your heart. And remember your humble friends in your duas as we remembered you. We all love you.

Ma'a Salaam,
Sheikh Suliman

Talib wept.

Chapter 15. The Forge.

The next morning Talib woke up, and for a moment couldn't remember where he was. He'd been dreaming, but couldn't remember what he dreamed. Only that he was involved with someone in some kind of task or search. He dressed, found his way to a washroom, and came back and made his salat. Then, grabbing his translator, he walked about, listening for the sounds of people. He found his hosts in the kitchen, eating breakfast. They were seated on cushions on the floor surrounding a low table. At the table's center, and on another table nearby, was a variety of food Talib couldn't identify; but it looked good.

"Ah! You're awake. We let you sleep late'" Firouzeh said, gesturing to an empty seat at the table. The children began bringing him food; more than he could comfortably eat. Their parents restrained them a little, with bemusement at their competition for generosity. Rasheema insisted upon sitting on Talib's lap; which he didn't mind, he being tenderhearted toward children.

After a hearty breakfast, the adults and Khalad sat and had coffee, while the children shared poetry and songs they'd learned in school. They were charming. Then Firouzeh and Anjjeliqh prepared to take the children to school, and leave for their own jobs. Rashidevqov, Khalad, and Talib were alone.

Khalad came to the point. "As soon as Sheikh Lateef had been informed of your credentials he had wanted to offer you membership."

"Technically, you're already a member" Rashidevqov said.

They approached the door. Talib said "After you"

Khalad was momentarily confused by the way the translator rendered "After you", and Rashidevqov had to explain it to him. They finished their coffee, and Khalad led the way.

It was a cool, overcast day. They leisurely made their way to the University where Sheikh Lateef taught. Talib had trouble identifying the group of buildings as a university. A beautiful mosque was the centerpiece of the incredibly large compound of the university. Several buildings with individual functions interwove into an aggregate of unified purpose. The architecture was breathtaking. The grounds surrounding the buildings were single multifaceted garden; with fields, forests, lakes, rivers, hills and valleys. The entire compound was designed for one purpose; to train Believers to reach their full human potential and prepare the vicegerents of Allah to assume the mantle of khalifah of humanity.

It was stressed that leadership was something that often assumed subtleties that were deceiving to the untrained mind. It was actually very rare that a man had to stand in command of armies and empires to be a true khalph.

They came to the music building, and once inside, the atmosphere seemed to coalesce into a stillness and serenity that was almost formidable. The architecture was beautiful, solemn and majestic. After being greeted by a caretaker of sorts, they were led to Sheikh Lateef's office.

It was more of a musical laboratory. Musical instruments of all kinds were everywhere. Talib was curious to examine them. Against one wall was what Talib guessed could be a recording device; but he wasn't sure. There were none of the cables, microphones, speakers, and the like, that a musician in Talib's time would associate with recording technology. Cushions and chairs were scattered about, and in one corner was a desk with neat piles of papers and devices of some kind. Behind it sat Sheikh Lateef.

Rising, Sheikh Lateef walked slowly toward Talib, his hand extended. They shook hands. After exchanging greetings, Sheikh Lateef said. " It's good to see you again. Your presence here is a great gift from Allah. I have many things to tell you.

"I imagine you already know that the Order that you belonged to still exists, and is quite strong. We would like to offer you membership. This we do not only because you are already one of us, but historical records of you survive, and your accomplishments are well known and well respected. So, would you like to take your place among us?"

"Yes" Talib said, without hesitation. What else could he do?

He was answered with a chorus of Alhamdulillah.

Sheikh Lateef said that there would be a brief ceremony of welcoming for him. He walked out, motioned for the others to follow.

They entered what could only be a conference room, except that there were cushions on the floor arranged in a circle around a large, low circular table made of some dark stone. The walls were a deep burgundy, and one wall had three archways that led to a balcony. They sat down, and after a while several men and women entered.

Sheikh Lateef briefly described the purpose of the Order. None of this was any surprise to Talib. After listening, he was asked if he understood what the Order was, what it expected of him, and if he wished to join – or rather rejoin – them of his own free will. Talib answered yes.

That was it! The men and women congratulated him. Taib was a little taken aback. He was half expecting a grand ritualistic initiation that threatened to destroy his mind!

That would come later.

*****

The day of his first lesson in this new world arrived. He carried his instrument to the place where Sheikh Lateef was waiting for him.

His instrument was called a bazhtaran. It was a staff like device designed by one of the ancestors of the Order. It was light, and perfectly balanced; and could function both as a musical instrument and as a weapon. It housed a double blade with a fractal edge that was actually longer than the length of the blade itself. Made of wood and a metal that resisted corrosion and damage, maintenance of the weapon was minimal. It also carried a static electrical charge that was extraordinarily powerful. This charge could recharge itself indefinitely. Worked within the design of the bazhtaran was a flute of a simple design; not very different from a ney or a shakuhachi. But in skilled hands it was capable of a wide variety of temperaments and timbres. It also had five strings spanning four octaves that could be bowed or plucked, as well as 40 sympathetic strings, that were hidden behind a series of sliding plates that could be moved away to facilitate playing. The strings, an alloy of titanium, silver, gold, and osmium, were incredibly strong, and with proper care, they would last several decades without significant wear or tarnish. The acoustic properties of the instrument were amazing. It had the capacity to produce harmonics in a wide variety of timbres and temperaments; all of which seemed to play not only harmonies, but at times counterpoints against the melodies being played. And it was very loud when it needed to be.

The bazhtaran was a gift from his friend Rashidevqov. It was his most prized possession, not only because it was such an amazing device, but because it was evidence of Allah's provisions, and of the compassion he was shown when he was at his greatest hour of need. He always remembered to show that same compassion himself, at every opportunity.

He was told that it was a tradition to give one's instrument a name. He called his bazhtaran "Zeinab," and later had the name engraved, in Roman letters, on the instrument in gold, emerald, and ruby inlay. He chose gold to symbolize the purity of the love his wife and him had. He added ruby and emerald to symbolize how he saw her beauty.

His music lessons opened up a new vista for him. One of the first lessons with Dr. Lateef, had pointed out a musical phenomenon that seemed in retrospect terribly obvious; but it was something he would never have thought of had he never left the earth. "The first this you must know" began Dr. Lateef "is that the diatonic scale's tuning resembles the arrangement of the planets in the solar system. The distances and velocities of the planets correspond to the basic scale." Here, he picked up his flute and played a simple c major scale. "Each note is analogous to a planet."

Talib interjected "Yes, I'm familiar with the idea."

Dr. Lateef paused, looking at him, and finally said "This scale," he played the major scale again "corresponds to the planets in *your* solar system. You are no longer in that solar system."

For a moment, Talib sat, stunned. The idea never occurred to him. Suddenly, he realized how the music at that concert had been so strange, yet beautiful. The theory behind it was fundamentally different from what he'd been accustomed to. Now, he would have to abandon his knowledge of music – again! - and start from a totally new foundation.

"This is how the planets are arranged in our solar system. There is our star, then a small planet called Qamb, then an asteroid belt, then Thuul, the gas giant, then Uq'Dyill, then a rock planet called Musharaab, which is slightly larger than Uq'Dyill, finally a gas giant called Layl. Beyond this, there is another asteroid belt with several dwarf planets and comets."

Dr. Lateef continued. "This scale corresponds to the first five Fibonacci primes: 2, 3, 5, 13, and 89. Now, the notes in our basic scale that correspond to the planets in this system, as your old theory system calls it, is as follows: Tonic, flat 2nd = 104.955 cents above octave - overtone half-step. median / neutral 3rd = 347.408 cents above octave - undecimal median third, augmented 4th (the octave reduced 89th harmonic)- 570.880 cents above tonic, perfect fifth 701.955 above tonic, median / neutral 6th (octave reduced 13th) 852.592 cents above the tonic, and return to the tonic. The tonic is always fixed; and while there are modulations at times, tonics are absolute.

"The thing you may notice about this scale is that on earth it would sound strange. Here, it comes across as perfectly natural."

Then, Sheikh Lateef taught Talib the scale, until he was able to play it to his teacher's satisfaction.

"A word of advice for the future, my dear brother "Sheikh Lateef said "try to avoid playing music in equal temperament, like most of the music of your age. People will find the sound to be uncomfortably alien."

Presently, he was brought to a dark room and asked to sit in the center of the room on a cushion. Talib was blindfolded, and his bazhtaran was placed in his hands.

He was doing a riyaz (an exercise to train his hands and ears). The exercise was a scale; the first scale Sheikh Lateef taught him. He would not be allowed to use his eyes; only his hands, ears, and inner senses would be used to pull music from this instrument.

The riyaz started in the late morning. He began playing the strings slowly, as he'd been taught, feeling his way around the new instrument and hearing the subtle nuances of the unfamiliar scale. His only interruption was the adhan for salat. After salat, he was to return to the riyaz.

The session lasted six hours.

He was tired and sore afterwards. The traditional playing position of the bazhtaran, while not uncomfortable for someone accustomed to sitting on the floor, did not allow any shifting or movement (there was a technique for playing it standing; but some purists disapproved of this. Sheikh Lateef was not among them). Talib took time to stretch and move slowly. He was hearing the scale over and over in his mind. For the next five days, he would do the same thing. After this, another five days of using the bow instead of plucking the strings.

After a day off, he was to do the same thing with the bazhtaran; but this time using the wind aspect, rather than the strings. He was taught breathing exercises that would help master the instrument; which he was also required to do if he was using the strings.

He was given another day to rest. Then the training cycle would repeat.

After three months of this, Sheikh Lateef began to teach him the indigenous music theory of Uq'Dyill.

The Order's traditions taught techniques that employed music and the use of musical instruments as a weapon and for medicinal purposes. While music as an artistic performance was common, the idea of music for the sole purpose of entertainment, to the exclusion of all other possibilities, was incomprehensible to them.

The lessons were difficult at first because he kept referring in his mind to the music theory of his world. Many of these references were almost completely useless here. Some elements of Indian raga survived; but the Hindu symbolism was long absent. This also held true for other music that existed in his time. Other elements arose in times and place Talib had no reference for. Yet they would use, again and again, temperaments, tunings, rhythms, and melodic patterns found in the nonlinear mathematical patterns that exist in sound and are found universally in the natural world, including the overtone series, fractals, the golden mean, the Fibonacci series, seashells, DNA sequences, solar systems, and galaxies.

*****

One day, after a little over a year, Sheikh Lateef offered Talib the opportunity to do a seven day chilla. He would be isolated, he would fast during the day, and apart from salat, bathing, eating, and no more than five hours of sleep a day, he would spend the entire time playing his bazhtaran. This would be culminated by the initiation into the Djjil'arghnab'vahaqq ritual.

The first day of the chilla, after sunrise, Talib was led to a room, a cell, actually. It was about four meters in each direction, with one circular window, a mattress, a lavatory, and a candelabra. This would be where he would spend the next seven days. Ayeesha, who tended to the cleaning and cooking, was assigned the task of supplying him with food and being his "timekeeper", i.e. marking when he would sleep, eat, etc.

When the door closed, he sat down, made a brief prayer, and went to work. He carefully tuned his instrument, and began with some simple finger exercises.

Four hours later, he was becoming bored. He resisted the temptation to play something that would amuse him. He kept playing, trying desperately not to think about eating – or anything that would break the monotony that was assailing his mind.

He thought about the stories he'd read about people doing chillas in his time, and tried to mentally compare them to what he was doing. And he realized his mind was drifting away from what he was there to do. His mind was constantly throwing images, thoughts, memories, and flights of fancy to the forefront of his consciousness; and each time it imposed imperfections upon his playing – and he would become frustrated, and try harder to play with concentration. After a while, his playing would become quite fluid, despite the physical discomfort he felt, and he would be pleased about this; proud, in fact. But suddenly he realized that it was his mind playing a different variation on the old tricks.

His body put up all kinds of protests. He was tired, and his muscles in his back were sore. His hands felt fatigued. Even his ears, it seemed, were tired of hearing the same things again and again.

During this time, he only stopped to make salat. Then, back to work.

Looking ruefully at the window, he thought "Isn't it time to eat yet?" And his fingers became sloppy again. He fought to regain his concentration, and after a while, fought sleepiness.

After what could have been a half hour or half of eternity, the room he was in was dark. The door opened, and Ayeesha lit the candles in the candelabra, went out, and brought a plate of food and a bottle of water. Talib broke his fast, made salat, and ate. The food was not very interesting, but in Talib's state of mind, he relished and savored every sensory impression the simple meal could give him.

Then it was back to work.

He played more complex finger exercises than what he'd begun with. None of what he played this first day was particularly musical. He took a break for salat, and then continued to play.

Finally, Ayeesha came in and blew out the candles. Talib placed his instrument in a corner, and crawled into bed, exhausted, welcoming the apparent escape of sleep. His dreams were plagued by images of his instrument, and the sound it made.

The adhan wrenched him from a fitful sleep. The second day of his chilla had begun.

Talib couldn't keep track of time anymore. He found his mind playing tricks on him. The notes would become like characters in a Shakespearian play; living their lives, working together, conspiring with each other, making love, murdering each other. Some of them even went so far as to include Talib in their dramas! He kept getting dragged into their internal power struggles. How they knew him, Talib couldn't figure out. Soon, the music he was playing became a real fight. He used his martial arts training with every note. Every musical idea he executed was a fight to the death. His breathing exercises that corresponded with his musical exercises were like waves crashing on a rocky shore. Then his bazhtaran took on the role of advisor and started telling him what to play. At first Talib was frightened, but then realized there was no reason why his instrument would want to hurt him. After all, they were friends.

After a while, Talib couldn't tell if he was awake or asleep; or if his eyes were open or closed.

Finally, Ayeesha entered with Sheikh Lateef, and informed him that his chilla was over. They slowly led him out of the cell, and Ayeesha helped him clean up and get dressed. A boy who was applying as a student and who did work for the order carried Talib's instrument for him. Talib slowly acclimated himself to the idea of walking, and of not playing his bazhtaran.

He went home and slept for almost 20 hours.

The night after the day following his chilla, at the time when he would really need rest, the night Talib anticipated, and dreaded, arrived.

He would finally, after all his training, have to pass through the Djjil'arghnab'vahaqq ritual. He'd been warned that it was dangerous, that he'd experience fear and a disassociation of what he thought he'd known and believed. He could go insane or die.

They told him that on the night of a violent storm that other people would seek shelter from, he'd have to venture out and survive a journey from the mosque to the music building. Should he prove strong enough to survive the walk, he'd have to participate in the Djjil'arghnab'vahaqq ritual.

Rashidevqov's wives had made him some food that would fortify and strengthen him without imposing upon his system. He ate the last of the food after sunset, slept a few hours, and after a solitary Salatul Isha, he prepared to go to the music building.

He reached the front door and walked outside. He was caught in a strong wind. Driving rain was coming down. Occasional flashes of lightning illuminated the surroundings followed by deafening cracks of thunder. The rain would let up occasionally, and then a violent deluge of hail would fall. Then the rain and lightning would continue. Gusts of wind would press against him; almost knocking him off balance. A piece of hailstone cut him across the forehead. Blood and rain got into his eyes.

Through all this, the crescent of Thuul was visible in the sky. It wasn't as large as the day of the eclipse, but it was enormous, terrifying in the way it dominated the night sky.

Suddenly, lightning hit a tree. The tree was split down the middle, and one of the pieces almost fell on Talib. It began to dawn upon him that this storm may kill him. He needed shelter.

After walking for about twenty minutes (which seemed like hours) he realized he was lost. This frightened him and threatened to engulf him in panic that could drive him to an act of desperation. He walked to a tree, held on (praying that it too wouldn't be struck by lightening) and looked around, straining to find some familiar sight. He noticed a stone structure that had caught his eye some days before, and remembered where he was. He soon had his bearings and returned to his path.

Far up ahead was the music building. He had to get there. The storm could kill him if he didn't make it. A gust of wind knocked him off balance, and he fell into a puddle. The wind became truly violent; the rain felt like knives stabbing at him. He literally had to crawl to the door of the building. Reaching for the handle, he prayed to Allah that it wasn't locked. It wasn't.

Opening the door, he staggered in, and closed the door behind him. He drank in the silence and calm in the building, and wondered how the architects had designed such a building that could withstand such storms, even preventing the noise from disturbing the quiet.

After wringing the water out of his wet cloths, Talib heard something faint and deep in the interior of the building. He walked towards it.

Stopping in front of the door of the Djjil'arghnab'vahaqq chamber, he heard something going on inside. He opened the door and quietly stepped in.

The chamber had eight sides At alternate corners were fireplaces. Between each fireplace was an incense burner; each one contained a different incense. At various places, according to the air currents, the smoke would mix, and produce subtle chemical changes that altered not only the aroma, but the subtle psychological associations with the aromas. The walls were carved with calligraphy; Qur'anic verses, Sahih Ahadith, Dhikr, and poetry in several languages and scripts. In the middle of the room, a circle of men facing each other sat on cushions. Each man had an instrument. was among them. Sheikh Lateef sat at the north.

Another man sat against a wall, a box next to him. He was the caretaker of the ceremony. His ears were plugged with wax of a type, and formed in a way that would prevent almost all sound from reaching him. Yet even he had to be prepared for exposure to the Djjil'arghnab'vahaqq music.

At a gesture of one of the men, Talib sat in the center of the room on a cushion. There was a wind instrument he'd been taught to play on the cushion; which now Talib held in his hands. He was surrounded by the musicians and Sheikhs.

They waited for the signal from Sheikh Lateef. He took a slow, deep breath, held it, then exhaled. The music began.

Once the music began, none of them noticed Talib's ego, only his essence was important enough to acknowledge. Talib was expected to master his own ego. The music occupied their attention and required intense concentration. One wrong or improperly executed note, and the whole performance would be thrown into chaos.

The music sounded strange, to be sure. It wasn't something he would ever have listened to, or went out of his way to hear, but it didn't sound dangerous. He felt fine. He tried to figure out why anyone would think this was perilous to listen to. Actually, it sounded nice. A little abstract, but nice. The melodies would wander and meander; almost like Wagner's "unending melody".. It was organic; like it had a life of its own.

The sounds of the instruments were as exotic as anything he'd ever heard. The strange tuning and temperament was difficult on Talib at first. Strings were plucked and sustained indefinitely, their harmonics cascading in unpredictable patterns. Wind instruments sounded like breathing and voices. Chimes tore through the tapestry of sound. Percussion became as loud as the thunder outside. Where did all these sounds come from, Talib wondered? The music became as thick as smoke, and seemed to envelope him; coming from all directions at once. Suddenly, he heard the music inside his head and inside his body. His veins and nerves vibrated like the strings on their strange instruments. His lungs became bagpipes, and his hollow bones became like flutes.

The music shook lose all manner of memories in Talibs mind. They rushed past him again and again. He tried desperately to make sense of it, to no avail. His senses were thrown to the winds. He saw images, ideas, sense impressions, memories; all scattered chaotic through his mind. The barrier between his conscious and subconscious was dissolved. He began to experience colors as aromas. Reaching out, he held memories in his hands and played with them. He could see the music vibrating in the air. He tasted the storm outside that almost killed him, and began to laugh. Then he remembered a deeply buried memory from his childhood, experiencing it as a visual and tactile sensory impression. He began to weep. Then he became angry.

He ran from the place, banging and crashing into walls and furnishings. Somehow, he found the door and ran outside. The storm was raging, and Talib's mind became even more disturbed by the sudden increase in sensory input. He saw things everywhere. Faces, things, ideas. People faded in and out of the shadows. Lightening would cause a sudden shift in his hallucinations: people and more people would appear; terrible, accusing figures. Pointing at him, denouncing him, passing judgment.

Staggering to his feet and moaning because of the pain he was in from the waves of diarrhea and coughing phlegm and blood from his lungs, he looked ahead. The lightning flashed again, and he saw all the people he'd known, angels, djinn, and the Prophets regarding him accusingly. This was the Final Judgment! Suddenly, Talib remembered a dream he'd had. A recurring dream, vague, yet frightening. A terrible crime he'd committed was coming back to haunt him. Justice was catching up to him. He fell to his knees; begging forgiveness. There was no place to hide. He screamed in emotional pain as memories of who and what he was bore down on him with terrifying intensity. Many conflicting mental images. Many moral dilemmas. The truths he denied, the realities he fought against. The lies he told and the lies he believed were unraveling before him. He couldn't stand it. All the wrong he'd done, all the pride and vanity he'd exulted in, all the pain he'd caused to the innocent were focused on him now.

Standing up, he yelled hoarsely "Everything is wrong! The world betrayed me! No! I betrayed myself! Those people, we wanted what was right! Don't you see? How did we know? How could we have known? It's all backwards! Can't you see that? It's all wrong! ALL OF IT IS WRONG!! WRONG! WRONG!!!"

Off in the distance, he saw a figure beckoning to him. It was Death; a terrible Destroying Angel. Talib ran, slammed into a tree, and fell down.

The music was increasing in its intensity. One of the men was now playing what looked like a wind instrument made of frogs and serpents; slimy, suggestive of disease and exotic poisons. It emitted a high pitched whistle that pierced every fiber of his being like long metallic needles. Most of the others played a percussion pattern of incredible complexity.

Then he saw something. A vague shadowy movement directly in front of him. It coalesced into a figure in the shape of a man. It was black with smoky streaks of purple light running through it. Three long tentacles emerged from its forehead, where the "third eye" would be. Talib realized that this was his djinn. He knew it's name.

It spoke to him in his own voice, or rather the voice of his thoughts. He engaged the apparition, commanded it, deflected its prevarication and lies. Knowing the djinn's name gave Talib a decisive advantage over it; but he still needed to be careful. Suddenly, one of the tentacles reached out and touched him. He was overcome by a wave of nausea.

Before he knew it, sharp pains struck his stomach and intestines like huge drums. Sweat poured from him. He vomited, and the man against the wall quietly and quickly cleaned it up. But before he did, Talib saw monstrous things coming out of his body. Things like insects, serpents with tentacles and wings, poisonous toads, scorpions with human faces contorted with rage and leering perversity.All manner of loathsome horrors were expelled that he realized had been dwelling within him his whole life.

And they were murderously resentful that they were being forced to leave.

Terror overtook him.

He closed his eyes. Shapes, colors, textures from his earliest memories filled his vision. He realized that his mind was being disassembled. He could finally see that these images in his mind were not what he was; yet for years he thought they defined him and were him. Now, he saw that it wasn't true.

What was truly frightening about this was that his personality was dissolving. He was terrified of this; a part of his "self" believed that this was all he had and all he could ever be. To lose this was the worst horror he could ever experience.

Yet at the same time, there never was a Talib. Talib was a phantom that never existed.

Then a being of light was present. And the music changed. This being of light was, Talib (or that which permitted itself to be known by other beings that were still trapped within these illusions by the sound of that name) realized, was "his" angel. It was, in reality, his higher self. It was not a being separate from "himself"- this had been a mistake he, and many others made. To see their human self and angelic self as two distinct and different ego / selves. Nothing could be further from the truth – once one was immersed in the truth.

This alarmingly powerful angel did not speak, it only looked at him with love and compassion. Talib wanted to speak to him; but within his heart, he was told "Not yet. Soon."

And the music changed again.

And Talib rose from the battlefield of his own heart.

A new Talib stood where the old one had died before death.

Talib fought to regain his bearings. When he opened his eyes, he saw that he was still sitting on the cushion, and had never left the room. The Djjil'arghnab'vahaqq ended. The laboratory was closed. The participants went their separate ways.

Talib walked with Sheikh Lateef for a while. Carrying his instrument was difficult; he was at the end of his physical and psychological limits. The clear night air and the quiet of his surroundings left him with a strange calm. The silence was a dominant presence that completely filled Talib's soul.

Sheikh Lateef spoke to Talib. "Brother, I advise you to spend some time recuperating. This may take the form of sleep, recreation, or solitude and retreat. You will have to find your own way; it is different with everyone."

The first moon was rising over a thicket of trees.

"It seems that all my adult life I experienced one big change after another" Talib said seemingly without provocation.

Sheikh Lateef's quiet voice filled the void. "I know of your biography. There are such people that empty themselves of everything, and then the vacuum that results is suddenly filled. It is a blessing from Allah that yours was filled with the most remarkable of adventures."

"It has been difficult, almost unbearable at times. But yes! What a fantastic life it's been! And the more I see, the more I know that Allah spoke the truth in the Qur'an when He said that we would never be able to count all His blessings. I know this like few men ever knows."

"You are an imago "Sheikh Lateef said. "You are like the ancient heroes of old Earth who embark upon great journeys and return transformed. In your time, such heroes were rare."

"I know" Talib said. "I've never known such freedom. It's a little scary!" He offered Sheikh Lateef a rueful and slightly self deprecating laugh.

Sheikh Lateef was not sure he understood the gesture or the emotional content behind it, it obviously being a residual effect of a cultural anomaly. But it felt right, so he simply smiled and said nothing.

As they walked on, Talib was silent. A sadness and homesickness descended upon him at the reminder of where he came from and what he lost. He knew that he was in a better place than in his former time. But there were many elements of his life that he loved, that had been a part of him, and were now gone forever. Friends, family, environment; all were gone. He felt this loss most acutely; and was on the verge of weeping.

"I can never return" he said, an unmistakable note of sadness in his voice.

The two men came to a fork in the path. Talib's home was on one path; Sheikh Lateef's home was on the other path.

Sheikh Lateef turned to the direction home. He knew what Talib was experiencing; and knew that the strain of the Djjil'arghnab'vahaqq experience had weakened his emotional defenses. Pausing, he said "We all return, Talib. The Source waits for us. The Source beckons us. There is no other destination. Asalaam alaikum wa rahmatuallah." He walked slowly into the night.

Talib stood and watched the elder slowly walk away. He thought about what he said. Could shirk be so subtle? Is there no end to the Jihad al-Nafs?

Yet he knew. Death is the end of the Jihad al-Nafs. There is no other way.

*****

Talib had been here five years. His training had gone well. He felt better than he'd ever felt in his life. His mind was clearer than ever, his health and physical strength were beyond what it was when he was 30 years old, and he was rightly considered a master musician.

He felt a presence approaching him from behind. He heard a slight sound of movement. It was Sheikh Ill'm Khayaam, his ruhaniya and martial arts teacher. He was of slight build, but possessed incredible physical strength. His skin was brown and his hair and beard were white and straight. His eyebrows were dark and hung over indomitable luminous eyes that have been known to change color; brown, black, indigo, dark violet, occasionally deep green. He wore an old but immaculately clean djalabia and turban. He was over 200 years old. At first, this had amazed Talib. It took him a while to accept that fact that people here lived very long lives..

The Order's system of martial arts was based in part upon the Qur'an and the shapes of the Arabic letters, and in part by the character of the subtle structure of the universe. It was impossible to understand their martial arts without some understanding of quantum physics. All their martial arts tied in with music, and all the musicians studied these martial arts.

The Sheikh, could move more silently than a slight breath of wind; sometimes passing through groups of people without being seen. He had allowed his presence to be known prior to his arrival solely as a gesture of politeness.

"You must leave and do not look back" the Sheikh said with finality. "The wave that forms far out in the ocean is not the same water when that wave crashes on the shore. But the wave is the same and the ocean is the same. You must know this; but Allah is the Best to Know."

Talib looked away. He stared for a moment at the distant horizon and the contrast between the earth and sky. He remembered the words of the Holy Qur'an "Between them is a barrier that they do not transgress." Yet Talib knew both sides of the barrier. He had been allowed to penetrate these secrets. But he still didn't know why.

He looked to the Sheikh. He was gone. He looked around and finally saw him at the top of a cliff, smiling.

"Asalaam Alaikum, wa Rahmatuallah" The Sheikh said, not shouting, but somehow perfectly audible. Then he disappeared.

Chapter 16. Testing the Waters.

Talib went to his small apartment after Salat-ul Fajr. He had gathered his belongings and prepared for travel. Yet there were a few things he needed to put into order first.

There were many books he had purchased and kept while here. His personal library was the subject of much attention from the murids. Their attitude was one of immense admiration; free of envy, but occupying their thoughts nonetheless. They would constantly ask to look something up or borrow one of the rare books for a few days. Talib never refused such a request. Knowledge increases as one gives it away. Now, he would give them away permanently. He didn't need them, as he had the entire collection committed to memory. His memory was flawless, as was anyone else who passed the initiation of the techniques of perfecting the mental process. His collection intact, he bundled them up and carried them to the library. Placing them before the master librarian, he told him that the books now belonged to the Order's library. The master librarian was an old man with animated and likable mannerisms. No stranger to Talib's esteemed collection; he was overjoyed, and passionately invoked the Blessings of Allah upon the young man for his generosity. Talib smiled, and replied "All praise is due to Allah."

There were two books he kept. One was his Qur'an. It was small, very well made. It was encased in an ebony box with gold and silver trim. It was rumored that the gold came from earth. The precious metals meant nothing to Talib; his attitude toward them was that they were insufficient to equal the Power and Majesty of the Holy Qur'an. The other book contained his personal writings. This included various tafsir on Qur'an (including his own) with correspondences with Hadith. His book also held theoretical mathematics, historical interpretation, astronomy, tassawuff, ruhaniya, mysticism; and a collection of his own poetry and musical compositions. This was a work in progress; one he would complete when he died. Both books were printed on platinum alloy paper that was expected to survive intact for thousands of years. The book he was writing in, and the stylus he used, were of a special design where he could fit an immense amount of writing on a single page; sometimes as much as full book's worth. A special magnifying device was built into the cover to allow the fine print to be read.

After Salat-ul Magrib, he returned to his cell. He checked his backpack. It contained clothing, writing utensils, paper, several items necessary for toiletry and basic survival, a cache of money, and a winter over garment. Talib cared nothing for "fashion" and preferred simple garments. But he loved that coat. It was a long, knee length, thick black coat with sheep's wool inside lining, a hood, a collar that could cover his neck, mouth, and nose, and several ingeniously placed pockets. One could sleep and move comfortably in it, it was easy to clean, waterproof, and could serve for him to hide in shadows if necessary. This coat would last him the rest of his life.

He also had his bazhtaran.

For years he had trained in all manner of arts and sciences. This information was available to anyone for the asking. The Order regularly sold, or made gifts of, any of their textbooks to whoever wanted them. The Order had no secrets from humanity. But here the manner of its presentation and application took on new meaning. The things he learned here were not accessible to everyone only in that few would understand its meaning, and fewer would know how to put it into practice without proper training.

What, for example would an uninitiated person make of the instructions found in the martial arts texts of the Order? In one page in a chapter on evading attack maneuvers is found the following:

In stillness, there is action.
In speech, there is depleted communication.
In form, there is imprisonment.
Your model is water and incense smoke.
Your teeth will fall out of your mouth before your tongue will.

Now he had finished his basic training. He thought briefly about the years of hard work he'd put into his studies and disciplines. He had reached the end of this phase of his development. He could have chosen to stay. Indeed, some of his friends did so. But he knew that his Path would take him far into the world.

Deep into the labyrinth of the dunyah.

And at the same time, far beyond the dunyah.

Which meant that his training and his Jihad, had really only begun.

In the late hours, Talib silently slipped out of the pavilion. A few noticed his exit, but held their peace. They respected Talib choice of taking his leave, and made silent prayer for his success.

As he walked, he realized that all of his training would be put to the test in every moment of the rest of his life. His safety net had been removed.

He was in a large forest that encompassed the grounds of the university. To the north was the I'Jass Mountain, where he'd had much difficult training. To the east was the river. He was walking west, keeping to the bank of the river. After walking for several hours, he decided to make camp and get some sleep.

After waking from a sound sleep, bathing in the river, and making salat, Talib walked along a path in the forest that ran southwest of the river. His eyes darted along the trees, shrubs, and animal life. He was intimately familiar with the wildlife of this area. He briefly wondered what kind of wildlife he'd encounter farther along on his journey. Under his breath, he recited "La Ilaha Ilallah" over and over. This became a habitual practice for him; after having read where Rasulallah (sas) said that on the Day of Judgment Allah will inform the angels of a good deed of His servant that they knew nothing about.

Talib had had training in the deeper meaning of Dhikr. He knew, as few men do, what power the act contains. He remembered his lessons and training in the science and art of Dhikr. He studied in detail the effects of each vowel, consonant, inhaled and exhaled breath, physical posture and movement, etc. He mastered the effects to the degree that he could control his bodily functions simply through Dhikr. His entire being resonated with the Holy words he chanted.

*****

Talib traveled through cities and countries. The majority of the populations of this world, as with all worlds, were ordinary folk. Most were decent people. Sometimes off-worlders arrived, also mostly good people. Yet, here and there, were to be found those who were lost in the worship of the dunya and who brought fitna. This had to be dealt with as the situation warranted. But always with subtlety. The Believing men and women almost never sat upon thrones, but they were the true leaders among humanity. They saw what most couldn't.

It was a cloudy day in the early spring. One of the moons had set. The other was visible as it rose over the ridge of the north mountain. The air was cool and crisp; Talib favorite whether; it reminded him of his youth to which he could never return. He stood and looked at the distant horizon, lost in contemplation. How different it looked to him now, he thought. Sunrise was once a melange of colors, an entertainment for the eyes. Now it held different meanings. Veils before secrets were removed; each impression carried a multitude of new meanings.

Talib mused as he walked. How he fought this day against the urge to give free reign to bitter cynicism! Folly! Futility! Politics; that ultimate monument to human stupidity! Armies, empires: blundering dementedly through the unknown millennium of human history like a blind idiot. And how reverently they offered their devotions to this pestilence that they lacked the power to control! A Frankenstein's monster wreaking havoc and senseless misery upon all it touches.

Yet he knew that defeatist cynicism is unworthy of the wisdom and insight of his station. It must be so; and as with all things created. Bound to the endless cycle of yin and yang; the element of entropy forever looming near. No permanence except with the Being of beings. Few men see this. Fewer understand what they are looking at. And even fewer possess sufficient wisdom to act correctly upon it. These things take time.

Chapter 17. You are Needed.

One day, after arriving in the city, Talib walked through the marketplace. Suddenly, he felt a presence. This was the signature of a true Sheikh. Talib walked in the direction of the vibration. Then, he turned around and faced a man who was standing almost directly behind him.

"Asalaam alaikum. Who are you?" Talib asked.

"Wa alaikum asalaam. You do not recognize me, but we are brothers. I have a message for you" the man said. "Let's go somewhere where we may speak undisturbed.

They walked a short way to a coffee house and waited until they were served. The place was not crowded. Most of the customers were scholars, artists, and scientists. In a corner two musicians played bamboo flutes. Intricate tapestries hung at intervals on the walls. The coffee house had many fine coffees; and one of the house specialties was a dark roast from the Thuul Mountain region, flavored with cinnamon and lavender.

A moment after savoring the masterfully crafted brew, Talib asked "Why do you wish to speak to me?"

The man put down his cup. "I have a communique from the council of elders of the Khaliphite. You are requested to return to your Order's headquarters. Transportation will be provided for you. I am authorized by the Sheikhs and Grand Sheikhs of the Order, and by the leaders of the world to inform you that they have chosen you to make the Hajj on behalf of the Uq'Dyill nations and their orders."

With all of the experiences Talib had, nothing could have prepared him for such a surprise.

"Me?" Talib said "Why me?"

The other man laughed. "My brother! The order knows what it's doing. Besides, I would imagine you would want to see your home world again. I was not born on Uq'Dyill; I was born on Hadhallya, and I relish every chance to visit my home world."

Talib was about to say something when the man, smiling modestly, interrupted him. "Please; don't think about it. Don't question your 'worthiness' or confuse yourself with a mere inverted ujb. Just make your preparations."

Talib sat silently. He had, indeed, come a long way in his achievements. He really wasn't living anywhere at the moment, and carried almost all worldly possessions on his back. There was nothing keeping him here, except friendships he could return to. Besides, he was a child of the Earth, and an adopted son of Uq'Dyill. He had kinship to both worlds. Logically speaking, he really was an excellent choice for the Hajj.

The man asked "When can you be ready?"

Talib said "I'm ready now. Let's go."

After returning to the headquarters of the Order, he'd received instructions on the Hajj, and what to expect from interstellar travel.

Rashidevqov was there. "This is a great thing you are doing, brother!" He exclaimed.

"Well, I hope I can pull it off!" This, he said literally translating the English idiom. He knew that Rashidevqov would not understand it and, unless he asked (Talib could imagine him asking "Exactly what are you trying to pull, and what do you wish to pull it away from?"), it would keep him busy with days of research. Such things were a private joke between them.

But he wasn't taking the bait now. "May Allah be with you! Remember me at the Kaba!"

"I will, Insha Allah" Talib promised.

*****

The spaceport was located in a secluded area, on the outskirts of a desert. Talib's trip to the spaceport had been uneventful. When he arrived, he was greeted by an envoy who escorted him to a processing area. He was given a medical examination, and treatments in the form of what 21st century society would understand as a seamless blend of Eastern and Western medicine to help his body adjust to the changes it would experience on the journey, and at his destination. This was followed by a brief orientation speech.

The space vessel would not leave for another seventeen days. He spent this time preparing himself, and also enjoying some recreational activities.

The day came when Talib boarded the vessel. His quarters were small and utilitarian; but decorated with colorful designs painted or etched on the walls and furnishings. He also had a window near his hammock, that allowed him to see the stars.

After the spacecraft left orbit and attained its full speed, it generated an artificial gravity which he judged to be about two thirds that of earth's. The vessel had to leave the solar system at a fraction of the speed of light before it could activate its drive that allowed it to circumvent relativistic space. This part of the journey took twenty days.

His biggest problem was getting used to the zero-g toilet. The strangeness of space travel upset his digestion.

*****

The spacefarers were a guild / order that was over two thousand years old, and were a political and economic force unto themselves. They formed their own autonomous society and sided with nobody. They charged for transportation, items, people. They would take any currency or barter for goods and services. While other planets and nations possessed space flight capabilities, none could equal the abilities of the spacefarers.

If they found themselves between two rival groups, they took no sides; and would do business with anyone, provided no aggressive moves were made against them. The squabbles of others did not interest them, but if they were attacked, they were formidable and utterly fearless warriors who would stop at nothing to win a fight. If they found themselves in a losing battle, they made sure that they took as many of their enemies to the death with them. It was rumored that they possessed secret weapons that were very strange and very powerful, and that they knew ancient ninja techniques that nobody else knew. It was also rumored that they themselves had started those rumors.

Nevertheless, most people avoided provoking them.

They would also go on salvaging missions, keeping whatever they find. If anyone else lay claim to what they find, they would either fight for it, or negotiate a salvaging fee. There were privateers of a sort among them, and some who were what can best be described as pseudo-pirates. These were not looked upon as being renegades and outcasts among the spacefarers. They were simply a little more "ambitious" than most.

Yet despite these idiosyncrasies, they were scrupulously honest. They never lied, never cheated, and always kept their end of the deal. They could also be extraordinarily generous and hospitable; and could always be counted on in an emergency situation. The stories of them coming to the rescue of other space travelers, or transporting emergency relief supplies free of charge were legendary.

Rank was usually assigned by the crews themselves; as there was no real economic incentive to attain rank, it was bestowed according to the merit and skill of the individual. In fact, in their whole society, there was absolutely no economic hierarchy whatsoever: beyond individuals earning what they could on the side. Even the privateers and pirates followed this economic model.

Energy was not much of a problem. Several centuries before, technologies were developed that were capable of harvesting energy directly in space. Solar radiation, stellar winds, and all manner of subatomic quantum energies, etc. were converted into energies that propelled and sustained the vessels.

They made a number of other remarkable technological innovations. The hulls of their spacecraft were made of a remarkable aggregate of substances. Nearly atomic size threads of gold, silver, platinum, titanium, osmium, and an ionic fusion of iron, ceramic and plastic were braided into lengthy strands. These were braided with other such strands into slightly larger strands, and so on; until they formed a fibrous material that was formed into the shape of the hull they needed, and fused into a solid mass. Nobody else possessed the technology to make this.

Their society could almost be described as a prototype anarcho-communism, except that they were also deeply religious. Despite this, the spacefarers were highly individualistic people. Each man and woman was a law unto him or herself, lived and died as he or she wished, and felt him or herself answerable to nobody: except in the general rules of their unique culture.

*****

Talib was standing in the common area of the vessel. A man walked toward him. He addressed Talib in the vernacular of the seasoned spacefarer. His name was Klee Ghaibal

"Salaam. I would borrow an hour of time, Hajji of Uq'Dyill"

"Yes" replied Talib. "What can I do for you?"

"Singular you go" the man said. "Be you a-hungered? I be. Viands await. Join me?"

Talib was glad for some company.

The meal the two men shared consisted of some of the usual fare a spacefarer would enjoy. Mushrooms, tubers, grapes, a leafy vegetable from another world that resembled kale, and slow roasted midget buffalo marinated in spices whose origins can be traced to ancient Mexico and Pakistan.

After the meal, Talib thanked him and asked why he was honored with the invitation to dinner.

"Hajji; you carry barakah. It flows through you like water. You go to the womb of our race. The mother of us all. The Axis stands there, and penetrates all worlds. Power, Hajji! Power more than the fleshy brain can hold stands there!

"I am a simple man, wanting little and holding less. Blessed I am with vision and blindness, no less and no more than any other. This humble wanderer's heart boldly begs a mercy and asks a sadaqa.

"Remember me. When you stand in the sacred place, remember me. Baraka, a drop of healing water! Implore the One to increase this Eternal Treasure in my modest coffers."

What else could Talib say but 'yes?' He promised to make du'a for Ghaibal on earth.

"Ahh! Gratitude and respect to you!"

Looking up, Ghaibal chanted "Oh Allah, look down upon the dead ones. Squinty eyed and blinded by their love of gravity hole tombs and false tomes of rules. Those who cringe in fear of empty words. Thrice enslaved they are; though they claim themselves free. It's worse yet; on horror's texts are accumulated new fears; deeds that call into doubt that which they stupidly cherish as truth. I say they have need of healing; for all their pride hastens them to ruin. Wretched dead ones! They think they know, but they know nothing!"

After a pause, Ghaibal said "Ah Hajji. I see a vast sojourn written upon your face. You face a path long and treacherous. Allah has many surprises for you, Hajji! If anything I may present as a gift, it is this. It is a vast truth that few will understand, and 'tis best you hold it close to your breast, or it will cry out and betray you to dead hearts.

"You see this true living Way. Most see little or nothing of this true living Way. Think about where you are now, Hajji. Feel what powers course around and through us! In Space, truly alive we be! Aware! The planet of our birth after we were born we left. Plans you have to return to your mother's womb? I think not. Not so destined are we! Allah told us as much when He destroyed earth! The Signs you see not? Listen and meditate, planetbound Holy man, and answer not me but in your own heart. Is not it best to die in the Ocean Infinite than to be slaughtered like lice on a rock? I tell you, and any blind one, perish not in the comfort of the cities of the frozen and living dead! Spend but little time on the islands, Hajji! Die among the Singing Infinite of the stars. The rocks are from stars; are we not as well? But gave to us did Allah much more, yes? Enough that the angels, djinn, and elements bow before us and that the Amir of the djinnatti and his own swore eternal envy? For therein upon your Path lay your apotheosis."

Chapter 18. Close to the Edge.

Talib entered the pavilion and addressed the class. "Asalaam Alaikum." They responded "Wa Alaikum asalaam,"

"Lets begin where we left off yesterday, shall we? I believe we were speaking about the period known among Interstellar Historians as the Great Calamities. Within a period of less than half a Terrestrial century, over two thirds of humanity was annihilated in a seemingly endless series of disasters.

"The Zindji people were originally of the community who settled near Olympus Mons during the pre-terraformation period of Mars. Their descendants were among the first interstellar colonists. They settled a planet orbiting a green giant. Their civilization flourished for centuries. They enjoyed peaceful trade and diplomatic relations with their neighbors. Yet, they began to develop strange ideas in religion. There arose among them a mythology based upon the entertainers and celebrities of old Earth. They believed that the imagery from capitalist society carried within it secret revelations that only they could interpret. This eventually became so extreme that religious scriptures were written describing them as being demigods who acted as intercessors with Allah. Temples were built in their honor and elaborate rituals were enacted. Figures such as the characters of centuries past television programs or popular musicians would be prayed to for inspiration and guidance."

One of the students, a young woman named Ghilta, asked "You were on old earth when these figures, or whatever they were, were created. What was it like?"

Talib smiled. "I saw some of them perform live concerts, in movies, or on TV. A few were brilliant; but their true brilliance seemed to be lost on the Zindji. Some of it was entertaining, but most of them were nothing more than talented artists. Which is fine. But they were not 'gods'! Some of them I met face to face and spoke to. I will tell you about them someday, Insha Allah.

"In fact, a man connected to the Zindji interviewed me about these people. He didn't want to hear what I had to say: his questions kept trying to pull me away from the truth, and get me to say what he wanted me to say.

"Anyway, the conflicts I mentioned before became so extreme that civil unrest arose. One intriguing example was when two cults declared a holy war against each other, each of whose leaders denounced the other as blasphemers. The war lasted for twenty two standard years, during which time, 350 million people were killed. There were countless examples of this, which you will find in the Archives, if you wish to examine them. Then their planet underwent a series of seismographic upheavals. Entire cities were destroyed. Shortly thereafter, a series of solar flares caused meteorological catastrophes, and permanently damaged the atmosphere. This resulted in ecological imbalances that caused famines and several epidemic diseases that no one was able to identify. Before the end of the fourth year after the solar flares, except for a

handful who were off-world, like the man who contacted me, the Zindji people were extinct.

"The Thala'an people of the Afgata world experienced similar ecological disasters. Unfortunately, due to several civil wars, economic upheavals, and mismanagement from despotic rule under a brutal and corrupt theocratic dictatorship, the Thala'an were so impoverished that they lacked the technology to leave their planet and save themselves. Even if they hadn't damaged their economy so, it would have been of small avail. Their scientists and intelligentsia were killed during wars and political purges. Their final years were spent in pursuit of tribal warfare that decimated their planetary population far below the point of viability. Within seventeen years the Thala'an followed the Zindji to extinction.

"An unknown disaster caused the extinction of the Rheem Ajna race on Hateem's Planet (named after the legendary Hateem Buu; a fearless explorer of African lineage who survived many perilous adventures). A little short of a millennium after the settlement of their planet, a convoy of space vessels from the world of the Twin Stars arrived to enact trade transactions with the Rheen Ajna. They found the entire world dead. No life of any kind survived; including microorganisms. On the trip home, the travelers in the convoy died while still in radio communication with the Twin Stars. By mutual consent of the leaders, their vessels were destroyed, and Hateem's Planet was quarantined. Robotic devices failed to find the cause of the disaster.

"As this was happening, a war broke out on Ghaa'Zaqi between the Kas and Qaaqalm nations. Before a peace settlement was reached, 89% of the planet's population was killed. Shortly thereafter, scientists found that the weaponry used in the war caused irreparable damage to their ecosystem. The survivors, mostly subcultures that had always opposed the war, banded together in an armistice, and emigrated off world. Some emigrated to other worlds. Others went elsewhere; their fate is a matter of speculation, but they may be among the nomadic spacefarers.

"On the planet Tat Baawuus, a scientist named Mikayal Zindam began experimenting with genetic engineering; a practice that most worlds had outlawed. He defended his theories by saying that his work enabled humanity to "better understand creation." After several years, he announced the discovery of a medical treatment that would increase human life expectancy by as much as 2000 years. The planet's population demanded that the government release it to the public. The government refused. Shortly thereafter, a black market operation began manufacturing and distributing a crude copy of the treatment. The plague that resulted from mutated viruses caused by sloppy manufacturing decimated over 90% of the planet's population. The survivors suffered serious damage to the brain and neurological system. They were little more than semi-conscious, and lived as animals. The planet was permanently quarantined. It was rumored that one of the survivors was Zindam himself.

"On the planet Riqq, the Uqdul race formed a sect that interpreted Shari'ah as being anti-technological and anti-science. At first, they lived a peaceful idyllic existence. After the first 200 or so years, their beliefs degenerated into empty ritualism that was strictly enforced. This innovation was due to the fanatical teachings of Imam Oussma Balayan. Science was forgotten. The arts were forbidden. Reading the Qur'an without official permission was forbidden; and interpretation was dictated by the despotic theocracy that ruled the planet. All attempts to bring about advancement of the society in any form were denounced as "Shirk", "Bid'a" and the "work of Shaitan." Punishments became cruel; to the point that singing a lullaby to a baby was punishable by flogging. Children were turned against their parents, brothers against their brothers. Historians later compared the planet's government to a Chinese Communist prisoner of war camp of old earth. The government became a degenerate and inefficient bureaucracy concerned only with punishing citizens that offended the law. Poverty, illiteracy, disease, and malnutrition were epidemic. The government did little about it. As long as the rituals were scrupulously observed and their power was secure, this was a matter of little concern for them. One night, an Imam whose name is not known had a dream that a mountain was descending from the sky. He tried to tell the people of his dream. The ruling class denounced him as a heretic and sorcerer, and sentenced him to death. As he was being led to be stoned, a comet twice the size of Olympus Mons appeared in

the sky. Three months later, the comet struck the planet on its north pole, and knocked it out of its orbit. It became a rogue body, and slowly sailed out of the solar system. The surviving population died when the planet's atmosphere froze.

"On Yyet'ex Y'Owd a group who were descended from Zionists of old Earth formed an underground political order called the Aliy Bakhari. After infiltrating the government by pretending to be Muslims and Christians, their leader and founder, a lunatic named Eliezer Karp who believed he was acting on orders from God, devised a plan to wrest political power on their world. If it worked, they would use it on other worlds until the entire universe was enslaved. A group of biochemists from among them went to work upon a chemical drug that would cause instant physical addiction. Withdrawal would be fatal. Their plan was to introduce this substance into the general population without their knowledge. Once the people were addicted, they would be told to submit to Aliy Bakhari rule. The slightest disobedience would be punishable by withholding the drug. At first the Aliy Bakhari succeeded in enslaving the planet's population. Communication and diplomatic relations with other worlds were severed. All mosques and churches were destroyed. The practice of any religion not officially sanctioned by the oligarchy became a capital offense. No political parties were allowed to exist. All communication and print that was not issued by the Zionist regime was outlawed. Muslim, Christian, Buddhist, and Jewish resisters went underground. After about five years of

intolerable oppression, a group of resisters formed suicide squads to commit acts of terrorism against the Aliy Bakhari. The tyrants were completely unprepared to deal with people who were not afraid to die. At first, they withdrew the drug from isolated regions; resulting in the deaths of everyone in the affected area. Yet they soon realized that their punishments were ineffective. Soon, more people joined the resistance. One hot summer day, during a national holiday (which was based upon a corruption of Yom Kippur) a group of resistors executed a highly organized strike against all of the existing laboratories that manufactured the drug, and all existing stockpiles. All production of the drug was halted, with no possibility of manufacturing enough of it in time to save the enslaved population. While they did this, another group of them commandeered a public communication facility and told the population what had happened; enjoining them to rise up and destroy the Aliy Bakhari tyrants: as they were going to die anyway, they should die as free men and women. They did just that. The Aliy Bakhari were powerless to stop them. Within days the Aliy Bakhari were annihilated. As their scientists had not thought it necessary to devise a cure for the addiction, less than a week later everyone on the planet was dead.

"These were followed by a disaster that shocked all of humanity into absolute numbness.

"On Earth, a series of ecological disasters, including seismographic disturbances, an enormous volcanic eruption beneath the North Pole, solar flares, undetected damage

caused by early man made damage, some of which dated back to the 20th century, and an eventual shift in the planet's polarity, which put the north pole at about 10 miles northeast of Japan, and an interruption of the North Atlantic jet stream, rendered Earth uninhabitable. Only 11% of the Earth's population survived to leave the world. It was decided to leave the solar system. Neither Mars nor the moons of Jupiter and Saturn could sustain the additional population. Venus was of little use; seventy years earlier the terraformation project had failed to render the planet uninhabitable."

A young woman named Thlabia asked "What were some of the man made damage?"

Talib said "Some of it was industrial pollution, automobile exhaust, inefficient farming and city planning, and careless waste management. Some of the industries that handled waste management were run by criminal organizations. There was also damage to the earth's environment done by industrialized genetic engineered food. These practices introduced biological factors into the earth's ecosystem that it could not handle."

"Didn't they know what was happening?" Thlabia asked.

"Oh, yes. They were perfectly aware of what was going on."

"But why did they do it?"

"Because" Talib said "They were making a lot of money from doing it."

Seif, a powerfully built young man asked "Are you saying they ruined their world only to make money?"

"Yes. They were only interested in the money. They pretended that the damage wasn't happening. And they had too many vested interests on these industries, and the powerful people who owned them. They would lose money; so they kept doing what they were doing, made more money, and the world continued to die."

"That's crazy!" Seif blurted out. Then he apologized.

"There are no words to describe how crazy they were." Talib said. "I'd actually spoken to a few of these people. There was no way to understand how they thought. The greatest hypocrisy of all was that the money they were earning wasn't even real. I'll tell you about that another day.

"Anyway, a group of people built an artificial environment in the vicinity of the Kab'a to protect it and enable people to make the Hajj. It had long since been impossible to make the Hajj in any normal manner. Now, the Earth couldn't support so much as 100,000 people. An annual Hajj from among the 90 billion people in the known universe was out of the question. The common practice was that nations and even entire planets would choose a representative to make the Hajj on behalf of the entire community. Such people would be revered as holy men or women. Each would be allowed to take with them a stone from the vicinity of the Holy city, and either place it at their world's own qibla, or use it as a qibla in the place of their choosing if they didn't already have one.

"The keepers of the Kab'a would have legendary status among the worlds; yet, owing to the hard work and

environmental hardships they lived with, would never enjoy it in this life. They never left Earth. Their duties ended only with death. Such deaths are believed to guarantee the custodian a place in paradise. Occasionally, a pilgrim from another world would arrive by whatever transportation was available, and offer his or her services as an assistant custodian of the kab'a. If they were accepted, they would have this job for life. Attempting to resign or leave their post was punishable by death. This being understood, nobody ever sought the position unless they were serious. And nobody ever violated the rule.

"Similar projects were undertaken to preserve the holy lands of Christianity, Judaism, Buddhism, and Taoism. These were successful. The Keepers of the Kab'a were instrumental in helping the People of the Book accomplish this, and their gratitude proved instrumental in easing thousands of years of animosity.

"Scholars and mystics were concerned about the effect upon the Unseen. It was known that only Allah knows the Unseen, but since the Kab'a has a counterpart in Paradise, it became the source of endless speculation, debate, Dhikr ceremonies, du'a, and meditation.

"After the Great Calamities, came the Great Scattering, or, as it is more commonly known, the Third Hijrah. Colonies separated from entire worlds and headed off into space. The survivors of Gheing Zaa were among the first to leave.

"Some traveled for centuries before finding a suitable world. Many people who settled planets had never known anything

except space travel. Some of these were further handicapped by long terraforming projects.

"Near the more populated areas of the galaxy, the transportation and shipping consortium we call the Spacefarers became extraordinarily powerful. They formed no alliances with any government. Their services were open to absolutely anyone. This was due mainly to the fact that, despite their having no monopoly on space travel, very few possessed the technology for interstellar travel.

"While many groups were intent upon building their worlds, some travelers eventually rejected the idea of planetary settlement and lived a nomadic existence of endless space travel. Like the Spacefarers. Soon, they banded together and formed nomadic nations; building fleets of ships that roamed endlessly through the cosmos. Some of these nomads, however, were never heard from again. Endless speculations of their fate made their way around the worlds. It was even rumored that one group had attempted to leave the galaxy. Although there was some evidence to support this, it was, for all intents and purposes, impossible to prove.

"The disaster on Earth created an unprecedented psychological reaction among the human race. It was as if humanity finally realized that its childhood was over. Yet it tried, on some cases, to cling to that childhood. Some desperately so; to the point of attempting to recreate cultures, architecture, governments, and even natural geographic characteristics from old Earth on worlds where this was

clearly impossible. One group of people even attempted to recreate mid 21st century New York City."

Another student spoke up "You lived in New York City, didn't you?"

"Yes," Talib said. "I was born there. Despite its many faults, I must admit, it was a great place. For better or worse, we loved that city. In all my travels, I've found nothing like it. It was unique, and had a character of its own. I haven't visited the recreation of New York City, although I've received invitations. I'd like to see it,,," He paused, reflecting. His students waited, silent.

A sigh. "But anyway. One of the Diaspora, an expedition composed of a cooperating party of the survivors of the Heyt, Soon Djii, Bithaq, and Fa'atim races, found a planet that needed no terraforming. They named the planet Uq'dyill. This is how our world was founded. Not long afterwards, some of the survivors of the Earth catastrophe arrived, requesting asylum. It was granted.

"Each of the four original groups formed their own nations. The Earth survivors split into several groups; some joining the Soon Jii and Hyat nations; others forming small isolated nations.

"The nations prospered as the centuries passed. The Soon Ji were the most advanced and wealthy. The Hayt and the Fa'atim were renowned for their cultural achievements. The Bithaq split into three nations after a brief civil war that

temporarily impoverished all three groups, and were almost annexed by one of the larger nations.

"Spiritual seekers from the three small nations banded together and formed an order of mystics. Most of these were Terrans, who formed an informal sort of metaphysical aristocracy. Soon afterwards, individuals from all nations applied for membership. Many were accepted. The order, known as the Order of Praiseworthy Light, became a formidable presence in the international scene. Other orders came into existence. They all held, for a time, a peaceful co-existence with the ruling governments.

Talib paused. His student waited. Such unorthodox teaching methods were, in this place, not unorthodox at all. Teachers pretty much did whatever they wanted.

"The hardest thing to do is to establish a religious government. Governments cannot be religious and proactive at the same time. Religion, with its emphasis on spirituality, is a spontaneous experience. Laws that governments produce inevitably attempt to suppress this spontaneity. Yet governments cannot exist without laws. Laws eventually attempt to replace morality, conscious, and even the spiritual principles of the religion it pretends to uphold. Ceremony always attempts to disguise itself as faith, and symbolism always attempts to disguise itself as morality. This is a dangerous paradox.

"Two days after I took my Shahada, a Muslim I met only once told me "The Deen religion, is in the heart." The heart, in

the sense of the Qalb wa qutb – the center / heart / spiritual foundation, and axis / neutral center.

"Personally, I am only interested in what a thing or concept actually is, and to act upon it accordingly. The popular "politically correct" definition of the word religion, or any politically correct idea, means exactly nothing to me - for the simple reason that it is, indeed meaningless."

At this, his students looked at him in utter confusion.

"Ah! Please forgive me. I occasionally slip back into thinking in terms of how things were in the 21st century. I can't help it,,,

"Anyway,,, The practices of Islam that are either obligatory and recommended are a means to an end. They are meant to produce a result. And its that result that is so vitally important.

"The word belief as many understand it, is treated in the Qur'an in a very different way than the way some languages describe it. In Arabic it would be translated as I'tiqad (belief) or Dhan (assumption) and the Qur'an explicitly criticized and dismissed these as inadequate methods of spiritual enlightenment / transformation. In the Qur'an, Surat Yunus 10:36, we're told, "And most of them do not follow [anything else] but assumption/supposition; the assumption/supposition does not suffice (replace) [as] the truth, Allah (is) knowledgeable of what they produce/do."

The word that refers to Faith in the Qur'anic Arabic is "Iman" and throughout the hundreds of times it is used, it is clear that it refers to the movement of the person in response to the Divine, it is not what people think or believe, it is who they are and by extension what they do.

"When you take the Shahada it does not involve belief. "Bearing witness" and not "belief" is what is required. Belief in the colloquial meaning is not enough to be a person of faith in Islam. Nowhere is this clearer than in Surat al Hujurat 49:14 : "The desert Arabs say we have faith, Say, "You have no faith; but you (should only) say, 'We have submitted our wills to Allah,' For Faith has not yet entered your hearts." "Enter your hearts" is translated from qulubikuum. Note the plural of its root qalb. This is an important point because it hints at spiritual principles as a cornerstone of social order. And the whole verse is an admonishment to those who would attempt to found social order based upon spiritual attainment they can lay no legitimate claim to."

Chapter 19. You Can Never Go Home.

The space freighter parked in a geosynchronous orbit directly above Mecca. Talib and the other Hajjis were told to gather their belongings and board the shuttle craft that would bring them down to earth. The was done with silence and solemnity.

Talib was filled with a strange melange of emotions. Finally he would make his Hajj. And in doing so, he'd be returning to his home that he left so long ago. He knew he was changed; how much more his home world would be changed!

He'd made arrangements that, when he'd successfully complete the Hajj ritual and then visited the Prophet's Mosque in Medina, he would take a tour with a group of archaeologists to some ruins of terrestrial cities; including New York City.

The shuttle craft descended slowly into the ruined and poisoned atmosphere, and through a yellow cloud covering. The Arabian peninsula grew larger and larger below him. Finally, the craft landed on a launchpad of what was obviously a spaceport, located in a remote area on the outskirts of the city. The launchpad descended into an opening, the roof covered it, and the area was depressurized, and filled with breathable air.

After disembarking, Talib and the other Hajjis were led to an underground shuttle train. This took them to their lodgings within Mecca, within walking distance of the Sacred Mosque and the Kab'a.

When the train got about halfway to its destination, it ascended into a transparent tunnel on the surface. For the first time, Talib saw the large geodesic dome that housed the Sacred Mosque, and the domes protecting Arafat,

Overhead, the sky was a poisonous yellow. Blue / gray clouds moved overhead at a moderate pace. The sun was rising.

When the train arrived and the passengers disembarked, they were greeted by the Imam of Mecca; Imam al Hajj Feisal Abdalsalaam. He was a stocky Arab of medium hight, and a direct descendant of Abu Musa al-Ashari. His family had been in Mecca since the time of the Prophet (sas), and resolutely refused to leave it.

It was cool when he stepped outside the train. Talib was surprised. He was expecting a sweltering heat. But then he remembered that not only were they in an artificial environment, but the climate of the whole earth was different. For a moment, he wondered how many other preconceived ideas he would be brutally reminded to abandon.

The Imam approached them and said "Asalaam alaikum, wa rahmatuallah wa barakatahu. Welcome to the city of Mecca."

*****

Talib stayed in a private tent. It was large enough to shelter a family of four, and was quite comfortable.

Talib and the other Hajjis entered into ihram, then repeated the Talbiyah prayer. Then walked a few miles to Mina and camped there overnight.

Upon arriving, they entered the Holy Mosque at Mecca, right foot first, and recites the prayer: "In the name of Allah, may peace and blessings be upon the Messenger of Allah. Oh Allah, forgive me my sins and open to me the doors of Your mercy. I seek refuge in Allah the Almighty and in His Eminent Face and in His Eternal Dominion from the accursed Satan." Then they performed the tawaf and kissing the Black Stone on each circuit. Then they performed the sa'i; running seven times between two small hills Safa and Marwah, commemorating the desperate search for water and food by Hajar, one of Ibrahim's (as) wives. As she searched, the Zamzam Well was revealed to her by an angel, who brushed the ground with the tip of his wing, after which the water of the Zamzam started gushing from the ground.

After the completion of Tawaf az-Ziyarah, they offered two Rakats at the Station of Abraham. They also drank water from the Zamzam Well; which somehow survived the ravages that the earth suffered. Then they returned to their tents. That night, Talib hared a good meal with some of the other Hajjis. Many were from worlds he'd never known about. They had many questions for him about what Mecca was like in the "ancient days." But this was Talib's first Hajj; so there wasn't much he could tell them; except that it was crowded. They were also curious about what it was like to be a Muslim in an "infidel" society.

The Day of Arafat arrived. Arafat was then what it had always been; an empty plain. Talib realized that this was a significant element of the three Abrahamic Faiths; they seemed to originate in places that had nothing. All this power and beauty originating from places that were completely devoid of any resource or interesting feature. It all made perfect sense to him. And now, of course, the whole earth was just as dead. They devoted the entire day to supplication and devotion, and recited the Qur'an, near the Jabal Al Rahmah hill from which Muhammad (sas) gave his last sermon. In the evening, they moved to Muzdalifa, where they camped overnight and offered more prayers.

Talib made dua for everyone he knew. He mentally visualized them all; Zeinab, Hassan, Sheikh Suliman, Rashidevkov and his family, Sheikh Ill'm, Sheikh Lateef, and many others. And he remembered his promise to Ghaibal. He wept, remembering the kindness they'd all shown him. If any man had friends and loved ones of half the quality these people were, he'd be a rich man, indeed. Allah is generous and compassionate!

On the tenth day of Dhul-Hijjah, they returned to Mina and throw seven pebbles at the three pillars that symbolized Shaitan's temptation of Ibrahim (as). Then they sacrificed a sheep, in recalling how Abraham sacrificed a sheep that Allah had provided in place of his son. The meat would normally have been distributed to friends, relative and the poor. But this aspect of the Hajj had changed, as there were, strictly speaking, no impoverished people on this world anymore. Thus, everyone had an equal share of the meat. Afterward, they returned to Mecca and perform a final tawaf and sa'i, and completed the Hajj by cutting their hair.

After returning from Arafat, and completing his Tawaf al-Wada. Talib stood in the Sacred Mosque, looking at the Kaba. It was an astonishing sight. Since it was first built by the hands of Abraham and Ishmael, it had been damaged and rebuilt many times, and undergone several reconstructions since his day. Now it seemed complete.

It was night. The Hajjis were making their circuits, as he had. It was not crowded. There were only about 500 Hajjis. But the area seemed charged with the immense power that would come from billions of souls all performing the beautiful act in harmony for centuries. Talib sensed / visualized / "remembered", the countless prayers offered in this place, the centuries of manifested power, the illuminated beings that walked this very land. The Kaba seemed an axis upon which the whole universe turned. And he sensed / visualized / remembered this same axis extending through the seven levels of Jenna, to al Kursi. Around it, humans, djinn, and angels revolved, were absorbed, annihilated, reborn in Unity.

All the while, Talib was aware of the responsibility of performing Hajj on behalf of an entire world. His training in mental concentration was useful; he couldn't afford to allow himself any distractions. On many occasions, he found himself weeping with joy, with regret for all his own imperfections, which he felt were held up in comparison to greater men and women who preceded him here, and in gratitude to Allah for the unimaginable blessings he'd been given.

When Talib came to his physical senses, he saw a man seated to his right. He was wearing a green djalabiah with a hood partially covering his face. The only part of the man's face that was clearly visible were his eyes; which shone from the shadow of his garment. He looked Talib in the eye. His soul sang to Talib's soul.

I ran away from my Beloved;
but wherever I ran,
My Beloved is already there,
staring into my soul.

Life brings me face to face,
with the pain of loving:
the loneliness of a loveless life,
is the pain of not loving my Beloved.

In the silence of my loneliness,

270

I chose not to love my Beloved;

the cold of silence made the loneliness brittle,

till it broke to end the silence:

To the jingling of the broken pieces,

I danced with my loneliness;

each piece became a company to my loneliness,

and my loneliness was lonely no more.

My Beloved stirs my soul

from behind the veil,

My Beloved evokes passions,

until I see my My Beloved through the veil.

Talib realized that this was no narrative; This man was singing Talib's own words. Words he was not aware of. Talib wept.

The man in green said "Soon you will know." Talib and the man stared at each other. Suddenly the man in green laughed out loud; a hearty and resonant laugh that penetrated the whole area. Talib felt the laugh as a physical wave though his whole being. He didn't understand the laugh; but it was not a laugh of ridicule. It was filled with love. The tears in Talib's eyes continued to flow; obscuring his vision. When he wiped away his tears, the man in green was gone.

Then began the first day of Eid-ul Adha: the Feast of the Sacrifice; the celebration after the end of the Hajj. The normally staid and sober Hajjis, and custodians of the Kaba suddenly abandoned themselves to a tumultuous celebration. Feasting, games, and poetry - that indestructible tradition in Arab culture – was enjoyed by one and all.   The men even took out dafs, that ancient instrument, and started playing and dancing. One man, Imam al Hajj Feisal Abdalsalaam's youngest brother Yusef was dancing on a rock, and got so excited he fell off and broke his leg. Despite the pain, he was happy and laughing the whole time. Imam Feisal said "He does this every Eid."

Everyone had a lot of fun.

*****

Talib had the opportunity to visit some of the remaining ruins of places that were reconstructed from the ravages of the 20th and 21st century. All the skyscrapers, hotels, and apartments from that age were gone. A few of the archaeological ruins that the Wahabbis destroyed in their zeal to eliminate what they believed to be idolatry had been reconstructed. The mosque at the grave of Hamza bin Abdul Muttalib, the Mosque of Fatima Zahra, the Mosque and tomb of Imam Ja'far al-Sadiq, the Grave of Amina bint Wahb, the Prophet's mother, and the Tomb of Umm Hawa in Jeddah were all restored as much as humanly possible. It made Talib sad to visit; but it seemed a strange justice that these would survive, and the skyscrapers, five star hotels, and shopping malls that the Saudi dynasty thought were more important than their own national and religious treasures (and which they destroyed under the pretext of preserving religious purity) were, without a single exception, obliterated without a trace. Archaeologists could find next to nothing of their remains beyond written historical record and a few photographs.

The Hajj now complete, they traveled to the city of Medina and the Mosque of the Prophet, which contains Muhammad's tomb.

The flight was short and uneventful. Medina, like Mecca, was protected by a geodesic dome. Within the dome, the Medina of this time bore no resemblance to the the Medina of Talib's time. The only exception being the Prophet's Mosque itself. The area was quite barren. About two and a half dozen sturdy, and attractive buildings surrounded the holy sites. Only about a hundred people lived there, all of whom cared for the place and maintained the life support technology.

The visit of the Hajjis was less formalized than Talib had expected it to be. The Hajjis all had their own ways of demonstrating their reactions for being there. Some were clearly influenced by Shi'ite sentiments. Others were more reserved. Talib, although not displaying excessive emotion, found himself moved to tears.

*****

When he left Medina, he headed to Egypt to visit the pyramid of Khufu and the Sphinx. He was assigned an environment suit, as these archaeological ruins had no domes for the environment. Greater Cairo's city limits once stood just outside the area of the. Now only a few ruins remain. A single building served as environment protection, housing, and maintenance and study of the archaeological site.

The pyramids themselves seemed to have remained unchanged over the centuries. Talib was amazed by the age of these structures. They were ancient when Jesus, the Son of Mary (as) was born! He spent a day exploring the inner chambers of the pyramids, and examining the entire complex from the pyramid to the Valley Temple. He also stood at the Sphinx. This sight aroused within him an emotion he'd been quite unprepared for – familiarity. He couldn't define or explain it. His guide, a wizened, ill tempered old man with a dour continence, said the Sphinx was over 25,000 years old. All things considered, Talib had no trouble believing him.

The ruin he would visit the next day would be Atlantis. It was located on the continent of Antarctica. His guide explained that maps dating back centuries suggested the location of the ancient civilization have existed, but Western historian authorities had suppressed them.

He was taken to a geodesic dome where archaeologists lived and studied the ruins. There were several buildings that had been excavated from the ground and what remained of the ice of the former south pole. Part of the city had been under water, as the earth's tectonic shifts changed the landscape. Large dams and walls were constructed to hold the ocean at bay and allow exploration of these ruins. Much of the architecture was remarkably well preserved. And according to the archaeologists, the ruins were over 70,000 years old. Which meant that the history of the world and the origins of humanity that was taught in the science books Talib had read was all wrong.

This was astonishing to Talib. He knew that ibn Arabi spoke of the thirty worlds before this one. He'd never given it much thought. Suddenly, it made sense.

Some of them were pyramids that were unlike any the Egyptians, Aztecs, Cambodians, and Colombians had built. They were grouped, Talib was told, in patterns that followed mathematical formulas based, as many had in the centuries to come, on the golden ratio. They also lined up with where specific astronomical bodies would have been at the time. One pyramid Talib explored had openings that, at each seasonal equinox, would, at the time of their design and construction, line up with Sirius. There were also buildings that had columns with almost fractal designs at their top and base. Some machinery and technology, some of which was more advanced than that of the world Talib had been born into, and amazing works of graphic art survived. One mural depicted the lives of celebrated people in the Atlantis history. Much of the meaning behind it, and a great deal of their writing – not quite alphabetic and not quite pictographs - was still unknown. And the physical appearance of these people, as depicted in their artwork, took Talib aback. They simply did not look like any race he could identify from his own time.

Talib was amazed beyond words.

He walked around for hours among the remains of these astonishing sculptures and improbable architecture. Walls that curved at bizarre angles, pillars that supported what was once large oval shaped basins of enormous size, spherical shaped buildings that were connected by bridges and tunnels, more pyramids that, despite being pyramids, their design owed nothing to any known predecessor. And these were so well preserved, as if the builders were conscious of their own mortality and built for the ages. Even something of their original color remained; after 70 centuries! White, green, and gold seemed to dominate; but here and there rose, dark violet, and vermilion asserted themselves.

His guide pointed out a bas relief that covered an entire wall about 30 meters by 18 meters. It was a depiction of the solar system. The accuracy was unbelievable. They knew of the planets that were not visible to the naked eye, the moons of the planets, and even the dwarf planets and other Trans-Neptunian objects in the Kuiper belt! But there were a few things he found puzzling. A planet lay between the orbits of Mars and Jupiter,

Neptune had three moons too many, Mars had three moons, and Earth had no moon. Could it be? His guide simply said that "things were different in those days."

And another unexpected surprise awaited him; an enormous black cube which seemed situated in the center of all these marvels.

What did it all mean?

With all this, the enormity of time itself pressed upon his mind, intoxicating and dazzling him. He wondered how these people kept their composure among all this.

He was scheduled to leave to visit New York City. On the way to his transportation, he was told about Jerusalem's archaeological finds.

So, the matter was finally settled.

The guide told him of ruins of cities Talib would have known of: Paris, Kuala Lumpur, Hiroshima, Rome, and Novosibirsk.

Los Angeles, Tokyo, Moscow, Bangkok, and Las Vegas were completely gone. Some people didn't seriously believe that Las Vegas ever existed. Talib assured them it did.

They told him about other ancient ruins unknown in his time. The underground network spanning the Himalayas and the Tora Bora mountains, the pre-Aztec cities in the Amazon, a city in North America believed to be over 9000 years old, and another place that was "terribly remote." Talib was also told exactly how remote this ruin was. He wasn't quite sure how to process this information. It completely shattered everything he thought he knew; and it was years before he could meditate clearly on the subject. All ridiculously ancient, all unknown in Talib's time - or so it was generally believed. Unfortunately, he never had the chance to visit them.

The aircraft that took him across the Atlantic ocean descended toward yet another landing pad that would descend into the ground. But this was no archaeological discovery to be savored as a new experience; this was a homecoming. He looked out the window, transfixed by what he was seeing. He recognized New York City. Most of the geography had not changed, except that much of the western part of Long Island was flooded, as were parts of Manhattan. In fact, the Hudson and East Rivers met in the general area where 125th street used to be. Uptown and the Bronx were a desolate island (but the Cloisters museum still stood atop Inwood Hill). A few ruined remnants of the old skyscrapers remained. He was told that visiting Brooklyn and Queens was inadvisable. There was not much left of it to visit anyway, and much was under water (some archaeologists were in disagreement as to where these two boroughs were actually located. None of them ever had the chance to ask Talib.).

Rikers Island was gone.

New Jersey was a desert. Absolutely barren.

After they landed and disembarked at their camp, which was located where the garment district used to be (of which nothing now remained, except a few ragged brick walls), Talib was shown to the room where he would be staying. Like the rooms in the other cities he visited, it was small and spartan, with a modest restroom. He lay down and tried to get some rest.

After a deep and refreshing sleep, he rose, had a breakfast of coffee, bread, and honeycomb, and prepared to explore the ruins.

The ruins of New York City. He still couldn't get used to the idea; even after all he'd been through.

Time Square still held some tattered remnants of its former glory. Movement among the area was difficult. There was no concept of tourism, and thus no need to make travel convenient. At Broadway and 42nd street, some of the subway stations had caved in. Parts of it were flooded. Further east, the ruin of Grand Central Station remained as a recognizable structure. All around it were piles of rubble, shattered walls, caved in subway tunnels and stations.

The whole of the UN Plaza was completely gone.

He went uptown a ways and stopped at Columbus Circle. The Time Warner building was completely gone. Evidence of Lincoln Center was still there. The ruin of the Museum of Natural History still stood. Central Park was a large mass of dead vegetation.

At length, he came downtown. He wanted to see what became of the Lower East Side. It was largely desolate, with some buildings still in evidence. But it was silent. Greenwich Village had a few ruins here and there, but mostly nothing. He wasn't even sure he could find the spot where once stood the apartment building where he and Zeinab lived. Almost all reference points were gone. Talib felt a bit sad; so much great music and art had happened there. Some great moments in his life. He was momentarily pulled by a desperate need to relive that time, to return to those "old days" - and painfully reminded of the absolute impossibility of this.

Then he ventured to the old Soho area. Not much was left of it. Some ruins of Chinatown were still standing. There was also a small river of brackish black water where Canal street used to be; which extended from where Mott street once was, to the Hudson river. A few fragments of the old buildings were still standing. No writing was visible on anything. A ways south, the financial district was gone. The place where the rebuilt World Trade Plaza once stood was barren. The courthouses to the southeast; sturdy, well built structures, were still there; but powerless.

Finally he found what he believed was the place where Hassan's building once stood. This was where he began his guitar lessons with Hassan. This was the place where he'd taken his first stumbling steps on the path he was now on – a Journey of No Return.

At that moment he would have given all the riches in the world for an hour to talk with Hassan, and to hold Zeinab in his arms once again.

He wept.

Of all the travels, all the strange places he'd been, this was the most emotionally trying – and that was saying a lot! He was experiencing something no human being ever experienced: seeing his own home as a ruin not from war or recent natural disaster, but as an uninhabitable ancient ruin thousands of years old. There was a finality about it that hung in the air like the tolling of a distant bell. Like a voice calling out in a vast wilderness, the words of the Qur'an inexorably, irresistibly hammered its words into his heart:

Is this not a warning to such men to recall how many generations We destroyed, in whose haunts they now travel? Verily, in this are Signs for those with understanding.

Talib understood this as few human beings could in the long history after Adam and Eve. And wept at all he'd seen, all he'd been given, and the enormous cost he paid for the gifts with his body, mind, and soul.

He reached down, and picked up a stone. Putting it in his pocket, he resolved to keep it until he died, if he could.

*****

It was time to leave. The shuttlecraft waited for him. Inside, the other hajjis waited too. They understood that he would need a little more time. They were, in fact, in awe of him. The enormity of what he was experiencing was not lost on them.

They had never been to earth, and none of their generations for centuries previous had walked on this world. For them it was a wonder; but an impersonal wonder. Talib knew it when it was alive. And now he knows it after it is dead, and all her ancient secrets unveiled.

Finally, Talib said his farewells to his mother world, boarded the shuttlecraft, and went his way.

In years to come, he would attempt to organize a trip to take his family and a few friends to earth and show them where he'd lived. None of his attempts were successful.

He would never see the world of his birth again.

Chapter 20. The Other Half.

After what seemed like centuries, Talib returned to Uq'dyill. He was unprepared for the reception he would meet.

He met with a group of representatives from the khaliphite. He was officially congratulated, and thanked for successfully completing the Hajj on behalf of the nations and peoples of Uq'Dyill. To Talib's utter surprise, a position of considerable political authority was conferred upon him. The privileges of his office were explained – although he was under no obligation to exercise any of them.

His old friend Rashidevqov and his family had arranged a beautiful reception. Once again, he would have to endure the role Allah assigned to him in the eyes of men. The reception was attended by all manner of dignitaries and their entourages. Food, entertainment, and speeches were plentiful. Talib was expected to make a speech as well. He was not really in the mood to be the center of attention and to receive accolades. He had traveled so far and seen and experienced so much. What he wanted was to quietly discuss what had happened with a few trusted friends.

But that would come later.

Several people wondered why Talib wasn't married. This was a matter of some concern. The world was not without marriageable women; and some of them made their status of availability quite obvious to Talib. He was flattered; and many of them were quite attractive. There was Bilqis bint

Ghaneemad, the daughter of an ambassador / envoy to the Spacefarers, whose beauty could only be described as distracting (one of Talib's friends said she could make Majnun forget Laylah). She almost swayed him; but, difficult as it was to do so, he resolved to finalize a few things in his life before marrying. This was a decision he would never regret.

One of the people invited to the reception was Hqiim Zalluh, and his wife. Zalluh paid absolutely no attention to the event. Instead he scowled and fidgeted nervously. He couldn't wait to leave and return to his work.

*****

Hqiim Zalluh was a controversial figure among the people. He was renowned to be the greatest mathematician of his time, possibly the greatest ever. Visitors and communications from the entire populated universe found their way to him, requesting assistance or begging to be taught. There was seemingly no mathematical problem that was beyond his understanding. His achievements caused him to be showered with wealth. This meant nothing to him, beyond freeing him to concentrate on his work.

Often, his behavior was downright bizarre. He was often required to return to places he'd visited to apologize for his earlier behavior. Neither king nor pauper were immune to his

284

outbursts of anger or incomprehensible behavior. But this and other eccentricities were tolerated. He was Hqiim Zalluh.

The only people immune to his behavior, and who invoked great tenderness in his otherwise scruffy exterior were his wife and two children. This was not well known. His wife Qaliya, whom many people felt sorry for as *"the poor woman who has to share a bed with this genius"* was an exceptionally intelligent woman originally from the Bithaq nation. She loved him enough to take care of him (he being somewhat neglectful of his personal habits) and tolerate his many eccentricities. He genuinely loved her, too, but was often so absorbed in his work as to give the erroneous appearance of indifference. Fortunately, she knew better. She understood as few women would that her man had a purpose and an importance to humanity that was greater than either of them. She was sufficiently selfless to devote herself to helping her husband in his purpose for the greater good; and sufficiently selfish to help him in his work to keep him close to her. He knew this, and loved her all the more for it. In addition to being an accomplished mathematician herself; one of the few who earned her husband's respect, she was also a shrewd businesswoman She not only handled the family's finances with finesse, but was also approached by many others for the purpose of consultation.

It was rumored that Hqiim was engaged in a project that involved the Qur'an. Hqiim believed that there was encoded within the Qur'an a mathematical language that would explain all of creation. In connection with this on-going project, he would petition all the Orders and the institutions of education and research on several worlds for obscure and arcane pieces of information.

Nobody was able to make sense of his requests; and he refused to be helpful in this.

*****

It was a rainy day in the city of Lanajd. A woman of the Fa'atim race walked briskly through the chilly downpour, intent upon getting to her destination.

Her name was Sudi bint Abdultawwab. Her family was highly respected among the people of Uq'dyill, having held position of importance in the offices of public service, education, and medicine.

She was a member, and a recently appointed Sheikha, of the Sisterhood of the Mountain of Light; an Order comprised entirely of women. No man was allowed entry into the Order. Some of its activities, while not suspect, were not made public. The sisterhood guarded its privacy. The Order of Believing Light once had the opportunity to learn some of their secrets and deliberately ignored the opportunity. The sisterhood learned of this gesture of respect from them; and relations between the two orders remained close ever since.

Sudi had made astonishing achievements in the order. So much so that she was the first to achieve the position of tekke leader at the age of 27. She mastered many of the mystic sciences, was fluent in seven languages, and was an acknowledged master of ijtihad. She was also proficient at yoga and medicinal arts involving chi.

By the time she reached the age of 32, she'd still never married. Some years before, she was informed in a dream that her husband would be a great and unusual man, from a far away place, who would be placed in her world to make a great achievement. None of her suitors answered to this description, so her answer was always no. Her family attempted to pressure her to marry, but she steadfastly refused. She had an aunt who was in the Sisterhood who understood Sudi's decision, and protected her (not that she needed a lot of protecting; she was a formidable woman, and enjoyed fighting with men.).

Sudi was exceptionally beautiful, with the golden brown skin and violet eyes common among her race. Most of her people had dark blonde or tan hair. Her hair was jet black. Her figure, which few people saw, was shapely, lithe, and athletic, and she moved with a silent, fluid grace.

*****

After Talib rested from his most recent journey, he resumed his business as a professional musician. There was plenty of work available and since his reputation preceded him, he had no difficulty finding engagements for performances. He soon found himself making a good living. His status as the Hajji of this world was technically not supposed to present him with professional advantage or monetary gain. But it didn't hurt.

One thing that Talib wasn't prepared for was for people to expect him to play ancient songs. He did so, but after his first awakening, he was more interested in forging ahead in his endeavors and exploring new music. He had no interest in being a curiosity for people who treated him as a historical artifact. Once he became upset with someone who, in the company of some wealthy people who'd hired him, demanded he play what they called "The Ancient Classics." Talib wasn't sure he knew what this meant; but found himself taking offense. He told the people that he had no interest in being their performing museum piece, and after some heated words were exchanged, he told them he didn't want their money, and walked out.

Fortunately, there were enough people who were just as interested in seeing where Talib's music would evolve to as Talib himself was. He performed all over Uq'Dyill, and had occasional engagements in major cities on other worlds.

He was also sought after as a music teacher. Students would appear out of nowhere, and beg to be taken as students. The student / teacher relationship on Uq'Dyill was something else Talib had to get used to. Money for music lessons was exchanged sometimes. But the relationship extended to the student traveling and living with the teacher, running errands, and learning about and sharing all aspects of life.

One of these was a young man named Musawa Mutawalrrajul. Musawa wanted to be a flute master, and approached Talib, begging him to take him as a student. He was very young, about 15, and very thin and nervous. Talib agreed, and the boy became his shadow.

Musawa came from a family of laborers. Nobody in his family displayed much artistic talent. Musawa's sudden interests in music was a matter of some concern to them, especially his father, who had difficulty understanding why his son would want to be anything other than a stone mason.

But Musawa was determined. He saved his money, purchased a flute, and went out in search of a master to teach him. He was delighted to find Talib, and after Talib agreed to teach him, much to Talib's embarrassment. he sunk to his knees, weeping, and thanked Allah for the honor. Talib told him "Stand up! Come on, kid; I'm not some kind of,,, whatever!" Musawa was, actually, in complete awe of Talib. He knew his biography, knew of all he'd seen and done. If he could achieve one small part of what Talib had, he would die a happy man.

It was the custom of this world that no music performances occurred during Ramadan. Talib stayed at a mosque in a small village in Mukhsama (a city about 30 km southwest of Lanajd), where he spent his days fasting, and his nights praying; occasionally teaching Musawa. Shortly before the end of

Ramadan, he was contacted by a group of wealthy people who wished to engage him to perform for their Eid celebration (they would pay for an enormous celebration; and all were invited, rich or poor, all schools of thought, all nations.) Talib happily accepted.

The offers for performances came again after Ramadan. He accepted an offer for a week's performances in Lanajd. Musawa came along, and took care of the mundane details, as he always did.

After Talib finished his performances, he spent a few days tended to some final business during his travels in Lanajd, and another few days resting. One afternoon during these casual days, he decided to get something to eat, and invited Musawa to join him.

Restaurants in Lanajd were a curious affair. It had taken Talib some time for him to get used to them. There were no menus. You were given a choice of three or four dishes; depending on what was available and what the cook was in the mood to prepare. Drinks were usually simple: water, or tea. Coffee was always available, but was most often sold in special coffee houses; places where artists, scientists and intellectuals tended to socialize. Laborers and the like tended to socialize in the restaurants. Juices may or may not be available. Soda did not exist.

The restaurant Talib went into was a very small, clean place, with stone walls and unremarkable features. The only item on the menu that day was a vegetable and squirrel meat stew served with bread. It was rather bland; Talib wished he has some seasoning (when Talib asked for some seasoning, the owner, a large bald man with a braided mustache, several earrings, and colored beads woven into his beard, asked him why he didn't bring any himself. He was not being sarcastic; that was actually how things are done in this district). But it would do.

At least the bread was fresh and tasty, and included in the price of the meal.

He was alone at one of the two low, asymmetrically shaped tables in the place. He sat on a cushion on the floor eating his stew. A woman came in, and sat at the other side of the table, facing the opposite direction of Talib. At first Talib paid her no mind. He ate his stew, absorbed in his thoughts. Musawa sat opposite him, and Talib largely ignored his attempts to start a conversation.

A moment later, Talib felt he was being watched. The man with no seasoning who ran the restaurant was washing a large pot, and paying no attention to anyone. The people at the other table were talking among themselves. But the woman at the other end of his table was stealing furtive glances at Talib.

Talib didn't know how to react. While women on Uq'Dyill were not as segregated as in some Muslim countries in his time on earth, they didn't do things like this in this world (as far as he knew) unless they were interested in marriage. She seemed a woman of good upbringing. Her clothing indicated she was educated and fairly well to do. He dared a look at her face. He was immediately captivated by her beauty. She seemed to have a strength and a delicacy of spirit enclosed within a supremely dignified bearing.

The spectacle of her small hands hit Talib like a ton of bricks. The golden brown color, smooth texture, meticulously trimmed nails, and perfectly shaped fingers were among the most beautiful things he'd ever seen. Her large violet eyes, perfectly placed above her high cheekbones and full lips held Talib's attention in a vicegrip.

They made eye contact. They seemed to try to break away from each other; yet couldn't. A powerful constriction gripped his breast. His breath left him, and his heart beat harder. The woman, finally looked away, seemingly as flustered as he.

Finally, Talib became bold.

"Mus" Talib said, "Go and find me some, uh, patchouli incense."

Musawa said "But master, there is none of this to be found in this area." The truth was, Musawa had no idea what patchouli was.

"Stop calling me 'master.' Do your best. Are you finished eating? No? Take it with you" Talib said, handing him some money. "Take your time, Mus. Keep the change."

Musawa was vaguely aware his master wanted him gone; but being inexperienced with women, he didn't see why. He took the money, and, left.

With Musawa gone, Talib abandoned the finer points of adab and threw caution to the wind, addressing her with a greeting.

She nodded and returned the greeting.

Talib said "Do I know you?"

She said "I'm not sure; I was wondering where I'd seen you."

In reality, she knew exactly where she'd seen him – and she'd seen him quite clearly.

Talib sensed this as well. He decided to take a chance.

"My name is Talib Ali Peterson" he began. "I'm a musician, and a traveler."

"Are you the man from Earth centuries past? The man who made Hajj for us?" she said

"Yes, that's me." Talib said with a modest smile.

"Alhamdulillah!" She exclaimed with a radiant smile, her eyes shining with delight and admiration. "I am indeed honored to meet you! My name is Sudi bint Abdultawwab."

"The pleasure is all mine." Talib said.

They moved a little closer to each other and began to converse. She told him about her work, and he told her about his music, and his travels. Their conversation continued for many hours. Fortunately, during this time, Musawa was still out in search of the incense Talib sent him for.

Finally the restaurant owner told them he was closing. Go away.

They walked for a while, and talked.

Finally they came to the place where they would part ways.

"I need to ask you something," Talib said. "Are you married?"

"No." Sudi said. "I assume you are also not wed?"

"That's right" Talib said.

A silence as profound as it was awkward, enveloped them.

"Let's meet again. Soon." Talib said.

"Yes; I would like that!" Sudi said, with more enthusiasm in her voice than she'd intended.

They made plans to meet the following day.

The next day, after Talib gave Musawa some money and told him he may visit his family (calling it an Eid Gift. Musawa apologized for not finding the incense, and promised to find it as soon as he could) he met Sudi. They'd originally intended only to have coffee or food. They ended up sharing the day together. They walked through villages, and in a forest; Sudi not the least bit concerned for her safety.

After more conversation, more periods of profound and awkward silence, Sudi said "Talib, I must tell you something. I am in love with you and always have been. You appeared to me in dreams and visions. Your coming was foretold to me, and I kept myself unwed so that I may be free to be yours and you may be mine. Our destinies are linked. I am a simple woman, a scholar and practitioner of the medical arts, and require nothing special in the way of lifestyle.

"Talib, I ask you to marry me. If you wish to take time and think of an answer that is fine. If you do not wish to marry me, we'll go our separate ways now. But I love you and wish to be your woman."

The bold, direct exclamation was quite unexpected – yet made perfect sense. Talib looked into her violet eyes, looking out at him with undeniable love - so beautiful against that golden brown skin! - and saw that she was, indeed, the woman he would share his life with. It all seemed so natural, so inevitable. Their spirits spoke to each other from a place the physical worlds could not touch.

Finally, Talib said "You are my wife. That's it; it can't be any other way, and I won't let another day go by unless you are my wife. I see that now. Let's wed today. Now."

Sudi raised an eyebrow "Ah! You are so impetuous!"

"Me, impetuous? Talib said, with mock indignation. "You meet me yesterday, and then ask me for marriage; and I'm the one whose impetuous? Young lady! You shock me! I blush to hear such words!" She started to laugh, and Talib continued "Admit it! You've been planning this for months! I'm a helpless victim of your wiles!"

They both laughed, and made plans to be married as soon as possible.

*****

Unlike his marriage to Zeinab, Talib and Sudi had a proper marriage in a mosque, although it was a simple and quiet affair. Talib was not comfortable being the center of attention at large gatherings, unless they were his concerts. Sudi's family, friends, and colleagues, and Talib's friends, naturally including the Rashidevqov family, were in attendance. According to Islamic tradition, a man is expected to offer a prospective bride a dowry. The dowry is hers to keep and do with what she wills. At Sudi's insistence, her dowry was a minuscule sum – although Talib insisted she accept more.

They had a wedding party; the first such that Talib had attended on Uq"Dyill. It was a happy affair. Anjjelliqh and Farouzeh made the arrangements for the event. Talib ended up playing a little music with the other musicians. Sudi didn't mind. She realized he was a musician, and this is what he does. Rasheema seemed a bit put out, and it took Talib years to realize she'd had a schoolgirl crush on him.

After a while, the newlyweds left the others to their revelries. Rashidevqov had started doing some kind of dance that threatened at any moment to do serious injury to himself and those near him. It seemed a perfect opportunity for a quiet exit.

They had made arrangements to stay at an inn. Such places were common; as travel was a common occurrence among the people.

During their wedding night, Sudi shares a secret of her Order. It seems the women have adapted the Kama Sutra and Tantric techniques in innovative ways, and to revive long lost techniques in these arts, to keep their health and vitality, and to keep their husbands happy. Some of this involved the use of breathing techniques, yoga postures, and dance in the form of tai chi type movements. Talib shared news of similar techniques he'd learned in his travels and studies.

They spent ten days exploring the potential of their matrimonial prerogative.

*****

Several months into their marriage, Talib told Sudi that he had to go away for a while. He told her to return to her tekke, and that he'd send word when he would return.

"You know that my life involves travel. I'd told you that, baby" Talib said.

Sudi had found Talib's use of the ancient terms of endearment "Baby," "Sweetheart," and the like to be quite curious. She's never heard of it's like in her culture, and wondered about what may be lost in the translation. She mostly liked it, although there were some moments of confusion.

"My love, I understand, and I find happiness in this.

"There is something you do not yet know about the women of the Fa'atim. We have no respect for men who seek nothing. We love warriors and greatness among our men. We want our men to be as free as the wind. We rejoice as much as mourn if our man dies pursuing a great achievement. My other self, I was with you when you evolved out of jahaliyah and into your evolved self. I shared your heart with Zeinab, and saw her as my sister. I was with you when you traveled through time. I was with you when you made Hajj and saw the ancient wonders of the mother world. You will travel, but we will never be apart. When our flesh is denied union, you and I will meet in the other worlds. We will make love among the stars"

Talib said "And the mountains and oceans will sigh in ecstasy, and the angels will brag to Allah about our love." Sudi loved poetry.

They delayed their parting another several hours.

Chapter 21. Danger on the Horizon.

As Talib walked through the Hemmat peninsula, he saw a stone building. It was small, yet well constructed. There were signs of agricultural activity about. However, no smoke emerged from the chimney. This was strange, as the late winter season held the area in its grip. Little or no snow would be on the ground here, but the nights and mornings would be cold. It would be best to keep the building warm. There were also no descriptive markings or calligraphy on the building to let the passerby know whose property he was visiting.

When Talib approached the stone building, he felt someone looking at him. While betraying no sense of alarm, he was curious as to how this person could so easily conceal himself from him. Soon, however, his alarm was traded for wonder. Emerging from the shadows was an old man.

The man moved with a silent stealth that conflicted with his age. His entire body was cloaked in a black robe with a hood. His skin was dark red (obviously belonging to the descendants of the Wati). His eyes were a deep violet. Upon the center of his robe was an embroidered calligraphy; of the type that few could read. Talib knew what it said. The man was an alchemist of the Order of the Ikhwan al-Jaza'a.

The Order of the Ikhwan al-Jaza'a were mystics who employed variations on the ancient practices of Dhikr and Yoga. They also engaged in a very controversial art: one of consciousness expansion through the use of entheogenic substances. While their practices were highly unusual, they existed in a state of general peace with the other Orders and Tribes. Few people knew what drugs they used. They kept this information a strict secret, and never propagated their beliefs about mind altering substances. Yet some bits and pieces of their practice leaked outside the order. The lavender of his eyes was indicative of an addiction to wa'atimq; a preparation of the extract of a flower that grew only on the planet Djemm Baat. It was believed that the drug enabled the user to perceive matter and time as a single phenomenon, and they employed it in the process of alchemical transformations. Yet its use was extremely dangerous. A single dose was addictive, and withdrawal was fatal. Since its sole source was a planet some 17 light years away, the user took a grave risk being addicted to a drug so rare and expensive.

Other substances they used for their rituals included yohimbie, igbotal root (indigenous to Hateem's World), and a mixture of hashish, belladonna, and yaghzi (a fungus that was found in abundant quantities on one of the planets orbiting Sirius. This was highly prized by them). One of their uses of yohimbie was to deliberately stimulate sexual desire while observing a fast of celibacy. The idea was to induce sexual energy, and channel it in an alchemical transformation into another energy form that could be stored and later summoned at will. There were rumors of other arcane and exotic substances in use by the order; as well as strange yoga practices that were kept a very strict secret. In the time the two men would spend together, Babbakh would not ever permit Talib to experiment with any of these substances.

The man walked up to Talib He extended his hand. "Peace be upon you, and welcome" he said. "I've been waiting for you."

The old man took Talib arm and led him to the building. As they walked, Talib noticed a scent resembling jasmine coming from the man's skin and breath. Another sign of wa'atimq addiction.

"I built this house 102 years ago. I saw you coming, and I began to build this house the next day. You're on time!" the old man said with a delighted chuckle.

Talib wanted to say that he was not alive 102 years ago, but thought better of it, and wasn't sure how to reply. He remained silent.

The old man smiled.

"My name is Babaakh Siddiq" the old man said. I perceive you know where I come from. There is a matter that requires your attention. Come, have some food, and I'll tell you all about it."

The simple yet very satisfying meal they shared (a soup of yogurt and cucumbers) was now a recent memory. Talib played a meditative tune on his flute while Babaakh smoked a pipe of blue lotus flowers. When Talib finished the melody, Babaakh chanted in an ancient language. It was not quite a prayer, but more than a poem. Talib didn't understand the language, but caught the general meaning from the association of linguistic sounds and inner interpretations.

Finally Babbakh spoke in their language.

"There is a powerful sorcerer named Oo'Myyah Mathars. He has mastered all the sciences except his own base desires. Shaitan is his god.

"He is a recluse of sorts. He kept people at arm's length. On occasion he would make pilgrimages of sorts to marketplaces or dwellings of the disreputable to indulge in carnal peccadillo." There are some who behave like this, as there always would be; people the ulemma classify as "sinners." But Mathars does so for reasons beyond simple sin. He delights in evil and loathsomeness; and practiced it with a finesse and virtuosity unequaled.

He continued "Mathars is an apostate of the People of the Book and a remarkably advanced - and dangerous - practitioner of sorcery. He is at work on a project that will contaminate the worlds and make his foul dreams a reality. All will suffer. Already his machinations begin to take effect. War threatens to break out. The nations of Soon Jii and Hyat have begun an argument over resources and territory. Neither will admit that this is the cause of the problem. They throw accusations at each other: and, in secret, they both conspire to acquire Hqiim Zalluhh's mathematical theories to use in weapons research and development. It was actually Mathars who pitted both sides against each other. He has followers in strategic places. And Mathars himself wants Zalluhh's work for his own ends."

Talib asked "Hqiim Zalluhh, the great mathematician?

"Yes" Babbakh replied. "He is at work on a great project. As we understand it, he has come across the means of unlocking a hidden code in the Qur'an"

"But hadn't there been other codes discovered before?" Talib asked. This was a matter of controversy among all Muslims in the universe. Nobody was in complete agreement about these "codes," and all kinds of theories, speculations, claims to fact, and fatwas were shared, published and argued about throughout the centuries.

"Yes, but this one promises to explain Allah's mysteries in a way that humanity hasn't understood before. It will usher in a new age for humanity. It also carries a responsibility that humanity as a whole has never held before; even as vicegerents of Allah.

"You have the potential to withstand the evil that men wish to use the new knowledge for and defeat them. I saw this before you were born. Signs that were written in creation foretold your coming. I can help you prepare for this war. We will summon other members of the Ikhwan al-Jaza'a. We must perform a ritual that involves leaving our bodies, and traveling between dimensions. All 18,000 universes will be visited simultaneously. We will combine efforts with their counterparts in the other universes to perform an alchemical transformation. This will prepare you for what must be done. You -are the sword in the Hand of the One. You are a Warrior.

I know who you spoke to on Earth; and this is no surprise to you.

Talib sat and thought. This was another great trial. Finally he asked "Have you ever seen Mathars?"

"Yes, once. I even spoke to him" said Babaakh. "It was a long time ago. I was among the al-Hasabsabb'ah. I was with a group who infiltrated their order. Their world was a harsh place as I remember it.

"They were strange; as were their customs" said Babaakh. "But what was truly strange was the ceremony of the Secret Order of the Yellow Sign that I witnessed. I was to prepare a report for a coalition of orders, including the Order of Believing Light. I was sponsored by a sorcerer whom believed I was a young neophyte. Later, I met Mathars. I shall never forget what I saw that day"

*****

The visitors from off world stood at a distance, clutching their garments around them and doing their best not to be carried away by the wind. A younger Babaakh was among them.

A man in heavy furs faced Babaakh, standing in a freezing desert. He removed the metal face piece that obscured his continence. He had long red hair and a beard. His skin was translucent. The men of their race were short and powerfully built. Their eyes, owing to the pale blue light of the planet's sun, were large, with large dilated pupils. Overhead, the blue-gray sky threatened to erupt in one of its violent storms. Clouds raced overhead with shocking speed. The cold wind assaulted the natives of this world with strong gusts that would have knocked them off their feet, had they not long ago become accustomed to its merciless nature. The sun was setting. Its blue light barely illuminated the unforgiving landscape.

The man had made introductions to the right people so they may be allowed to attend the ceremony that Mathars led. Soon the ceremony began.

After a pregnant silence, a nerve shattering music pierced the air. The music was, by any standards, bizarre. It consisted of mostly percussion instruments. Three men sat on chairs playing drums that resembled djembes. Another three men played a counter rhythm on dafs that had small chains on the edges with bells on the ends of each chain. One man played a bell and a gong at irregular intervals; another had a large set of cymbals that he used in a manner reminiscent of the ancient Chinese opera of old Earth. An old man sat at a large log that had been hollowed out and had slits cut into it that he struck with sticks that had bells attached to the opposite ends. One man stood playing what looked like a modified didgeridoo. Another played a large wooden flute. Two men played loud piercing reed pipes. The tuning and degrees of the scales they used seemed nonexistent; or followed a pattern that seems to deliberately conflict with human biorhythms. There were no string instruments.

It was thought among the people of this world that the use of musical instruments was dangerous, and thus were forbidden to women and untrained men. Yet they were encouraged to sing and chant. The women in the back of the group did this; occasionally howling at the top of their lungs. The men would do the same. Almost everyone contributed to the vocals of the music. Mathars stood on a large rock and led the ceremony with his incantations, and intricate hand gestures which were actually perversions of yoga mudras. His voice somehow cutting through the incredible noise everyone was making.

At one point during the ceremony, a man wearing a white robe and turban, and whose face piece had been painted black walked into the circle. He sat down in front of the musicians and swayed back and forth to the beat of the music. He didn't chant like the rest of the group. He simply swayed to the odd rhythm of this bizarre music. The music suddenly changed. It was accompanied by louder chanting from the men, and syncopated screaming from the women, who still kept their distance. The man in white stood and swayed to the music. He reached into his robe and pulled out a knife with an ornate handle and curving blade. Still swaying and dancing, he began to whirl in a circle, waving the knife over his head in a counter directional circle.

Without warning, he began to tear at his clothes with his free hand. He ripped off his face piece and threw it into the fire. Suddenly, in time with the music, he cut his arm just above the wrist with the knife. Again and again, he cut himself on his arm, his other arm, his leg, and his other leg. All the while the dancing continued. Then, he cut his scalp. Again and again, until he was covered with his own blood, and the blood from his scalp ran into his eyes, obscuring his vision. He cut his chest, abdomen, and shoulders. Still, he kept dancing. The musicians played louder and in a more frenzied pace. The man danced and ran around the circle, weaving in and out of the people. Never once did he collide with anyone or anything, despite the fact that his eyes were filled with blood. Then the man did something truly unexpected. He thrust his hands into the hot embers of the fire, picked them up, and began rubbing them against his face, and even eating them. His skin and hair seared and scorched, filling the air with a nauseating smell. He showed no signs of pain.

The infiltrators were shocked beyond words; but controlled their emotions. The rhythms of this bizarre ceremony were intoxicating and infectious. No matter how shocked or bewildered one was by the goings-on, one was caught up in it and escape was impossible.

Then, without warning or, it seemed, preparation, the musicians and the chanting abruptly stopped. All motion stopped. At the same time the man who had cut and burned himself fell to the ground with a wet thud. For a few seconds - or an eternity - no one moved or made a sound. During this eerie silence, snakes, large worms, and insects appeared within the dancer's blood soaked garments until the whole body was covered in the loathsome creatures. Then, two women walked to the man and covered him with a sheet of burlap. They walked away, and slowly, silently, the rest of the congregation did so.

Mathars approached Babaakh. Looking him in the eye he said "Do you understand what you have just seen?" He chuckled and shook his head "No, clearly not."

Babaakh said "But, what of the man who hurt himself?"

Mathars laughed. "What of him?" and walked away. Babaakh turned and looked toward where the dancing man had collapsed. The sheet lay empty on the ground. No sign of the dancer.

*****

Silence fell upon the two men after Babaakh concluded his story.

Talib knew. He knew that what Babaakh said was true. Pieces of dreams and visions he'd had over the last several years fell into place and made sense now. He also saw several signs that told him that Babaakh need not be tested.

Before retiring, Talib asked Babaakh "How will I know Mathars?"

Babakh said "You will read the signs on his face and in his qalb which will suggest a darkly shining void. He is of the Khwasill race. He also wears an amulet in the shape of a serpent coiled around a gecko lizard seated upon a throne. His clothing will have much red coloring. His smell will simultaneously attract and repel you. Wear your shields when you're near him. He can read people well, and can leech your qi and drain your willpower. This is why he's so old, yet does not appear to age; yet what people see when he is near is not always real. He has been trained in several martial arts, and can also kill with his spirit."

"Get some rest" Babaakh said. "We will begin tomorrow." Babaakh left. Talib made his bed, and went to sleep.

The next morning, Talib and Babaakh waited outside the house. After a while figures appeared in the forest. They came closer to reveal themselves as members of the Ikhwan al-Jaza'a.

Most of them had pale skin, red hair, and green eyes, and were of short stature. Two of them had the red skin and violet eyes that Babbakh had. Three looked Chinese, and were taller than the others. They all wore dark purple robes with gold embroidered calligraphy that blended with some of the plant life in the area. There were seventeen of them in all. Babaakh introduced them; and Talib was slightly amazed to learn that most of them were Christians, and that the three Chinese were Jews. They were an unexpected addition. Talib had had little contact with the People of the Book since his arrival in this world and time. Yet now, these men were pledged to stand at his side in a great battle. He was impressed.

As time went on, the Alh al Kitab in the group proved themselves to be knowledgeable, wise, utterly trustworthy, and in the end, formidable warriors. The Christians were more circumspect, almost like the image Talib held in his mind of a medieval monk. The three Jews were especially hardy and resourceful men; and given to outbursts of good humor. One of them, a woman named Shuzh Ti, whose likable exterior and sublime knowledge of medicine drew attention from the fact that she was a feared and respected martial artist. Only the most skilled (or foolish) fighter would dare face her on a level playing field. As she and Talib got to know one another, she occasionally played small practical jokes on him, to everyone's amusement.

Soon, Talib found himself not only learning a great deal from them, but developed an urge to protect them. From what, he wasn't quite sure; they were quite formidable warriors. But these were among the finest human beings he'd ever met. He cherished their acquaintance and company.

They sat in a circle around a fire, and discussed how to proceed.

"We should proceed with the assumption that Mathars knows that he is going to be attacked" Babbakh began.

Luthur, one of the Christians said "Yes, he'll know. Doubtless his divination will alert him. We will make shaduat so his information is inaccurate and misleading."

"His information will not be very accurate to begin with" said Pauqal, another of the Christians. "But this is a good idea. Arrangements should be made immediately."

310

"Babbakh said "It's been difficult to assess the strength of his followers, although we have a general idea. We will need to cut off their ties with Mathars. My guess is that they do not, and probably cannot, operate in an autonomous manner. We know Mathars is obsessed with exercising absolute control over his followers. And they could be sent against us. We will have to be ready for that as well."

Shuzh Ti said "We could make some kind of action, some overt provocation. Then, we watch and see how those in a position to move against us react. They will give away their positions."

"That could be a good idea," Talib said. "But what kind of casualties can we expect on our side, and how can we reduce them?"

She said "We can position warriors to await the kuffar's reaction to the initial stimulus. Then, should they make offensive moves, we can cut them off before their actions can have significant effect.

After a thoughtful pause, she added "Talib should not be involved in the dunyah fighting." Talib was about to protest when she interrupted him. "No, brother; you will be fighting him on a spiritual level. You and he will meet in the Other Worlds. This is where the greatest part of the Jihad will take place. Mathars has command of forces that can laugh at any weapon. He embodies and wields these unseen weapons, as you do. This is where you will face him. Everything will depend upon you."

*****

At the rampart of a large luxurious mansion overlooking the sea, Oo'Myyah Mathars, dressed in a scarlet silk jacket and kilt, stood looking out at an approaching storm. He held a flagon of spiced wine, his fourth of the night. He was noticeably intoxicated, but not so impaired that he couldn't function. Near him was a large shisha wherein he had been smoking a mixture of tobacco, belladonna, opium, and crushed pearls. Inside his bed chambers, the ravaged body of a teenage boy lay dead upon a pile of silk cushions.

Mathars indulged in perverse levels of luxury at every conceivable opportunity.

The storm was not a large one, and it would not be necessary to take shelter. Presently, he turned his back upon the sea and returned to his home. He summoned a servant and gave orders that the boy's body be disposed in the usual manner, and the place cleaned up. The servant, a middle aged man, obeyed; he was too frightened of Mathars to ever question him or even consider escape. Only once did he question Mathars. His question cost him his right eye and the power of speech.

Oo'Myyah Mathars was born into a noble family; in one of the Christian communities on Uq'Dyill. His mother died in childbirth. His father, a deacon in a church, was one of those who equated sexual frustration with good morals. Such people are often given to acts of unprincipled machinations and incredible cruelty disguised as religious piety. He treated his only son with a mixture of tenderness, indulgence, ruthless discipline, and didactic oppression that can only be described as bizarre.

The young Mathars was noted for his exceptional intelligence. His scholastic achievements were remarkable. Yet he was also noted as being reclusive, secretive, and adept at manipulating those around him. Some believed him to be prescient. He eventually learned how to manipulate his father, when the elder Mathars grew older. He also showed talent in athletics and martial arts; although he did not display good sportsmanship.

It was in his late childhood that he began to investigate and experiment with sorcery. His early experiments had some frightening results that the maladjusted boy interpreted as success.

When Mathars was 17, he killed his father, using a rare poison that would resemble the effects of a brain hemorrhage, leaving no trace. He inherited his father's property, and immediately went to work performing similar operations upon his relatives. By the time he was 19, he was practically the sole surviving male in his family, and owned his family's entire estate.

He pursued his studies of sorcery a single mindedness that was easy to interpret as obsession. When he was not increasing his knowledge of sorcery and skills in its practice, he was pursuing wealth by whatever means he could, including outright theft and usury (which he was very good at concealing).

His budding sexuality took on dimensions of perversion that were, in this time, rare. His experiments were not confined to gender; and he even had dalliances with djinn.

When he was 23, he joined an underground group of similarly minded people; and by age 30 became its leader. They were called the Secret Order of the Yellow Sign. They believed that through alteration of human will, manipulations of the yogic sciences and mystic traditions both ancient and contemporary, the detailed use of ritual and symbolism, technological method, and the assimilation of life-force energies, they could become god-like beings based on the promptings of their base selves. They practiced what could best be described as a metaphysical gangsterism, and a spiritual vampiric usury.

Their existence was kept secret. They were outlawed on every world; yet had members on several planets: some in positions of political influence. The SOYS's membership was not large. This was true partly because of the secrecy necessary to their survival, and partly because they were constantly feuding and murdering each other.

Their secrecy extended to many of their "followers." Most of the people who served them had absolutely no idea what they were involved in, believing themselves to be serving a noble cause. Their ignorance and naiveté were meticulously cultivated by the SOYS.

314

As the years went by, Mathars' writings were venerated by the SOYS's brethren, and rumors of his books circulated on several planets. Few copies ever fall into the hands of anyone outside the SOYS. Those that did were scrutinized by doctors of religious and secular law. As they were written in a code, they were not understood by anyone outside the SOYS; beyond being sorcery and absolute abomination. These books were not considered publishable.

Some of the members became jealous and envious of him. The stories of the battles with magic were legendary. Mathars always emerged victorious; and was feared.

Mathars became famous among the SOYS for a remarkable accomplishment. He learned how to kill djinn, and absorb their energies in a vampiric fashion. This was not unusual to do to other humans; the SOYS saw this as required study for their practices. But Mathars was the first to do so with djinn.

One document that circulated among the leaders of the SOYS was an outline of a project that Mathars wishes to enact. It involved the summoning and enslavement of a powerful djinn believed to inhabit Uq'dyill. According to theory, this djinn could hold the key to dominating a great percentage of the corporeal worlds, and the unseen. Mathars had been at work upon this project, until it became an obsession. He soon assumed the guise of a medical researcher and emigrated to Uq'dyill.

Many of those who were aware of Mathars designs suspected that he was deliberately withholding data concerning the project, and that some of the data had been deliberately falsified. They were right. Mathars was attempting to play the resources of the SOYS against itself in order that he alone may possess the rewards of his work. One man who attempted to compile evidence against him disappeared. Through subtle legal wrangling, Mathars took possession of all the man's property. Soon thereafter, his family died, in accidents or from rare diseases.

One item in his reports to the SOYS that he did not lie about was that the name of the djinn he sought which was central to his project was unknown. This, it was believed by the other sorcerers, was an extremely dangerous undertaking. One must be able to identify any djinn one is planning on enslaving. A few tried talking Mathars out of this perilous operation. They died soon after.

These problems didn't worry Mathars. He was ambitious, ruthless and greedy, but not careless or sloppy.

Mathars worked at this for over 80 years. Finally, everything was in place. He prepared for the operation with meticulous and leisurely care. He didn't believe that failure was possible.

The resources that Mathars commanded were quite impressive.

His wealth was enormous. He'd set up various economic mechanisms that would direct the flow of wealth to him. Some were usurious interest executed in the most subtle and undetectable ways imaginable. Some was outright theft. He had a network of thieves who would execute his plans – Mathars always taking care to limit his own exposure to the operations – they would steal money, take their cut, and deliver the rest to Mathars.

Mathars had also kept a great number of people in his debt in other ways. He had a genius for cultivating and exploiting human weakness. He would lure people in positions of authority and influence into compromising positions. Then, he owned them. If they refused, or attempted to speak the truth at the cost of their own careers or reputations, Mathars killed them. These assassinations always looked like accidents or deaths by natural causes, and never followed a predictable pattern. Those who were so exposed to Mathars, and who would not speak against themselves, had no choice but to occasionally knowledge the "favor" he did them by covering up their shortcomings. There were other ways Mathars manipulated people psychologically, some of which dated back to the PSY-OPS techniques developed on Earth during the late 20th century.

In these ways, Mathars adroitly manipulated money and politics.

Mathars was also very interested in technology. In this society, religion and science were not seen as two separate things. There was no conflict between them. This also held true with technology. There was no difference between the development of technology and the development of the intrinsic human potential: except that "external" technology (i.e machines, computers, vessels, etc.) was seen as entirely subservient to "internal" technology (i.e. dhikr, meditation, yoga, mastery of mental processes, etc.). The idea of developing technology that would interfere with human free will fascinated Mathars, and he expended considerable wealth and resources in attempting to develop this for his own use. The main idea he kept in the forefront was how to reverse the status of "internal" and "external" technology.

He often experimented on people, with varying results; most of which were disastrous to the subject. Mathars was not worried; he was confident he could cover his tracks.

Yet these were mere accessories compared to how he'd directed the SOYS. Its members were aware of Mathars' power, and some saw within him an almost messianic personality. Mathars had published several writings, conducted elaborate ceremonies, and conducted personal interviews (many of which amounted to brainwashing sessions) that outlined the evolution of the SOYS from a secret society into an oligarchy that ruled human civilization. Drawing on the models of zionism, the religious / mystical elements of nazism, and every example of metaphysical colonization that history had to offer, he built the SOYS into an order of mystic warriors who saw themselves as the only possible rulers of humanity and the djinn. All of the "lesser" populations existed only to serve. And the SOYS would march forward, trampling upon the corpses of all who did not submit. For those who had backgrounds, training, and that particular mindset found among the SOYS's membership, Mathars' diatribes were irresistible, hypnotic and intoxicating.

The comparison between Mathars and Hitler is particularly instructive. Hitler was a 'front man" for people like Haushofer and Ekchart; and they served a dark power that was beyond human. Mathars was different: he served nobody. He was attempting to conquer and absorb those dark powers and make them his own personal slaves. And in so doing, make himself a power greater than all of them. In other words, he was a spiritual cannibal, a metaphysical vampire. And if he couldn't have it, he didn't want anyone to have it. His heart was the essence of pure envy.

Mathars understood the nature of djinn and his effect upon them as well as any human did; perhaps better. He established himself as a formidable presence in their world. Many djinn followed him for the same reasons that humans followed him. He appealed to their metaphysical vanity; offered power and a position of higher purpose.

As for the followers of lesser rank, he found that, despite the strong presence of Islam, he could induce people to accept his ideas if they bore the appearance of Islamic orthodoxy. It was the same as with any despot; find poor, uneducated, frustrated young men, tell them how "special" they are, give them weapons, and tell them "Obey, fight, and die. Do this and attain glory. That's all."

But it was too early to implement this phase of his plan. He was still cementing his own power. And so far, it had gone well, and, with the exception of those who were after him, he'd not attracted unwanted attention to himself.

He would deal with that problem presently.

But the most important piece of the puzzle now was the djinn. It is an ifrit; a powerful djinn that possesses a quality – its being attuned to a unique combinations of harmonics - that will enable Mathars to achieve his objective.

That harmonic came to Mathars' attention through the work of Hqiim Zalluh.

Chapter 22. A Well Planned Strategy.

"So," Babbakh said to the group "We have a plan."

"Yes," Talib said. "Insha Allah, we have a good chance to emerge victorious."

The others made scattered comments in agreement.

For a moment, Talib was silent. The enormity of the task he found himself facing suddenly seized him with horror. He was to go face to face with an enemy that not only could kill him, but had not a shred of mercy or honor. He was assailed with doubts.

He was afraid.

Babbakh sensed this. But said nothing. He knew this would be something Talib needed to work out himself. He'd intervene only if it became necessary. Perhaps when he returned home to his wife,,,

Finally, everyone bid each other farewell, and went their ways. Talib started on his way home.

*****

After traveling two days, Talib returned to Lanajd and rejoined Sudi. His journey had been a quiet one, except for the fear he struggled with.

He'd told her to purchase a house near her tekke, which was also near transportation to Talib's old tekke. He'd only seen the place once, before he had to leave again on his travels. Taking a moment to look at it, he realized it was actually a nice place.

He entered the house they shared, announcing himself. She silently stepped into the room, her vermillion garment flowing around her like an opaque mist.

"So, my husband," Sudi began "what wonders did you meet on this trip?"

"Sit down, my own" Talib said. Sudi sat, knowing something important had happened.

Talib shared the story of what happened, and what he must prepare to do.

"Beautiful one," he said "I am overcome by how big this is! Why me? Why did Allah put me here? I'm not up to such tasks!"

Sudi caressed his face. She knew that even the strongest of men need support and reassurance; especially in the face of such monumental dangers. She looked into his eyes and said "My warrior. My king. Insha Allah, I will contact the elders in the Sisterhood. They must pledge their help to you. They will."

It always seemed to have a calming effect on Talib when Sudi called him "my king." It took the responsibility he felt toward her and directed the effect toward her as recipient of what he could give, as opposed to calling attention to himself as the one who must meet that responsibility. It made his ability to act effortless.

She continued with a liquid tenderness "You ask 'why me?' Why not you? You have been chosen and you have been given all you can possibly need. Allah will not abandon you. Do not abandon yourself to fears that will only strengthen an enemy that can have no mercy. Did not the ancient Prophets all face overwhelming tasks? Allah mentions Musa (as) more than any Prophet. He had great enemies surrounding him at all times. Yet he prevailed, and his enemies were forced to accept humiliating defeats. Your enemies will also be forced to accept humiliating defeats.

"My own; I see your victory. It is my Knowing that tells me this – no less and no more than my love for you."

She pressed the tips of her small fingers into his ears, pressed her other fingers against parts of his temple and face, and smiled. She pressed her forehead against his for a long moment, held her breath, then released him and her breath at the same time. Why she did this, Talib didn't quite understand. He suspected it was part of some energy meridian stimulation technique she'd invented, or experimented on him. Or maybe she simply liked his ears. She never told him. But Talib didn't mind; he rather enjoyed it.

Suddenly Talib realized he wasn't afraid anymore.

*****

Mathars had a large room he'd set up as a temple / workplace for his sorcery. The room was filled with all kinds of images of forms of djinn, reproductions (and sometimes authentic archaeological pieces) from old polytheistic religions, magical implements and weapons, symbols, and altars displaying bizarre items and technology. He lit some foul smelling incense and sat in silence, concentrating his mind on the task at hand.

He then stood and picked up a sword. Intoning an incantation (a haphazard mixture of chants in several languages, devoid of the true essence of the plainchant of ancient religions, and blended into a metaphysical mess), he waved the sword in specific patterns in the air. The air was charged with a noticeable energy that became stronger moment by moment. Mathars placed the sword on an altar, and continued his intoning. The air took on a cold, greasy feeling.

On one of the altars was a deck of cards, a corruption of the old tarot cards Mathars designed and crafted, and a large jet black trapezoidal obsidian with one side polished to a mirror smoothness. Mathars shuffled the deck, and placed four cards face up in front of the mirror. He looked at the images on the cards; a red and black bird feeding on a dead corpse surrounded by three lotus trees, a small man hiding in a dark doorway, a high priest at an altar, and lightning bolts striking a black tower. Memorizing the sequence, he stared into the dark mirror. The shifting images he saw, infused with lies and foulness, told him what he needed to know.

Someone was hunting him. He closed down the ritual, and went to his study to ponder a course of action.

After the ritual, Mathars stood at the base of a tree that grew on his property. Few plants seemed to grow on his property, and nothing else would grow near this tree. It was covered with a sickly black bark, with twisted and misshapen trunk and branches, inedible fruit that damages and corrodes the digestive system, and thorns grew from it that secreted several different poisons. Mathars had often sampled these poisons in small amounts in the form of drugs he'd concocted; oblivious to the real damage they were doing to him.

After all, he believed himself to be invincible. He thought he couldn't die.

He had summoned his assistant. Presently, a boy of about 16 ran to him, stopped, panting to catch his breath, and bowing.

His name was Faar Taearradhib. He was tall, thin, and had a shock of black, greasy hair that hung limp over his head almost to his shoulders. He wore a brown tunic and pants that needed washing. His face was a pockmarked; but an appealing shade of ivory. His eyes were deep blue, and quite attractive; which contrasted with a slightly oversized mouth, and a large, slightly protruding set of teeth. His nose looked as if it had been broken. He fidgeted, and nervously shuffled his feet and wiggled his long fingers.

Faar's mother had died in childbirth. He had unpleasant memories of his father, an irresponsible man who was addicted to opium derivatives who'd abandoned him at the age of nine, and soon after, died from his addiction. Mathars found Faar at an orphanage, and, bribing the caretaker of the orphanage, took him in. Having had no children of his own, Mathars wanted an heir. He'd begun the boy's training at an early age.

Faar having learned much, had become a sorcerer of some skill and power on his own, and believed he was all but assured to inherit everything. The truth was that despite this, he hated Mathars and was always looking for a way to kill him.

Mathars was, of course, perfectly aware of this. It often amused him to occasionally present a feinted weakness, and then remove the opportunity an instant before Faar tried to take advantage of it.

"It took you much too long to answer my summons" Mathars said. The boy began to sweat. They both knew precisely how long it would take for him to arrive. Mathars was playing with him, and Faar didn't much like it. The pattern was predictable; Mathars would point out some flaw or error that was real or imaginary, upbraid the boy, threaten a severe punishment, toy on and off with forgiveness, then usually end up administering a punishment anyway. All the while, making it seem as if Mathars was doing Faar a big favor by "correcting" him.

Despite this, Mathars would always include some kind of useful instruction in the ordeal, and even occasionally offer some gift or reward for "a job well done." In truth, Faar was the only human being Mathars had any feelings for; and this was the only way he knew how to demonstrate it. He seriously thought of placing Faar in the position of public figurehead once the warriors of the SOYS were ready to move against the khaliphite. The boy could be taught charismatic techniques to lead people. Faar would sit upon the throne, and Mathars would be the power behind the throne, pulling the strings.

Faar was aware of all this; and it only increased his deep rooted resentment. It was very dangerous to be disliked by Mathars. Being loved by him was hellish.

This time, however, he did not begin any variation on the sorry, wasteful psychodramas Mathars inflicted upon him. "I have learned" Mathars began, "that someone is attempting to end my career."

Faar knew exactly how this information came to his teacher. For a moment, he thought that Mathars believed that it was he who wanted his demise. Which was marginally true, of course. But Faar had implemented no definite plan. Either a djinn or another sorcerer was betraying him, hoping to gain Mathars' favor, or Mathars was lying, and this was another of his sadistic games.

Unless there was someone else who was plotting against his master. It took Faar a while to arrive at this conclusion; his paranoia being honed to a fine point.

Mathars continued "As far as I have been able to gather, there is one person, supported by a group of people, who are planning to do me in. Evidently they are among Uq'Dyill's *sacred* orders. I do not know which order, or what art or science they emphasize. But they've already set their plans in motion. It is possible they are aware of my *magnum opus*.

"You will go into the cities. Hemmant, Lanajd, and Qalm are most likely where they will be found, one of the nearby retreats will contain the people we're looking for. Look for someone who has experienced a recent initiation of some kind. He will be followed by powerful people and weaklings such as yourself alike. I shall begin to fortify our defenses, and gather our forces for an attack."

"Yes; at once, master" Faar said.

"And Faar," Mathars added, putting his hand on the boy's shoulder "see to it that you are not seen. You attract entirely too much attention to yourself."

"Yes master" Faar said, suppressing his rage, and wishing he'd not touch him. Faar hated it when Mathars touched him, especially at night,,,

*****

Farr had spent time listening to new, to the talk in the restaurants and coffee houses. There had been a great deal of talk lately of that man he'd heard about. The one who traveled through time, and who made Hajj for Uq'Dyill. Of course! He had to be the one. Master would be pleased with this. Faar knew he'd have to check it out, but he was quite sure of his suspicions.

But now he had to get close to the sources of information. How would he get close to this man? He was too famous, and would be surrounded by people who would protect him from casual admirers.

Perhaps he could infiltrate the group in the guise of a follower or a murshid. Perhaps he could even kill him. Mathars would be pleased.

After several days of searching, he found an associate of the Order of Jaz, with whom this man, Talib Ali, belonged. His name was Musawa.

After stalking Musawa for a few days, he figured him to be a relatively weak person who could be induced to surrender all kinds of useful information about this Talib.

One day, he found Musawa in a marketplace. Musawa was searching the vendors for some specific kind of incense. Farr slid up next to him.

"Salaam" Faar said. Musawa returned the salaam.

"You seem to be looking for something that you can't find."

"Yes, "Musawa said. "I am looking for some incense for my Master. It is called 'patchouli', but I cannot find any. It's been a long time I've searched on and off when I could; but I can't find any!"

Faar was thoroughly amused by this innocence and naivete on the part of this little weakling. Why should he concern himself with what his master wants, unless he faced a severe punishment for not finding this patchouli stuff?

"I will help you. My name is Faar Taearradhib."

"Alhamdulillah!" Musawa said. "My name is Musawa Mutawalrrajul."

They went off in search of the mysterious and elusive patchouli.

After another day and no sign of patchouli to be found, Faar made a suggestion.

"I have an idea. We don't know where to find patchouli because we don't know what it is. Why don't we ask your master what it is?"

"I can't,,," Musawa said softly.

"Why?" Faar asked. "Will he beat you?"

"No! My Master treats me with kindness! And he is teaching me everything! I have learned so much from him. I love him. And he is a great man! You don't know the gifts that Allah gave him! It's just that I cannot let myself appear ignorant in front of him. I would be ashamed, especially after all the kindness he has shown me!"

Faar was confused. Why all this frantic searching for this stuff? There was no threat of punishment and no promise of gain that he could see. The idea of it being a labor of love was beyond Faar's comprehension.

Nonetheless, he had to figure out a way to get close to Talib.

"Listen," Faar said. "Why don't you just ask him? I will go with you. He will probably appreciate your honesty." It was a flimsy lie, but it just might work.

After a pause, Musawa said "Very well. Let's go."

*****

"Master!" Musawa called to Talib when he found him with Babbakh.

Talib smiled when he saw Musawa. He really liked the boy a lot, and saw great potential in him, once he overcame that awkwardness.

The boy with him was another story. As soon as Talib and Babbakh looked at him, they knew there was something wrong. He was,,, dirty. Unbalanced. Sexually twisted, as if from being helpless in the face of constant molestation. Foul. Contaminated by something,,,,

Talib and Babbakh glanced at each other. Mathars. Of course.

"Asalaam alaikum!" Talib called out. "Where have you been?"

"I got Master Babbakh the herbs he wants." Musawa said, handing Babbakh a satchel of the herbs. "But Master, I was unable to find any patchouli. In fact,,," he hung his head, "I do not know what patchouli is. Perhaps if my Master could tell me what it is,,,"

Talib looked at him and looked at Farr. Faar was clearly trying to hide both amusement and disgust with a well executed facade of false humility.

"Well," Talib said "don't worry about it. You can look later. We have other more important things to do. You brought a friend, I see."

Musawa said. "This is Faar. I met him while collecting the

items you needed and looking for patchouli. He was helping me."

"Asalaam alaikum, Farr." Talib said. "I thank you for helping my murshid." he held his hand out to shake.

Faar was taken aback. "Masters" (as he understood them) did not make such polite greetings to disciples of low station. And he also knew that if Talib touched him, he may know what is in his mind. The true danger he'd put himself in was becoming apparent to him.

But there was nothing to be done. He held his hand out, and said "Wa Alaikum asalaam."

They shook hands. Talib and Babbakh both noticed the boy's hesitation. And once their hands touched, Talib knew that Mathars was behind this greasy disheveled boy.

In fact, Talib was a bit angry, because this kid exploited Musawa's innocence. His mind raced back into his memories of how many such ruined boys insisted upon taking others down with them. He'd seen so many of his kind.

Faar suppressed both his fear of being detected, and his hatred of being touched. At least this Talib, when he finally got around to - he couldn't say it - probably wouldn't be a brutal as Mathars. But his thoughts had been so absorbed in these unpleasant memories that he wondered if his real motive for being there had been detected. He couldn't tell; he couldn't penetrate Talib's defenses. And who was this other man,,, what was his name? Yes; Babbakh.

Talib released Faar's hand. "Welcome. Would you like something to eat?"

"Yes, thank you." Faar said. He was actually quite hungry.

As they ate, Faar was amazed that Talib and Babbakh ate the same food as Musawa and he. He'd not expected this. Talib and Babbakh spoke to him as if they were interested in him, and as if his opinions carried weight. They could be setting him up.

The conversation went in directions Faar was having trouble following. They were discussing how matters of the spirit affect worldly / material affairs, and vice verse. The general tone of the conversation implied that everyone must be aware of their responsibility toward others, and how what they do affects the spiritual state of others. Faar had no experience with this. Talib brought the conversation around to how many people miss the true meaning of their own spiritual nature, and how they misunderstand the nature of Islam.

"Yes," Talib said, looking gently into Faar's face. "Some people are like stones in the water. You break them in half, and inside they're perfectly dry. The hearts of some people are like stones: surrounded by Islam for centuries, and yet Islam has not penetrated their hearts."

Faar wished they would talk about something else. The thread of this conversation was making him uncomfortable (which Talib and Babbakh noticed). His patience in waiting for information that Mathars would find useful was wearing thin. Unknown to him, Talib and Babbakh were wearing down

Faar's paranoia, and, when the wound in his soul was properly "cleansed," they would "disinfect" it and proceed with the healing process. Faar was in desperate need of this; and at the same time resisted it with every ounce of strength he had.

After five days of this, he'd found no information his master could use against his enemies. In truth, Talib and Babbakh were giving him every piece of knowledge that he needed to understand what they were doing (without exposing themselves to attack). Faar was spiritually and psychologically incapable of seeing what they were doing. He expected details of their attack; magical or otherwise. What they gave him were clues to the true Source of Power. And he could not understand.

Finally, after a few days of this, Faar's patience broke. The pain of his psychic wounds, and the initial process of exposing himself caused his soul to cry out. This took the form of an uncontrolled and utterly irrational attack.

He waited in ambush in a wooded area for Musawa to return from an errand. When he saw Musawa, he struck him in the head with a large stick, kicked him in the leg (just missing the knee), and pulled out a knife to kill him. Musawa, having had martial arts training, partially blocked the blow, but was still dazed but it. Had the kick to his leg been better aimed, he would have lost his balance. He stood firm, but his leg was hurt. He saw the knife coming at him, and managed to deflect its trajectory; but not enough to prevent a large cut on his right forearm. Faar took a step back, and hurled himself toward Musawa. Musawa turned to his right, caught Faar's right arm with his left, pulled him off balance, and with his right hand, slammed it into the back of Faar's right hand, forcing him to release the knife. Then, grounding his right foot, back handed Faar in the face, swung around, and slammed his bleeding forearm into the back of his skull, knocking him out.

Musawa called for help. Pauqal had been within earshot, and had sensed something was wrong during the brief fight. He arrived to find Faar unconscious and Musawa hlding his bleeding arm. Improvising a bandage, Pauqal sent Musawa back to the camp, tied Faar's hands behind his back with some cloth he tore from his tunic, and dragged him back to the camp.

Talib was not there, having left to inspect one of Luthor's defenses. Shuzh Ti tended to Musawa's injured arm. The whole time, she made jokes about amputations, leeches, and other mad medical procedures in such a way that Musawa laughed his way through an otherwise painful experience. Pauqal and Babbakh secured Faar, and when he came to consciousness, began to question him. He would tell them nothing; and cursed them for what he believed was their naiveté.

Soon, Talib and Luthor arrived. After having been informed of what happened, and being assured Musawa would be OK, Talib and Babbakh exchanged glances. Babbakh was thinking that Faar was too dangerous to let go free, and too much of a drain on resources to keep as a prisoner. His solution to the problem was as obvious as it was grim. Talib had another idea.

"Faar" Talib began "you could not have just come out of nowhere. You are not simply some criminal." Faar stared at him. He'd expected a question: something like 'Who do you work for? Why are you here?" Talib started with a statement. How much did he know? Had Talib known all along what he was doing? Did he know he worked for Mathars?

As if on cue, Talib said "You work for Mathars."

"I'm not telling you anything!" Faar hissed. The defiance he tried to project could not hide his desperation and fear. Talib said "And I'm not asking. I knew what you were up to the minute I saw you. There's nothing you can tell me that I don't already know. You were sent by Mathars. You are spying on us, and when you couldn't find what you were looking for, you lost control, and gave yourself away."

Faar's blood ran cold. He was truly trapped. His enemies had him, and knew he couldn't return to Mathars. He ran out of options. In the past, he would often play khosos with Mathars. Mathars was a brilliant player, and often beat him in the most cruel and humiliating ways he could devise. This was that same feeling, of being trapped, helpless, and seeing in hindsight how he'd been manipulated into walking into a trap. But there would be no game after this; the stakes were final.

"As you can see, I have a problem to solve" Talib continued. "This is what I'm faced with. You infiltrated my community to spy on us and use whatever intelligence you could find against us. You also attacked and injured a dear friend."

Faar was confused. Friend? How could a servant (or slave) be a friend? This didn't add up. What was going on that he couldn't see?

Talib continued "Now, after you gave yourself away, I have to make a decision what to dod with you. It would be simple to kill you, I suppose." At this Faar gave up. He resigned himself to his fate. He was dead. There was nothing he could do, no way out.

"There's another option,,," Talib said.

Faar went cold. He was going to be tortured. He'd seen how Mathars handled such situations. The sight repelled and disgusted him; but he had to do his part and dared not disobey his master. Now, he would be on the receiving end. Doubtless the others, especially Musawa, would take great delight in their part in this. Death would be better.

Talib immediately sensed Faar's interpretation of what he'd said. Truthfully, he had not meant to imply or threaten this. Such was not in Talib's nature. What Talib really wanted from Faar was something very different.

Talib walked away from Faar. He watched as Talib took Musawa aside and spoke to him. Now Faar was convinced he'd be tortured. In desperation, he tried to think of a way to commit suicide. But his mind would not function analytically now. He was close to being reduced to simple animal survival.

After what seemed like an eternity, but was only ten minutes, Talib, Musawa, Babbakh, Pauqal and Luthor surrounded him. This was it, thought Faar. He was close to blacking out.

Talib spoke. "I offer you an option. Renounce Mathars and everything he ever taught you and all his beliefs, and tell us all you know about what he is planning. Take your place at our side. Swear allegiance and service to us. In exchange, we will protect you from him, and you will be treated with the dignity and respect Mathars never gave you. All you did and tried to do will be forgiven."

Faar didn't understand. He literally could not believe his ears. "I,,, I don't understand." he said after a long pause.

"You heard me. This is the offer. Join us, and live as one of us, with all the rewards and responsibilities. The other option, well, I need not elaborate. The choice is yours alone."

Talib said this with an unmistakable tone of clinical coldness; but in his heart, he was desperate to find a way to avoid having to kill Farr. He truly believed that his ruined life could be salvaged.

"You'll protect me from Mathars? You can do this?" Faar asked.

Talib said "I swear it."

Tears fell from Faar's eyes. His defenses were breaking down as fast as his preconceived ideas. He was at the mercy of a man who not only could kill him, and had every reason to do so; but also defied and posed a real threat to Mathars, whom Faar had seen as all powerful and invincible. Yet, Talib was offering mercy. It took a moment for Faar to realize what was happening; it was only with effort that he recognized an act of mercy for what it was.

Faar said "I have never known forgiveness or mercy. When you spoke of these things, I didn't understand you. I'm still not really sure what you're talking about; I don't know what forgiveness or mercy is,,,"

Talib stood, waiting; his companions at his side.

"What do I do? How do I,,, I mean, how do you live like this? What is it? What am I supposed to do,,,,?"

Talib said "Your answer, Faar."

A long pause. "I accept your offer." Faar said in a half whisper.

"Untie him." Talib said, to nobody in particular. Musawa untied him.

As Musawa was undoing the binding, Faar said "I'm sorry about what happened."

"Let it go. We have more important things to do." Musawa said. Faar looked at Musawa. There was no anger, bitterness, or hidden hate in his eyes. Was this forgiveness?

Babbakh said "Sit." Everyone sat in a circle. "Now," Babbakh said. "Tell us everything you can about Mathars."

Faar kept his word, and told them everything. His narrative went on for hours. It was more like a confession and an emotional catharsis than a report for use as a battle plan. At times he would weep, incapable of speaking. Much of what he revealed shocked and disgusted them. But what he told them was of incalculable value.

*****

In the crowded marketplace of lower Lanajd, Talib and Musawa (whose injuries were healing nicely, despite walking with a limp, and bearing a scar he would have the rest of his life) stood outside the coffee house that was patronized by the thinkers, scientists, and artists of the city. Items were bought and sold. People haggled over prices, money was exchanged, bargains struck. Talib knew someone was watching him, but couldn't pinpoint who.

Suddenly, a man appeared near him, made his presence known.

It was Mathars.

Their eyes locked. Mathars said "I'm pleased to meet you."

Talib looked at him. So, this was Mathars. His great enemy. Would he begin a fight here? Would he attack him in a crowded place like this?

Musawa was an instant away from attacking Mathars; but Talib made a tacit command to hold back. Mathars was amused, and impressed at how disciplined the young man was. Talib was still quite wary of his enemy, and stood ready for anything.

Out of habit, Talib almost said "Asalaam alaikum," but the words stuck in his throat.

Mathars sensed Talib's apprehension – took it as a compliment, in fact – and said "Not to worry, confused wanderer. I will not start an altercation here. This material realm is so vulgar an arena for so glorious a battle. May I buy you a cup of coffee?"

Talib looked at him, and said "I'm buying."

"As you wish!" Mathars said decorously, with an indefinable sarcastic overtone.

They entered the coffee house. Talib bought two cups of inexpensive coffee, never taking his attention from Mathars; never permitting Mathars to touch his cup. They sit down at a corner table. He placed a cup in front of Mathars with his left hand; and Mathars understood the gesture.

"Will you begin, or should I?" Talib said

"Tell me," Mathars said "did you enjoy seeing your former home on earth? Was its present stage of development to your liking?"

"You invited me here to taunt me with stupid questions?"

"Just trying to become acquainted" Mathars said.

"That aside, I'm going to be as candid with you as possible" he went on. "Your career has been of great interest to me. I've studied your progress since your arrival. Your performance has been, to say the least, impressive.

"No doubt you have heard of the Secret Order of the Yellow Sign. Admittedly, we are, shall I say, somewhat unorthodox and arcane. But our doctrines and philosophies are not what people believe them to be. I want to make our beliefs and objectives clear to you before the situation between us passes beyond a point of no return.

"We believe in the same thing you believe in. Our cosmology is like yours. The area where we diverge is in humanity's place in this cosmic hierarchy – and specifically, in the idea of will. Free will and all the possibilities and potentials that go along with it.

"You have doubtless noticed that most of the human race is not quite 'human' in the sense of their understanding of the self. They have no capacity for intellectual or spiritual growth, or for independent thought. They are like livestock. Now, before you say anything, please hear me out on this. You know I'm right. It doesn't matter if it was during your time in earth's antiquity or now that we have traveled the cosmos and accomplished so much. Mankind has changed very little, and never will.

"Yet within man is the essence of what we are as evolved beings. Our animal nature will never go away. It is indestructible; and all the efforts of the so-called mystics have accomplished nothing to bring mankind as a whole to a higher state. Therein is the truth: this indestructible aspect contains the key, the potential for the next stage of your evolution. The truth is, the spirit serves the flesh; not the other way around.

"You think you are serving Allah; but Allah made us what we are, and in all my travels, studies, and efforts, I have seen that it is our nature we must serve, as it will serve us.

"Thus, the next stage of evolution is not something we must wait for, blindly, like an animal, or the livestock humans that work, procreate, and wait to die. They are useless as anything but slaves or food; and you know it. We have the power to understand and direct that evolution according to our will.

"This is what I have devoted my life to.

"Now; as I said, I have seen what you have been through. It amazes me how far you have come! To be sure, we meet here as enemies under a flag of truce; but I must confess you have more than earned my respect and admiration.

"So, I have a proposal. Let us end our hostilities. I will overlook all you have done, including brainwashing my former heir. You may have him. But rather than merely ceasing hostilities, why not unite our efforts? Let us join forces. If I am any judge of what your own objectives are, yours are not all that dissimilar to mine. So why should we fight? We are already like brothers – and we are bonded in many subtle ways.

"I will even give you a leadership position in the Secret Order of the Yellow Sign. You will enjoy a position near to my station.

"I am offering you much more than I ever offered anyone else. All I ask in return is an alliance. All I require is for you to be honest with yourself, and realize we were always on the same path, headed toward the same goal.

"Think it over. I will be in touch with you soon for you answer."

Talib looked at Mathars. His performance, his body language, vocal inflections, facial movements, all designed to invoke trust and the illusion of sincerity. All were perfectly executed. Yet Talib was not taken in by any of it.

"Mathars, the answer is no. I will not accept your offer, nor will I stray from my path. You have nothing I want, and I will surrender nothing to you."

Mathars stared at Talib. His face a mask. Taking a slow drink from his coffee, and taking a deep breath, he stood.

Calmly, he said "So be it. We shall meet at the appointed place. You shall regret your decision. And I will do what must be done. But know this; I will do it with some reluctance. I still see within you a kindred spirit – at least potentially so. But there is a truth I'd overlooked. We are not only warriors, we are predators whose function is to thin the herd. We must kill in order to become what we are destined to. So shall it be."

Chapter 23. Jihad: its Realities and Results.

Mathars walked out. Talib and Musawa went out, taking a different route back to their headquarters. Talib gave Musawa a special dhikr to make while they traveled.

When they returned, Talib told Babbakh and the others what had happened and what Mathars had said. Faar was among them. He was still fearful of Mathars; and in awe of the fact that Talib could face him, and walk away.

Shuzh Ti said "He could have been lying."

"Or he could have given me enough of the truth to try to invoke fear. His offer to join him was an interesting tactic" Talib said. "Maybe he's not as sure of himself as he thinks he is. This could be an advantage."

"Brothers" Babbakh said with a tone of command in his voice. "The time has come. Everyone to their positions. Musawa, alert the Sisterhood, and return here immediately with whatever message they have to give. And if they give anything to you personally, do not refuse to accept it. When you return, I have a special job for you."

"May I know what it is now?" Musawa asked.

"Your master Talib will be leaving this world and invoking baraka on himself; and engaging the foulness of the Unseen that Mathars commands and embodies. You will stay and protect his physical body. Construct a strategy, I will give you men to command. This will be your part."

"Me? In command,,,?" Musawa asked, astonished.

Talib said "Mus, I trust you with my life."

Babbakh added "We all trust you. I can think of no one better suited to the job than you."

*****

The Sisterhood of the Mountain of Light, led by Sudi bint Abdultawwab, assembled their dhikr group immediately after Musawa left.

Before he left, Sudi said "You will tell the men that all is in place, we have our part of the Jihad ready. And you will tell Talib something. It is in his mother language. repeat after me,,,"

She enunciated a phrase in 21st century English that she'd learned, which Musawa didn't understand. He memorized it and repeated it to her satisfaction.

"Musawa, "Sudi said "This is for you." She handed him a signet ring made of a silver and iron alloy covered with a thin, hard ceramic. It had Ayatul Kursi engraved in nearly microscopic calligraphy. "Know that you have earned my eternal respect and gratitude for what you are doing. Talib loves you like his own son, and so do I. Be the warrior we all know you are. No, Musawa: do not protest and do not say anything. Just act. The truth is that many great deeds throughout human history have been done by common people. All of history bears witness to this, Masha Allah. You will, on this day, rise to the heights of the elect."

Musawa was speechless. Despite Talib's encouragement and instruction, nothing could have prepared him for the honor that these great people had done him. All this because he insisted upon learning to play the flute! Allah is indeed the Subtle!

He had nothing else to say or do here; so he gave his salaams, and left.

The women began with a lengthy meditation.

The practice of dhikr among the Sisterhood of the Mountain of Light was both a monument to sincerity toward Allah, and a mathematical and linguistic masterpiece. Intricate rhythms derived from the traditions of ancient earth and the surviving records of music theories of the Gheing Zaa, and methods from the Djjil'arghnab'vhaqq were masterfully used. Their dhikrs were effective on a subatomic level.

The dhikr that Sudi led consisted of a chant backed by percussion. The percussion parts used a rhythm based on multiples of varying tempos based on a rhythmic cycle of 19 beats. The phrasing and beat groupings were derived from the first five Fibonacci Primes 2, 3, 5, 13, and 89. There were always 17 participants in such dhikrs, each having a specific function. The words of their dhikr consisted of Qur'an (in a tajwid style that their ancestors devised over a thousand years ago), and a series of words or phrases in Arabic, Hebrew, Sanskrit, classical Zaa'ee (an old language from Zaa), and modern Qamath.

*****

Mathars cloistered himself within his temple, facing his alter. He lit candles of various colors at specific directions and intervals form the center of the room. Within the center of the room was a circle inscribed upon the floor in lead and gold, with arcane names in arcane symbols. Next to the circle, Mathars had drawn an asymmetrical shape in red and black paint made from a variety of substances. Within its center an iron cauldron burned a hand crafted incense that hung in the air, undisturbed by drafts in the sealed room. Carefully, Mathar's used his ceremonial dagger, and slaughtered a dove, a cat, and a small primate forming a triangle around the incense. Then, entering the circle, and invoking his own energies with gestures and incantation, he ascended to a realm more subtle than the physical world. There, he commanded the djinn he's long sought to visible appearance. It appeared, and Mathars, nauseated, commanded it to assume a pleasing form, and to keep its smell to itself.

Grudgingly, the djinn obeyed. It watched Mathars; studied him, searching for weaknesses. It was resentful of having been summoned from its place. It was, as many djinn are, out of harmony with itself, and with creation. It held on to secrets, a disordered scrap heap of bits of hidden wisdom it never examined or put into a useful context, which it guarded with a demented jealousy. Yet now, it was being forced out into the open; and it didn't like it one bit.

Mathars was aware of this, and didn't care. The djinn was his to command. He would wield this weapon against his enemy, and then against all humanity.

Talib and Babaakh sat in deep meditation. Babaakh had prepared a mixture of incenses and an infusion of herbs that would assist Talib in his astral travels. This infusion did not contain the same psychoactive substances that Babaakh would use for himself, as Talib's body chemistry could not withstand them, and he lacked the training to properly control their effects. Talib would never have ingested it in any case. It would, however, help to open the channels and facilitate the changes in the Ruh that was needed for the task at hand. Babaakh had also set up several sound producing devices about the room to entrain the mind and body.

At the tekkes of the Ikhwan al-Jaza'a, and the Sisterhood of the Mountain of Light, the believers kept a powerful dhikr. Their concentration focused upon Talib and his jihad. They began with a lengthy meditation. A single idea focused into the area beyond space-time. The ancient scientists of earth called this subatomic energy. The advanced Sufis of these times could summon them, and other forces, by a conscious act of will. Technology was a matter of developing the self: external machinery had become for the spiritual teacher and student a mere accessory: a prosthetic of human consciousness and imagination. But not always a necessity. This explained why a people who could travel among the stars and build architectural impossibilities preferred to sleep in tents and cook their food over an open fire.

The dhikr continued with a chant in rhythms based on multiples of varying tempos based on the same rhythmic cycle and patterns the Sisterhood of the Mountain of Light used. They used flutes, membranophones, and metallophone percussion instruments. Each one was hand made and build to specific dimensions and from exacting combinations of metals and woods. The musical parts played on these complimented the vocal chants.

The dhikrs of all the gatherings at all their locations were meticulously timed and synchronized. This was difficult; they'd never attempted anything like this before. But it worked quite well.

Musawa was among them. He had a group of twenty seven men; all trained in the warrior arts. He positioned them in strategic areas, and assigned them areas to protect. It would have been impossible for anyone to approach the area without being detected. and with Musawa's distribution of forces, any individual group could help no less than three groups in their immediate vicinity. He took the greatest advantage of the landscape and foliage, and even made use of the whether patterns. In truth, his strategy was flawless. Everyone saw this, and were impressed with his natural aptitude for military operations.

*****

At the house of Babaakh, the two men, knowing that the two orders were supporting them, consecrated the area they were working in. Talib chanted several ayats from the Qur'an, and Babaakh lit candles and the special incense he'd crafted for this occasion. Then they began their dhikr and meditation.

Talib saw the walls surrounding the circle dissolve. The furnishings flew away.

He stood at the peak of a mountain. Clouds, red like blood, flew across the dark sky. Stars reached out to him from their terrible distances. He approached a precipice, and dove over the side. He glided down and down into a deep valley surrounded by sheer rock. At the bottom was a river of emerald green water. He hovered over it, reached down, and drank. The river spoke to him; myths, histories, warnings, poetry.

Angels looked on. Djinn hovered in dark corners, hoping to see or hear something, searching for a weakness. But frightened; never daring to come too close.

Talib flew to the axis of the universe and intoned verses from the Qur'an.

The firmament answered him back.

He spoke the names of the things around him, names of angels. Old names, known to Adaam, and forgotten to all but a few.

Finally, Talib made a dua to meet his angel.

Then, standing before him was the very angel that Allah had assigned him at the dawn of creation. They knew each other.

It is beyond the capacity of the English language to describe what an angel "looks like." And the fact that their forms are transient in a way that is more subtle than that of a human body makes the act of describing one "form" somewhat futile. Nevertheless, suffice it to say that Talib saw the higher essence of his self.

The angel stood before Talib, and emitted a name consisting of 2182 letters.

It was Talib's True Name. The Name his father Adaam would have known him by.

Finally, after this ceremonial greeting, the angel spoke. The words the angel spoke were of such power that they reverberated and penetrated Talib's entire being. He briefly remembered the famous Hadith where the Prophet (sas) described receiving Qur'anic Revelation like "a bell." Talib finally understood what this meant; and wondered how the Prophet (sas) tolerated 23 years of this.

In English, the angel's statement was, more or less, as follows:

The Angel embraced the Soul in potent embracing, set him in an office.
The Soul, frightened, but resolute.
Thus his heart spoke:
"Brother, with favor look upon me. Remember me in the Life's Presence."
The Angel replied

"Wake up and meet yourself.

You, who give ear to Discourse, the Truth and the Light has risen upon us, and our honor is approved in the Realm of Light upon Light.

Everyone who gives ear to your voice, will be in the pure region included.

In Life's Treasury will he be included and splendor will rise over him tenfold.

For everyone who gives not ear to your voice, wakefulness and sleep will be in ruins.

I and thou will circle aloft and, victorious, mount to the Heights.

But you will tower over your own charges who shall receive the Mysteries of the Ineffable.

They will be on your right and on your left, and you are they, and they are you.

But not yet.

Through the Beautiful Names find praise and assurance.

In each Beautiful Name you may ascend and behold the Light's region.

Refutation of all heresies and vanities.

Life's Treasury awaits you; power irresistible.

Humble yourself! Did you author this power?

Wear the cloak; it is a command irresistible. Decisions have been made.

"Fear you hearsay - lest you witness the chains of Law broken?

*No; banish all fears. They do not break, for they are not
chains; they are tethers of safety.
Enter the waters still, and drink deep.
The disciplines are a tent that protects the tribe from the
midday sun,
And the overwhelming mysteries of the night.
But of what use is a tent in a rose garden?
Or a prayer rug on a sinking ship?
What does this mean? Soon you will know."*

*"Oh Soul; heir apparent;
An abyss waits before you, and death waits behind you.
Do you fear the precipice?
Safe havens kind to frail human mortality call you like a siren;
But I am stronger.*

*"Oh Soul:
Know; you are not Musa! You are not Muhammad!
Do not lay down any law like a lawgiver;
Do so, and be constrained by it, to your ruin.
But you shall wield a weighty position.
Do you wonder at this, if matter will be destroyed or not?
All nature, all formations, all creatures exist in and with one
another, and they will be resolved again into their own
primordia.
For the nature of matter is resolved into the primordia of its
own nature alone.*

354

There is no sin of the world, but it is you, oh Bani Adaam, who make sin when you do things that are unlike the nature of your own essence, which is within and without all things.

Forget our Sajdah to you?

No! All things are remembered.

Matter gave birth to a passion that has no equal, which proceeded from something contrary to nature.

Then there arises a disturbance in its whole body.

It is a wild beast you ride! Be strong! Beware that no one lead you astray saying; here! or there!

For the whole universe is within you, but you do not see it."

"The Struggle is engaged; there is no turning back.

The Soul is assailed at every step and as the struggler struggled, the Soul saw the dark power

It asked the Soul, "Whence do you come and where are you going? In wickedness and entropy are you bound. Do not judge! I did not see you descending, but see you ascending. Why do you lie since you belong to me?"

The Soul answered and said, "I saw you. You did not see me nor recognize me. I served you as a garment and you did not know me. Why do you judge me, although I have not judged you?

"I was bound, though I have bound no one.

"I was not recognized. But I have recognized that the All is dissolving both the earthly things and the heavenly things.

"These injustices I suffered, and I burned, as gold in a furnace.

"What binds me has been slain, and what turns me about has
been overcome,
"But my desire and ignorance have not died; for they were
never alive.
"I was released from the yoke of oblivion which is transient,
and powerless.
"I attain to the remainder of time in silence.
"The light that was created is a rainbow split from darkness.
"A new world will arise; creation is not yet complete."

"When the Soul said this, it went away rejoicing greatly.
Yet a further trial awaited.
There is war. There is a gate, and before it is a gatekeeper;
furious like a jealous lover.
There is a slave of his inner "nowhere" that lies and covets and
envies and betrays his own self.
Cut the tether; and fear nothing.
He will fall in shame and cowardice when his falsehood is
exposed.'

"Oh Soul; who hears the Call of the Ever Living,
Oh Soul; of open heart and discerning mind.
Oh Soul; renouncing the illusions of this world
Oh Soul; embrace the Gnostic, walk on the Path of Peace
Oh Soul: prepare to ascend.
The Garden you were promised is close,
The Bridal Chamber of the Word and Spirit from Allah is close,

And the One is ever closer.

Remember, and remember.

What is hidden from you I will proclaim to you.

Soon you will remember the Thirty Worlds before yours.

Soon you will remember the Worlds yet to be.

You will never have need.

Blessed are you that you did not waver at the sight of of the Struggle.

He does not see through the soul nor through the mind, but that which is between the two that is what sees the vision

For beyond this gate is a Treasure.

Power within Light.

Light within you."

Each word the angel spoke was an experience that transformed him. Each truth the angel revealed was now and forever written within the fabric of Talib's being. This was initiation into a new mystery.

A staircase appeared in front of him. The angel told him to ascend.

As he ascended, always approaching each level with great caution and reverence. Each step revealed new truths and confirmed truths he already knew.

His angel accompanied him. When they reached the top of the staircase, another angel appeared. He handed Talib a staff and a sword. The staff was two staffs intertwined. He realized that these were of the same kinds of staffs of Musa and

Suliman. The sword was a two blade sword of light, like that of Hazrat Ali. These would be his to wield in his battles. Nothing could withstand these weapons and seats of authority.

At this, Talib heard a Chord. This Chord consisted of twelve Notes that interchanged and harmonized, and re-harmonized with each other; the overtones shifting to form new harmonies every fraction of a nanosecond. The whole of creation was represented and symbolized in this Chord; but this was no dead symbol. It was a living thing that spoke a vast Truth again and again, always new, always alive. And beyond the twelve Notes was a thirteenth Note. Nobody knows what that Note is: only Allah.

This Chord preceded a Book. It was the Qur'an.

The Qur'an opened.

Each verse in the Book manifested as doorways. Each letter was a universe in itself. The shape of the ancient script revealed secrets that few human beings anticipated and fewer would ever comprehend.

With great humility, Talib approached and invoked the 99 Names of Allah. The verses opened, and invited him to enter.

What he saw is beyond the capacity of human language to describe. Talib would never have words for it.

He was now ready to face Mathars.

*****

A place in a different dimension, a realm normally veiled from physical senses, was prepared for the battle. Physical bodies wherein Ruh had been condensed were of secondary consideration (yet not without their importance, and effect); their lack of spatial proximity was not important. Talib arrived, and saw Mathars standing in a circle of yellow light diffused with changing symbols. An asymmetrical shape of lights of ugly contrasting color was to Mathars' immediate left. Instantly, Talib gathered his own energies, and commanded into existence a sphere around himself. The sphere contained the qualities and attributes of his angel, and the weapons that Allah had given him. There were no weak points.

All around them, beings human and otherwise who were loyal to Talib, and other such beings in bondage to Mathars stood, separate, unable to participate as anything but witnesses.

Talib took his sword in his right hand, and his staff in his left. The battle began.

Mathars first attack was straightforward. He was testing Talib; almost insulting him with the simplicity of his attack. Talib responded with a block, and a feint. He followed with a "blast" of energy that harmonically countered what he sensed came from his enemy. The two combatants exchanged blows like this for a time.

The djinn snarled. A flaming burst of blind hate flew from the djiin toward Talib. Talib deflected it, and attempted to neutralize it. He was fighting defensively, Mathars noted. He interpreted this as a tactical advantage, and a sign that Talib was frightened. He commanded the djinn to read into Talib's mind. This was not easy; as Talib's defenses were quite formidable. But the djinn, at Mathars' urging, probed, looking for weaknesses.

Talib gathered his energy, invoked Baraka, set his breath into motion, and began a dhikr that synchronized with the movement of his sword and staff. He used a fighting technique his teachers taught him of getting his opponent into a rhythmic pattern, then, abruptly changing the pattern to throw off the opponent's balance. This had the desired effect; Mathars was weakened, disoriented. He countered with recitation of Qur'an, but outside the verse's context, and with select words altered or removed. Talib was ready for this, and countered with the real ayats. Mathars invoked a harmonic of his qi, and created a blast of dissonance in Talib's own qi. Talib struggled to regain his balance. Pain shot through one of his meridians, as the normal flow of energy was disrupted. With some effort, he redirected the normal flow of his life energy; and he readied his weapons.

While this was happening, the djinn probed Talib's mind and memories. Finding something he could use, it waited until Talib was at a crucial point in his defense. Then, it took the form of Talib's mother and father.

"Russell!" the djinn said in his mother's voice. "Why did you do this to us? Why did you abandon us the way you did?" The djinn assumed the appearance and voice of his father; "Your mother and I loved you, Russ. You went off and wasted your life with that rock band. You embarrassed us, and made your family a disgrace! Then you joined that stupid religion, and just left us! Your mother's heart was broken! I died of cancer, and your mother was all alone!"

Talib knew this was a lie. He's taken good care of his mother after his father's passing. But the words still stung in a sensitive area of his emotions.

"Russell," the djinn said in Talib's mother's voice and form "Your father and I love you!"

The djinn shifted back to his father's voice and form. "We loved you and gave you everything. And you wasted it, you threw it all back in our faces! How could you be so selfish and ungrateful?"

The djinn then assumed the form of Talib's grandfather, who'd died when he was in his teens. "Russell, where were you when I was dying? I was all alone. You were off somewhere having fun or playing that damned guitar, I suppose. I was in that nursing home, waiting, hoping to spend just an hour with you. And you left me there to die!" As he said this, the image became progressively weaker, and more decrepit and decomposed, until a skin and bones corpse stood in its wake; pointing an accusing finger.

Suddenly the djinn took the form of his old friend Eddie. "Russ! You let me die. You knew I was too drunk to drive that night! You followed me, and just hung back, and waited for me to kill myself. I'm in hell, Russ! I'm in hell, and it's your fault! You let me go here! You didn't even try to save me! You never even wanted to give me a way out of this, even though you could have done it any time you wanted!"

Then the djinn took the form of a woman Talib knew in his jahaliyyah. She was one of Russell's lovers; a woman whose sexual attractiveness was nothing short of astonishing. The physical features that Russell found most appealing and memories of their peccadilloes were paraded before Talib's mind.

All of this was, Talib knew, an illusion and a lie. He knew that this was the deceptions of an intelligent ifrit in bondage to his arch enemy. But it still gnawed at his emotional sensitivities.

Mathars attacked again. Talib was dazed by the blows to his life force; all to areas opened up by the djinn's illusions.

The djinn's illusions took a decidedly cruel turn. Standing before him was the image of Zeinab. She met Talib's eyes. She was crying. She held a dead baby in her hands. "Our son" the image of Zeinab said. The baby opened his eyes and made a pitiful whine.

Talib held his ground and ignored the pain, knowing it was all a lie.

Then the djinn attacked. Its attack was more akin to that of a wild animal. The speed and ferocity of it started Talib; the djinn was not behaving as it had. It's first attack was intelligent, strategic. Now it was losing all composure, and simply lashing out. Talib interpreted this as a good sign. He saw the real reason for it; the djinn hated its bondage to Mathars, and wanted its freedom more than anything. This was a weak spot for both of them. He held his ground against the djinn, holding it at bay with his staff, and continued to deflect Mathars' attacks.

Apart from the intense concentration necessary to fight these two enemies simultaneously, the most difficult thing he found was in controlling his anger and sorrow. The images of his long dead loved ones continued. Family, friends, loved ones, all appeared and disappeared in succession while he fought. The effect it had on him indicated an area he'd not mastered; and now his life was in danger because of it.

There was a volley of blows which temporarily disoriented Talib. He slashed at Mathars with his sword, and Mathars had barely deflected the attack; but this was less controlled, wild and almost random. Not good; he needed control. While Talib struggled to regain his guard, inner balance, and mastery of his weapons, Mathars blasted him with qi. Talib was blinded; this was more than he'd expected, and nothing in Mathars' previous attack indicated he'd possessed such power. Mathars had been toying with him; this blow was his way of saying "Well done, boy. You have a little talent. Now, let us play this game for real stakes." Talib was concerned, but did not relent. His own strength was waning, his defenses were seriously challenged. The possibility of him losing this battle was showing its face – and for the first time, Talib was worried. His very soul was threatened by a level of danger he'd not been prepared to face.

A vicious series of attacks, feints, deflections and blocks followed. Talib was becoming angry. Mathars sent him a vibe that seemed to express amusement at his anger. The djinn was becoming more and more mindless, completely immersed in a blind rage that was becoming more and more difficult to withstand, and, Talib began to notice hopefully, more and more difficult for Mathars to control. He sensed that much of this blind rage was actually directed toward Mathars! The demented sorcerer was simply redirecting that rage at Talib.

But Talib was wondering how long he could keep this up. His very soul was becoming fatigued. His weapons were becoming heavier and more difficult to wield. His vision dimmed.

Suddenly, without warning, a wave of light, of renewed strength filled Talib. His defenses became strengthened and his senses and awareness were sharpened to the point of utter clarity. He recognized this: it was Sudi's presence that shielded and revitalized him. She "stood" in a place far from the battle and was in no danger; but she lent her own strength to Talib; and it was in the form of pure love.

*****

Musawa was at his post, camouflaged and silent. His partners, two men, Seif and Hameed waited with him. Pauqal and Luthor held their positions to the north and west of Musawa's post. The others were in their positions.

Musawa had devised an interesting series of subtle communications between the groups. Natural ambient sounds would be imitated; forming a code. Soft rustling of the foliage from specific directions that changed at unpredictable patterns determined by the direction of the wind were used to indicate that all was well. No sound was to be investigated as a possible sign of trouble. If someone saw a possible danger, one of the members of group would make a sound imitating a kudota (a small mammal indigenous to the planet) in patterns of three. If an individual or group was attacked, either the imitation of a pukkhwa bird, or all out fighting would indicate this.

For almost two hours, there was no sign of trouble. The signals were all good.

Suddenly, Musawa saw a color, very briefly, in a bush that didn't belong there. He pointed it to Seif. Seif was more skilled at imitating a kudota than he was and gave the signal. The other group responded, and crept in the shadows to investigate.

A figure in the dark leaped forward toward Seif. Seif side, but not quickly enough to prevent being cut on his left biceps. The man attempted a backhand with the knife hand, but Seif deflected the blow, and Musawa leapt at him, and snapped the man's neck. Pauqal's group had moved in to help. While this was happening, three men took advantage of their moving away from their post and tried to get past the defenses. Musawa signaled silently, despite Pauqal's group being immediately aware of the breech in the parameter, and he and Pauqal's men intercepted two of the three intruders, killing them. The third managed to make his way almost to the building where Talib and Babbakh were engaged in their ceremonial battle; but he was caught. One of Pauqal's men was going to kill him, but Musawa commanded him to be taken prisoner.

Luthor's group, meanwhile, had intercepted two other men. A third man from among the intruders had managed a retreat. They were taken prisoner.

All three prisoners were bound and gagged. Seif was assigned to guard them. A bandage was improvised, and the bleeding wound was under control, and he assumed guard.

When Musawa, Pauqal, and Luthor returned with their groups, they found five other men breaching the parameter. They outflanked them and, after some minutes of savage hand to hand combat, defeated them. One man was injured. There were no survivors among this group of intruders.

Meanwhile, Shuzh Ti's group to the south, seven men under her command, encountered a group of invaders. Their battle was victorious, and the intruders had no reinforcements. One man from the group Shuzh Ti commanded, Mahmoud, suffered a broken collarbone, and a man named Jafar was killed.

But the ceremonial area was safe.

*****

Talib was no longer part of the battle. There was no Talib. The malignancies that fought what they thought was Talib now opposed a force of nature whose every movement was as natural as water seeking its level. They found no target, no flesh to sink their knife into, no spirit to poison. The entire momentum of the universe was behind every move, every breath, every expenditure of energy. The sword in the right hand met no obstacle or resistance, the staff in the left hand could not be moved, but could move whatever the hand that held it commanded.

Mathars was becoming concerned. For the first time in his life, the possibility of failure and defeat came to his mind. This was not something he'd ever thought possible. His previous successes had seduced him, lied to him, and made him utterly unprepared for what he was now beginning to understand.

Mathars, desperate to gain the upper hand in the fight, commanded the djinn to attack.

Talib readied his weapon. The djinn dropped his guard and could have been hurt by Talib. To his utter astonishment, Everything Talib did was purely defensive. He could have wounded or killed the djinn, and didn't. It was confused. Talib had several perfect chances to burn the djinn, yet showed it mercy. None among any of the Bani Adaam had ever shown this djinn mercy, kindness, or respect before now. It struck the djinn to the core of its being that this Bani Adaam was not like the foul master he'd been forced to serve.

There was nothing in the djinn's experience that could have prepared it for this exposure to love and light. Something was different now. Something was not as it had been before. The djinn felt its own being changing. The djinn finally realized that Talib was not his real enemy.

Mathars repeated his command to the djinn. Although the djinn could have attacked (to little real effect, as Talib had not let his guard down for an instant), it held itself.

Mathars made several angry gestures that would silently command the djinn to kill Talib. The djinn ignored him. This enraged Mathars as much as it confused him. Djinn were not supposed to disobey! He repeated the ritual gestures; and in his haste he became careless, and part of his garment entered the djinn's circle. The djinn snarled, and pulled on the garment. Mathars lost his balance and fell out of his circle. He pulled Mathars into his own circle, and seized him by the throat with its left hand. Mathars couldn't move. He gasped and tried to speak. His body made slight convulsions. His fingers twisted in grotesque attitudes.

"The chains of your geometry and your poetry no longer bind or compel me! Your curses are impotent!" the Djinn said, its voice hissing and sibilant; vowels like steam and consonants like broken glass.

While this was going on, the other Believers who witnessed this battle from a far away place intensified their dhikr. Talib made his dhikr within, as he was always doing. A good deal of this dhikr, and some well placed dua, invoked baraka on the djinn; which the djinn felt as a flow of pure pleasure and fulfillment beyond anything of its experience before. The confusion and disharmony it knew for millennium were suddenly relieved for a time – with the promise it could be permanent. This Bani Adaam bore gifts and freedom from bondage. Mathars brought pain and slavery.

From a far away place, those engaged in dhikr perceived through the veils of time / space what was happening, and held themselves still. None of them moved. They were too well disciplined to act out of panic. There was nothing they could do to save Mathars anyway,

Nor, strictly speaking, could they think of a reason to try.

The djinn suddenly cried out "The Bani Adaam disrupts order and brings chaos! Veils are penetrated and mock the centuries of our rule. Your presence here speaks strange poetry: will you not hear it? You bring your own essence! You are invaders into territories you can't see! There are wars raging around you and you are not aware. Is our world so inaccessible to you?"

To everyone's surprise, the djinn began to sob.

"Did the One make you so blind?" the djinn continued. "Two bodies of water are in bondage. We could not cross the barrier between them. You did! You sailed across them like the ships you build. We suffered because of your journeys. Why do you force yourself upon our nation? We don't change like you must! We never wanted you here!"

Talib recited from Qur'an:

"Behold! We said to the angels, "Bow down to Adaam": They bowed down except Iblis. He was one of the djinns, and

he broke the Command of his Lord. Will you then take him and his progeny as protectors rather than Me? And they are enemies to you! Evil would be the exchange for the wrong-doers!"

The Djinn was stunned, as if it had been caught in a compromising position.

Talib paused,,

"Behold, We turned towards thee a company of djinns (quietly) listening to the Qur'an: when they stood in the presence thereof, they said, "Listen in silence!" When the (reading) was finished, they returned to their people, to warn."

After a pause, Talib and the others recited again:

"I have only created djinns and men, that they may serve Me."

Talib took a careful step forward. "Hear me well, Djinn, whose name I do not know. You knew from the first that we were given station and rank. We bear the great responsibilities. We have the great struggles. My kind faces a great danger. Our custodianship over our worlds and what we do with it changes the condition of our Ruh with every step. Our Ruh, mind you! The beautiful loan from the One with the most Beautiful Names. We are answerable for this; and are scarcely aware. Those of us that are aware must learn difficult tasks.

"We meant you no harm. We still mean you no harm. We command your tribe with justice and compassion as is our right and our duty, by Allah's command. The human named Mathars enslaved you, and tried to use you as a weapon against those who seek the next step on the Path. He came as a thief and an assassin. We came as friends and by command from the One. You know this as truth, though are loath to admit it. Our quest is for the Glorification of the Beneficent and Merciful. We seek to know Hu's artistry. It is our right; and you must help us or be gone. We are inspired by the Science of Love and the Art of Reality."

The Djinn didn't move. He changed his facial expression slightly. The mouth softened, and the teeth no longer showed. His eyes became larger. His complexion changed from blood scarlet to verdant green. His bearing became calm and dignified. The humming sound that came from him became quieter and modulated to a slightly higher pitch. The revolting odor that usually emanated from him (which Mathars had commanded to keep to himself) became like a floral perfume. His right hand raised at the elbows, palms upward. Flowery fractal shapes of gold, rose, and green danced just above his fingertips. His clothing solidified into a blue robe with gold calligraphy that none but Allah and the race of Djinn could read.

The Djinn said "You who are flesh and Ruh. I heard your words. I am powerless against them. Look upon my robe. The words thereupon declare no god but the One and the praiseworthy carries His Words. I clothe myself in this promise. I stand abased before this Great Truth. In all the worlds are those who would speak outrageous lies. I will not hear them again. I will not live by these foul paths. I will help you, Bani Adaam. I will bring the treasure you seek. Your new structure will have the final pillar it needs. I grow weary of that-which-is-not-Truth. My misery is meaningless and profits me nothing! I thirst for Love and all it begets. Assist me! I claim this as my right."

Talib replied "Seek the One without expectation of anything but Annihilation in Unity. All else is illusion and idolatry. You need no more help from me than this; may Allah guide you. I will remember you in my supplications. Let our affairs together end profitably and let us go our way in peace. May Allah look favorably upon you, Djinn."

And the Djinn told Talib his true name.

And Talib told the Djinn his true name.

Now, they were closer than brothers. A trust has been established that would not, could not, ever be violated.

"Peace to you, Bani Adaam. Upon the fate of my self, and as Allah as my witness" said the Djinn.

And with that, Mathars died. Utterly. His body broken in all its capacities to contain life, his mind and intelligence shattered like glass, his soul poisoned, diseased, and torn to shreds.

The Djinn let him fall in a messy heap upon the floor. Out of respect to Talib and in keeping with his word, the Djinn ignored the breach in the circle.

The Djinn departed. The ceremony was closed, and the battlefield was vacated. An intense fire appeared and purified the place, as it returned to its former essence.

*****

After the battle, Talib needed to rest. Yet he was glowing, radiant.

Babaakh bowed before him and said "Welcome back, Master."

It was true. He could see how he'd changed in these few hours. These aeons.

Musawa came in , disheveled, and bleeding from a few cuts, but otherwise unharmed. "Master!" he cried. The two embraced.

"Mus! I am forever in your debt." Talib said. "Were any of the others hurt?"

"Yes. Two men were injured, one of them seriously. Jafar was killed, may Allah grant him peace and paradise. The injured are receiving medical attention. And we have three prisoners."

"Have two of the men prepare Jafar's body for burial. We'll have his janaza. I will deal with the prisoners. Bring them here, I want to see them" Talib said.

Talib approached the prisoners. They had been bound and were on their knees, guarded by seven young men with weapons.

Two of them were strangers to Talib. They both looked frightened. It was almost certain that they had no idea who they were really working for, and had been duped; but Talib would make sure before deciding what to do with them.

One, however, was familiar to him. He was Qadi, a judge, Khalil ibn al-Qasmana. This was distressing; Mathars' influence seemed to extend to very high places in government.

Ordering the Qadi separated from the other two, Talib sat down in front of them and asked their names. One was Tariq and the other was Houmam.

Talib began "Do you know who I am?"

Houmam looked at him and, with some defiance in his voice, said "No."

Tariq said "I'm not sure who you are. I can guess; are you the Hajji who traveled in time?" His companion looked at him, angry.

"Yes" Talib said.

The two men looked at each other. "You are the one we were sent to fight?" Houmam asked.

"Yes. Who do you work for?" Talib asked.

Tariq began to say something, but Houmam silenced him with a look. "Why should I believe you? How do we know you are who you say you are?"

Talib told the young men guarding them to release the two prisoners.

"You're free. Return to your families." Talib said, and stood up and began to walk away.

"Wait!" Tariq said, as Talib started to walk away. "You're going to release us?"

Houmam said "Why would you do such a thing? You could kill us! We tried to kill you."

Talib paused a long moment, turned, and said "You," pointing at Tariq "you believe me. You are beginning to see that you were fooled into attempting to kill someone who did no evil. You failed, and now see what you did, and are repentant. You," pointing at Houmam "don't know what to believe. If I keep you prisoner, I would have to waste time in vanities to prove who I am. If I executed you, it would be of little or no profit to me, and you would die without the opportunity for repentance. Releasing you is the only way to prove who I say I am.

"The man you were working for told you lies. The lies sounded beautiful; such was his talent. He probably gave you money, and made promises that were alluring to you. He was never going to be true to his word. He would have killed you when he was finished with you.

"You read Qur'an? Even a little?" They both nodded yes, with some hesitation. "Then you remember Allah's account of the story of Moses and Faroun. The man who seduced you was probably more evil than Faroun. This was who you obeyed. I'm actually quite happy that you survived your battle, and have the chance to regenerate and heal your life. I pray that you do."

With this, Talib went to his shoulder bag, pulled out some money, and gave each of them ten gold coins; a considerable sum.

"If this is the reward of repentance from a mere man, imagine what rewards await you when you meet Allah. Go, and live good lives. Asalaam alaikum."

The two men, shocked beyond belief, stumbled over exclamations of thanks, salaams, and promises to return to the Sirrat ul Mustikeem and went home.

For the remainder of their lives, they were true to their word.

Qadi Khalil ibn al-Qasmana was still bound and on his knees when Talib approached him. For a long moment the two men stared at each other. Fear and hate radiated from al-Qasmana's eyes, his mouth in a sneer.

"Mathars is dead." Talib said.

"Did you kill him?" al-Qasmana asked.

An unconscious confession – or tactical error. Why would al-Qasmana ask this about Mathars was unless he were involved with him?

"No. We were engaged in a fight to the death. The powers he tried to control betrayed him when they realized they were no longer constrained to obey him."

Al-Qasmana said "You lie!"

With a gesture from Talib, two men walked away, and a moment later returned carrying a human body. A nod from Talib, and they threw it on the ground in front of al-Qasmana. It was Mathars.

"It seems you no longer have the authority you once had."

Al-Qasmana thundered "I am still Qadi of the region! You can't take that from me!"

"I have several reliable witnesses that will testify that you engaged in sorcery, corruption, and attempted murder. And I am al-Hajj of Uq'Dyill, which places considerable authority over you in this matter. You know the law; I speak the truth."

Al-Qasmana knew the law. Hajjis of Uq'Dyill had a lot of power. He knew he was running out of options.

"Tell me," Talib continued, with a touch more sarcasm in his voice than he'd intended "when you sold your soul to Mathars, what price did you get?"

Al-Qasmana was becoming truly frightened by this time. The reality of his situation was becoming clearer with every moment.

"I swear I didn't know what Mathars was doing!" Babbakh and some of the men laughed. "It's true!" he went on, as he began crying "He approached me, and asked my help in a business deal. I helped him. At the time, I should have known it was illegal, but I just didn't see it! I was bewitched! Yes! I was! Then when I realized what happened, there was nothing I could do! Mathars told me he'd help me. He covered up the incident, and I was free. But then he would ask my help in other things. I didn't know what all this work was about. I didn't know what he was doing, I didn't understand any of it. It all got so,,, so complicated,,, How did it happen so,,, fast?" His voice trailed off.

Talib and Babbakh glanced at each other. There was something he was hiding. Something he was lying about.

"Is there anything you can tell me that will be of any help?" Talib asked.

Al-Qasmana thought a moment, and said "Hilal Ghyrut and Jubal ibn Adaam were close to Mathars. They will probably try to go into hiding or commit suicide when they hear he's dead."

This was no lie.

Hillal Ghyrut and Jubal ibn Adaam were highly positioned men in the caliphate. Ghyrut was involved in the treasury and the mint. His charges actually minted the nation's coinage. Ibn Adaam was highly placed in the nation's military.

Al-Qasmana was betraying whoever he could; doubtless to use as a bargaining chip to save his own life. But of course he knew that there was really no life worth going back to; nothing really worth saving.

"Thank you." Talib said. "Now I have a difficult decision to make."

Al-Qasmana began to feel faint.

Talib summoned two of the young men, two of the Christians, and two of the Jews. Appointing Shuzh Ti as scribe, he dictated a document outlining al-Qasmana's crimes; all of which were witnessed by the men here. A copy was made, and all of them signed the document and the copy. Then Talib dictated the sentence he pronounced upon al-Qasmana, and signed it. Talib kept the copy, and ordered Shuzh Ti to to deliver the document to the office of the Khaliphite.

Talib had never before exercised his authority as Hajji al Uq'Dyill. He did not enjoy it one bit.

There remained one last thing to do.

"Bissmillah, ar Rahamn, ir Raheem. Qadi al-Qasmana, owing to your crimes, your willing association with the proven leader of the Secret Order of the Yellow Sign, and the position of authority and trust that you violated, resulting in harm done to countless innocent people, and incalculable damage done to our civilization, I sentence you to death." Addressing the young men, he commanded them to untie him. One did so, the rest repositioned themselves so al-Qasmana couldn't run.

Addressing al-Qasmana, Talib said "Make two rakats, and a dua."

Al-Qasmana made ablutions, and made his peace with the Creator.

The sentence was carried out quickly, efficiently, painlessly, and with as much dignity as humanly possible. Talib performed a brief janaza for him: tears were in his eyes the whole time.

By this time, Jafar's body had been properly prepared for his janaza. All the men involved knew what they were risking, and accepted it. Talib performed the janaza ritual for his fallen comrade. His eyes still wet with tears, his heart heavy with the sense of an almost unbearable responsibility. All this blood so that he could perform the task Allah assigned to him. To be sure, Jafar was a martyr, and would be greeted in the next world as a beloved of Allah. Still, Taib was almost overwhelmed by the enormity of the position Allah placed him in.

After the janazas and the burials, Talib asked to be left alone a while.

"Master Talib" Babbakh said, when Talib returned. "It is over! Allah had given us a decisive victory. Even if some of Mathars' people survive, it will be a while before they will be able to ruin anything but themselves.

"Alhamdulillah!" Babaakh continued. "I have waited so long for this! My master, I learned at an early age that I was born to no purpose beyond your ascension and initiation. Now the purpose of my life is complete. I may die in peace and with dignity."

Talib heard all this, yet was unmoved, beyond simple gratitude and gracious friendship toward Babaakh. There was no pride, no exultation. Only a knowing. He smiled, his whole being radiating love.

Suddenly, Babaakh looked old and tired. The life energy and spirit rapidly and inexorably drained from his physical vehicle. He walked slowly to the door, staggering slightly, and went out. Talib followed. They walked until they came to a stream. At the bank was a circle of flowers of various species. The sun began to rise. Babaakh sat down among the flowers, looked up, and with a great effort, said "La illaha ilallah, wa Muhammad-ar Rasulullah!"

Silently, in unutterable peace, the Angel of Death greeted Babaakh Sidiq as a beloved friend.

Tears fell from Talib's eyes. Babaakh's passing was the saddest and most beautiful thing he'd ever witnessed. Talib made salatul fajr, and made a dua for his friend that lasted almost two hours - for what better friend could any man hope to have? Then, he walked to the house, found a shovel, assembled Musawa and the others who remained behind, returned to the stream, conducted another janaza for yet another departed friend, dug a hole, and sent Babaakh home.

Babaakh was at peace. Resting, waiting for a great event in spacious comfort, guarded by powerful and beautiful friends.

In the years that followed, a beautiful tree grew next to his grave. It bore sweet fruits that fed people for generations.

*****

The Djinn returned to his abode, transformed. His nation and his race saw this, and were struck with wonder. They'd always respected and feared him. But now, after this interaction with the Bani Adaam, he was so very different. Some of them approached him to learn from him, to be like him. These were treated with love and generosity. Some of the lesser djinn, inspired by his example, assembled as an alliance attempting to improve themselves through a collective activity of becoming a whole being. This was rare among the djinn, but not unheard of.

Others were too frightened, and fled. The Light that emanated from him was too much for them. They preferred the darkness.

Some cursed and raged and ridiculed, and even plotted to kill him; or at least ruin his life. The Rejected former Amir of the Djinn races who inspired Mathars and his theories and career was among them. The Djinn was too powerful for them to harm; and too much at peace to be affected. After all, how can fire burn fire?

Among the djinn, of this world, he would be known as their greatest saint.

The power of the Djinn achieved a state of balance, a state of Fana. In this, Talib accomplished what Mathars could not; except that Mathars' psychic cannibalism was proven as unnecessary as it was spiritually and morally reprehensible. They were all "absorbed" in an Absolute Power. They were the drop that became the Ocean.

*****

Throughout human civilization, almost all the remaining members of the Secret Order of the Yellow Sign acted in concert. Their lives, as they understood them, were now without meaning. Their life's work and purpose for remaining alive were destroyed with the death of Mathars. According to their beliefs, they would need to fall back and regroup in a "new form." Their present "form" was disgraced. Their honor as mystic warriors fighting to establish their beliefs was in ruins, and only one thing could restore their honor. So, on exactly 1/333rd of a standard year following the death of Mathar's, these members of the SOYS committed a mass act of synchronized suicide. The Muslims, Christians, and Jews who knew them, and were unaware of their association with the SOYS were shocked and traumatized by the event.

*****

Mathar's body was taken to his estate, dumped in a pit of trash and sewage, and burned. The area stunk abominably. The smell was so intolerable that nobody could go near it for years. Until the end of time, nothing would grow near the spot except disease and foulness. No prayer was ever made for him, no tear shed at his passing, nobody mourned or loved him.

His torment in the afterlife cannot be imagined.

*****

A few days later, Hqiim Zalluh was paging through the catalog of the Book Repository of Thyral Hijazz. His eye caught a listing of a title of a book, "The Unique Vessel" by Shams N'Quturas. Acting upon an impulse, he contacted the repository and ordered a copy. It was terribly expensive, but Zalluh had more than enough money for such expenditures.

Three months later, the book arrived. Zalluh paged idly through it when his eyes fell upon a symbol. He read the inscription below it, and went to his own books. Suddenly, the pieces fell into place. Here was the key to what he had been looking for. It all made sense. In a flash, a lifetime of hard work paid off.

The missing piece was that there was no single mathematical formula encoded in the Qur'an; there were several. Each one wove in and out of the other in a complex lattice structure of numbers and formulas that function on multiple dimensions simultaneously; each iteration forming an integral part of the structure. Each of these tied in with every science, every religious body of work and Revelation, every philosophical concept, every art, every moment in history, all that exists. It went on forever; yet it had a recognizable pattern – or more specifically, a meta-pattern.

He worked non-stop for 56 hours, without sleep, and not nearly enough food and drink, writing his notes. Then, after completing his task, he collapsed in exhaustion.

He had a dream.

Talib was asleep and had a dream.

They met in the same dream.

Zalluh said to him "It was you who helped me?"

"Not exactly" replied Talib "I helped the one who helped you."

"Here" Zalluh said, holding a book in his hand. "Take this."

384

The book became a light. Talib absorbed it and was absorbed in it; and he understood.

"How can I thank you?" asked Zalluh.

"All praise and gratitude is due to Allah."

Then they turned and looked. Off in the distance, the Djinn whose name is known only to Talib looked down upon them from a slight elevation. He smiled and walked away into a passageway of light.

Then Zalluh woke up.

Within months of the publication of his work, he was flooded by requests from the populated planets to speak or teach. Some denounced him as a charlatan, a lunatic, or something dangerously near a kufar. Others showered him in adulation.

Zalluh didn't care about any of this. His work had only begun.

*****

After what seemed an eternity, Talib returned to the Order of the Mountain of Light. Sudi waited for him. She ran into his arms and they embraced; quite unaware of the spectacle they were making of themselves. The others overlooked this minor breech of adab, the circumstances permitting some forbearance.

"My warrior! My king!" Sudi whispered, tears welling up in her eyes.

Talib held her and said "My queen! My guide and inspiration! I know you were with me. You helped me, you fought at my side. Allah reward you without end! I could not have survived this without you."

After a brief, powerful kiss, Sudi placed a small kiss on Talib's lips, as if sealing a sacred document. Then they regained their composure, and made their way into the order's building.

The leader of the order, a very old woman named Aisha bint Yathriq, greeted Talib.

"You have done well, little brother. You have experienced a great hijra and a great jihad. Few have seen such as you have. You are among the elect. You have the Sisterhood's gratitude, and we stand at your side as a friend forever."

Talib sighed. The weight of what had happened – the weight of *everything* that had happened, centuries of enormous mind shattering events - was focused upon him. He wished only a time of peace. Everyone there knew it. "Alhamdulillah" Talib said. That was all he could say, and all that needed to be said.

After offering his thanks to the women, and exchanging salaams, Talib took Sudi's hand, and they walked out. Transportation had been arranged, and they were taken home.

Talib and Sudi wanted some peace for a while.

Chapter 24. Without the Sacred Letter Waw, They Would Be Worthless.

Talib addressed the students for what would be the last time.

"The principles discovered by Hqiim Zalluh had universal repercussions throughout humanity. The effect opened unimagined perceptions within the minds and hearts of countless people. Cultures, subcultures, and schools of thought arose from this new paradigm and all of humanity was in a state of peace and heightened awareness that it has not collectively known in its whole existence.

"But it wouldn't last. History is not linear; it is cyclical in a spiraling pattern.

"This meant, of course, that Islamic civilization faced the only crisis it ever faced: the lack of fertile ground within the human heart in which to grow. Uq'dyill became the capital of the civilized worlds, and Lanajd became its center. The psychological processes and entropic instabilities of the individual and collective soul of humanity ran wild. As it always will. It's mad desire for an image to assign its worship to requires constant attention. It will fall to pieces one way or another. But this is not the way of Islam, and not the Way of Allah. We are to go beyond that.

"Everywhere in the worlds, things are breaking down. After an all too brief golden age, the structure of society began to

crumble. Within two generations, much of the greatness that had been achieved is being lost. Chaos is fomenting everywhere. Do you wonder at this?

"Humanity, being what it is, still has many lessons to learn. and many old lessons to re-learn. Much is forgotten among us. We live in a realm of forgetfulness. Our people, blessed with gifts that few lay claim to, cultivated higher truths in this world. Those who could not follow us we treated with compassion and mercy; as was the example of the Compassionate and Merciful. We were, to them, as doctors speaking in the presence of a terminally ill man. He could hear us perfectly, but our meanings were always unintelligible to him. It had to be this way, as we searched out those among them who would rise to greater heights. Many in the past have done so with cruel intrepidity. We could not do this, nor would we.

"We still have so much left that is undone. But we have reached a limit. The nature of this corporeal realm cannot follow us where we are now going. You who study music will know of polyrhythms. Several different rhythmic patterns playing simultaneously will create a dense tapestry of sound and movement. They intermingle and weave in and out of each other. But they inevitably meet on the 'One'. And the cycle begins again. So it is with the universe, with creation. Infinite dimensions have been at work, unfolding their rhythms, their harmonies, their melodic inventions. And soon, they will land on the 'One.'

388

"This will be a Great Event. Nothing that exists will be unaffected, except Allah. For Allah is neither the cause nor effect of anything, being beyond all things. As for Hu's creation, its multidimensional polyrhythms will land on the 'One" and all we knew or could ever understand will end.

"Our station in this abode is the result of two qualities meeting; each quality differentiates us. These are the qualities that force us to the Jihad an Nafs – the Struggle to master the ego. When some of these qualities remain with us when we are called home, some will be secure on the Great Event, others will not. All will be arranged in ranks. Among those who will not be secure, some will experience hell as a deliverance from these qualities that meet in this abode. Some will never be delivered. But all, no matter who, will experience the Light of Allah as either a blissful love or a fearful exposure to immense truths they are not prepared to face. It is where the corrupt meet themselves and find no place to hide.

"This is what the hellfire truly is.

"Most people are blind to these realities. It has always been like this.

"Little brothers and sisters, don't be shocked, and don't be sad. Just remember. Most people say that Allah will punish. But this is not exactly how it works. We punish ourselves. When the Bani Adaam deny the gift of their fitra, their true nature, they re-harmonize their selves to the harmonic of hell. If our beings were truly aligned with the Being of beings, we would

not experience hell if we stood within its worst place. It would have no power over us.

"They ignore the tone of the Qur'an: it is not angry, but sad and compassionate. Never despair of Allah's mercy. Return; even if you broke your vows a thousand times. Return and remember. Allah loves to forgive."

The lesson ended.

Talib walked out, and headed up the path in the forest where his house was located. He took his time walking, occasionally going off the path to visit a particularly attractive sight. But he would return to the path, and head home.

Far away, the sunlight shone bright white-blue through the clouds. Then the sunlight dimmed as the larger of the planet's two moons eclipsed the sun. Wind blew across the mountain peaks. Chunks of ice and rock were dislodged from the enormous cliffs. The few stars that were visible at daylight held their lofty places appointed by Allah; their light intensifying as the sky darkened.

And unseen by any eyes, a leaf fell from a tree into a river. It stayed there for a long moment. Impossibly, miraculously defying the current.

Then it floated away.

****

Talib was old. He recently observed his 187th birthday. His aging body, despite the inconvenience, was a matter of small concern for him, as he was now closer to Allah. He had fewer distractions, and saw what others could not see. The purity of his *Ruh* grew to such an extent that the flesh was becoming more and more inadequate to contain it.

Sudi had been called home by Allah nine years ago, and he never remarried. Her passing had been peaceful, easy, and dignified. There was no pain, and in subsequent dreams wherein Talib saw her, she was always at peace and radiated Light. Despite this, Sudi's departure was hard on Talib, as he truly loved her, but all things pass away. His children, grandchildren, great grandchildren and their children (did they have children too? He couldn't remember. He would have to ask someone) all lived in the city nearby. He was visited often, and enjoyed the company of those who visited him.

His firstborn son by Sudi, Hassan, became a warrior. Most men were trained in martial arts. But Hassan became a master. His Order / Dojo was respected throughout the known universe, and Hassan was acknowledged as a master's master by everyone. Many challenged him; nobody ever defeated him.

Talib's second son, Suliman, became a political leader. He achieved a position within the upper levels of Uq'dyill's government. He was known for his incorruptibility, and his absolute intolerance of social injustice. This made him many enemies, but he handled himself well; even surviving three assassination attempts in the recent downswing of civilization.

Talib's daughter Suhaila became an engineer specializing in spacecraft design. She married a colleague at her institution, and they had four children.

All his children and grandchildren played music. They loved to do so.

Among his visitors were students whom he'd once taught, or young students who wished to ask of him some specific thing. He loved his students like his own children and always made time for them. He was thoroughly amused by his "legendary" status among the people. He knew better than to be flattered by such kudos.

But he also enjoyed his solitude. He spent a great deal of time in prayer and meditation; and still played music on the same bazhtaran he had for years. The only significant change on it was that he'd engraved the name Sudi in gold and black diamond on the instrument.

His friend Rashidevqov died a half century ago. His son Khalad was still alive and active as a medicinal musician. M'Daud visited him often. He'd become a scholar of metaphysics. Amandla became a master of martial arts and a military philosopher. Djunal earned a position in Uq'Dyill's treasury, and was an expert in finances. Rasheema became one of Talib's students, and later studied with Hqiim Zalluh; who, despite continually addressing her half humorously as "You Idiot" praised her brilliance and respected her. She achieved a great deal in the realm of mathematics and astronomy, like her mother. Her children and grandchildren were frequent visitors of their "Uncle Talib."

In fact, the nickname "Uncle Talib" was more than a casual honorific. Malik Rashidevqov had not known he was one of Talib's distant descendants. When he learned this, he was overjoyed. His entire family had marked the occasion with an elaborate celebration.

But this was a long time ago.

The others who'd joined him in his battle had enjoyed good lives. Shuzh Ti became a Rabbi, a rare title for a woman, and made a good living as an agricultural engineer who helped farmers.

Pauqal married a woman named Zakiyyah, and Luthor married her sister Yasmin. After spending some years in business together doing spacecraft repair, were invited to join the Spacefarers. They accepted the invitation, and they and their families lived in a large spacefarer community. Five years ago, Talib heard that Pauqal and his family had died in a disaster that claimed the lives of over 3000 people.

After several years in public office, Seif became a Shiekh, and lived a relatively secluded life on Khulazh: a remote world that had only very recently been colonized.

Hameed died while working in a town that was suffering from an epidemic disease.

Faar's life was greatly improved, although his experiences with Mathars had left scars. While he made an admirable career for himself as a metallurgist and chemist, he had several personal difficulties that plagued him the rest of his life. Nonetheless, he bore his trials well, and kept in touch with Talib from time to time until his death at the young age of 97. He died saving the lives of two small children who had fallen into a river.

Musawa eventually did become the wind instrument master musician that he wished to be. Talib was proud of him. Musawa, to this day, referred to him as "Master;" even though he was long since Talib's musical equal. Musawa still seemed the skinny kid he always was; but by now, this ceased to be a liability for him. Musawa had married four women from among the Sisterhood of the Mountain of Light; two of whom were among those whose dhikr / meditation had strengthened him during his fight with Mathars. Talib was aware of many other women who would have gladly married him – somehow, as he matured, women found him quite attractive, even irresistible. Some women would flirt with him before they were aware of what they were doing. And even now, despite his advanced age, women felt drawn to his presence.

During a recent visit, the two men spoke for hours about music, and of the long years they spent together. Then, as the hour became late, Musawa got ready to leave.

"Before I leave, Master, there is something I need to do. It is quite important, and I've been neglectful of it too long."

"Yes, what is it?"

"This is my gift to you" Musawa said. He reached into his cloak, pulled out a box, and handed it to Talib. Talib took it and opened it.

It was patchouli incense.

After a moment's pause, the two men laughed heartily. In fact, Talib hadn't laughed this much in years. No joke could have ever surpassed this in sublimity and acknowledgment of friendship earned through endurance of hard times, and perfect trust.

When the laughter ebbed enough for both men to regain their composure, the two men stood. Hugging and exchanging salaams. they parted ways, and Musawa left Lanajd.

This would be the very last conversation they would ever have.

*****

Talib continued to perform and compose music. His compositions were published, and were popular on several worlds. some of them were written in a highly specialized form of musical notation that he needed to invent himself. He also taught classes in this notation, as well as in his theories on music. His concerts also featured his improvisations. A Talib Ali Peterson concert was considered an event of special importance; because not only was he a highly respected man, the music he would improvise would never happen again for all of eternity. Missing such an opportunity was unthinkable.

Many of these concerts took on a legendary status. People would talk about them for years afterward.

Talib also spent a great deal of time writing. He had published several books. One of them was quite controversial; it was an epic poem that described the thirty "worlds" that existed previous to this one in terms that resembled erotic love (without being overtly so). This got some of the more strict adherents to Shari'ah upset with him. He had to write another book explaining the poem, line by line. Despite his position, he was still in slight disfavor over this: because while his explanation was perfectly acceptable, the introduction and epilogue of the book made his detractors look like idiots. They didn't like that very much. There were also text books on music that were well received, memoirs of his life and travels, and a series of novels.

There had been times he was visited by his angel. These were enjoyable moments. His whole being was filled with peace on these occasions; and all he'd learned in those cataclysmic events of the past would be renewed for him, refreshed and revitalized as he needed them. He was also occasionally visited by the Djinn he met during his battle with Mathars. The Djinn would mostly visit in dreams, and sometimes in places at night that were subtly illuminated by fire or moon light, appearing exactly as Talib remembered him, with no subterfuge or malice. They would exchange greetings of peace, and go their separate ways in peace.

On occasion, he would pay attention to news reports. Madness and chaos, corruption, war and famine, and disasters natural and manmade arose everywhere like a plague of locusts. On Earth, a drastic shift in the planet's polarity created a complete reversal in the rotation on its axis; which meant that the sun rose in the west. Talib was, mercifully, insulated from all this. It never touched or affected him. But he could feel its presence. It could only mean one thing,

Epilogue: The Comedy is Over.

One clear Friday, in the late afternoon, Talib was preparing to plant a tree. He'd come to his garden to do a little work after jumma. The light from the sun was bright. Shortly thereafter, clouds appeared, almost out of nowhere. It began to rain. This happened on occasion in the post cold season they were in. Rain storms could come without warning. It is Allah Who sends the rains.

It was a light rain, and it seemed unnecessary to Talib to seek shelter. Talib actually found the sensation quite pleasurable.

The tree he was planting required delicacy. It was a rare sapling with three main trunks supporting thirty six branches. If properly cultivated, it would bear thirteen different wondrous fruits. But care was needed in more than the tree's cultivation. If the fruit wasn't properly harvested, it would become poisonous.

As he was digging the hole, his mind was filled with wonder. He perceived the interaction of all things, the delicacy and strength of life and the beauty of the evidence of the Creator that all these things bore. Allahu Akbar! All the experiences of his life were a single moment that led to an eternity of peace and truth. But he was not a mere observer, as many seekers and seers are. He was it and it was him. No difference. And no barriers between him and Allah, except what must be so that he still has an "I", is still an individual being named Talib. What peace! A light burst from his heart and upon his continence. What could possibly be more important than this?

The "I" of Talib was moved. Carried by a momentum more powerful than he. In an instant, every event of his life returned to him. The weight of centuries was upon him; yet it was all so brief!

How fragile, delicate, and rare,,,

Such poetry,,,,

As his heart began to soften and tears welled up in his eyes from this quiet yet intense meditation, the Hour of Judgment came upon Creation.

Talib stood up, brushed the dirt from his hands, and faced the direction of the qibla.

Suddenly a thought occurred to him and he turned around. Kneeling down, he finished planting the tree. He watered it, and used the last of the water to make wudu. Again, he faced the qibla, with the tree to his left, made two rakats, and made du'a and dhikr.

As he sat making dhikr, in his peripheral vision, to his right, he saw his old acquaintance, the Djinn, making sajdah. All around him, he sensed the presence of his angel, the angel's wings surrounding him, and also making sajdah.

Without warning, a man in a green robe appeared and sat next to him to his right. Talib recognized him. The man smiled and said "At last!" and resumed his dhikr.

Then the universe was rolled up like a scroll.

www.ingramcontent.com/pod-product-compliance
Lightning Source LLC
Chambersburg PA
CBHW020652110726

47901CB00001B/159